PASSION'S PROMISE

"Elizabeth." He cupped her chin with his forefinger and thumb, and forced her to turn toward him. Her gaze locked with his, and burned.

"Is this what you require in payment for rescuing my person, Mr. Cantrelle?" she asked nervously.

A smile nipped at his mouth, but he refused to rise to her bait. "No, darlin', but that's as good an excuse as any." His head lowered toward hers. "If I need one," he added, the words so soft she almost didn't hear them.

Elizabeth looked up at him helplessly, suddenly paralyzed by a wealth of emotion she was at a loss to understand. She knew he was going to kiss her. Yet she made no effort to escape his embrace. *It's wrong,* her mind screamed, *slap him, hit him, push him away.* But somewhere, in a tiny, secret place within her heart, where even she had never gone before, Elizabeth was not listening.

His lips took possession of hers in a kiss that was so gentle, Elizabeth felt a shiver of surprise. His tongue traced the outline of her lips, softly caressing, stroking, and awakening feelings within her she had never known existed . . .

PASSION BLAZES IN A ZEBRA HEARTFIRE!

COLORADO MOONFIRE (3730, $4.25/$5.50)
by Charlotte Hubbard

Lila O'Riley left Ireland, determined to make her own way in America. Finding work and saving pennies presented no problem for the independent lass; locating love was another story. Then one hot night, Lila meets Marshal Barry Thompson. Sparks fly between the fiery beauty and the lawman. Lila learns that America is the promised land, indeed!

MIDNIGHT LOVESTORM (3705, $4.25/$5.50)
by Linda Windsor

Dr. Catalina McCulloch was eager to begin her practice in Los Reyes, California. On her trip from East Texas, the train is robbed by the notorious, masked bandit known as Archangel. Before making his escape, the thief grabs Cat, kisses her fervently, and steals her heart. Even at the risk of losing her standing in the community, Cat must find her mysterious lover once again. No matter what the future might bring . . .

MOUNTAIN ECSTASY (3729, $4.25/$5.50)
by Linda Sandifer

As a divorced woman, Hattie Longmore knew that she faced prejudice. Hoping to escape wagging tongues, she traveled to her brother's Idaho ranch, only to learn of his murder from long, lean Jim Rider. Hattie seeks comfort in Rider's powerful arms, but she soon discovers that this strong cowboy has one weakness . . . marriage. Trying to lasso this wandering man's heart is a challenge that Hattie enthusiastically undertakes.

RENEGADE BRIDE (3813, $4.25/$5.50)
by Barbara Ankrum

In her heart, Mariah Parsons always believed that she would marry the man who had given her her first kiss at age sixteen. Four years later, she is actually on her way West to begin her life with him . . . and she meets Creed Deveraux. Creed is a rough-and-tumble bounty hunter with a masculine swagger and a powerful magnetism. Mariah finds herself drawn to this bold wilderness man, and their passion is as unbridled as the Montana landscape.

ROYAL ECSTASY (3861, $4.25/$5.50)
by Robin Gideon

The name Princess Jade Crosse has become hated throughout the kingdom. After her husband's death, her "advisors" have punished and taxed the commoners with relentless glee. Sir Lyon Beauchane has sworn to stop this evil tyrant and her cruel ways. Scaling the castle wall, he meets this "wicked" woman face to face . . . and is overpowered by love. Beauchane learns the truth behind Jade's imprisonment. Together they struggle to free Jade from her jailors and from her inhibitions.

CHERYL BIGGS

MISSISSIPPI FLAME

ZEBRA BOOKS
KENSINGTON PUBLISHING CORP.

To my husband Jack,
for giving me all the love and romance
a woman could possibly want,
for giving me your faith and encouragement,
for always listening and understanding,
but most of all for being my own special hero.

ZEBRA BOOKS

are published by

Kensington Publishing Corp.
475 Park Avenue South
New York, NY 10016

First Printing: May, 1993

Printed in the United States of America

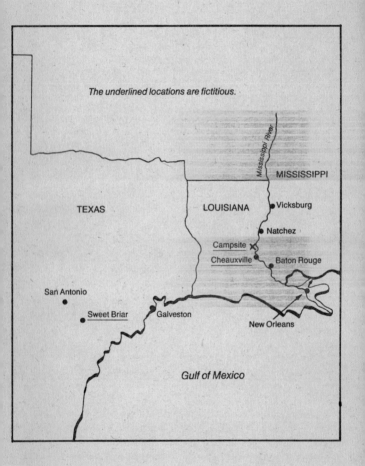

Chapter 1

"Ohhh, I hope Aaron Reynaud is struck by lightning and . . . and . . . and burns to a crisp!" Elizabeth mumbled beneath her breath. One of the four heavy satchels she struggled to maintain a grip on began to slip from her arms, and she shifted its weight. A lock of blond hair fell loose from the mass of pinned curls atop her crown, bounced onto her forehead, and dangled down before her nose.

"Hey, watch yerself, lady," a loud voice commanded from behind her.

Startled, Elizabeth jumped at the barked order and glanced over her shoulder. Her gaze met that of a grizzled roustabout, whose dirt-smudged chest and muscled shoulders glistened with sweat. He paused long enough to purse his lips and propel a spit of tobacco juice to the ground, then swept around her, and pushed a dolly loaded with wooden crates toward one of the docked riverboats. "Gonna git yerself runned over, standin' around like that," he called back.

Suddenly, she felt the planks beneath her feet tremble, and a loud rattling sound filled the air. Elizabeth whirled about and found herself standing within inches of a passing dray. Two huge workhorses lumbered past near enough to where she stood that the smell of their sweat-covered bodies caused her nose to wrinkle in distaste; one of the wagon's large wheels brushed her skirts.

"Eek!" She jumped back and glared up at the driver, but he paid her no heed. Gritting her teeth, Elizabeth silently damned all men in general. She had begun to believe there wasn't a decent one in the entire world. One of her satchels slipped a little from beneath her arm, and she tightened her grip on it. She stalked her way toward the docked boats.

Ten yards from the *River Belle*'s gangplank, Elizabeth dropped her reticule.

"Drat!" She stomped her foot in frustration, and the small heel of her shoe became wedged between the rough planks that made up the wharf. She tried to jerk free and almost lost her balance. "Aaron Reynaud, if I ever see you again, I'll kill you!" She yanked again and the shoe pulled free. This day was definitely the worst of her life. Everything had gone wrong. And now she even had to carry her own bags. She mumbled a string of oaths beneath her breath that would have mortified her older sister's sensibilities, and looked down at the small handbag.

Obviously it was too much to hope that one of the roustabouts scurrying about the busy docks was gentleman enough to notice and come help her. Elizabeth looked around. No, there wasn't a gentleman in the whole disreputable lot.

It was then she noticed the man leaning against a tall stack of baled cotton only a few yards from where she stood. Thin streams of white smoke drifted upward from a cheroot he held between the fingers of his right hand. His thumb was hooked casually over the belt of a holster that slanted low across one hip and was tied securely to his thigh.

Suddenly, Elizabeth realized *he* was watching *her*. Watching her? No, she fumed, that was the wrong word. Scrutinizing her. Undressing her with his eyes, *that's* what he was doing!

With a toss of her golden curls she turned away, but her curiosity was not to be denied. She looked back, her nose held high in the air, her own expression haughty and contemptuous.

Her gaze swept him from head to foot and back again. *Rakehell* was the first thought that jumped into her mind. *Gunslinger* was the second. Yet there was something about him that intrigued her, a hint of tempered savageness, a wildness slightly tamed and reined in, but unbroken.

A black Stetson rode low on his forehead to shade the deeply bronzed face. The cocky angle of his hat did nothing to soften the harsh lines of a square jaw and rigidly carved cheekbones.

A buckskin vest stretched taut over broad shoulders and contrasted starkly with the whiteness of his shirt, well-worn leather *calzoneras* wrapped around long, lean legs, and thin strips of fringe streamed from the centers of six highly polished silver conchos that ran down the outer length of each legging. But it was the Colt Peacemaker strapped to his thigh that caused Elizabeth's eyes to widen and whip back up to meet his.

Her china blue gaze was caught by his earth-rich brown one, and she felt a nervous fluttering sensation within her breast.

The hard-set line of his lips softened, and one corner curved slightly upward. As if he'd sensed what she felt, the dark eyes sparkled with momentary warmth and amusement.

The loud shriek of the *River Belle*'s whistle suddenly filled the air, and the sound jerked Elizabeth from her reverie. If she didn't hurry, the paddle wheeler would leave without her. Oh, if only she'd brought her servant Serena, she wouldn't have to carry these horrid satchels.

Remembering the reticule that lay at her feet, she bent to set down one of the satchels. Out of the corner of her eye, she saw a pair of black boots moving toward her, and heard the jingle of the roweled silver spurs attached above each high-wedged heel. The boots stopped beside her, and she tensed. A lean, work-roughened hand appeared above her reticule. Strong fingers wrapped around the figured velvet bag and lifted it from the ground.

"Give me that, you thief!" Elizabeth cried. Almost every cent she had with her was in that bag. She released her tenuous grip on the other satchels, oblivious of their thudding crash to the ground, and swung out with the one valise still clutched in her hand. It slammed against the man's chest with a loud *thump,* just as he began to rise from his bent-over position.

He dropped the reticule instantly and staggered a step backward, holding his stomach and gasping for breath, his eyes wide with surprise. The heel of his boot rammed against the edge of a protruding plank and threw him further off-balance. He flailed the air with his arm in an effort to right himself, but it was too late.

Elizabeth, eyes blazing with self-righteous indignation, jammed clenched fists upon her hips and glared down at him. "That will teach you to try and steal from a lady."

Grayson Cantrelle sat awkwardly sprawled within the midst of her discarded satchels and stared up at her. His flash of temper quickly turned to utter disbelief. When he'd spotted her walking across the deck toward the *River Belle*, he'd thought she was pretty. Now he realized she was beautiful, despite the fact that she'd just clobbered him, accused him of being a thief, and continued to stand over him like a fire-breathing dragon.

With a toss of her head, Elizabeth adjusted the green plumed hat that had fallen askew on her crown, and bent to retrieve her satchels. "The nerve of some people," she grumbled softly.

Gray moved to get to his feet, and reached for one of her portmanteaus in an effort to assist her. "Listen, ma'am, I was only—"

"Get your hands off of that!" She brought her closed parasol down soundly atop his hand.

Gray jerked it away. "Dammit, woman! I was only going to—"

"I know what you were *only* going to do—" she whacked his arm again for good measure, "and you're not! So just leave my things be." Elizabeth quickly retrieved her bags, turned on her heel, and stomped toward the *River Belle*.

Gray watched the saucy hellion flounce her way up the gangplank and quickly disappear. "Wild little firebrand," he muttered, his words contrary to the smile that tugged at his lips. Next time he got near that little lady—and he knew there definitely would be a next time—he'd make sure she didn't have any weapons in hand, like a heavily packed valise.

He picked up the wide-brimmed Stetson from the ground where it had fallen when she'd hit him, ran a hand through his thick black hair, and then covered it with the hat. He got to his feet and started to follow her up the gangplank.

"Hey, Cantrelle! You on this boat?"

Gray paused and looked up toward the passenger deck. "Travis?" He stared up at his old friend in disbelief. "Travis Planchette? What the hell are you doing here? Last I heard, you were in California."

11

"Yeah, well, never stay in one place too long, that's what I always say."

Gray took the stairs two at a time. With each step the silver conchos on his *calzoneras* reflected the sun in a myriad of dazzling brilliance.

"Well, you don't look any worse for wear," Gray said, and grabbed Travis's extended hand. He gave his friend a quick once-over and smiled.

In stark contrast to Gray's well-worn leathers, Travis wore an impeccable suit of black broadcloth. Thick waves of dark blond hair surrounded a softly cut, handsome face, which was complemented further by warm blue eyes and a well-trimmed mustache.

"You don't look so bad yourself, Gray." Travis leaned against the rail and returned Gray's once-over. "Still wearing your leathers, I see, even when you're not on the back of a horse."

Gray laughed. "You know me, Trav, never did have much use for getting all fancied up. Where you headed?"

"New Orleans. How about you?"

"Home to Texas. You traveling on business?"

"You might say that," Travis said with a wide grin. He ran a finger over one corner of his mustache. "I make my living off the boats now. Doing pretty good, too."

"Why, you slicker! You're a gambler?"

"Not just *a* gambler, Gray. I'm one of the best." Travis smiled proudly and tucked his thumbs within the arm cuts of a silver-threaded brocade vest.

"One of the best, huh? Hell, Trav, quit jawin' me. I remember when we were riding together, you couldn't bet your way out of a chicken coop, let alone win a hand."

"Yeah, well, things change. Tell you what, I'll take you on at the tables tonight, what d'ya say?"

12

"You're on, my friend." Gray laughed and clapped a hand on Travis's back. "It'll be one hell of a pleasure to take your money again, Trav, one hell of a pleasure."

The shrill blast of the boat's whistle startled Elizabeth awake. She bolted from the narrow bed, and looked about the dimly lit cabin in confusion and panic.

Then she remembered where she was, and why. She slumped back on the bed and listened to the steady *whoosh-whoosh* sound of the packet's huge red paddle wheel, as it churned through the water. Another whistle sounded from somewhere in the distance. Elizabeth stood, crossed the room, and paused before a small window. She opened it, and the tangy scent of the river, a blend of sea and forest, rushed in to surround her.

At first she saw only blackness, but her eyes soon adjusted to the night, and the horizon began to take shape: a ragged black line in the distance. The dark scene was momentarily interrupted by another riverboat passing alongside the *Belle* in the opposite direction. Its decks were alight with the soft glow of several dozen lanterns. A whistle blasted again, and suddenly the air was filled with soot from the passing boat's smokestacks.

"Oh, heavens." Elizabeth waved a hand in front of her face, coughed, and slammed her window shut. She turned toward the dressing table mirror and let out a shriek of temper. Her face was a mask of blue-black grit.

She moved to the side of the bed and reached for the servant's cord, only to realize there wasn't one. "Oh! This is all Aaron's fault," she said, and cursed her ex-fiancé for the umpteenth time since that afternoon. "If

13

he hadn't been so hateful, I wouldn't have left without a servant. Now I have to do everything myself!"

Just then her stomach growled, and Elizabeth realized she was hungry. No, famished, she decided. Hopefully she hadn't missed dinner. With tepid water from the pitcher that sat on the dressing stand, she washed the soot from her face. She threw her wrinkled batiste wrap onto the narrow bed and struggled into a lacey camisole and pantalettes, hooked a huge hoop-cage around her waist, and pulled a flowing gown of apricot-hued silk over her head. With Serena's help dressing took only ten minutes—by herself it took Elizabeth nearly thirty frustrating, curse-filled minutes. She ran a brush through her long hair, and secured it at her nape with a white ribbon. Within seconds a halo of wispy golden tendrils curled about her face. She sighed in frustration, yanked the ribbon off, and allowed the thick strands to cascade over her shoulders in soft waves.

Minutes later, in the dimly lit passageway, she paused. Would they allow her into the dining salon unescorted? She hadn't thought of that before. She knew it wasn't proper for a lady to travel alone, but what choice did she have? It wasn't as if she'd planned this trip.

"Oh, fiddle, they'll just have to let me in. After all, I do have to eat." With chin held high, she marched up the stairs, determined to make the biggest scene the captain had ever seen if the steward refused to seat her in the dining salon.

She passed several empty lounge areas before she located the door to the dining room. At the arched doorway she stifled a giggle. It was the most audaciously decorated room she had ever seen. The walls and ceiling were a collage of carved woodwork painted white, several crystal chandeliers hung from

14

the ceiling, a huge mural of a plantation scene was painted on one end wall, and red curtains edged with gold fringe adorned every window. The tables and chairs were all of highly polished rosewood, their cushions covered in red brocade, and all seemed to be occupied.

Elizabeth's stomach growled again, and she instinctively straightened her back, hoping no one had heard.

"Can I show you to a table, Miss Devlin?"

She turned, relieved to see the young steward who had directed her to her cabin earlier. "Thank you, sir. I would truly appreciate that."

"You're a mite late, ma'am, there's not too many chairs left, but I can seat you at that table near the window over there." He pointed across the room. Elizabeth placed her hand on the steward's arm, and allowed him to guide her through the maze of tables toward the one he'd indicated.

Two men and a woman were already seated at the round table. The trio looked up and smiled at Elizabeth's approach, but neither man rose from his seat.

Elizabeth's opinion of the men was swift: obviously not true gentlemen.

The steward pulled a chair from the table, bowed toward Elizabeth, and excused himself. She ignored the drawn chair, which was next to one of the men, and settled into the one next to it, leaving an empty seat on either side of her. With a cool smile to her dining companions, Elizabeth turned her attention to the menu.

"I'm Zachary Montrose," the older of the two men said. He wiped a napkin across his heavily joweled chin and sat back in his chair. The pearl buttons on his shirt front strained to remain within their holes. He stared at

Elizabeth and waited for her to look up and acknowledge his introduction.

It was just about the last thing she wanted to do, but she forced herself, not wanting to be outright rude.

"This here's my wife, Anna." Zachary nodded toward the thin, almost nondescript woman who sat beside him. "And that strapping young man next to Anna is my brother, George."

George smiled and Elizabeth shuddered. He was as skinny as his brother was fat. A hawklike nose protruded from a face in which cheekbones stuck out like ragged cliffs, and brown beady eyes looked back at her with cold, calculated interest.

She nodded and quickly looked away.

"We're from Galveston," Zachary said, demanding her attention once more. "Texas. I own a general store there. Took a little time off, so we could go see my wife's sister up in Boston. She's sickly. George here," he nodded toward his brother again, "he's got his own business, too. Trade and supply." George chuckled softly, as if Zachary had just told a joke. "Where might you be going, little lady?"

"New Orleans." If that's any business of yours, she added silently.

A dining steward appeared at her side to take her dinner order.

"Don't believe we caught your name there, missy," Zachary said, the minute the steward walked away.

Elizabeth gave a mental sigh. The man was going to insist on being chatty. "Elizabeth." She refrained from providing her surname.

"Elizabeth, a beautiful name. You traveling alone, Elizabeth? Pretty little thing like you shouldn't be traveling alone. Don't see a ring on your finger, guess you're not married, huh?"

16

Elizabeth felt a flash of alarm and glanced at George. A rather sly smile creased his face. "Huh, actually, my . . . um, husband is . . . uh . . . not feeling well this evening."

"*Actually,* darling, I feel much better. Even somewhat hungry," Grayson said. With his hands on the back of her chair, he leaned over her shoulder and brushed his lips across her cheek.

Elizabeth nearly jumped out of her skin. Her head whipped about, and her jaw hung agape. She stared up at the handsome stranger, and was instantly assailed by a wave of conflicting emotions, not the least of which were outrage, indignation, and curiosity. She didn't know whether she was grateful to the man for saving her from what she was sure were the amorous attentions of George Montrose, or furious with him for pretending to be her husband.

You certainly could do worse, Elizabeth, a little voice said at the back of her mind. But a niggle of apprehension at the base of her neck would not be denied, and the word *dangerous* screamed itself at her over and over.

Thick waves of rich sable hair glistened beneath the glow of the chandelier overhead, and laughing, golden brown eyes looked down at her expectantly, waiting for her to deny him. He smiled at her hesitancy, and the lines about his mouth deepened.

She had seen that face before, she knew it, but where?

"I see you've already met my beautiful wife," Gray said easily, and offered his hand across the table to Zachary. "I'm Grayson Cantrelle."

He shook hands with both men and nodded an acknowledgement to the woman who sat silently between them, with an added "How do, ma'am."

Elizabeth remained silent, and continued to gawk at

17

him in an effort to remember where she'd seen him before.

Broad shoulders were encased within the confines of a rich black broadcloth jacket that tapered down to a narrow waist and flared slightly over long, lean thighs. His white shirt was minus any ruffles, and proved to accentuate the deeply bronzed face that seemed almost harshly cut in comparison to the elegant attire.

She suddenly remembered him. The docks! The man in leather. He was the cowboy who'd tried to steal her reticule. "Great, saved by a thief," she mumbled under her breath.

"Pardon me, darling, what did you say?" Gray settled into the empty chair on her left, a look of feigned innocence on his face.

With a quick glance back at the Montroses, Elizabeth forced a smile to her face, and a sweetness to her voice so false that it almost dripped sugar. "Oh, I was merely giving thanks to see that you've recuperated so quickly from your . . . ah . . . *illness.*"

"Oh, it was nothing, really, a little stomach upset from that . . . um . . . *problem* we had earlier, that's all." He smiled at her, his dark eyes alight with amusement.

"Well, sweetheart," Elizabeth cooed, and batted her eyelashes, "you probably should be more careful of whom you try to . . . ah . . ."

"Assist?" Gray offered.

Chapter 2

"Hey, Gray, thanks for saving me a chair."

The deep voice drew Elizabeth's attention. She turned to see a tall, blond, elegantly dressed man step up behind the rogue who pretended to be her husband, and slap him jovially upon the shoulder.

Gray nearly choked on his wine at the sound of Travis's voice, but managed to hide his sudden fluster behind a smile.

Travis settled into the empty chair on Elizabeth's right and leaned toward her. "He doesn't usually let me get this close to his lady friends." He winked mischieviously.

"Travis, I want to—"

"Sorry, I'm late, Gray," Travis said. He looked around Elizabeth. "I was playing poker with a gent who didn't want to lose, but I finally convinced him it was inevitable." He laughed again and turned an appreciative eye back to Elizabeth. "I sure would have hurried it up a bit, if I'd known what a beautiful creature I'd be seated next to at dinner."

"Travis, I—" Grayson's words were sterner, but again, effectively cut off.

"Why, sir, what a nice thing to say. I do appreciate it

19

ever so much," Elizabeth purred, and smiled her most flirtatious smile. She glanced over her shoulder, confirmed Grayson Cantrelle's unease, and felt a sense of satisfaction. He wasn't the only one around here who could playact. Imagine, she fumed silently, inviting a gambler to their table! It was just too much!

Of course, why she should have expected more of *him*, she didn't know. The situation had been bad enough with Zachary Montrose and his brother George, but now she was ensconced between a gunslinger and a gambler . . . if her mother were alive, she'd faint away at the shock of seeing Elizabeth in such scandalous company.

Travis took Elizabeth's hand in his and raised it to his lips. "I assure you, ma'am, never have my words been more truthful. You are a most beautiful woman."

Gray saw the look in his friend's eyes, recognized it, and struggled to prevent the amused smile that itched at the corners of his mouth. It had always been that way between him and Travis. If they were together and a woman came along, it was rival time. Afterwards they would always share a drink and a laugh, and resume their good-natured friendship, usually without further thought to the woman whose favors they'd each just fought tooth and nail to win.

"Seems your wife and friend get along quite nicely together," George sneered. His black gaze darted from Elizabeth to Gray and back again.

Gray glanced at Elizabeth. Her attention seemed riveted on Travis, who was whispering something in her ear.

"Why, I never," she said, and laughed softly. A faint pinkish hue flushed her cheeks, and she smiled coyly up at the gambler.

"Yep, pretty good friends, if you ask me," George snickered.

20

Gray looked back at George Montrose and could almost envision a river of drool snake down the man's chin as his beady little eyes stared at Elizabeth. Gray leaned forward and looked around Elizabeth to his friend. "Travis, you keep flirting with my wife like this, and she's going to run off and leave me for you. Then I'd have to kill you." A wide grin creased his handsome face. "I sure wouldn't want to do that to my best friend."

Travis's teeth clunked down atop the rim of the wine glass he had lifted to his lips, and he let out a choking gasp when the liquid slid down the wrong pipe. "Wife?" he echoed, too shocked to say much more. He stared at Gray in disbelief.

"Sorry I didn't tell you, Trav, but, well, I was going to explain things later." He turned to Elizabeth and draped a proprietary arm around her shoulders. "Sweetheart, I've got a little surprise I've been saving to give you, and tonight's the night." He smiled widely and rose to his feet. "Ready?" he asked, offering her his arm.

Suddenly, Elizabeth wasn't so sure of herself anymore. Going off into the darkness alone with a gunslinger, or cowboy, or whatever, was not something she'd counted on. Her mind raced to find an excuse to turn him down. "Well, honestly, dear," she said finally, refusing to meet his penetrating gaze, "I had planned on returning to the cabin right after dinner. I . . . I'm rather tired."

"Well, I'll be damned!" Travis swore. "You really did it?"

Gray ignored his friend and kept his gaze riveted on Elizabeth. "Well, returning to our cabin is exactly what I had in mind, *sweetheart*," he said. An insidiously satisfied grin curved his lips. "But after we take a little stroll about the decks."

"I really don't feel up to . . ."

"Come now, darlin'," he drawled smoothly, "we're on our honeymoon." His smile was devastatingly wicked.

"Oh, all right!" Elizabeth snapped. She rose from her seat so quickly that her chair toppled over and crashed to the floor.

Four pairs of eyes stared at her in surprised astonishment, and Elizabeth felt a wave of chagrin. She forced a smile to her lips. "Good night, everyone," she said sweetly, and tipped her head to the silent Mrs. Montrose. "I'm sure we'll all meet again."

Gray stifled the laugh that desperately wanted to burst from his throat, and after righting her fallen chair, offered her his arm.

She stared down at it as if he were offering her a rattlesnake instead of his arm, but after hesitating a moment, Elizabeth slipped her hand around his crooked elbow. Gray, with a satisfied little smile, led her toward the door to the outer deck.

"I can't really go out there with you," she whispered frantically, overcome by a sudden spurt of propriety. Helene Devlin had diligently taught both her daughters the rules of being a *proper young lady,* and Elizabeth had learned them well, although she wasn't timid about breaking them any time the need arose. *This,* she decided angrily, was not one of those times.

Gray patted her hand and smiled again, but said nothing, and continued to walk toward the door . . . with her in tow.

"Mr. Cantrelle," Elizabeth said. "Didn't you hear me? I cannot go out on deck alone with you!"

"Would you rather go with old George back there?" Gray asked innocently. He already knew her answer.

She caught the spark of amusement that lit the golden brown eyes and bristled. Maybe she could find a way to toss him overboard, she thought. A smile pulled at her lips, as her mind conjured up a picture of Grayson Cantrelle plunging over the riverboat's rail. That would teach him. And serve him right, too!

They approached the door, and Elizabeth tried to pull her hand free again, but the fingers of his other hand moved to cover hers. He held her in place with a casual possessiveness that infuriated her.

"You know, both times we've been together, Elizabeth, you've been angry. And yet, both times I've found you quite fascinating. I wonder why?" He held the door open, and they stepped out onto the night-shrouded deck.

"Oh, really!" She flashed him an icy glare. "Are you in the habit of forcing your attentions on unattached women who travel alone, Mr. Cantrelle?"

Gray's laugh echoed on the air, and blended with the lulling sounds that surrounded them: the night sonance of the small animals and birds that lived on the distant shores, the gently lapping waves created by the boat's movement, the rhythmic whoosh of the huge red paddle wheel at the boat's stern, and the piano music from a nearby lounge.

Once the door closed behind them, Elizabeth stopped and dug her heels into the deck. She looked up at him with a defiant glint in her eye. Any pretense of joviality or flirtatiousness was gone from her face. It had been a bad idea anyway. All this man seemed to do—handsome or not—was stoke her ire and make her see red! She jerked her hand free of his arm. "Thank you, Mr. Cantrelle, for your gallant rescue of my person, but I believe I can make it back to my cabin on my own from here. Good night." She turned to leave.

"Darlin', your temper's flaring again," Gray baited. "Now, how's it going to look to our good friends, the

23

Montroses, if such a loving couple like us spends the rest of the voyage to New Orleans *estranged?*"

Elizabeth stiffened and turned back. She smiled, but refused to rise to his gibing remark. When she did answer, her voice was sugar sweet. "Well, I'm sure they've had their share of marital misunderstandings, Mr. Cantrelle. They'll understand."

"George might not." Gray struggled to maintain an air of seriousness. "In fact, I'd say he just might not care whether you're married or not. He looks the sort to me, gets his mind fixed on having something and he means to have it, no matter what."

Elizabeth remembered the lascivious gleam in George Montrose's eye, and shuddered. She felt an urge to give in to Gray's invitation of protection, and then bristled at the mere thought. She'd relied on a man to take care of her before, and look where it had gotten her. No, she would not do that again. As far as she was concerned, men could just all die a dastardly death and rot in hell. Forever! She turned a cold eye to Gray and lifted her chin. "Thank you, Mr. Cantrelle, but as I said before, I can take care of myself. I don't need some gunslinger, or cattle drover, or whatever-you-are, to protect me."

Gray allowed himself a genuine smile and took a step toward her, closing the distance between them. What he intended to do, she never found out. In a whirl of silk and lace, Elizabeth spun around and hurried back toward the open doorway.

"Ungrateful little vixen!" Gray mumbled. He watched her disappear within the shadow-engulfed passageway. In his entire life he'd never met a woman with so much sass in her.

Elizabeth paced the small confines of her cabin, too

agitated to even think of sleep. Her emotions were in such a turmoil, she couldn't have defined them if the good Lord himself had come into the room to ask her what was the matter. In the last few days everything that *could* have gone wrong in her life, *had* gone wrong, and she seethed with rage at having no control over any of it. There was nothing she could do, and that stoked her fury even more. If only her father hadn't died, then none of this would have happened. She wouldn't have agreed to marry Aaron Reynaud, only to find out in the nick of time that he was a blackguard, and she certainly wouldn't be on this boat headed to her sister's home in that forsaken place called Texas. And, Lord knows, she wouldn't have been forced to put up with that gunslinger and his gambler friend. Or those leery-eyed brothers, George and Zachary Montrose.

"Ohhhh!" She stamped a foot on the thick area rug that covered the floor. "Why didn't I wait and bring Serena with me?" Well, at least, she mused, she'd had the good sense to leave a few dollars and instructions for Mrs. Reynaud to put Serena on the next packet to New Orleans.

Suddenly, Elizabeth felt the need for a bit of fresh air. She grabbed a wrap from the armoire and left the cabin, intent on taking that stroll about the decks she'd missed because of Grayson Cantrelle. A warm spark of emotion flared to life deep within her breast at the thought of the cowboy, and she quickly doused it. He's probably nothing more than a no-good drifter, she told herself. Penniless. Unreliable. Most likely the type that shoots a man just for looking cross-eyed at him, and expects a woman to grace him with her favors just because he smiled at her and mumbles some pretty words.

"Well, well, what d'we got here?" a voice echoed from the black shadows of the stairwell.

Startled, Elizabeth spun around. Now what? she fumed, too agitated to be frightened.

George Montrose sidled out from the darkness, his lips curved in a grin that left her with no doubt about the thoughts that occupied his sleazy mind.

The smell of stale whiskey and tobacco surrounded him, and permeated the air in the narrow passageway.

"You shouldn't be out walking all by yourself, Missus Cantrelle," George slurred. "Or is that really who you are?" He took a step forward, swayed, and caught himself. The grin returned. He grasped both lapels of his frock coat and puffed his thin chest out. "See, I find it mighty peculiar that Cantrelle fella was on this here boat long before you got on. Why's that, you suppose? If you're his missus, that is."

Elizabeth instinctively took a step back, and found herself pressed into a small alcove that was built into the wall of the passageway. "What do you want, Mr. Montrose?"

"Why, just for us to be friends, ma'am, that's all." He raised a hand toward her face.

Elizabeth cringed, and revulsion blazed from her eyes.

"What's the matter, honey, ain't I good enough for you?" George jeered. He took a step closer, and brushed his long bony fingers across her cheek.

She flinched. How dare he act so bold! Outraged propriety swept over Elizabeth, and filled her with reckless courage. She smacked his hand away, and glared at the ugly little man who stood in front of her and blocked her path. "Get out of my way, Mr. Montrose. Get out of my way or I'll—I'll—"

"Oh, I like a woman with spunk," George chortled. His hand slid down her arm intimately.

Repugnance washed over Elizabeth, and she saw red, her rage and indignation making her oblivious to

26

any need for caution. She'd had enough of men and their wanton lust. Her father had gotten himself killed because of it, when he'd made a fool of himself over some saloon whore. It had been the cause of her mother's untimely death, when she'd tried to please her husband by having a son to carry on the *great* Devlin name. And only two hours before their wedding, Aaron had ruined everything, because of his need to go to bed with some little trollop. Was that all men ever thought about? Elizabeth bristled. Well, enough was enough!

She raised an arm high in the air, her reticule clutched tightly within her fingers, and swung the satchel down toward George's head with all her might.

George was too busy gaping at the rapid rise and fall of her breasts, which had accelerated with her wake of heated emotion, to notice Elizabeth's movement. He never knew what happened. Her reticule connected with the side of his head. A dull *thunk* echoed in the air, and with a look of utter shock on his face, George sagged, unconscious, to the floor.

For one brief second, Elizabeth stared down at the prone figure in dismay, afraid that she'd killed him. She had forgotten all about the tiny gun nestled within the beaded evening bag. Carrying the derringer was a concession made to her late mother, and over the years it had become a habit, something she did now without conscious thought. Though Elizabeth had always conceded to her mother's wishes, she had repeatedly found better things to do on the afternoons when she was supposed to practice her aim with the plantation's overseer. Thus, Elizabeth would be lucky if she could put a bullet into the side of a barn three feet away.

George stirred, and Elizabeth quickly pushed her old memories aside. Well, at least he wasn't dead. But he might think twice the next time he got the idea to approach her, she thought smugly. She stepped past him and proceeded on her way toward the open decks, confident he wouldn't follow. If she guessed right, George Montrose would have a headache the size of Mississippi for a few days.

Only a few yards away, Gray stood behind his barely opened cabin door. He'd been just about to rush to her defense, when she'd knocked George unconscious. He quietly closed the door and finished pulling on the *calzoneras,* strapped on his holster, and grabbed several cheroots from a satchel that sat on the bed. After spending the last few hours at a poker table practically giving his money to Travis, he needed a good smoke. A little loving wouldn't hurt either, he thought.

He left the cabin and stepped gingerly over George, but once out on deck, he saw no sign of Elizabeth. At the rail Gray leaned a shoulder against a support pillar. To get back to her cabin, she'd have to return through the same doorway she'd exited, he reasoned. He'd just stay put, enjoy his cheroot, and wait for her. He gazed out at the slowly passing shore. The low, black landscape was only faintly discernible through a heavy layer of ground fog that had settled upon the earth.

Gray inhaled deeply from the thin, brandy-soaked cheroot, and the simmering orange red tip of the cigar glowed brightly against the night. The sight of the tiny flame stirred memories to life within Gray's mind, and his eyes grew thoughtful and distant. He had failed in his trip to Washington. For all the weeks of searching, of questioning one person after another, he had turned up nothing. What the hell was he going to tell Dana?

The thought of having to tell his sister he'd failed brought a soft curse to his lips. He slammed a fist down on the mahogany rail. "I'll find that bastard if it's the

28

last thing I do. Someday, I'll find him, and he'll pay for what he's done."

He sighed and forced himself to calm down. Nothing on this trip had gone right. He'd thought for awhile that he would at least have the pleasure of some female companionship on what was left of the voyage to New Orleans, but the blue-eyed minx he'd set his sights on had proven to be a real firebrand. He grumbled his way through another string of oaths. That was surely one thing he didn't need, and yet here he was waiting for her to come past.

He tossed the cheroot out into the air with a flick of his thumb, and watched the tiny missile disappear within the sheer clouds of gray fog that floated over the water's surface. High above, the dark sky shone clear. Hundreds of stars nestled amid the velvety blackness like tiny specks of ice, and a crescent moon glowed a soft yellow, its pale rays cast down upon the landscape in a futile attempt to light the night-shrouded earth.

The river fog obscured any image of the huge boat in the murky waters, but Gray didn't need to see the *River Belle*'s reflection to know exactly what she looked like. He'd boarded in Louisville, and had been a passenger for almost a week now. The *Belle* had three decks, the main two furnished with wide galleries of fancily carved woodwork and painted white. The bottom deck was stored with crates of goods, bales of cotton, and livestock. The top deck supported the wheelhouse from where the pilot maneuvered the boat, the crew's quarters, and the two tall black smokestacks which continually choked out billowing clouds of gray smoke and soot, leaving a trail in its wake a blind Indian could track if he had a mind to. The deck in between was for passengers: salons, cabins, dining, and gambling theatre.

Gray turned toward the rear of the boat, and lifted a

29

booted foot to the rail, his back still against the pillar. The sudden clang of the ship's bell brought him instantly to his feet, alert. He gripped the rail and braced himself for the inevitable jolt of the boat, when she would ram whatever obstacle lay in her path.

At the bow, Elizabeth jumped at the sound of the bell, her eyes wide with alarm. The boat jerked, she screamed, and swung around to grab the rail.

The *River Belle* lurched sharply to the left. Her timbers creaked from the sudden movement, and the huge paddle wheel furiously churned the water as the boat shuddered.

Elizabeth's fingertips brushed the rail at the same time her feet flew out from beneath her. In a swirl of fabric, she fell to the floor, her ruffled gown and petticoats a mound of tangles about her legs. The whalebone spines of her hoop-cage crested wildly at all angles, and pushed at the heavy fabric that crushed down atop it. Her mantua cloak twisted about her neck, and one end of its long fold draped over her head.

The paddle wheeler swerved to the right, and then straightened out to once again glide smoothly over the river.

Gray released his grip on the rail and looked down into the water. A huge, dark snag of tangled tree limbs poked through the surface only a few feet off to the side of the boat, directly in the center of what had been their path. If the *Belle* had hit it, the snag would have ripped a hole in the bottom of her the size of Kentucky.

Elizabeth sat in a turmoil of frustration. Tears stung her eyes, and she tried to blink them back. Why, oh, why was all of this happening to her? Eugenia never had these kind of problems. Of course, she thought with a sigh of angry envy, everyone had always said she and Eugenia were exact opposites. Eugenia Devlin Kane lacked the fiery temper and streak of independence that had always gotten her younger sister in trouble. She was also six years older than Elizabeth, married, and the mother of three children. The imminent arrival of her fourth child had prevented her attendance at Elizabeth's wedding in Vicksburg.

"Thank heavens for that!" Elizabeth muttered angrily. She never would have been able to walk out on Aaron so splendidly, if Eugenia had been there. Her sister would have made her talk to Aaron and settle things in what she would consider a proper manner. "Proper? Huh!" she grumbled. "Aaron Reynaud doesn't know the meaning of the word!"

Elizabeth straightened her cloak, punched down her skirts, and reached out to grasp one of the balustrades.

"Well, my dear *wife,* what kind of trouble have you gotten yourself into this time?"

Chapter 3

Gray's deep, satin smooth voice startled Elizabeth. Her heels slipped on the smooth planks, and her derriere once more connected with the deck with a soft *whoopf.*

Elizabeth glared up at him, and Gray fought to suppress the laugh that was about to strangle him. "Can I help you up?" He offered her his hand.

With a sniff, Elizabeth turned away, took hold of the balustrade with both hands, and struggled to her feet.

"Do you always sneak up on people, Mr. Cantrelle?" she said snippishly, once upright and stable. She began to slap at the rumpled mass of her gown and petticoats.

"Only beautiful ones." He chuckled, undaunted by her sharp tongue. "But I really didn't think—"

"That's right, you didn't. Most men don't!" She threw him a baleful glance and then wished she hadn't. Grayson Cantrelle was probably the most gorgeous man she'd ever seen, gunslinger or not, and that fact was not helping her to remember that she considered men—*all* men—no good wastrels.

Even dressed in his buckskins, or whatever they were, Elizabeth thought there was a virility about him she'd seen in few other men, if any. Strength emanated from him, and she sensed that this was a man who knew no fear, and who would readily challenge the world to hang onto whatever he felt was his. She also sensed a gentleness about him, and that was the dangerous part, the thing that she knew could be her undoing. What would it be like, she wondered, to kiss him? How different would it be than the chaste kisses she'd shared with Aaron Reynaud?

"Are you going to put any words with that smile?" Gray asked teasingly, while he watched her gaze slowly slide over the sinewy length of his body.

Elizabeth flinched, appalled at her own errant thoughts. The man had the uncanny ability to make her forget all propriety. After all, she would never have thought such things if he were a gentleman! She glared up at him anew, all the more angry to feel the heat of a blush rise to her cheek. "I was merely wondering if I were strong enough to lift you and toss you overboard!"

A roguish smile creased his face and warmed the amber-sparked brown eyes. "You can try."

He leaned one shoulder against a pillar. His gaze blatantly swept her from head to toe, and paused to admire every inch of femininity that was in-between. Elizabeth had the beauty of an angel, and the disposition of a dragon. She was trouble. He sensed it, felt it, knew it as well as he knew his own name, yet she intrigued the hell out of him. And no woman had accomplished that for a damn long time.

"Ohhh! You are a . . . a *blackguard!*"

"So I've been told before." He chuckled softly, an action that drew another baleful glare from her. Damn, the woman was all sauce and fire, wrapped up in the most breathtaking package he'd ever seen. Grayson knew a lot of men might shy away from a woman with that much sass and spit in her, but it drew him. She was like an unbroken filly: beautiful, wild, and free-spirited, and trying her damndest to be independent.

He felt the heat of desire begin to burn within his loins, and a sudden hunger to know the woman that lurked behind the sharp tongue and fiery temper.

Elizabeth moved to stand at the rail, and wrapped her arms around one of the support pillars. She stared out into the night, tried desperately to ignore him, and failed miserably. Every inch of her body was aware of him, intensely aware. It scared her, and when she got scared, she got angry . . . which seemed like all she'd been doing lately.

But she wasn't about to let some smooth-talking cowboy get near her, even if he was handsome, and virile, and strong, and . . . and . . . *Stop it!* she told herself sternly. She couldn't trust him, she couldn't trust *any* man.

On the wall just a few feet from where she stood, a candle burned steadily within a glass-enclosed brass sconce. The soft glow of the flame gilded her hair, and turned the pale blond tendrils to flowing streams of flaxen silk, the shimmering threads of her apricot orange gown to the rich, hazy hue of an August sunset.

As if sensing his stare, and drawn to it against her will, Elizabeth looked back at Grayson. She opened her mouth to speak, and then clamped it shut. There was no need for words. By tomorrow she'd be in New Orleans and never have to see him again, or put up with his boldness. She lifted her heavy skirts and turned toward the door to the passageway.

Without conscious thought to the reason behind his actions, Gray stepped in front of her and effectively blocked her exit.

She didn't back away, but stood her ground, hands clenched at her sides. Defiance and outrage flashed from blue eyes that reminded him of a Texas sky on a cool spring day.

The control she had on her temper was strung taut, and tenuous at best. She struggled not to flinch beneath his penetrating gaze, and steadfastly tried to ignore the accelerated beat of her heart.

His hands slipped around her waist, and their heat seared through the thin silk fabric of her gown. He pulled her to him and felt her tense, noted the nervously clasped hands held tight to her sides, and the full creamy curve of her breasts exposed by the low-cut bodice. His gaze rose to her face, strayed to the corner of her lips, and then moved to her eyes, which were looking everywhere except at him.

"Elizabeth." He cupped her chin with his forefinger and thumb and forced her to turn toward him. Her gaze locked with his, and burned.

"Is this what you require in payment for *rescuing my person,* Mr. Cantrelle?" she asked nervously, as if suddenly finding the bravado she sought to defend herself against him. But her voice cracked when she spoke, and her words came out breathless and faint, rather than haughty and cold as she had hoped.

A smile nipped at his mouth, but he refused to rise to her insult. "No, darlin', but that's as good an excuse as any." His head lowered toward hers. "If I need one," he added, the words so soft she almost didn't hear them.

Elizabeth looked up at him helplessly, suddenly paralyzed by a wealth of emotion she was at a loss to understand. She knew he was going to kiss her, she knew it. Yet she made no effort to escape his embrace. *It's wrong,* her mind screamed, *slap him, hit him, push him away.* But somewhere, in a tiny, secret place within her heart, where even she had never gone before, Elizabeth was not listening.

His hands moved to caress her neck, his fingers entwined within the golden waves of her hair, and he tilted her head back to receive his kiss. Her hands rose of their own accord to rest upon his chest, and her fingers spread wide over the crisp whiteness of his shirtfront. His lips neared hers, and Elizabeth suddenly stiffened. A snap of reality invaded her thoughts without warning. She pushed against his chest, but he was too strong, too intent on his purpose, and she was no match against his strength, against the wild longing of her heart.

His lips took possession of hers in a kiss that was so gentle, Elizabeth felt a shiver of surprise. His tongue traced the outline of her lips, softly caressed, stroked, and awakened feelings within her she had never known existed.

Hands, warm and powerful, slipped to her waist and pressed her body to his, forcing her curves and swells to contour to the hard, muscular planes and valleys of his own length.

Mind-shattering waves of tingling, pulsating heat rippled through Elizabeth, and her heart started to hammer against her breast like a drumroll on the Fourth of July. Nothing in life had prepared her for the surge of passion Grayson Cantrelle's touch had unleashed within her.

Her lips parted in a soft moan and, taking full advantage, Gray's tongue darted forth to fill her mouth in heated exploration. With provocative slowness his tongue encircled hers. It teased and tempted, dared her to reject him, and invited her to respond to him.

Elizabeth clung to him. She had been kissed before, but never like this, with such brazen need and power. His kiss was one of firm mastery and expertise. His tongue caressed the innermost secret places of her mouth, and sparked a feeling deep within her that both scared and excited her, and ignited a heat that at once burned and chilled her oversensitized flesh.

Consumed by a flood of strange, new sensations, lost

36

in a world of dreamy sensuality that vanquished awareness of everything real and sane, Elizabeth found herself oblivious to all but the man who held her in his arms. A tall, dark man, a dangerous man, whose kiss pulled her into an unchartered region of emotion and desire.

Gray lifted his mouth from hers, and a soft whimper of protest escaped her lips, unbidden. He gazed down into her face, aflush with passion, and knew then that he wanted her, wanted to claim possession of more than just her lips.

At the other end of the deck someone opened a door and music wafted out onto the night air, cut off a few seconds later when the door was again closed.

But it had been enough.

Sanity returned with brutal force. Gray drew himself away from Elizabeth. He forced his arms to relinquish their hold on her, and fought to control the desire that rushed through his veins, to deny the sharp hunger that still ached within his loins.

What the hell was he doing? He'd never forced his attentions on a woman yet, and he sure wasn't going to start now. Anyway, she wasn't his kind of woman. He'd known that the moment he'd set eyes on her. She was too refined and proper. Women like her weren't strong enough to survive in his world, and most didn't even want to try. He'd known all this about her with one look, yet he'd been drawn to her, and rationalized away his misgivings by reasoning that he wasn't looking for a wife, merely a little warm-hearted companionship for the remainder of his journey to New Orleans. A few hours, no more. After they arrived in New Orleans, he'd probably never see her again, and that was all the better. Wasn't it?

He longed to touch her once more. His arms felt suddenly empty. Unconscious of the movement, his hand rose toward her face, and the tips of his fingers lightly brushed a caress across her cheek. For Grayson, it was a gesture of gentleness rare in its offering, rarer still in its occurence.

Dazed by his sudden abandonment of her, Elizabeth stared up at him, her eyes still luminous with passion, her lips slightly swollen from the sweet ravishment of his kiss.

He felt like an absolute heel. "Elizabeth, I'm sorry," he muttered, even though he knew it was a lie. He wasn't sorry he'd kissed her, and damn it, if he didn't get away from her, he knew he was going to do it again—and maybe a hell of a lot more.

His apology, like a splash of icy water dumped over her head, instantly brought Elizabeth back to her senses. How could she have been so wanton? So loose? It had only been mere hours since she'd walked out on Aaron, and here she was in the arms of another man! And a cowboy, at that. Did she never learn? Mindless fury seized her, but whether at Gray for his advances, or at herself because she both allowed and responded to them, she wasn't sure. Her hand pushed his aside, swung through the air, and connected hard with the lean, chiseled curve of his cheek.

For a brief second, the sky filled with a rainbow of stars, and Gray's ears rang with the peel of a hundred church bells, while the skin where her hand had hit burned like the searing heat of a branding iron.

"How dare you!" she sputtered indignantly, and stared at Gray as if he had just sprouted horns, tail, and pitchfork. She stamped a foot for emphasis of her words. "I should have known you were no gentleman."

Gray rubbed a hand over his cheek and, with a glint of amusement in his eyes, watched her stomp away. He didn't know what it was about the saucy blond hellion that drew his attentions like a magnet, but he was beginning to wonder if he really wanted to find out. It could be dangerous.

Suddenly, the deck beneath his feet trembled, and the pillar he had leaned against shook with such force he almost toppled over the rail. A deep, low rumble filled the air, and the boat seemed to rise up, and then dropped back into the murky river a second later. Water flew up and sprayed all around the boat in large waves. Gray grabbed the rail and turned toward the passageway. His gaze quickly scanned the deck in search of Elizabeth. A loud blast rocked the boat, and it began to sway violently. A wooden crate stashed beneath the stairwell careened across the deck and smashed into Gray's leg. With a muffled curse, he fell to one knee and nearly lost his grip on the rail.

Elizabeth screamed and clung to the doorway that led to the cabin area, fear etched in every feature. Her face was deathly white, rivaling the lace which trimmed her gown.

A fine cloud of black soot spewed from the choking smokestacks to rain down upon both river and boat. Gray heard Elizabeth's scream and staggered toward her. He had to get to her. The deck beneath his feet shuddered again, and the *River Belle* began to jerk like a bucking horse. Gray lost his balance, slid across the deck, and slammed against the bulkhead wall. Pain shot through his shoulder, but he ignored it.

Intent on nothing more than reaching Elizabeth, Gray was momentarily unaware of the thunderous rumble that had begun to reverberate from the central depths of the big boat.

The shrill whistle of the *River Belle* sounded, even as her bell clanged loudly to alert everyone, both onboard and anyone on shore near enough to hear, that the huge boat was in trouble and needed help. In seconds the decks were filled with people: scared, bewildered, panic-stricken people. They ran in every direction, jostling and pressing against one another in an effort to find a way off the heaving boat.

Gray pushed his way through the mass of hysterical humanity. He had almost reached Elizabeth, when a large man stumbled through the doorway, his arms full of satchels, his eyes wide with fear. One of the satchels he carried rammed into Elizabeth and knocked the breath from her lungs. She lost her grip on the doorjamb and fell to her knees. Others surged around her in a screaming stampede, and within seconds she was lost from Gray's sight.

"Son of a—Elizabeth!" he shouted. The sight of her on the floor, and then her disappearance beneath the press of panicked passengers, filled him with sheer terror. He ruthlessly shoved people from his path. "Elizabeth!"

She huddled against the doorway, her face turned toward the wall, hands raised to cover her head. Gray bent down and took hold of her arms, his relief at finding her almost overwhelming. His iron-strong grip wrapped around her, and he pulled her to her feet. "Come on," he yelled.

Maintaining a tight grasp on her arm with one hand, he used the other to try and shove his way through the throng of bodies that pushed against him. But it was no use. He looped an arm around the frame of an open cabin window, and drew her to him as he flattened them both against the cabin's outer wall.

The rumbles that echoed from the bowels of the boat grew to a deafening roar, and with a final shudder the paddle wheeler burst at the seams. An ear-piercing explosion rended the air, and the sound turned the once serene setting to a paroxysm of panic and disaster.

The *Belle*'s woodwork flew in all directions, and the ornate balustrades turned to a deadly hail of splinters.

Gray wrapped his body around Elizabeth's to shield her. He looked up just in time to see the wheelhouse disappear in a sudden blaze, and the huge black smokestacks on either side of it break in two. The large funnels fell over and hurtled down past the panicked passengers, to quickly sink beneath the murky depths of the river. Fire sprouted from nearly every doorway and broken window, and hot, orange flames leaped upwards toward the sky. Gray felt Elizabeth tremble, sensed the silent scream of terror suppressed within her breast, and tried to ignore his own fear. He tightened his arms around her, and lowered his head against the crown of hers.

In that instant the world went mad.

One entire side of the boat splintered, and was instantly engulfed in flame as another boiler exploded. At the stern the huge red paddle wheel hung crookedly from its brace, the paddles now only ragged pieces of wood. People surged to the edge of the deck and threw themselves into the blackness beyond. Their screams filled the air and wrought the night with horror.

Within minutes the deck was empty. Everyone who could escape had done so, except for Gray and Elizabeth.

The riverboat began to list to one side, while hot flames incinerated everything in their path. Gray tried to pull Elizabeth away from the wall and toward the broken remains of rail at the edge of the deck, but she resisted his efforts. She shook her head in denial and made to break away from him.

He pulled her to his chest again and lowered his head next to hers. His lips brushed her ear as he spoke, his words urgent and rushed. "We have to jump, there's no other way. It could blow again—the boilers."

41

"I—I can't!" She tried to twist away from him.

The words had no sooner left her mouth when there was another explosion, and the entire rear portion of the *River Belle* fragmented into a cloud of debris and wood. Bright tongues of fire rose from the wreckage to turn the midnight skies a fiery orange, and the river to a glistening pool of silver-tinged redness.

"Elizabeth, there's no more time!" Gray yelled, and yanked her toward the edge of the deck.

"I can't!" she screamed. "I can't swim!"

His head whipped around and his gaze met hers. The horror he felt at her words was mirrored in her tear-filled eyes.

"Stay here!" He pushed her back and forced her arms to encircle a beam that protruded from the cabin wall. "Hang on to that. I'll be right back." Before she could utter a protest, he disappeared within the darkness of the black smoke that was everywhere.

Elizabeth clung to the board and strained to see through the dark acrid cloud that stung her eyes and throat. He'd left her! She was alone on a boat that was on fire and sinking! She choked back a sob of fear, and nearly screamed at the sound of glass breaking behind her. A window had shattered from the heat, and shards of ragged glass flew out into the night.

The screams and cries of the other passengers filled her ears and sent a ripple of chills up her spine. She stared out at the river through the haze of smoke that surrounded her, and was horrified at the sight that met her eyes. Faint light from a thin sliver of crescent moon blended with the fiery glow of the flames, and shone down on the few survivors who floundered about in the murky depths. With the black water covered by fog, and the distant shoreline obscured by darkness, many of the people in the water could not discern which direction to swim.

Suddenly, Gray was back. His strong hands gripped her shoulders, and once again he pushed her toward the open edge of the deck. "No!" she shrieked, barely able to control her hysteria. She choked on a lungful of smoke and struck out at him.

"Damn it, Elizabeth, stop it!" He gripped her shoulders. "This is the only way. I thought if we could get downstairs, closer to the water . . ." He shook his head. There was no time to explain what he'd hoped they could do, or that the stairs no longer existed. "We have to jump!"

She looked up at him with sudden comprehension, and her body sagged in resignation. What did it matter anyway, she thought with numbed dismay. If she stayed on the boat, she'd be consumed by fire. If she jumped into the river, she'd drown. Either way she was going to die.

He bent down, lifted the hem of her skirt in his hands, and jerked at it. Several long, thin strips of ruffled fabric came away in his hand and he twisted them together, one around the other, like a rope.

She found a small ray of hope and clung to it. "What . . . what are you doing?"

"Hopefully this will keep us together." He tied one end around her waist, the other to his belt, then grabbed her hands and forced her to grasp the length of fabric that hung between them. "Hang onto this like your life depends on it, Elizabeth, because it does. I'll be right beside you. Just kick like hell, when you get into the water." He turned her toward the edge of the deck and stood beside her. "Now, jump!"

Chapter 4

Elizabeth plummeted through the air toward the dark water, her voluminous skirts ballooned about her. She gripped the twisted strip of material, knuckles white from the pressure, fingernails biting cruelly into the flesh of her palms. She squeezed her eyes closed, as if blocking out the sight of what she was doing, of what was happening, might make it all nothing more than a nightmare, not real. Heaven help her, certainly not real.

She was still screaming when she hit the surface of the river. Black water surged up all around her, as her weight dragged her down into the murky depths. Suddenly a voice seemed to shout in her mind, commanding her to do something, to move, to help herself. Remembering what Gray had said, she began to kick furiously, but her legs and feet instantly entangled within the folds of ruffled pantalettes and undergarments that swirled around and clung to her legs like grasping tentacles.

I am *not* going to die like this! I am not!

The weight of the huge hoop-cage pulled her ever deeper. The coldness of the water seeped into her body to chill and numb her. She released her hold on the cloth rope and beat at the water with her hands in an effort to claw her way upward, out of the water. She needed air! Her lungs screamed for relief, seared with hunger for oxygen, but the more she reached for the surface and forced her tired legs to kick, the farther away it seemed to become.

Gray shot up through the gently lapping waves with a gasp. He gulped in air and whipped about in search of Elizabeth. She was nowhere in sight, and alarm gripped his rapidly beating heart. Then he felt the tug of weight at his waist, the insistent downward pull. Taking a deep breath, he dove, and, unable to see far in the dark water, followed the long loop of material with his hands until he found her.

She was still struggling against the water, but barely.

Gray pushed her skirt and petticoats aside, and fumbled at her waist for the hooks that would release her from the hoop-cage. Why in thunderation did women wear these damn things? A stream of curses ran through his mind, and he once again felt his lungs begin to burn. He saw the swoosh of bubbles that escaped Elizabeth's lips, as she finally gave up the air she had been holding within her chest.

There was no more time. He had to get her to the surface. His fingers closed about the waistband of the hoop-cage and he pulled. The wet fabric, now twisted and resilient, resisted. He yanked furiously, and finally the small fasteners broke apart. He ripped the offensive garment away, frantically pushed it down over her hips and legs, and released it into the oblivion of the river.

His own clothing had also become a burden; the leather *calzoneras* turned his legs leaden, and the gun on his hip had begun to feel like an anchor, but he refused to give them up. There was no time anyway. Summoning every ounce of strength he had left, Gray wrapped an arm around Elizabeth's waist, kicked his legs, and propelled them both upward. They broke through the surface, and clinging tightly to each other, gasped and choked in great gulps of air.

Debris floated all around them, pieces of the boat's balustrades, support columns, window sashes, broken furniture . . . and bodies. Many of the passengers had made it into the water only to find it their grave.

One of the *River Belle*'s railing support columns floated past. Gray grabbed it and pulled it to his chest, then wrapped an arm around its wide girth. "Elizabeth," he drew her to the wood. "Grab this! It will keep you afloat."

She forced her arms over the wood and lay her head upon its rough surface. If only she could rest, just for a little while. She closed her eyes.

"Elizabeth, you have to help me. We have to get to shore. Now kick, come on, kick."

Gray heard a faint cry to his left, and turned just in time to see an elderly man several yards away disappear below the water's surface. He remembered the old timer from the gaming salon.

"Aghhhhh!" Elizabeth screamed, her voice one of pure terror. She thrashed about and jerked on the wooden column.

Gray whirled around. "What the hell . . ."

Wide-eyed with horror, Elizabeth pushed at the water in front of her with one flailing hand and scrambled toward Gray, as the body of the *River Belle*'s captain, draped over a tangle of broken wood, floated past. The man's sightless eyes stared up at the dark sky, while his mouth hung agape in a silent scream.

Gray pulled Elizabeth to him, her back pressed tight against his chest. He kept one arm around the column and wrapped the other about her waist. He felt her tremble, and sensed her terror. "It's alright, Elizabeth, it's all right," he soothed, his lips close to her ear. "I'm here, come on, sweetheart, I'm here with you, calm

46

down. We'll be all right." He let his head lean against hers. Lord, he was tired. But there was no time for that now, they had to get to shore.

As he coaxed Elizabeth back to the wooden column, Gray caught his first glimpse of the *River Belle*. The boat was no more than a bonfire of red and orange against the inky blackness of the night now, her bow having come to rest atop a sand bar only a few hundred feet downriver.

The broken remains of a cherrywood ladies' chair washed up against Gray's arm, and drew his attention back to the matter at present. He took Elizabeth's cold, shaking hands in his, and forced her to wrap her arms around the thick beam of wood again. "Come on, Elizabeth, kick," he said. "Kick."

"I'm kicking, I'm kicking," she mumbled, and threw him a quick glance. Thank all that was saintly he'd been there to save her, or she'd have been a goner for sure, she thought, and with a shiver remembered the fear she'd felt only moments earlier. But, did he have to be so . . . so demanding now? Why couldn't they just let the current carry them to shore? She was tired, for heaven's sake!

They moved slowly through the water, the lapping waves all around them glistening orange, red, and silver in reflection of the tower of flames behind them. Before they had managed to move more than a few feet toward the river's edge, another explosion rocked the skeletal remains of the riverboat.

Gray turned back to look. Flames flew high up into the darkness, followed by a shower of wooden planks, splinters, and broken glass. One of the ornately carved deck balustrades shot through the firelit night toward them, and Gray instinctively raised his arm to protect himself and the woman beside him.

Elizabeth tried to scream, but the sound was silenced within her throat by muscles paralyzed with fear. She was going to die! The thing was shooting directly toward her.

The balustrade glanced off Gray's arm with jarring force, then struck the side of his head. He was thrown violently back against the wooden column, and one of his arms smashed down on Elizabeth's neck. Darkness enveloped him in one swift surge, and his last conscious thought was that he had not meant to strike her.

The air in Elizabeth's lungs flew out at the impact, and she nearly lost her grip on the beam of wood. She struggled to secure her grasp, and then turned an angry glare to Gray. The scream that had been on her lips earlier now burst forth, short and panicked. A long, jagged gash cut across his temple, and blood ran down the side of his ashen face. The makeshift rope about her waist instantly began to tighten and grow taut, as Gray, limp and unconscious, started to slip beneath the water.

"Gray!" Elizabeth screamed. His head bobbed up and down in the current, and he slowly began to slide from the beam of wood.

By chance, since Elizabeth was frozen with shock and a strong sense of having just been dealt the most unfair hand since this whole miserable day began, Gray's shirtsleeve caught on a nail that protruded from the column, and momentarily halted his descent into the river's depths. Under Elizabeth's morbidly fascinated gaze, each minute strand of cotton slowly and inexorably strained against Gray's weight, until it was too much, and each thread, one by one, broke. Startled out of her stupor, Elizabeth shot into action. She grabbed a handful of his shirt collar and locked her fingers about the wet cloth. As her fear usually brought forth anger, his sudden helplessness brought forth her strength. With one arm wrapped securely about their wooden "raft," she tugged, pulled, shoved, and pushed him back onto the column, until he lay with his head on the wood and both arms draped over it.

"Grayson Cantrelle, don't you dare die on me!" she threatened, and fought to hold back the tears that filled her eyes.

Her lungs burned from inhaled smoke and exhaustion, and her limbs were numb from both the coldness of the water and the pain of exertion. Elizabeth ignored all of that and commanded her legs to move, to kick against the river's sluggish current. It was a long journey to shore, made longer by the fact that every few seconds she was forced to stop and rest, to allow her heaving chest to calm, and her madly thumping heart to slow.

She lay her head against the wet, fire-scorched column of wood, and closed her eyes. She wanted to cry, she wanted to scream, to curse the captain of the boat for getting them into this mess, to pound the breast of the engineer who'd allowed the boilers to explode, but most of all she wanted to kill Aaron Reynaud. If it hadn't been for him and that . . . that *strumpet* she'd found him with, she wouldn't have stormed away from his plantation and taken passage on the first riverboat headed for New Orleans. And if she hadn't done that, she wouldn't be bobbing around in the middle of the river, clinging to a half-charred log and trying desperately to get herself and an unconscious gunslinger to shore.

The thought of putting a bullet through Aaron's forehead brought with it a sense of delight, and a strong determination to survive.

"Just wait, Aaron, you'll get yours."

She began to kick again.

"Grayson Cantrelle, will you please wake up," she ordered, and threw her unresponsive companion an angry glower. He remained limp, unaware of the world around him, unheeding of her demanding request. A worried frown tugged at her brow. She turned back toward the distant shore and forced her leaden legs to again propel them onward. "I'll never make it. I'm going to die, I just know it. I'm going to die out here in the middle of nowhere, tied like a bale of cotton to a gunslinger." She kicked angrily at the water. "Poppycock! What did I ever do to deserve this?"

Long minutes later, or perhaps it was centuries later, she wasn't sure, Elizabeth felt solid earth beneath her feet and nearly fainted in gratitude. She didn't know how long they'd been in the water. Minutes? Hours? She'd kept expecting some horrid creature to loom up out of the inky depths and take a bite out of her, to sieze one of her legs in a powerful, tooth-lined jaw and pull her down into the murky depths, or wrap slimy, sucking tentacles around her waist and squeeze until she burst. She turned and shook Gray's shoulder.

"Grayson Cantrelle, wake up!" She shook him again. Nothing. "You're not dead. You can't be." She suddenly felt weak with fear for him, and not quite so sure of herself. "Oh, please wake up," she moaned, but he didn't stir.

Elizabeth sighed heavily and began to push him toward shore. When the water became too shallow to swim through, she dug her feet into the soft earth of the riverbed and inched forward, convinced that moving a mountain couldn't be any harder than moving Grayson Cantrelle halfway across the Mississippi River. She struggled ashore, and her feet instantly sank into the thick quagmire of earth that lined the river's edge. Her ankle-high leather shoes disappeared as the mud sucked at her and enveloped her feet. Elizabeth pulled one foot free, made to step forward, and fell to her knees when her foot sank below the earth's surface again, this time to her calf.

"Help, I'm sinking! Somebody help me!" She twisted and jerked about. "Help!" She pulled on her leg, and grimaced when the suction held her in place. "Somebody?" She yanked again, and one leg popped free of the mud. Not wanting to return her foot to the muck, but seeing no alternative unless she wanted to remain rooted in the middle of this mire for the remainder of her life, Elizabeth said a quick prayer, wrinkled her face in distaste, and put her foot down again. She watched in dismay as it immediately disappeared. The squishy, oozy sensation and the feel of cold, wet earth seeping through her shoes was enough to make her want to sit down in the bog and weep.

Instead, she twisted about at the waist, grabbed hold of the material rope that was still attached to Gray's belt, and heaved. He barely moved.

"Oh, drat!" She wrestled about and nearly lost her balance. Once fully turned around, with her feet again sunk far below the mud's surface, she used the earth as leverage to hold her in place while she pulled on Gray.

She managed to drag his body from the water and within a few feet of the dry, weed-covered ground that sloped upward toward the elevated bank. Completely out of breath and strength, she paused and wiped a hand across her forehead, leaving a smear of mud over her brow. Her gaze scanned their surroundings. The river and immediate shoreline were bathed in a hazy orange glow, a combination of pale moonlight and the reflection of the flames that still crackled loudly on the riverboat. The tree-covered landscape beyond the riverbank, however, was left in a shroud of darkness.

Wheezing heavily, Elizabeth stumbled forward. She had to sit down, to rest, just for a few minutes. She collapsed to her knees, and let out a screech when a small rock dug sharply into her leg. She picked it up, and threw it toward the river with a curse. A long sigh escaped her lips as her utterly exhausted body began to relax. She slipped her feet from her wet, mud-encrusted shoes, pulled off her torn stockings, and with a muttered oath of disgust, flung them aside.

A tiny lizard darted out from a tall clump of weeds near where her hand rested on the ground. The reptile paused and stared up at her, assessing, and then, as if he'd decided caution was the better side of valor, raced for cover . . . directly beneath Elizabeth's skirts.

The movement caught her attention. "Ack! Get away! Get away!" She scrambled to her feet and furiously whipped the wet, mud-caked skirts about. She danced frantically from one muddy foot to the other, while her gaze shot in every direction. Finally, satisfied that the lizard was not clinging to her, and not about to dash up her leg, she stopped and stared down at the moonlit ground, fully expecting the tiny creature to loom up and attack her.

A soft moan broke the silence, and Elizabeth's head snapped up. Her gaze flew toward Grayson. "Oh, thank heavens, you're awake!"

Gray moaned again, a deep sound that brought with it a stream of choking, gasping coughs. He tried to rise up on his elbows, and his chest heaved in spasms as he gulped for air, then collapsed weakly back onto the wet ground. The movement aggravated the gash on his forehead, and blood began to trickle from the torn flesh, snake its way past his still closed eye, and over his pale cheek in a thin rivulet of red.

Never one to mince words, especially when in situations not to her liking, Elizabeth flounced across the short distance that separated them and stopped to stand above him. "Grayson Cantrelle, you stay awake," she demanded. "I can't carry you up that bank. I won't, you hear me? I'll let you lie here in this muck until you sink!" But even as she said the words, she knew he had already succumbed to unconsciousness again. "Oh, balderdash!" Tears swelled in her eyes, and she quickly wiped them away. Whatever was she going to do? She didn't know a thing about tending injuries or sick people. Was he hurt worse than she'd thought?

she wondered with a sinking heart. "Gray, please wake up," Elizabeth whispered, suddenly full of compassion and worry. She dropped to her knees beside him and lay her hand gently on his cheek. She'd like nothing more than to indulge herself with a good cry and tantrum, but worry and concern now held her tears at bay. At the same time, she wanted to pound his chest with her fists. This was the worst, most horrid predicament she'd ever been in, and it was all *his* fault!

He could have left you on that boat to burn to a crisp! a little voice within her piped up.

A twinge of guilt pricked at her conscience, but as was usual with Elizabeth, she rebelled against giving in to it. "Well, he didn't have to go and get himself knocked out. He should have been more careful. We could have both drowned!" she retorted aloud.

You would have, if he hadn't saved you by cutting off your hoop-cage.

"Oh, alright, he saved my life. I'll help him, I'll help him," she mumbled, and bent down to push Gray onto his back. She grabbed him under the arms, and as before, began to tug. It was like trying to pull a two-hundred-pound sack of rocks.

Time to change tactics.

She paused and waited for her breathing to calm, then clasped both hands about one of his muscular arms and began to pull again, dragging him inch by slow, agonizing inch toward the dry, weed-covered ground.

"Grayson Cantrelle, you're going to pay for this," she huffed, and gave his arm another pull. "Imagine, throwing me into the river like a sack of potatoes." She took another deep breath and tugged. "I might have drowned!" Another huff. "Men! They're all alike." Huff. "Good for nothing. Always pushing their will on women, acting so high and mighty." Huff, huff. "They act like they have all the brains, and we've got nothing but mush!"

With a series of gasps and desperate gulps for air, and more than a few curses and oaths of retribution, Elizabeth, bedraggled and muddied, hauled her unwelcomed burden up the bank.

The morning sun peeked over the horizon and bathed the landscape in a misty haze of golden yellow rays that touched the treetops and awakened the land to a bright, new day. The air was crisp, cooler than normal for June, and the pungent odor of fire and destruction was unmistakably present. A short distance downriver from where Elizabeth lay within the tall weeds, more passed out from exhaustion than cradled in mere sleep, the charred, skeletal remains of the *River Belle* stuck grotesquely out of the water, mute testimony of the night's disaster.

The broken evidence of what had once been the boat's beautiful furnishings and adornments, as well as what was left of the passengers' belongings, and in some places, the passengers or crew themselves, were scattered along both sides of the wide river. Here and there small animals scurried about the soggy debris, the lively chirrup of a mockingbird's song filled the air, and the sun continued to slowly rise, its sultry heat finally beginning to warm the cold earth.

Elizabeth stirred, the arm that had been draped across her forehead fell back, and her eyelids fluttered open. Dull pain throbbed through her shoulder. She struggled to sit up, and her stiff limbs instantly screamed in anguished protest at each movement.

For a brief second, she forgot where she was and gazed around in disoriented confusion. Then she saw what was left of the boat, and the burned or water-soaked luggage and broken wood mired within the mud at the river's edge. And Grayson Cantrelle.

She bolted forward, ignoring the agony of sore and bruised muscles, and scurried across the damp earth on hands and knees. Tentatively, almost fearfully, she lay a hand lightly on his forehead, and then quickly drew it back. His skin was as cold as marble.

"Oh, God, don't let him be dead! Please, please, don't let him be dead," she murmured, unaware she'd spoken the words aloud. "Gray? Gray, can you hear me? Are you awake?" He didn't answer. She prodded at his chest and leaned down to press her ear to it, half-afraid of what she wouldn't hear.

His heartbeat had a steady rhythm.

Gray's lashes lifted slightly while Elizabeth remained bent over him, the ends of her long hair brushing across his chest. He focused blearily on the wheat-colored strands, and the first thing that came to his mind, which seemed to be filled with a thousand men hammering away at his skull, was that she was alright. He tried to move, and a stab of pain shot through the left side of his head. He snapped his eyes closed, sucked in a sharp breath of air, and wished instantly for the darkness to return.

Elizabeth heard the soft hiss of breath and sat up. "Gray?"

His eyelids opened again and he squinted up at her. "Elizabeth?" Everything was a blur, but what he did see made him groan and close his eyes. There were two of her. Two Elizabeth Devlins. He let out another groan. From what he'd experienced so far, one Elizabeth Devlin was almost more than any sane man could handle. Two was just downright cruelty.

"What's wrong?" Elizabeth leaned over him anxiously. "You're not going to die, are you? You can't die! You can't!"

Gray forced his eyes open again. "I'll try not to." He made an attempt to smile, but the movement caused a shower of stars to erupt in his head. The frown deepened. "Where'd your sister come from?"

"Sister? What are you talking about? I'm the only one here."

He closed his eyes in relief and sighed. "Thank the Lord." She was safe, but at least there was only one firebrand for him to contend with, not two as his eyes told him.

"Thank the Lord?" Elizabeth echoed. "For what? Letting that fool boat explode? For stranding us out here in the middle of nowhere? Thanks? Humph!"

His whole body hurt like hell. His head throbbed, his chest felt like it had been kicked by a mule, and muscles he hadn't even known existed ached. At the outer edges of his consciousness, blackness swirled about, ready to consume him again. It beckoned and promised comfort and rest, a haven from the pain that pounded within his head, and he couldn't resist it.

Elizabeth reached out to touch his leather vest, as much from curiosity as concern. It was cold, as were the buckskin leggings, and his white shirt—which wasn't really white anymore, but more an ugly brown—was still damp. The once glistening walnut handle of his gun was covered with mud and half-buried in weeds.

She stared down at him, uncertain what to do. A soft, self-indulgent moan escaped her lips. She wasn't good at this type of thing, not like Eugenia, who was always practical and efficient.

Elizabeth glanced at the blood that had caked over the wound on his temple. The skin surrounding the injury was purple, bruised and swollen. She touched the torn flesh with the tip of her finger.

"Aghhh!" His head jerked back, and his hand swung up and out to slap hers away.

Startled, Elizabeth jumped. "Gray?" She poked at his shoulder.

He groaned and tried to open his eyes, but it was too

much of a strain, too painful.

"Drat, damn, and thunderation!" Elizabeth pounded a fist on the ground in exasperation, and tried to deny the fear that caused her body to tremble. "We need a fire . . . maybe if he's warm, he'll wake up. Then we can get out of here." She leaned forward on her knees and began to dig through Gray's pockets in search of a box of lucifers. She'd seen him smoking a cheroot; he had to have lucifers to light it. And he did. But the small box was still wet, and the sulfur-tipped sticks crumbled uselessly when she tried to strike them.

Tears of frustration welled within her eyes. Later, she told herself, later she could bawl her eyes out, but not now. She needed to find a way to get him warm, and then get out of this mess, and obviously *he* wasn't going to be much help. She looked down at Gray, and again, felt a sharp twinge of guilt at her uncharitable thoughts.

"I know, I know, he saved my life!" she mumbled before the little inner voice could remind her.

Elizabeth stood up and scanned the horizon for other signs of survivors. She found none. They were alone. If anyone else had made it off the boat and managed to get to land—alive—they were either nowhere nearby, or already headed inland in search of a town or farmhouse.

She stumbled back down toward the river. Wreckage was everywhere. It lined the shore and lay anchored in the mud. She picked up a dead tree branch that had fallen to the ground, and used it to push aside some of the smaller debris in her search. There seemed an accumulation of just about everything: portmanteaus of every size and shape, satchels, reticules, a vendor's case, broken chairs, a table, chinaware, clothing, and . . . bodies. She skittered about several poor souls who had drifted ashore and settled amid the refuse. Nausea closed her throat.

"I'll never set foot on a boat again, *ever!*" Elizabeth swore, as she paused before the body of the young steward who had shown her to her cabin. He couldn't have been more than thirteen years old, and now, she thought sadly, he never would be.

Denying herself the tears she knew would leave her a limp, useless mess, she moved on, searching for something to help them, but still uncertain as to exactly what it was she was looking for.

Then she saw it.

A broken bottle. Memories of a long-ago summer picnic flooded her mind. Holding her skirts high, she stationed one foot atop a satchel that was stuck in the mud, and leaned over to grab the bottle. She'd been only a child that summer, but she'd never forget how her cousin Fredric had held the glass over the ground and let the sun's rays shine through it. Long moments later, to both her surprise and delight, the dry pile of twigs and grass he'd brushed together burst into flame. She let out a soft snort. How *could* she forget? The fire had leapt upward and caught at the hem of her dress. If her sister, Eugenia, hadn't lifted her up and tossed her in a nearby river, Elizabeth would probably have gone up in smoke that day.

She picked the broken bottle up by its throat and swished it around in the water to wash away the mud, then rubbed it against her skirt. Once back on the bank near Gray, she knelt beneath the shade of a tall oak tree and raked several dozen dry leaves into a pile with her hands. She held the bottle over the small mound, maneuvered it to catch the glint of the sun, and directed the magnified beam onto the center of the leaf pile. Then she waited. Long moments passed. Her arms grew stiff and sore, every muscle ached to relax, but she wouldn't give up. It would work, she knew it would . . . in time.

A thin stream of white smoke drifted upward and

spiraled around her hands. "Yes!" Elizabeth yelled, excited at her success. She'd done it, she'd really done it. Her chest swelled with pride. She carefully placed several dry twigs across the mound to help feed the fire and make it stronger, then she ran back to Gray and knelt down beside him.

"Gray?" She nudged his shoulder. "Gray, can you hear me?" She nudged him again, harder this time.

He moaned and made to roll over. A stab of pain shot through his ribs, and Gray winced. He forced himself to remain still and wait for the aching to stop. "Elizabeth?" he whispered, finally.

"Gray, you have to get up. You have to try and get to the fire." She slipped an arm under his in an effort to help him rise.

He rolled to his side and tried to ignore the dull throb in his head, and the sharper ache in his chest. He pushed himself up to a sitting position, and groaned. The world spun sickeningly around him for a few seconds.

"Are you all right?" Elizabeth asked anxiously.

"Yeah, just . . . just dizzy." His voice was little more than a raspy whisper. He struggled to his feet. The world tilted crazily, cymbals crashed inside of his head, and his stomach turned over in a violent somersault. He leaned hard on Elizabeth and on legs that threatened to buckle beneath him at any moment, walked over to the fire.

"How . . . how did you build the fire?" he asked, in an effort to keep his mind off of his agonizing limbs and skull.

"My cousin taught me," Elizabeth said between puffs, and tried to shift the sinewy arm draped across her shoulder.

"Huh?"

She shook her head. Lord, the man was heavy. She was about to wither beneath his weight, and all he

59

could do was question her about how she'd made the fire.

"Are you all right, Elizabeth? You're not hurt?" Gray muttered with an effort.

"I'm fine." But she wasn't fine. She was tired and dirty. Her dress was reduced to rags, her hair was a mess, all of her luggage and money were at the bottom of the river, and she was stranded in the middle of nowhere with a . . . a cowboy. And a helpless one, at that. She was a very long way from being fine, she thought, but there was no use dwelling on it at the moment.

Once beside the hot flames, Gray loosened his grip on her and crumpled back to the ground. He released a long sigh and lay his head on a mound of dry leaves, using them as a pillow. He was bone-tired, and he hurt. Damn, did he hurt. His head was filled with stars, the side of his chest felt half-caved in, and every muscle in his arms and legs ached. But at least he was alive. And Elizabeth was safe and unhurt.

Elizabeth dropped to her knees beside Gray and gazed down at him. She flexed her shoulders to relieve the cramp in them. "Gray? Gray, we have to get you out of these damp leather things, before you catch your death."

He didn't answer, and made no move that he'd heard her.

"Gray, are you awake?"

He still didn't answer.

"Oh, Lord, why me?" she whined softly. "What did I ever do to deserve this?" Elizabeth reached toward the ornate silver buckle of his holster, and felt the heat of a blush rise to her cheeks at what she was about to do. She fumbled with the buckle, and finally managed to release the clasp, then gently tugged the holster's belt from beneath him and tried to pull it away from his hips. It wouldn't come. She looked down and saw that the holster was still secured to his leg. Untying the leather thongs from around his thigh, she pulled the holster loose, wrapped the thick belt around the gun, and carefully set it aside. She unclasped the buckle that was settled just below his stomach and which held the leather leggings taut across his hips. Suddenly, she paused, then forced herself to continue. This was no time to worry about feeling embarrassed. It wasn't as if she were going to strip him naked. A sly little smile curved her lips. She'd never seen a man naked before. She shook herself, shocked at her own thoughts. No, she was just going to get these leather things off of him.

It took Elizabeth several minutes to untie and release the threads of each silver concho. How did he ever get the leggings on? she wondered curiously. That done, the unusual coverings slid easily from his legs. She carried them to a nearby log and spread them out atop it to catch the warmth of the sun so that they'd dry, then returned to his side to continue her chore. His boots, along with the mud-encrusted silver spurs, came off easily.

His trousers were secured with another buckle, and she reached for it, only to stop, startled by what she'd intended to do. She'd actually been about to remove his trousers!

Gray stirred again, and, torn between hope and embarrassment, Elizabeth's gaze shot to his face. "Oh, it would just solve everything, if you'd wake up and stay awake," she murmured fervently. "Gray?" Then a bit sterner, "Grayson Cantrelle, can you hear me?"

He took a deep, ragged breath, but his eyes remained closed. The rising movement beneath her hand drew her attention, and Elizabeth looked down at his chest. Her fingers lay atop the damp and soiled white shirt. Less than an inch from her hand, the fabric spread open to reveal burnished skin and a light sprinkle of silky dark hairs.

For the briefest of moments, she wondered what it would be like to run her fingers over that hard wall of muscle, to feel the short strands against her own flesh. Her hand moved toward the edge of his shirt.

"Elizabeth Catherine Devlin, whatever is the matter with you? For mercy's sake!" she chided, and yanked her hand away from his chest as if she'd just been burned. Her face reddened at her own errant imagination.

Gray clenched his fist at his side and held his jaw rigidly clamped shut, his teeth tightly ground together. It was all he could do not to laugh, but then, that wouldn't have been a wise move. Not only would it antagonize *Miss Elizabeth Catherine Devlin* further, but the movement would surely aggravate his rib cage, and the pain there had just begun to subside into a dull ache. His head still hurt like hell.

Too upset with herself to remember to be gentle, Elizabeth rolled Gray onto one shoulder and began to tug at his vest and shirt in an effort to get them off of him. His ribs screamed in protest, and Gray grimaced and nearly bit his tongue. There was no admitting to being awake now, not with her temper. If she knew he'd been conscious while she undressed him, well, his imagination didn't want to even think what she'd say, let alone do. This was one little hellcat he didn't want to aggravate while he wasn't in exactly top shape.

Elizabeth gave a firm yank on his shirt and pulled it and the vest over the crest of his shoulder, then slipped her hand beneath the material, and forced it down over his arm. She felt the rock-hard ropes of muscle that corded his shoulder, and tried to ignore the current of feather-light shock waves that swept through her, as her hand slid slowly over the smooth bronze flesh. By the time she worked him free of the offending garments, Elizabeth could only excuse her erratic heartbeat, the dryness of her mouth, and the heat that surged through every cell of her body, by blaming them on the exhausting job of stripping a deadweight.

Gray remained still, although he suddenly felt a little guilty. It was not enough now to admit that he was awake. In her present mood, he figured he'd probably go from injured to dead. But more than that, he was curious as to what the peevish and obviously pampered Miss Devlin was going to do next. From beneath his thick brown lashes, he peeked up at her. In spite of her inexperienced and sometimes painful administrations, he had to admit that he was far from immune to her touch. If anything, a part of him was responding all to well to the angelic face and body that still hovered over his, despite the fact that she was no longer the perfectly coiffured belle he'd spotted on the docks of Vicksburg only hours before. Her dress was torn and muddied, her blond hair curled wildly about her shoulders, and the haughty air of superiority was, at least for now, gone. Yet, she looked beautiful to him.

Elizabeth rose to her feet, and Gray was surprised to see her reach under her skirt and pull down her petticoat. The heat within his loins intensified, and he shifted uncomfortably. With a quick jerk of her hand, Elizabeth ripped one of the ruffles from the petticoat hem. She held them before the fire for several long minutes, then turned and draped the undergarment across his chest. She knelt down beside him and gently covered the ugly gash on his forehead with the ruffle, careful not to move him while she tied the ends of the cloth loosely about his head.

She was afraid to move him. The wound might start to bleed again, and she wouldn't know how to stop it. Or maybe his skull was cracked, and she'd cause him to die. Oh, he couldn't die. She felt a rush of panic and fought to quell it. She moved back to sit beside the fire, and bit her lip in nervous uncertainty. She didn't know what else to do for him. Her heavy skirts were still damp, but just barely, and despite the warming of the morning air, she felt suddenly cold.

Elizabeth glanced back at Gray. Lord, what if he really did die? She felt tears sting her eyes and quickly disspelled the gruesome thought, never stopping to think about why his death should bother her so much. It wasn't going to happen, she told herself. It couldn't. It just couldn't! Not after she'd gone through so much trouble to save him. She lay down, pulled her legs up, and wrapped her arms around them. Weariness screamed from every aching bone and muscle. She had to rest, just for a while.

The sudden stillness brought Gray's eyes open in alert wariness. Something was wrong. He lifted his head to look around, and ignored the pain that throbbed in his temple. For a brief instant he felt panic, and then he saw her, huddled on the opposite side of the fire.

He laid his head back down on the leaves with a sigh, and felt a stab of remorse. The sight of her like that evoked a strong rush of protectiveness within him. He shouldn't have pretended to be unconscious. He should have helped when she was trying to undress him and care for him. A devilish smile tugged at his lips when he thought back to the scene.

The soft *whoosh-whoosh* continued to sound like a gentle drumroll on the still air. Elizabeth stirred slightly, but refused to awaken from her sleep. Three steamboats passed the wreckage of the *River Belle* that morning. Each captain looked out at the charred, burnt remains of the boat and the debris that lined the shore, and wished that they could stop and search for survivors, but none did. It was too dangerous. Highwaymen were too commonplace along the river. They hid within the thick foliage and small inlets, just waiting for a chance to jump the steamboats and rob everyone aboard. In some cases the passengers and crew were killed to eliminate any witness to the crime. So each captain said a prayer for the unfortunates, and another of thanks that it hadn't been his boat. The tragedy would be reported at the next port, and someone more equipped and armed to deal with the mishap would come to investigate.

Gray saw the boats pass, but made no move to wave them down. He knew it would do no good. He wondered if Travis had made it off the *Belle*, and prayed that he had. It'd be a stupid way to die. Texans were supposed to meet their maker in Texas. On the back of a horse, with a gun in their hand. Not be blown to bits by a riverboat's boiler. He closed his eyes and let memories of Travis and the adventures they'd shared together overtake him.

A few hours later, Elizabeth woke and hurriedly knelt beside Gray. Once reassured that his breathing was steady and strong, she stood and stretched the kinks from her muscles. For a while she wandered along the shoreline, hoping to spot another survivor or a passing boat. She saw neither. Instead, she began to sift through some of the debris, careful to stay far away from the bodies of those who had been washed ashore, and from the deeper mud near the water's edge. Finding one of her own satchels, and several belonging to other passengers that she felt might come in useful, Elizabeth picked them up and turned back to climb the sloping riverbank. Halfway up she stubbed her bare toe against a tree root. Pain shot up her leg, and she crumbled to the ground. The bags tumbled back down the slope.

"Damn!" Angry, self-pitying tears welled in her eyes. "I hate this! I hate this! Why is this happening to me? What did I do?" She glared down at the satchels. "This whole mess is all Aaron's fault! Aaron's, and Papa's, and . . . and—" she looked up toward the small campsite, "Grayson Cantrelle's! Men! Rot! The world would be better off without them! Rot, rot, rot!"

Feeling a little better at venting some of her frustration, she snatched up the satchels and scrambled back up the slope. Near the fire she opened her arms and let her burden drop to the ground, not caring if the noise woke Gray. Why should he sleep, while she did everything?

Because he's hurt, silly, the little voice reminded her.

He's not hurt that bad, Elizabeth silently retorted. She stared down at her muddy bare feet, and her nose wrinkled in disgust. "Heavens! Mama would absolutely shudder if she could see me now." Tears burned her eyes again, but something else distracted her from a good bent of weeping.

Her stomach began to growl. "Now what do I have to do? Hunt my own food?" She threw another handful of dry twigs onto the fire. "Aaron Reynaud, if I ever see you again, I'll kill you. I swear I will. And it'll be a real slow and extremely painful death."

Gray glanced furtively at Elizabeth. Who the hell was Aaron Reynaud?

Chapter 5

Elizabeth looked down at the holster cradled in her lap, then slipped the gun from its tooled leather sheath. Dried mud and bits of weed were thickly caked on the smooth wooden handle. The weapon felt awkward and heavy in her hands, much more so than the tiny derringer she'd carried in her reticule. She shoved the gun back into its damp, muck-covered holster. Hunting was out of the question. She'd never be able to hit anything with Gray's gun, except maybe her own foot. Her stomach growled again, and Elizabeth threw both gun and holster down into the weeds. She drew her legs up to her chest, hugged them to her, and stared out at the wide river, its surface turned silver and gold by the morning sun.

Gray watched her silently, his vision still a bit blurred. At least now there was only one of her. But his physical condition was not his foremost thought at the moment. Instead, his mind kept asking the same questions over and over: who was Aaron Reynaud? Why did Elizabeth sound so angry when she spoke his name? And what was this Aaron Reynaud to her?

Suddenly, the faint echo of a familiar sound filled the air. Elizabeth's head snapped up, and her entire body jerked to attention. A smile lit her face. They were saved! She scrambled to her feet and rushed down the bank toward the river. She paused at the edge of dry land, just as a large steamboat came into view from around the river's bend. The steady *whoosh-whoosh* of the huge paddles plying the water was a more than welcome sound.

"Here! Stop the boat!" She began to jump up and down and wave her hands frantically over her head. "Stop! Stop the boat! Help me!"

Gray pushed himself up onto his elbows. "Elizabeth." His voice came out little more than a hoarse whisper. He cleared his throat and tried again. "Elizabeth, they won't stop."

She didn't hear him. Her attention was riveted on the passing steamboat. A woman on the deck waved back.

"Stop! Stop! Oh, you ninny woman!" Elizabeth shook a fist in the air, and glared at the stern of the boat as it continued downriver. "You peabrain! What do you think I was doing, lady? Wishing you a good trip?" She stuck her tongue out at the disappearing paddle wheeler.

"Elizabeth?" Gray eased himself back against a nearby tree trunk. Beneath the petticoat that still draped his chest, he lifted an arm, and his rib cage burst alive in a sharp stab of pain.

Through clenched teeth, his eyes still closed, he called out again, louder. "Elizabeth."

She spun around. He was awake. Relief surged through her, and she hurried back up the riverbank. At his side, she dropped to her knees, and her stomach suddenly growled loudly.

Gray opened his eyes at the sound. "I take it you're hungry?" He couldn't help the smile that curved his lips, despite the pain in his ribs.

She ignored his comment. And his smile. "I was trying to flag down some help for us, but they act like they don't even see me!"

He shifted his position and merely made the pain worse. "The boats won't stop, Elizabeth. They're afraid of highwaymen."

She looked at him scornfully. "Do I look like a robber?"

Gray made to open his mouth, but she continued before he could comment. "Well, at least you're all right. Now maybe you can get up and hunt us some food, and then we can get out of here." She took a better look at him. He *wasn't* all right. His brow was knit in a frown, and his jaw was clenched and rigid. "What's the matter? Are you hurt somewhere besides that cut on your head?"

She pulled the muslin petticoat from his chest. An urge to touch that solid wall of muscle seized her, and she tore her gaze away. Her mind instantly registered the tightly knotted fist at his side, the other hand pressed to his ribs.

"I think my ribs are cracked," Gray said finally. "And my head feels like it's been split open with an axe."

"Not an axe, a piece of wood from the boat. It knocked you out while we were trying to get to shore." She lifted the bandage on his forehead and peeked beneath the bloodstained fabric. "It's bleeding again."

"How did . . ." Gray paused.

She began to remove the bandage, and he sucked in a deep breath at the sting that shot through his temple when the fabric pulled crusts of dried blood from the wound.

"You really got us ashore alone, huh?" he asked, a teasing note to his voice.

Elizabeth bristled. She should have known better than to expect gratitude. She snatched up the petticoat and began to tear a long strip from its hem.

"No, Mr. Cantrelle, actually we're both dead. We drowned," she retorted sarcastically, and glowered at

69

him. "Of course, I got us to shore *alone*. There wasn't exactly a whole lot of help out there, you know, and since I had no intention of dying, and you tied yourself to me, I didn't see where I had much choice but to get you to shore, too."

"You could have untied the rope."

"And let you drown?" She stared at him in shock.

"Some people would have."

"If I'd have known how much trouble you were going to be, maybe I would have done just that," she said, but the smile that tugged at each corner of her lips made an instant lie of the words.

She slipped a hand behind his neck. Her fingers became lost within the black tangles of his hair, and she pulled his head forward to wind a clean strip of cloth around it.

A rainbow of bright colors instantly assaulted his mind, as a parade of marching drummers banged their way through his skull.

Elizabeth folded the remainder of her petticoat into a small wad, and placed it against the tree trunk, then gently lowered his head onto it. "*Now* what are we going to do?"

"I don't think I'm up to doing much of anything just yet," Gray mumbled. He wished he had a good, strong shot of whiskey.

"What about your . . ." her gaze strayed downward toward his ribs, but became detoured by the sight of his bare chest—a sight that she was no longer able to ignore. The broad expanse seemed a landscape of strength and virility, even while he lay injured, and the mat of short satiny curls sprinkled across it glistened in scandalous exposure. Elizabeth felt sudden color suffuse her cheeks with a heat born of embarrassment, but she couldn't help her thoughts.

She had an overpowering desire to run her fingers through that silken forest, to feel the sinewy planes and

70

valleys of his flesh beneath her hand. She had to clench her fingers together tightly in order to stave off the urge.

Gray watched her, and amusement lit his eyes. His vision was still slightly fuzzy, but he could see enough to define the situation and interpret what she was thinking . . . and he liked it. He liked it very much. Too bad, at the moment, there was nothing he could do about it.

Elizabeth shook her head, pulled her gaze from his chest, and looked back up into his eyes. Another mistake. Her mind seemed to have gone blank, and her body tingled with a warmth she didn't understand. What in heaven's name was the matter with her? She searched for something to say, something safe. Then she remembered his injured ribs. "Huh . . . your ribs, shouldn't we, huh, do something?"

"There's not much that can be done. I'll just have to stay still for a couple of days, and let them heal." He took a deep breath, and grimaced a little more than was necessary.

"Well, what are we going to *do?* We can't just sit here." Her frustration was getting the better of her again, now that she knew he wasn't going to up and die on her. And that silly tingling feeling was annoying. After all, he was just a gunslinger, or cattle drover, or some such type. Not someone to go swooning over. Her stomach growled. "I'm hungry!"

"You're beautiful."

Elizabeth started and her eyes locked with his. She felt a warm languor steal into her limbs, and turned away to hide her confusion. He wasn't going to get to her. She wouldn't let him. She'd had enough of men and their pretty, but hollow, words. "I look like something the river spit out. And, I'm hungry!"

Gray smiled. "Anything from the boat wash ashore?"

71

"Yes, lots of things. Satchels, broken furniture, and lots of burnt wood. But no food."

"I meant pans or pots. Things to cook with. I guess it would be foolish of me to think you could shoot a gun." He was careful to keep any hint of amusement from his voice.

"As a matter of fact, I *can* shoot a gun, but not that cannon you carry." Elizabeth caught him trying to look at her from between scrunched eyelids, and momentarily forgot her pique. "You still can't see clearly?"

"No." He closed his eyes, but not before he saw, or at least thought he saw, concern on her face. He'd definitely heard it in her voice. "Can you fish?"

"Fish? You mean catch them?" Now she knew the bump on his head had jarred his brain.

"Yep, that's what I mean. Have you ever fished?"

"No, and I never wanted to. I saw my cousin do it once. It was disgusting. Slimy, icky things . . . ughhh!"

A crooked smile lifted one corner of Gray's mouth, and he let his eyelids slowly open. Still a bit fuzzy, but definitely clearing. "You eat fish, don't you?"

"That's different. They're dead. And cooked."

"Well, we could probably eat nuts and berries, but since I can't see too good, I don't know if there's any around. And even if there are, without looking at them I wouldn't be able to tell if they're poisonous. Of course, that wouldn't be any guarantee anyway, since I'm not all that familiar with this part of the country."

"Are you sure you should be sitting up? I mean, your head . . ."

"I'll be all right, Elizabeth. I won't die on you, I promise." He chuckled softly. "But I'm not going to be able to do much moving around for a while."

The smile almost did her in. It turned his square jaw into a curve of pure strength, softened the sharply cut cheekbones, and revealed a dimple within the deep

72

groove of his left cheek. But it was his eyes that held her momentarily spellbound. Deep, dark liquid pools of brown, speckled with slivers of brilliant gold where a warm reflection of the sun danced. A nervous flutter began to beat within her heart. She tore her gaze from his and stood up.

"I . . . I really do look a sight." Oh, why had she said that? It was a stupid thing to say, but she couldn't think. Not with *him* staring at her like that. Of course, it was true. She did look a sight. Her hair was a mass of unruly curls that fanned out to drape over her shoulders in a wild mane. Her hairpins had been lost in the river. She was barefoot, her dress was dirty and torn, and the folds of her skirt hung like a limp rag around her legs from lack of a hoop-cage and petticoats.

A giggle slipped from her lips. The woman she'd hailed on the boat that had passed earlier must have thought she was some poor little river waif.

She moved a few feet away, paused halfway down the elevated bank, and stared upriver. The afternoon sun gilded her hair and turned the blond curls to shimmering strands of platinum, the soft white shoulders that rose above the apricot gown to rich, magnolia ivory.

Gray watched her as best he could, and the desire that had been there ever since he'd first set eyes on her at the dock, intensified. With each second that passed, the need to know the passion of the beguiling creature whose life he had tried to save, and who in turn had saved his, grew stronger, and Gray grew more puzzled. What the hell was there about Elizabeth Devlin that intrigued him so much? Could the knock on his head have addled his mind? She was like no woman he'd ever met: soft and angelic one minute, a curse-spitting hellcat the next. She was too stubborn, too independent, and too damn innocent for her own good. She

73

was also gentle, sensitive, high-spirited, and breath-takingly beautiful.

She took a few steps toward the river, and the movement drew Gray's attention. The skirt of her silk gown swayed provocatively with each step. She moved further into the bright sunlight, and her legs became silhouetted against the fabric: long, lean, exquisitely well-curved legs.

He sucked in his breath at the sight, closed his eyes, and let his head drop so that his chin rested on his chest. Maybe if he blocked the tantalizing scene from his vision, his pulses would slow down. Maybe the heat that simmered within his groin would cool and go away.

Elizabeth heard his sharp intake of breath, but mistook it for one of pain. With a sudden twinge of guilt at her obstinance and bad temper, she rushed back up the hill and dropped to her knees beside him. When Gray didn't raise his head or open his eyes, a frown of worry knit her brow, and she reached a hand to his chest to reassure herself he was still breathing.

She knew her fear was silly, but she couldn't help it. He might be convinced he wasn't going to die . . . she wasn't.

Her hand on his bare chest was like a sudden smattering of hot sparks strewn atop his skin, that stoked the fire which already smouldered within him. Gray jumped, and his eyes shot open in surprise, only to snap shut as a dull pain erupted within both his head and chest at the sudden movement. He paid it no mind, and opened his eyes again. Damn, he'd been so intent on trying to ignore her, that he hadn't heard her approach.

"Are you alright?" She lifted her hand from his chest, and he immediately caught her fingers within his.

A shock wave of warmth exploded within the fingers that lay cradled in his large hand, tiny bolts of heat that streaked up her arm to merge with the accelerated beat of her heart. Butterflies burst to life within her stomach, and a wild keening surged in her veins, dark, urgent and indescribably sweet.

Gray's gaze held hers. The look in his eyes was at once savage and wild, yet gentle, commanding and hard, yet full of doubt and uncertainty, questioning her, questioning himself.

Elizabeth felt unable to breathe, to look away, to pull her hand from his. She was suddenly overcome with desire and wanted nothing more than to throw herself into his arms, to feel the warmth and protectiveness of his body close to her own, to be kept safe and cherished in his embrace. At the same time, she desperately wanted to run away, to flee, to race through the woods in search of the nearest farmhouse, plantation, or town, and never look back, never see him again.

She felt his fingers tighten around hers. Without conscious thought to what she was doing, Elizabeth slowly leaned forward. Gray felt himself being drawn into those deep, china-blue eyes, and the need to have her, to make her his, almost overwhelmed him. Awareness of the discomfort and pain that had tortured his body for the past few hours was suddenly vanquished from his mind, no longer of concern. With his free hand, he reached up and twined his fingers into the thick mane of golden curls at her nape. Her lips brushed his, tenderly, lightly, and Gray groaned with the effort not to crush her to him. The hand at her nape pressed down, strengthening its grip, pulling her to him. His mouth claimed hers, and he drank in the sweetness of her lips.

Elizabeth's mind struggled to resist the euphoria that swept over her, but her traitorous body yearned only for more.

She pulled her mouth from his. "Gray." Her voice

was ragged with emotion. "We mustn't . . ."

"Don't fight it, Elizabeth. Don't deny what I know you feel." His lips covered hers again, and his tongue darted forth to fill her mouth and wreak havoc with her senses.

A pleasurable ache consumed Elizabeth, and though she knew she should resist him, fight him, she surrendered to the need to be in his arms. She had been kissed by other men, she had heard many a pretty word and husky plea whispered in her ear, but none had touched her, tempted her, like his. Startled by her own newly awakened passion, but helpless to deny it, all thought of resistance left Elizabeth, and her arms slipped up to encircle Gray's shoulders.

His lips left hers and moved to the long column of her neck, his face buried within the soft curls of her wild mane. His warm breath against her skin was like a caress that heightened her longing, while his lips kissed, teased, and tantalized. "Ummm, my beautiful angel is also a temptress," Gray murmured huskily.

Forgetting his injuries and the need to be gentle and slow with her, Gray's mouth returned to hers in a kiss that was meant to brand her, to let her know he had staked his claim and declared her to be his. Like it or not, Elizabeth Devlin had gotten under his skin, and at this moment he was more than willing to admit it. His hand slid from her neck to the smooth skin of her shoulder, her back, her breast. His warm fingers cupped her bosom and softly caressed the subtle mound, while his thumb began to move in a rhythmic circle atop her already taut nipple.

Elizabeth stiffened at the intimate touch. The reality of what she was doing suddenly invaded the sense-routing enchantment. She moved to pull away from him, but Gray's embrace tightened, and his kiss grew more devastating. Within seconds reality again vanished, propriety was forgotten, and all Elizabeth could feel, all she could sense and know and want was his touch. The delicious ecstasy his touch invoked swept through her limbs, through every muscle and cell of her body. A small moan escaped her throat, and her arms tightened around his neck. She ran her fingers through his hair and felt the warmth of the sun on each silken strand. She returned his kiss and tasted the savage wildness and gentle tenderness that was Grayson Cantrelle, and she snuggled closer, closer.

"Ouch!" Gray yelled, and abruptly jerked away. His features were contorted in a grimace of pain. He clutched at his side and mumbled beneath his breath.

Elizabeth sat sprawled beside him in a not too dainty heap, the blue eyes that only a moment ago had blazed with passion, now glared at him in ice-cold anger. Whatever had she been doing? She raised a hand to her lips. They felt tender and a little sore. They were also slightly swollen. Good Lord, she had kissed a gunslinger! No, her mind instantly argued, *she* hadn't kissed *him*. He'd taken advantage of her, forced his attentions on her. Well, it wouldn't happen again. She'd just have to keep her distance from him, that's all.

The pain in Gray's ribs slowly began to subside, and he let out a long sigh of relief. Damn, of all the luck! And then with a start, he realized that what he'd been about to do would have made him no better than the man he'd been hunting for the past four months. The man who had seduced his sister, and then run off and left her when he discovered she was with child. Gray had been totally prepared to seduce Elizabeth, but he was far from prepared to offer to marry her. He opened his eyes just in time to see Elizabeth scramble to her feet. He'd have to control his desires from now on. At least with her. "Elizabeth," his voice was still heavy with emotion. "Elizabeth, I'm sorry, I didn't mean to—"

She turned a cold eye on him. "Well, you should be! How dare you kiss me! We may be stuck out here together, *Mr.* Cantrelle, and I may have to play nursemaid to you, but I don't have to be your . . . your trollop! Just you remember that!" With a toss of her head, Elizabeth spun around and stalked down the elevated riverbank.

"Where are you going?" He felt apprehensive, but certainly not guilty. Well, not *too* guilty. Gray watched her flounce toward the river. She might be angry, and a little hard to take for a while, he reasoned, but that kiss had sure as hell been worth it. Even now his body reacted to the mere sight of her, and the kiss lingered on his mouth, the fine, sweet taste of her like an intoxicating wine in his blood. "Where are you going, Elizabeth?" he repeated, a bit more sternly.

"To find some food," she said without a backward glance. "I told you before, I'm hungry."

Gray laughed softly at her petulance, which was oddly endearing—another sure sign that the knock on his head had jumbled his brain. "Find a hat pin, or something like that," he called out to her. "And see if you can locate some more clothes, women's skirts or petticoats. And a pail, you'll need a pail."

"Just why do I need those things?" she asked icily and turned to stare at him, hands on her hips.

"To fish."

The loud crash brought Gray awake with a start, which in turn caused a burst of pain in his head. Once the stars cleared away, he opened his eyes.

Elizabeth stood over him, arms crossed beneath her breasts. "There are the things you wanted. Now you can go fish."

Gray pushed himself to a halfway sitting-up position, and leaned back against the tree trunk. "If we're going to wait until I can get down to the riverbank, we're going to be mighty hungry for a while."

"You want *me* to do it?" she exclaimed in shocked disbelief.

"Take that—" he pointed to the small bucket she'd found, "and see if you can find some worms."

"Worms?"

"Worms."

"I'm not eating worms. I'd rather starve to death. That's absolutely disgusting. Only someone like you would eat worms."

Gray bit his bottom lip in an effort not to laugh. It would only make matters worse, and anyway, it would probably hurt like hell. "They're not for eating. They're for bait . . . for the fish."

"Oh." She looked at him skeptically, not sure whether to believe him or not.

"The worms," he reminded softly.

She grabbed the pail. "Just where am I supposed to find them?"

"Probably over there, that bank of dirt just below those trees." He pointed to a copse of oaks a few feet from where she'd made their fire. "I'll try to bend this hat pin into some semblance of a hook, and fasten it to a couple of strips of material. You see if you can find yourself a spoon or something to dig with."

"Dig with? Why am I going to dig?"

"You have to dig into the earth to find the worms. Then put them in the pail. Come back after you've got five or six."

"What? I have to dig them out? And how do I get them in the pail? Can't I just put it down by them and let them crawl into it?"

Gray stared intently down at his hands. Don't laugh, he told himself. Whatever you do, don't laugh. "No, Elizabeth," he shook his head, "I don't think they'll willingly crawl into the pail. I doubt they're too crazy about being used as bait."

He pretended not to notice her stomp away, pail in hand, and set his attention to the hat pin and petticoats Elizabeth had found in one of the portmanteaus.

Minutes later her angry mumbles caught his attention, and he turned to watch her.

"Horrid little creature, get into that pail!" She pushed at one end of a gray worm with the fork she'd found, but it slithered in the opposite direction from where she'd laid the bucket on its side. She slipped the tines of a fork beneath the wiggling creature and flicked it toward the pail, then watched in horror as it did a somersault in the air and landed on her bare toes. "Ahhh! Get off! Get off!" she screamed, and shook her foot wildly. Again the worm flew through the air, this time to land in a clump of weeds and promptly disappear. Elizabeth threw the fork down, grabbed the pail, and stalked toward Gray.

"Here." She dropped the pail on the ground beside him, "There's four of those filthy, slimy creatures in there, and that's all you're getting, unless you want to go dig them up yourself!"

Gray rubbed a hand over his mouth to hide the smile that ached to appear. Why he found himself so attracted to this little blond spitfire, he couldn't figure. She hadn't said more than a handful of nice things to him since he'd met her, if that many.

"Okay, sit down and let me show you how to bait the hook. Then you can go catch us some dinner."

Elizabeth remained standing, and gasped in horror when he reached into the pail, picked up one of the worms with his fingers, and proceeded to calmly spear the squirming body with the hat-pin hook. He picked up the loop of fabric in his other hand, and held both out to her.

"I'm not touching that thing," she said, her gaze glued to the speared worm.

Gray let go of the worm and hat pin, and they dangled from the fabric strip he'd ripped and tied together to form a line. "Just take this down to the river, and toss the end with the hook on it into the water. When you feel a tug on the line, pull it back in quickly, or our dinner will get away."

Elizabeth reached a hesitant hand toward the fabric, trying to stay as far away from the hook and worm as possible. She held it at arm's length and hurried down the bank toward the river.

The first worm fell off the hook before she reached the river's edge.

The second worm disappeared from the hook as it hit the water.

The third worm managed to stay on the hook, but when Elizabeth felt the tug Gray had told her about, and began to draw the line in, the tussle got hard. By the time she finally pulled the hook in, it was empty.

"This is the last worm, Elizabeth. Lose this one, and you'll have to go dig up some more."

"I'd rather go to sleep hungry."

Elizabeth marched down to the river, a curse muttered with each step. "Aaron Reynaud, this is all your fault. If I ever see you again, so help me, I'll skin you alive! I'll feed you rat poison! I'll . . . I'll make you eat worms!"

Five minutes later, the line jerked, and Elizabeth was nearly pulled off her feet, which was something, considering she was sunk in mud up to her ankles.

"Hang onto it!" Gray called.

"What do you think I'm doing? Waving the stupid thing on its way?" Elizabeth mumbled under her breath, as whatever was on the other end of the line tried desperately to drag her into the river. What in blazes had she caught anyway? A whale? Despite her sullen anger, she felt a thrill of accomplishment. She'd actually caught a fish! She'd really done it!

She looped one hand over the other to retrieve the line a foot at a time, until finally the fish lay in the mud at her feet. Its blue green eye stared up at her accusingly.

"Well, it's not my fault!" She suddenly felt like a murderer. "We have to eat." She wound the line about her hand and carried the fish up the bank.

"Here. I caught it, you cook it." She held the still-flapping fish out to Gray.

Before he could reach up and take the line from her hand, she released it, and the fish fell onto Gray's stomach and began to jump about crazily.

"Elizabeth!" He jerked upward and grabbed at the fish. A stab of pain shot through his ribs, and he nearly bit his tongue. "Damn little vixen! Needs a good spanking, that's what she needs," he muttered softly to himself.

He heard Elizabeth giggle and looked up to see her watching him. Gray pulled his gun from its holster.

"You're not going to *shoot* it?"

He didn't answer. Instead, he gripped the fish firmly in his lap and whacked it over the head with the handle of the Colt. The fish instantly fell still. Gray returned the gun to its holster and looked back up at Elizabeth. "I'll forgive you that one, Elizabeth, but I won't forget it." A slow smile softened the dire promise. "Now, do you think you can get me that pan you said you found?"

Elizabeth wrapped the remainder of the cooked fish in what was left of her shredded petticoat, and placed it back in the pan beside the fire. At least she wouldn't have to worry about breakfast. Lord, if anyone ever found out she'd had to fish, or that she'd actually dug in the earth for worms, she'd just die.

Evening approached, and with the sun's descent below the horizon, the warmth of the day quickly faded. A blaze of scarlet color filled the sky, and streamed down through the branches of the tall trees. An almost imperceptible haze floated above the river, and all about them the forest began to come alive with a buzzing, humming, chirruping cacophony of sound.

Elizabeth felt a shiver of unease, and threw a furtive glance over her shoulder into the growth of trees and brush that surrounded them. What was in there, in the darkness, that only came out at night? She moved to the fallen tree trunk she'd used to lay their clothes on to dry, and retrieved two velvet cloaks she'd found in one of the portmanteaus that had washed ashore. She wrapped one about her shoulders, fastened its small broochlike clasp at her neck, and carried the other cloak over to Gray. She knelt and draped it over him. "This should help to keep you warm tonight."

He'd been deep in thought, but her words pulled him from his reverie. A sadness etched the corners of his mouth, and dulled the bright spark that was usually in his eyes. He'd been overcome by memories of himself and Travis, and fear that he'd never see his boyhood friend again. Suddenly, Gray felt very lonely.

His hand reached up and closed around her arm, and his gaze bore into hers. "I can think of a better way to keep warm."

Chapter 6

Elizabeth snuggled deeper into the circle of Gray's arm, then realized what she was doing and tried to pull away. His hand on her shoulder stopped her.

"It's all right, Elizabeth."

"But I might hurt your ribs."

"If you do, I'll let you know. Now go to sleep."

But she couldn't. For some reason, even though her body was weary and sore all over from using muscles she had been unaware she even possessed, she was not sleepy. She lay back against his arm and stared up at the black blanket of sky, dotted with a thousand diamondlike stars, and a pale half-moon.

In the distance she heard the soft *whoosh-whoosh* sound of a paddle wheel plying the waters of the wide river, but made no move to look up. Gray had been right: they wouldn't stop.

Elizabeth closed her eyes and tried to relax.

"Go to sleep, angel," she heard Gray murmur a few minutes later, as the soft sounds of the night began to drift away from her consciousness.

Gray remained still until he was certain Elizabeth was soundly asleep, then he carefully shifted his position, and tugged at the inseam of his pants with one hand. Having her this close was playing havoc with his body, and it was damn uncomfortable.

The next morning Elizabeth was up bright and early, moving about the small camp quietly while Gray slept. She'd awakened to find herself still wrapped in his embrace, but shocked to find her own arms securely clasped about his waist. Shaken, she had scurried to her feet and begun at once to fan the smouldering fire back to life. Gray needed to rest, she'd decided. That would help him recuperate from his injuries, and the faster he recuperated, the sooner he could move. Then they could leave this godforsaken riverbank clearing and get back to civilization. Elizabeth sighed at the thought. She had never realized how much she'd taken all the little luxuries in life for granted, until now.

Wrapping a swatch of material she'd torn from a salvaged petticoat around the handle of the pan, she carried the warmed fish over to Gray and bent down beside him. His eyelids fluttered open immediately. "Good morning, beautiful," he said smoothly.

"Beautiful?" Elizabeth laughed. "If what I look like now is your idea of beautiful, then I know you still can't see very well."

"I can see just fine," Gray countered. "And smell, too." He eyed the fish.

"Here. I've already had mine." She held the pan out to him. "Do you need help?"

"Depends on what kind of help you had in mind," he answered. A wicked little smile curved his lips.

Elizabeth stood. "I think you can do just fine on your own," she said coolly.

Gray shifted position and his ribs screamed to life. He grimaced.

"Is it really bad, Gray?" Elizabeth asked, suddenly

worried again. She dropped to her knees and reached out to touch the bandage on his head, lifting it slightly to peek at the broken skin beneath.

"Ouch!"

"Oh, I'm sorry." She pulled her hand away quickly. "I've never been good at this sort of thing. Too bad you weren't stranded with my sister Eugenia. She always knows what to do."

"Is Eugenia as full of spit and fire as you are?" Gray asked, and tried to ignore the urge to set aside the pan of fish and pull Elizabeth into his arms. What he really wanted to taste this morning were her lips, but he knew that if he did, he wouldn't be able to stop with just a kiss.

"Eugenia's perfect," Elizabeth said. "Everyone says so. She's pretty, and polite, and always, always, knows the right thing to do."

"You've done all right for us here, considering."

Elizabeth looked at him quickly. "Considering what?" she asked defensively.

Gray smiled. "Well, considering you're probably used to being constantly waited on hand and foot by a half-dozen servants, for one thing. And that you're stuck in my lowly company, for another."

Elizabeth jumped to her feet. "I'll have you know, Mr. Cantrelle, that I don't *need* servants to wait on me. I'm perfectly capable of taking care of myself, which, at the moment, is more than I can say about you. And secondly, I could always leave you here, if I had a mind to."

"You'd get lost," Gray said, unable to resist the impulse to tease her further.

"I would not." Elizabeth whirled and hurried down the slope toward the river. The nerve of the man! After all she'd done, he acted as if she were nearly helpless. "Ohhh! I could strangle him," she muttered under her breath. "Just who does he think he is, anyway?"

"Better catch us another fish before too long," Gray yelled.

Elizabeth spun around. "You just ate."

"But we'll need dinner, and fishing's always better in the morning."

"Oh, for heaven's sake. Fish can't tell the time. How would they know whether it's morning or not?" She climbed back up the slope and bent down to retrieve the pail and fork from beside Gray, where she'd dumped them the night before.

The tall bushes that edged one side of the clearing rustled, and Elizabeth froze. Gray, in a movement so swift she didn't see it coming, grabbed her arm and jerked on it. Yanked off her feet, Elizabeth flew through the air and landed on the opposite side of him, the contact of her derriere with the hard ground producing a solid *thunk*. Gray's other hand shot out and wrapped around the butt of his Colt. In a flash, he slipped it from the holster and held it ready, his gaze riveted on the still rustling bushes.

"What do you think you're doing?" Elizabeth demanded, trying to straighten herself and get to her feet. His arm, held stiffly across her midriff, and his hand gripping her forearm, prevented her from rising.

"Ssssh," Gray hissed.

"Why I never!" Elizabeth sputtered. Then she noticed the drawn gun, and Gray's intent stare at the wall of thick bushes that were no more than eight or nine feet away. "What . . . what's in there?"

"I don't know," he whispered.

She cowered beside him, trying to make herself smaller, and snuggling up against his shoulder. "Is it a . . . bear?"

"You don't have bears in Louisiana. More likely a wildcat."

Elizabeth made a whimpering sound and clung to

the back of Gray's shirt. A wildcat? Oh, merciful Lord in Heaven. She was going to die for sure now.

A hint of movement fluttered within the bushes again, a few leaves fell to the ground, and the branches parted. A small deer poked its head from the foliage.

Too terrified to look, too overwhelmed with a dreadful curiosity not to, Elizabeth peeked over Gray's shoulder and felt a wave of relief at seeing the soft brown eyes and huge ears of the tiny doe. But, just as relief began to wash over her, she was abruptly engulfed in a rush of horror.

She jumped up and pushed at Gray's outstretched arm.

The gun went off and, with an explosion that was deafening in the silence of the river wilderness, a bullet slammed harmlessly into a tree a few yards away. The deer instantly bolted from the bushes and disappeared. Gray spun around to stare at Elizabeth. "Why the hell did you do that?" he demanded.

"You were going to kill it."

"Of course, I was going to kill it. That deer could have been our dinner for the next few nights. Or don't you like venison?" he asked, his tone a bit snarly as his mind conjured up an image of a thick steak.

"Well, of course, I do, it's just . . ."

"Just what?" he demanded.

"She looked so sweet. I didn't want you to kill her."

"Where do you think venison comes from, Elizabeth? Trees?" he challenged, sarcasm practically dripping from his tongue.

Elizabeth glowered at him, but didn't answer.

He picked up the pail and fork from where she'd dropped them. "Here, go catch us some dinner."

Elizabeth snatched the pail and fork from his hand and got to her feet, but looked back at the bushes before turning toward the river.

Gray caught her gaze. "Don't worry. The deer's

gone. We'll have fish again . . . or worms if you don't catch anything."

Too furious to retort, Elizabeth stalked across the clearing and knelt down at the same spot where she'd dug for worms the day before. "The gall of the man," she muttered. "No account, shiftless drifter. Gunslinger, that's what he is, I just know it. Probably raised by savage Indians."

This time Elizabeth managed to get down to the river with her first worm still skewered on the hook. But it took three more before she caught a fish. By midday, she had caught another and presented both to Gray to gut and clean. That was one thing she adamantly refused to do. Even the mere thought made her cringe with disgust.

Gray decided to try and atone for his earlier words. He *had* been a bit rough on her. "Tell me about yourself, Elizabeth. Have you lived in Mississippi all your life?" he asked, curious to know more about her and wishing he wasn't. He slit the belly of one fish, thankful he didn't have to move much to get the job done.

Elizabeth sat down on a log opposite him and watched him prepare the fish. "I was born and raised in Vicksburg, but my parents are dead now. Our plantation was sold a few months ago, just before my father died, and my sister, Eugenia, who's married, lives in Texas, of all places."

"I'm sorry."

"So am I. Why anyone would move to that uncivilized territory is a mystery to me."

"I meant about your parents."

"Oh."

"What happened?" Gray asked.

"Mama's been gone now for about three years. She died of the fever. Papa passed on a few months ago."

89

"Sick?"

She shook her head. "No. He . . . he got in a fight over a lady he was seeing." She almost gagged on the word lady. "The other man was drunk and whiskey mad. He pulled a gun and—" her voice broke, "and my father was killed."

Gray saw the shadow that darkened Elizabeth's eyes, heard the catch in her tone, and quickly changed the subject. "What about your sister? Why'd she move to Texas?"

"Virgil's home is there. That's her husband."

"I would have thought, with your mother also dead, that you would have gone to your sister's place right after your father's passing. Being alone and all." Gray looked at her questioningly.

"Oh, I wasn't alone. I had—" Elizabeth abruptly snapped her mouth closed and rose to her feet. "I think I'll go see if I can find some berries to have with our dinner."

Gray watched her as she hurried toward the trees beyond the clearing. What had kept her in Vicksburg after her father's death? If it had merely been the sale of the Devlin properties, or a reluctance to leave her home, he felt confident she would have said so. Instead, she'd skittered away like a nervous kitten. And what had she meant about not being alone? Was that where this Aaron Reynaud guy she'd been muttering to herself about came in? It was obvious that Elizabeth didn't want to talk about who or what she'd left behind in Vicksburg, and that only proved to pique Gray's curiosity all the more.

Standing beside a huge mound of tangled vines and interwoven leaves, Elizabeth gathered part of her skirt together and dropped a handful of berries into the fold of material, then popped one into her mouth. She closed her eyes and savored the sweet taste on her tongue and the cool juice that filled her mouth. Lord, she was so sick of fish that the berry tasted like a gift from heaven. If anyone had told her a week ago that she'd so thoroughly relish the taste of a simple little piece of fruit, she'd have told them they were crazy.

When she had a small mountain of berries cradled in the fold of her skirt, Elizabeth returned to the campsite. She stepped into the clearing and immediately stopped. It was empty. Gray was nowhere in sight.

She took a hesitant step forward and dropped the berries into a pan. "Gray?"

No answer.

"Gray? Where are you?" she called louder, her voice edged with panic.

Gray stepped out from behind a tall bush, while at the same time fastening the top button on the front of his trousers. He looked up, startled to see her standing there watching him. "I thought you were off looking for berries."

Her eyes narrowed in suspicion. "And I thought you couldn't move. What were you doing?"

Gray walked to the fallen tree trunk he'd been using as a backrest and, supporting himself against it with one hand, slowly lowered himself to the ground. A hiss of breath escaped his lips.

"Well?" Elizabeth demanded.

"I was watering the trees." A grimace of pain creased his face, as he shifted around and tried to get comfortable.

"Watering? The trees don't need watering." Elizabeth took several steps toward him and propped clenched fists on her hips. "You said you were too hurt to move. You said it'd be days. You said—"

"I was going to the privy," Gray said, interrupting her tirade. "Or would you like to help me do that, too?"

"Oh. Well, why didn't you say so?" A flush of warmth swept over Elizabeth like a tidal wave, and she felt her cheeks redden.

"Did you find any berries?" he asked, trying desperately not to laugh at her look of embarrassment.

She hurried to retrieve the pan of berries.

He took it from her stiffly outstretched hand and set it down beside his thigh. "Let's save them for after dinner." With that he lay his head back on the log and closed his eyes.

Elizabeth felt suddenly chagrined for yelling at him, then bristled against the feeling. Why did she always feel guilty around him?

Because he's hurt, and you're acting like a selfish little shrew, her conscience screamed.

I don't care, she retorted silently, then felt a wave of guilt. "I'll cook the fish," she said, and turned away. She felt the need to stab something, and the fish was a safer choice then Grayson Cantrelle.

He didn't answer, but remained still, lying against the log, his eyes closed.

She knelt beside the rock-encircled campfire and poked at the small pile of logs with a stick. "Oh, piddle, it went out." She threw an angry glare at Gray. He'd probably fallen asleep while she'd been fishing and didn't stoke it. Her shoulders sagged at the thought of starting the fire all over again.

Come on, Elizabeth, the chiding little voice in the back of her mind said.

"Oh, all right!" The words snapped off her tongue. She brushed some dry leaves together, sat down, and held the shard of glass up so that it was angled between the pile of leaves and the sun, and waited.

Gray moaned softly, and Elizabeth tensed. Oh, God, what would she do if he got worse? What if his moving around, his going to the *privy,* had done something to his insides? What if he died? She'd be out here all alone. A knot of fear formed in the pit of her stomach, and her heart fluttered. Did he seem weaker? She stared at his face, but couldn't decide if he looked as if he was in pain, or merely tired from the effort of getting up. Had the movement aggravated his injuries? Was he bleeding inside? Was he dying? She felt a sudden sense of panic. "Oh, why is this happening to me?" She nearly mashed a fist on the ground in frustration and anger, but caught herself and glanced at Gray. Tears filled her eyes, and she wiped them away with the back of her free hand. "Please don't die, Gray," she whispered softly.

The leaves began to smoke, thin wispy white trails that curled up to wrap around Elizabeth's hand and pulled her attention from her worries. She placed the shard of glass aside and bent toward the fire, carefully blowing on it in an effort to fan the tiny sparks that had caught. Within minutes the fire was ready for the pan of fish, and a few minutes later the fish was ready to eat. Elizabeth slipped the meat onto a tin plate she'd found and carried it to Gray. She sat down, facing him.

"Gray?"

His eyes opened and he lifted his head. "Ummm, smells good." He took the plate from her hands, and his fingers brushed over hers.

Elizabeth felt a shock of skin-prickling currents rush up her arm at the touch, and quickly withdrew her hand.

"Are we dining together tonight?" he asked, a teasing glint in his eyes.

"Oh. I forgot my plate." She made to get up.

Gray caught her arm. "No. This is fine."

She hesitated, suddenly unable to think. His hand on her arm was like a circle of fire that burned her skin, turned her blood hot and molten, and left her breathless. Her mind whirled in confusion. What was there about this man, that he had such an intense affect on her?

"Come on, sit here beside me." Gray urged her to turn around, pulled her to his side, and wrapped an arm around her shoulders. "You'll have less to clean up this way." He set the plate on his lap and speared a piece of fish with his fork, then lifted it to Elizabeth's mouth.

Her lips parted and she accepted his offering.

Gray gently pulled the fork from her mouth, watching the way the silver tines slid from between the soft, pink flesh of Elizabeth's lips. He felt his body tense slightly as his groin tightened.

Elizabeth felt his movement and turned to look up at him. "Am I hurting you?" she asked. "I didn't mean to lean against you. I'm sorry."

"You didn't hurt me," Gray answered, and in spite of the discomfort he was experiencing from having her so close, urged her, with the arm he still held around her shoulders, to settle back against him. He jabbed his fork into a large chunk of fish from the plate that lay on his lap, shoved it into his mouth, and handed the fork to Elizabeth, but kept his gaze focused on the darkening line of trees a few yards away. He tried to ignore the way her body fit snuggly against his, the way her hair brushed across his arm and shoulder, like soft, teasing strands of silk, and the way his skin felt seared by her touch. It took all the self-control he possessed not to drag her up against his chest and take what he wanted from her. Why in hell's name was he torturing himself like this?

He remembered what her lips had tasted like when he'd kissed her before. He could recall the feeling of her body pressed to his, her breasts crushed against his chest as he'd held her tight, drinking from the sweet nectar of her passion. The memory filled him with aching need and sent his blood racing, scorching his veins and hardening his male flesh until it was almost unbearable.

Stop it! he demanded silently. He had to control himself. He had to. Once he would have taken, without a second thought, all she had to offer. How many women had he seduced with sweet words and gentle hands, and then left, never looking back? But no more. He could not allow himself to do that to a woman again. Not after what had happened to his sister Dana. Yet, hadn't that been exactly what he'd planned to do with Elizabeth, when he'd made advances to her on the boat? He'd known she wasn't his kind of woman. She wasn't cut out for the type of life he led, nor was she the type to give herself freely to a man with no strings attached. He'd known that, sensed it the moment he'd laid eyes on her, and he'd gone after her anyway.

Gray sighed and rubbed a hand over his eyes. He could still hear his sister's sobs, as she'd told him about the man she'd fallen in love with while visiting friends in Washington. A man to whom she'd given her heart and body, on only the promise of marriage. A few months later, when it became apparent she was with child, her lover denounced Dana as a little trollop he wanted nothing more to do with, and promptly deserted her.

"Gray?"

Elizabeth's voice pulled him from his thoughts. He turned to look at her, and nearly groaned aloud. She held a berry with the tips of her fingers, and had lifted it in offer to his lips. Didn't the woman know she was driving him crazy with want?

Elizabeth smiled innocently and pressed the berry to Gray's lips. "Taste it, Gray, they're delicious."

All his tautly held self-control and willpower, all his hard-learned self-discipline and good intentions,

95

suddenly vanished. A surge of emotion and need that he could no longer ignore swept over him, and Gray found himself unable to deny the luxury of exulting in Elizabeth's touch and tasting her sweet lips.

Knowing that he shouldn't, but unable to stop himself, Gray pulled her to him until she lay across his lap. His ribs ached at the pressure of her weight against him, but the pleasure of feeling her body molded to his outweighed the dull pain. Elizabeth gave a squeak of surprise that was cut short as his mouth covered hers in a kiss that was more a tender caress.

She moved to push away from him, but found herself held firmly in place by the steel strength of his arms around her. Her lips parted as she made to protest, and Gray's tongue darted forth into her mouth.

The shock of the intimate act caused Elizabeth to stiffen, but the warm pressure of Gray's hands on her back, stroking, circling, petting, was a tantalizing reassurance. A burst of hot, burning pleasure erupted deep within her, glowing through her limbs, engulfing every nerve, every cell, and bringing with it a hunger for more. All thought of resistance was swept from her mind. Her hands crept up his chest, felt the hard mesa of muscle beneath her fingers, and slid over the rippling plane of his shoulders.

Her subtle surrender sparked a rush of desire in Gray that raced through him like a prairie fire, turning every cell in his body into an atom of fiery heat, and filling him with a hunger like none he had ever known before. All awareness of the pain of his injuries faded, replaced by desire for Elizabeth. His lips deepened their seductive caress as his tongue explored the dark caverns of her mouth, teasing, and tempting her to respond.

Lost in a world of languid pleasure, Elizabeth began to return his kiss without conscious thought.

The glide of his tongue against hers was a rapturous torment that fueled the yearning need within her, while each brush of his hands on her back was a sensuous caress that caused her body to tremble in anticipation.

His lips left hers and skittered across her cheek, her jaw, and down the side of her neck, leaving behind a burning, tingling trail of flesh that ached to know his touch again.

"God, you're beautiful," Gray murmured as he buried his lips in the hollow of her throat.

A soft moan escaped Elizabeth's lips, and she clung to him. Her slender fingers moved through his hair and held him to her, as the sensual heat that was building in her body grew hotter, and hungrier.

He nuzzled her ear, and his warm breath wafted through the soft tangles of her hair and turned her skin into a blanket of goose bumps. One hand slipped from her back and moved to cup her breast, his long fingers wrapping around the taut mound. His hand moved in a kneading motion over the hardened nipple, that strained against the fabric of her gown as if reaching for his touch.

Elizabeth let her head drop back, the feel of his lips on her skin a sweet pleasure she wanted to last forever. "Oh, Gray," she murmured, holding to him tightly.

The sound of her voice, heavy with passion and surrender, and the feel of her breast cradled within his palm, caused Gray's loins to harden with a savage swiftness that brought with it a shock of reality. What in God's name was he doing? He was nearly out of control. This was exactly what he'd sworn not to do ever again. And it was exactly what he'd wanted to do since the moment he'd seen her. Summoning all the willpower he could find, Gray dragged his lips from Elizabeth's, gripped her shoulders, and forcefully moved her away from him.

Chapter 7

After a long moment of total puzzlement, mixed with a lot of chagrin at sudden comprehension of what she'd just done, Elizabeth scrambled to her feet. A look of anger glinted from her eyes, confusion creased her brow, and the bruise of passion still lingered on her lips. "That is the second . . . no, the *third* time you have taken liberties with me, Grayson Cantrelle, and I will not stand for it. You hear me? Your attentions are not welcome."

Gray, abashed at what he'd *almost* done, had been on the verge of offering an apology, until he heard her words. Not welcome? Hell, he'd kissed saloon whores who hadn't been as responsive as Elizabeth Devlin had been while in his arms. An angry retort rested on the tip of his tongue, but he held back from uttering the words, realizing that he should be grateful she was upset with him, that she didn't want him. It would make it easier for him to keep his hands off of her. He watched her whirl around and stomp toward the river. The red rays of the setting sun fell on her thick mane of blond hair, and turned it into a halo of fire around her head. He pulled at his trousers as they tightened further. Damn, what kind of allure did the woman have for him, anyway? It was as if the more fire she spit at him, the more he wanted her.

"I've gone loco," Gray said to himself. "Plumb loco. Must have been the hit on the head. Probably turned my brain upside down."

He lay back against the tree trunk, but the image of Elizabeth that disappeared with the closing of his eyelids did not fade from his mind. And the taste of her lips on his, her tongue sliding into his mouth, her body cradled against his length, lingered to tease his senses and give him no peace.

Suddenly a scream split the air, and was just as abruptly cut short. Gray felt a chill of fear sweep up his spine, and jerked up from his reclining position. Elizabeth.

Moving without caution or heed to his injuries, he lunged for the Colt that lay only a foot from his hand. Fingers, long used to the curve of the walnut gun barrel, wrapped around its length, as his index finger slid over the trigger. His thumb cocked back the hammer, and the weapon was pulled from its leather sheath. At the same time, in one fluid movement, he rose to his feet and began to run in the direction Elizabeth had taken toward the river.

His ribs throbbed in agony from the sudden movement, and it felt like a drumroll had erupted inside his head, but Gray ignored the pain and hurried toward the river. He scrambled over the slope of uneven ground, losing his footing and sending dirt and pebbles flying as he sat back on his haunches and slid down the small hill. Almost before reaching the bottom, he was on his feet and running across the flat mud bank. The air was quiet now, which made him more nervous and urged him to hurry.

"Elizabeth?" He plowed into a thick copse of scrub trees, and stopped short when he saw her only a few yards away, her arms held tightly across her breasts, clenched hands tucked under her chin. She didn't turn at his voice, but he could see that her entire body was trembling, and she stared at the weed-covered ground as if expecting it to open up and swallow her.

Gray inched forward, gun ready, his body tense with alertness. Whatever she was staring at, it had scared the bejesus out of her, and he wasn't too sure it wouldn't do the same to him.

When he was only two feet behind and to the side of her, the tall weeds just in front of her moved, and a soft squeaking sound broke the air. Gray frowned and moved closer. The weeds rustled again. Behind the clump of weeds was a cluster of large rocks. Gray realized instantly that whatever she was staring at, she had it unwittingly cornered. He pointed the Colt at the moving foliage and inched forward, his leg brushing against Elizabeth's skirts. But she didn't seem to notice, or take comfort from his presence. She just continued to stare in horror at whatever was hidden in the tall reeds of grass and weeds before her.

Gray knelt next to Elizabeth, and pointed the gun into the weeds. A grayish brown head suddenly poked up from within the green blades, its long, pointed snout wriggling feverishly as its beady brown eyes stared back at Elizabeth, Gray, and the moonlit steel of the gun barrel. The animal grunted several times, then its nose touched the cold metal; it emitted a panicked series of snorts and grunts and lowered its head to push at what looked like miniatures of itself that lay in the nearby grass.

Gray smiled and tried not to laugh when Elizabeth let out a startled yelp at the animal's warning sounds.

"Hey, little mama, you've got quite a brood there," Gray said, uncocking the gun and lowering it to his side. He stood and wrapped an arm around Elizabeth's shoulders.

She remained stiff, all her attention riveted on the ugly little creature who had begun to frantically burrow into the ground.

Gray hugged Elizabeth to him. "It's only an armadillo. She's just letting you know not to bother her family." He let his hand slide up and down Elizabeth's arm in an effort to relax her.

"Fa . . . family?" she finally sputtered. She leaned against him weakly, feeling faint with the realization that he was there and she no longer needed to be afraid.

Gray urged Elizabeth away from the armadillo and back toward their campsite. "Yeah. Those four little ones were her babies. Normally they run away from whatever scares them, or make for their burrow, but you had them cornered. That's why she stood up to you like that."

"I've never seen one of those things before. What did you call it?"

Gray chuckled. "An armadillo. I doubt there are many this high up in the valley. Most are down in Mexico, Texas, and the lower regions of Louisiana. Maybe this little mama's just got the wandering bug, or someone brought her up here to raise for food and she got loose somehow."

"Food? People eat those things?" Elizabeth asked, then shuddered at the thought.

"Yep. Meat's real good and tender."

"Yck."

Gray laughed. "You might not turn that pretty nose of yours so high in the air if you tasted it. But that little mama's lucky. If she hadn't had those babies, I would have sacked her for our dinner."

"Thank heaven for small miracles," Elizabeth muttered. She sat down next to the campfire and pulled a heavy cloak over her shoulders. Though the air was still warm, she felt chilled to the bone.

Now that the episode was over and he was no longer

tense with alertness and fear for Elizabeth, Gray became suddenly aware of the pain hammering at his ribs and head. Gritting his teeth, he lowered himself to the ground. A hiss escaped his lips.

Elizabeth's head jerked upward, and she saw the knit of his brows as he frowned. "Are you all right?"

"No, I'm not all right," Gray said, snapping the words off tersely as his rear settled onto the ground, and his back came into contact with the toppled tree trunk. "I've just played knight to a damsel who wasn't in real distress, and I hurt like hell."

Elizabeth bristled. How was she supposed to know that scaley-looking creature was harmless? "Humph! I guess I should have just waited to see if that thing was going to take a bite out of my leg."

Damn. He hadn't meant to snap at her, but his head felt like a mule was inside of it, trying to kick his way out. His ribs didn't feel much better. He tried to soften his tone. "She wouldn't have hurt you unless you'd gone after her babies."

"That thing was hissing and snarling, and she took a swipe at me with her claws. Big, long, ugly ones. And I wasn't going after her babies."

Gray chuckled, then grimaced when the movement brought further pain to his ribs.

"I fail to see any humor in the situation," Elizabeth said. Both her tone and her blue eyes were as icy as a northern sea.

Hell and tarnation, Gray thought. He'd be damned if Elizabeth Devlin wasn't the most ungrateful little minx he'd ever met . . . and the most beautiful. Even with her hair tousled and flying wild about her shoulders, and her gown little more than a ragged, mud-stained piece of sorry cloth, she was the most gorgeous woman Gray had ever laid eyes on. And the most contrary, he reminded himself.

*   *   *

Nursing a somewhat bruised ego at Gray's rejection, Elizabeth spent almost all of the next morning and afternoon down by the river. It was better to keep some distance between herself and Gray whenever possible, she'd decided, especially after her wanton response to his attentions. She neither wanted nor desired to get involved with his type. All she needed Grayson Cantrelle for, she told herself, was to get her out of here.

When she wasn't fishing, she rummaged through the debris that had washed ashore from the *River Belle*. Occasionally, when she opened someone's portmanteau or valise, she'd feel a bit like a thief, but she as quickly shrugged those feelings away. Whomever these trunks belonged to would either never need them again, or had gone off and left them with, most likely, no intention of returning to search for them. In one trunk she found a small sack of gold coins stuffed amid some men's clothing. In another, a comb, brush, mirror, and several bottles of scents and soaps. She looked at her reflection in the mirror, and her face screwed into a scowl of disgust. "Mercy, I look like a street moppet. And a filthy one, at that."

Carrying her newfound treasures up the slope, Elizabeth placed them near the still smouldering fire, grabbed one of the large pots she'd found earlier, and ran back down to the river. Within minutes she'd returned to the fire and began pacing beside it, impatient for the pot of water to heat.

Gray watched her from the corner of his eye, curious. He could ask her what she was doing, but he didn't feel like getting his head bitten off again. He'd made the mistake of trying to talk to her over their breakfast of berries. The first time he'd received only a cold glance.

The second time she'd lashed out at him with a few choice words he was surprised she even knew.

Determined not to pay him any mind, Elizabeth went about her business without so much as a glance in his direction, let alone a word. She removed the pan of water from the fire and immediately placed another in its place. Then, kneeling before the hot pot, she bent over and submerged the top of her head in the water. Within seconds she had lathered her long mane into a crown of lilac-scented soapy foam. A soft mew of pleasure escaped her lips at the fragrant scent that surrounded her, and the pleasurable feel of the silky soap on her hair and hands. She ran her fingers slowly through her hair and massaged her scalp, totally absorbed in the joy the small luxury afforded her. She worked with her eyes closed, her head tilted back, and a small smile of contentment curved her lips.

Within seconds Gray found himself mesmerized. With each slow, caressing stroke of her hands through her hair, with each small moan of enjoyment that escaped her lips, his body hardened further, the hunger in him grew, gnawed at him, until he thought he'd burst from want of her. Just when he thought he'd die from the unquenchable demands his body was making of him, when he knew he could stand no more, she removed the other pot from the fire, and moved to sit at the edge of the clearing. She dipped a cup into the clear hot water, lifted it in the air, and poured it over her bent head to rinse away the soap. She repeated this continually. Gray groaned softly and turned away, his body on fire. But the temptation to watch her was too great, and he looked back.

Toweling her hair with a petticoat—that judging from its size must have belonged to a very hefty woman—Elizabeth returned to the fire and set a pan of fish on it to cook. Then, leaning back, she draped her long strands of hair over the trunk of a dead tree to allow the still warm rays of the setting sun to dry them. She thought about changing into the gown she'd found in a valise down by the river earlier. She missed feeling pretty. Though the idea to change was tempting, she discarded it. She knew the dress would fit, but it already smelled terribly of the river, though she had lain it out to air. Also, if she wore it now, it would get covered with dirt and mud. Anyway, there was no one out here to look pretty for.

She threw a glance at Gray, caught him watching her, and quickly looked away. Primping herself for a gunslinger was unthinkable. Besides, he didn't care about her. He only needed her to tend his injuries and provide his food. She'd wait to change until they were ready to leave this place and find a town, or farmhouse. She might not smell too good when she wore it, but at least she'd look halfway decent.

Her hair dried quickly, and Elizabeth rose to remove the fish from the fire. She turned toward Gray and found him gone, but this time she didn't panic. He was probably watering the trees again. She settled down to eat, pushing half the fish into another pan for Gray. He returned to the clearing minutes later and, rather than resuming his usual seat several yards from the fire site, moved to sit beside her.

"You look as if you feel better," she said, forgetting that she'd decided to talk to him as little as possible.

"I do." He retrieved his dinner from the fire and sat back against the tree, surprised not only by the fact that her tone was pleasant, but also because he suddenly realized how much he'd missed hearing her voice all day.

He knew she'd stayed down by the river most of the day to avoid him, and for a while he'd been glad. But that feeling had slowly disappeared. By midday he'd found himself watching for her return. "It still hurts like hell when I move, but at least now it's tolerable. I wouldn't have said that yesterday morning. I might even be able to move around enough tomorrow to get us a rabbit for dinner."

Elizabeth tried to keep her eyes from straying to the open vee of his shirtfront, but the temptation was too strong. She peeked at him from the corner of her eye, trying to camouflage her movement by lowering her head slightly and lifting a piece of fish to her mouth. Her pulses began to race when she stared at the wall of chest that his open shirt revealed.

She looked away quickly, but not before Gray had seen her. He smiled to himself. Bedding Elizabeth Devlin would certainly be a pleasure he'd never forget, he mused. The image of his sister's tear-streaked face suddenly loomed in his mind, and Gray remembered, with a swell of disappointment, that he couldn't go around bedding every beautiful woman he desired anymore. Well, he could, he reasoned, if he wanted to be considered no better than the blackguard who'd seduced his sister, impregnated her, and then deserted both her and his own child.

The thought left a vile taste in Gray's mouth. He felt as if he'd been plunged into a cavern of gloom and emptiness. So what the hell was he supposed to do? Go without a woman for the rest of his life? Of course, that was impossible. So, he had two choices left to him: whores and prostitutes or marriage. He snorted softly at the last thought. He had nothing against marriage, he had just never given it any consideration where his life was concerned. One woman. Kids. Family. Responsibility. The mere thought scared him silly. Sure, he had responsibilities already, but not that kind. Just the ranch, and his mom. And Dana, of course. But that was different, they'd always been there. And they didn't actually *depend* on him. Hell, the ranch practically ran itself. And his mom was about as independent as they come.

Gray smiled to himself. Well, whores and prostitutes it is. He sighed contentedly at his decision.

Elizabeth heard the soft sound and ignored it. He was probably only trying to get her attention, so that he could say something crude and nasty again. Or sweeten her up to accept more of his improper advances. Her cheeks warmed as she remembered their kiss the night before. Then she remembered that he had pushed her away. Obviously her kiss hadn't pleased him, and that suited her just fine. It hadn't pleased her either.

Placing her pan down by the fire, Elizabeth grabbed the cloak she'd been using at night for a blanket, sat forward, and draped it around her shoulders. "I think I'll retire early." She lay down with her back to him.

Gray looked at her suspiciously. Early wasn't the word for it. The sun, though sinking quickly, was still slightly visible over the tops of the trees. So what was her problem? He'd tried to be nice. Flipping his pan, he tossed the remainder of his fish over the sloping bank. If he never had fish again, it would be too soon. He rested against the tree trunk, closed his eyes, and willed sleep to come. It didn't.

Grabbing his Colt, he pulled the gun from its holster, broke the cylinder, and emptied it of bullets. Then, with a piece of ragged cloth, he began to clean the weapon. When he finished, an hour later, he started in on the holster. Then his belt buckles. His spurs. His boots. The conchos on his *calzoneras*. Finally, with nothing else to clean, and no one to talk to, he leaned back against the tree again and looked up at the sky. He glanced at Elizabeth's sleeping form. Why was she mad? She wanted him to leave her alone, and he was. So what was the problem now?

Sleep came slowly, but at last it did come.

Elizabeth's eyes popped open and every cell in her

body tensed. She wanted to jump up and shake her arm, to fling away whatever was on it, but instinct held her still. Without moving her head, she tried to look at the arm that, in her sleep, had stretched outwards. A cast of pale yellow moonlight illuminated the clearing, and Elizabeth could see the long, slender shape that draped across her arm just at her wrist.

A snake! her mind shrieked. A snake was on her arm. It moved again, and Elizabeth choked with fear. She held her breath, afraid to breath. *Oh, Gray, wake up. Please wake up,* she prayed. The snake's head moved to point toward her face, and Elizabeth nearly strangled on a scream stuck within her paralyzed throat.

The snake's head swayed back and forth, his blackish forked tongue poking at the air, testing it. When the reptile obviously had decided there was no immediate danger, it once again relaxed and slithered forward, but not enough to free Elizabeth's arm.

Moving so slowly it was almost painful, Elizabeth began to turn her face away from the snake. "Gray?" she whispered. She waited. Neither the snake nor Gray moved. She tried again, a bit louder. "Gray?"

A soft snore escaped his lips, his eyes opened for a brief second, and then he rolled over, turning his back to her. "Go to sleep, Elizabeth," he mumbled curtly.

Tears stung her eyes. Oh, God, she was so afraid. She waited a long moment, ordering herself not to cry, and called to him again, softly. "Gray, please?"

He rolled back toward her. "What?"

Her lips trembled. "There's a—"

Gray frowned. "There's nothing to be scared of, Elizabeth. No bears, no wildcats, no—" Then he noticed the look of sheer terror on her face. With infinite slowness he rose up on one elbow and peered over her. "Oh, shit," he mumbled, and stared at the large king snake. Its black and red striped body glistened in the moonlight, but for all its reptilian beauty, Gray knew it was deadly. Damn deadly. "Stay still, angel. Whatever you do, don't move." He eased a hand behind him and reached for his Colt.

He held the gun ready, waiting for the snake to move so that he could get a clear shot of its head. If he didn't kill it instantly, those huge fangs would strike out in search of whatever had harmed or threatened it, and sink into the first thing they found, which would be Elizabeth's arm. Sweat broke out on Gray's forehead. She'd be dead in seconds if his aim wasn't perfect. He slowly pulled the hammer back until it cocked into place.

Elizabeth waited, suddenly felt nauseous, and closed her eyes. A tapestry of her life unfolded within her mind. Birthday parties and picnics, adventures with her sister and cousins, soirees and carriage rides with courteous admirers who'd left her ego satisfied, and her blood lukewarm. In the brief flash of a few seconds she saw it all, her mother and father, who'd always indulged her every whim, her sister Eugenia, who'd always watched out for her, Aaron Reynaud, the childhood friend and blackguard she'd almost married, and Gray, the man who'd saved her life, and God willing, was about to try and do it again.

A soft whimper escaped her lips, and she shuddered.

"Hold still, angel," Gray whispered.

She felt the snake move, its coils sliding across her arm, peeked from within scrunched eyelids and saw Gray's finger pull back the trigger of the gun, and the world exploded in a thunderous roar. Gray lunged across her, knocking the breath from her lungs, and grabbed the snake, whose body, caught in the throes of death, twisted and jerked atop Elizabeth's arm. With a quick swing of his hand, Gray sent the lifeless reptile flying through the air toward the river.

Scrambling off of Elizabeth, he pulled her into his arms. She covered her face with her hands and trembled violently. A series of deep sobs wracked her, as she finally released the panic that had built up within her.

"It's all right, sweetheart, it's dead," Gray said gently, tightening his arms around her. He began to rock her back and forth. "Come on, Elizabeth," he kissed her temple, "hush now, angel, it's all right. It's all right."

Elizabeth clung to him, her fingers clutched tightly to the front of his shirt, her head pressed against his shoulder, her legs drawn up tightly. "Oh, Gray, I was so afraid," she sobbed, unable to stop her trembling. "That thing . . . I thought . . ."

"I know, sweetheart, I know. But it's over now. You're safe." His lips caressed the soft tangles of her hair, brushed repeatedly over her temples and across her cheek. "You're safe now. Nothing's going to hurt you. I promise."

In the dark, dense fog of Elizabeth's fear, Gray's voice pulled at her and began to ease her panic. The comforting feel of his hands on her back, tenderly caressing, helped to ease her trembling and urge warmth back into chilled limbs and skin.

"I almost lost you," Gray whispered huskily. "I can't believe I almost lost you." His embrace tightened, and Elizabeth snuggled closer.

Her hands crept up to his shoulders, she turned her face to him, and her arms wrapped around his neck, holding him to her. "I . . . I was so afraid. I thought I was going to die."

The words tore at his heart, nearly ripping it from his chest. He looked into her eyes, those brilliant blue eyes that reminded him of a clear spring night, a cool desert lake, and the endlessness of the ocean, and felt his breath catch. He knew then, no matter what the price, he had to have her.

Chapter 8

Knowing that what he was about to do would haunt him for the rest of his life, but also knowing that he couldn't help himself, Gray cupped Elizabeth's chin in his hand and turned her face up to him. His lips brushed across hers lightly, and his tongue traced the curve of her mouth.

Then, as she had been doing since the moment he'd met her, she surprised him further. Her lips opened invitingly to his, seemingly eager for his seduction, hungry for the hot, sliding caress of his tongue.

Gray felt the hesitant, almost fearful, touch of Elizabeth's tongue against his like a flick of fire, felt her hands slide over his shoulders and through his hair like fiery irons, searing into his flesh, branding him.

"Elizabeth, let me love you," he whispered against her lips.

Love you. Those were the only words Elizabeth heard. The only words she wanted to hear. They were wrong for each other, she knew, but now, at this moment, it didn't matter. Nothing mattered but that she was in Gray's arms, and that he loved her. The gentle brushing of his lips on hers sent a shiver of pleasure coursing through her that left her without the ability or the desire to deny him.

"Yes," she breathed. Her lips moved against his. "Love me, Gray, love me."

Every muscle in Gray's body tensed with a yearning anticipation, every cell flamed with demanding hunger. Somewhere deep down inside of him, a warning beckoned for his attention, echoing a message for him to stop before it was too late, but he ignored it, knowing it was already too late. It had been too late since the first moment he'd spotted her on the docks of Vicksburg.

His mouth ravaged hers, taking all she had to give and still demanding more. With deft swiftness, his fingers released the buttons of her gown and slid the soft material from her shoulders. He pulled at the ribbon of her camisole, and it fell loose, baring her breasts to his touch.

Every brush of his flesh against hers was like a burning caress that reached to her soul, imprinting it with his mark of possession and left her aching for more.

His lips left hers, and before she could utter a protest at the desertion, she moaned in ecstasy as she felt the hot wetness of his tongue circling her nipple. He pulled the taut peak into his mouth, laving the small velvet pinnacle, flicking the tip of the hardened spire until she cried out his name over and over, instinctively begging for more, and yet not knowing what it was she begged for.

Her cries fed the savage need in him, fed his hunger for her, and fanned the flames of passion that clouded his mind and consumed his body. "I need you, Elizabeth. More than I've ever needed another woman. I need to love you." His hands pushed at the limp folds of her skirt, and the small hooks that held it closed at her waist broke free of their thin threads. He half-lifted, half-pulled her from the confines of material, until there was nothing left between them, nothing separating them but his own clothes.

Lost in a world she had never visited before, had never known existed, Elizabeth exulted in the stirrings of pleasure that assailed her body. "Yes . . . love . . ." she gasped, her ragged breath breaking the words.

Gray turned and, ignoring the pain that throbbed in his ribs at the movement, pushed her gently backward until they both lay on the soft grass-covered ground.

Elizabeth's hands slid over Gray's shoulders, kneaded the hard, muscular flesh, felt the power within him, and slipped to comb through the dark, silky mat of hair that covered his chest.

Gray's breath caught in his throat. He wanted the exquisite sensation of her touch to go on forever, and at the same time, he wanted to thrust himself into her and ease the gnawing hunger that was slowly tearing him apart. His hand moved over the shadowed curve of her waist, across the ivory plane of her stomach, until his fingers slipped amid the soft triangle of golden curls at the apex of her thighs.

A ripple of tiny tremors swept through Elizabeth. "Gray?" His finger moved amid the delicate folds of flesh, and found the sensitive nub that was the center of her pleasure. Elizabeth stiffened reflexively, pressing her legs together and unintentionally imprisoning his hand.

"Don't hide from me, angel," Gray whispered against the long column of her neck, pressing his lips to her hot skin. "I won't hurt you. I just want to love you. All of you."

Elizabeth drew a shaky breath, and opened her mouth to tell him she had never been with a man before, that she didn't know what he wanted, what she should do, when the gentle, skimming caress of his

113

finger sent a river of hot, torrid pleasure sweeping through her.

"Oh, Gray," Elizabeth cried, nuzzling his shoulders with her teeth as her body continued to tremble with the tender convulsion. Her arms clung to his neck, her lips sought his, and her legs pressed together, holding his hand to her, wanting never to lose the blissful feeling that washed over her with his touch.

"Yes, angel, feel it, let it flow through you," Gray murmured, urging her legs to open further for him. With one hand he tore open the buttons of his trousers, pushed them over his thighs, and struggled out of both them and his boots.

He moved into her gradually, sensing without knowing, that he needed to be gentle, to take her with tenderness and care. His body quivered from the tautly held control of his restraint, hungering to have all of her, but forcing himself to move with infinite slowness. The hot moistness of her passion welcomed him, enveloped his aching shaft and drew it within her. He felt the fragile barrier of skin that silently said she had never been with a man before, and damned himself for what he was about to do. But it was too late. The hounds of hell could threaten to rise up and pursue him for the rest of his life, but he could not stop, he could not deny himself what he wanted so badly to possess. He pushed against the frail veil of flesh, withdrew slightly, and pushed again.

Her small cry was swallowed in his mouth, and the momentary stiffness that flexed her body quickly subsided as his hands caressed her ivory skin, gliding over the soft curves and satin planes. His fingers moved over the tiny nub of her desire, and his lips pressed fiery kisses over her face, her neck, her breasts, until, once again, she was lost in her need for him. He buried himself deep inside of her, and then paused, and lifted his lips from hers.

Elizabeth's hips moved against him in a silent plea. When he didn't respond, she opened her eyes and looked up at him.

"You are the most beautiful woman I have ever known," Gray said huskily, and before she could reply, his mouth caught hers in a kiss that was both tender and savage, infusing her with need, and filling her with pleasure.

His kiss, his caresses, and his lovemaking combined to create an unbearable sweetness, a torture of her senses that radiated through her entire body, enveloping it in a cloud of bliss.

He moved in a gentle rhythm, a sensuously hot advance that fed the seething, volcanic hunger that burned deep within her, and a teasing retreat that increased her yearning for his return. Each thrust became deeper, heightening the sensual heat that engulfed them both, and pushed them farther up the mountain of pleasure that sprawled before and between them.

Elizabeth scaled the ragged peak first, falling from its tip and spiraling into the endless void of mind-routing pleasure. She clung to Gray, and rode the crest of rapture, his name tumbling from her lips over and over as a burning fire exploded deep within her, showering her with sparks of pleasure, and sheathing her in an avalanche of raining ecstasy.

When he felt the near violent shiver of her climax wrap around him, heard her cry his name while in the throes of passion, Gray covered her mouth with his, swallowed her cries, and let her ecstasy consume him until it was his own, and he, too, spiraled from the mountaintop, rode the waves, and touched the stars.

Long moments later, when both lay quiet, limbs entwined, hot, passion-slick bodies pressed tightly together, Elizabeth listened to the heavy rasp of his breathing, caressed the steel-hard bands of muscle that made up his arms, and wondered how she could ever have thought to deny her love to this man. He was from a world unlike the one she had known, a world where grand homes and fine furnishings didn't exist, where the land was rough and unyielding. He was a different breed of man than any she had ever met, powerful and independent, with both a will and body of iron, yet a touch that was at once strong, gentle, and loving, and he was all that she could ever want.

Elizabeth snuggled deeper against him, her hips pressing to his as she savored the deliciously sweet feeling of him still inside of her. She luxuriated in the warmth and intimacy of his embrace, and felt her breasts tighten in anticipated excitement when his hot breath wafted across the exposed peak of her nipple.

Her movement caused a stirring of renewed hunger in Gray, a yearning that surprised him in its intensity. Never before, with any woman, had his desire stirred to life again so quickly after having just been satiated. His hand moved to her breast, his fingers encircled the already taut mound.

Elizabeth turned toward him and smiled. Gray blinked several times in disbelief, as he saw her golden hair turn dark and her green eyes turn blue. Suddenly it was his sister Dana's face only inches from his own, tear-streaked and drawn with grief, Dana's hair that caught the moonlight and shimmered, Dana's eyes that looked up at him, trusting, loving him. His fingers froze on Elizabeth's breast, and those of his other hand, raised to caress her cheek, paused in midair. He jerked away from her, pulling himself from that sensuously warm womb of desire, deserting the silken plane of skin that had been pressed to his, and the lips that, only

116

moments before, he had ravished without a thought or care to the consequences.

The vision of Dana's face disappeared, and reality rushed back at him with stark clarity as he stared at Elizabeth. He almost groaned, caught himself, and reached for his trousers. Now what the hell was he supposed to do? Offer to marry her? He felt a knot form in his gut. Elizabeth Devlin might be everything he'd dreamt of for his bed, but she was far from what he envisioned for his wife, if he ever took one. Elizabeth would never be able to cope with his way of life. He tugged on his trousers and then rammed his arms into his sleeves, pulling the shirt up over his broad shoulders. No, the best thing to do in this instance—for both of them—was to keep his mouth shut. Tightly, firmly, resolutely shut.

He tugged on his boots, reached down for the gun and holster, and fastened them around his hips. His ribs hurt like hell, his head throbbed, and his leg felt as if it were going to splinter and turn to sawdust at any moment. Gray bit down on his bottom lip, and tried to ignore the small rivers of sweat that had begun to trickle over his temples.

Damn, what was the matter with him? He chanced a quick and furtive glance at Elizabeth, and damned himself again when he saw the look of bewilderment in her eyes.

He had to get away from her, had to put some distance between the gnawing hunger for her that was still eating at him and her beautiful, tantalizing, and willing body. Otherwise, he'd lose control again, and he couldn't let that happen. "I'm going to find us something to eat besides fish," Gray said gruffly, and took a step away from her.

"Now?" Her voice was barely more than a timid squeak. "In the dark?" She had covered herself with the

draping fabric of her gown and, arms drawn up, clutched it to her breast with both hands.

He heard the fear in her voice, sensed the hurt she felt at his brusqueness reach out and touch him; and the disgust he felt at his own lack of self-control nearly doubled. "Animals don't all sleep at night like we do." Or ought to be doing, he chided himself. "There's nothing to be afraid of, I won't be far." He walked toward the edge of the clearing and into the dark, inky shadows that the light of their fire could not reach. Memories of Dana swam around in his mind, haunting him. He could still see her tears, hear the despair and anguish in her words, feel the pain that filled her heart. Dammit. Was that what he was doing to Elizabeth?

He left me, Gray. He told me he loved me. He said we were going to be married. I thought he'd be happy that I was with child, Gray. I thought he'd be happy. Dana's voice echoed in Gray's mind, the words burning into his brain, searing into his conscience and feeding his guilt, until he thought he would go mad.

Shut up, Dana, he silently screamed back. *Shut up!*

Something scurried across the ground in front of him. Gray stopped, narrowed his eyes in an effort to pierce the darkness—made even blacker by the dense growth of the trees—and held his hand ready over his gun butt.

He sighed softly. Whatever it had been, it was gone, as was any real chance of him bagging them anything to eat. That had disappeared along with the light of the moon, when he stepped into the overgrown brush that surrounded their clearing. About the best he could do now was to shoot blindly at whatever moved, but with the way his luck was running lately, it might shoot back.

His body felt like one big ache. Everything hurt. If he didn't get off of his feet pretty soon, he was going to fall off of them. His ribs were screaming in agony, worse than they had been earlier that day. The throbbing in his head was beginning to sound and feel like thunder trapped within his skull, and his leg was quickly turning to rubber. If that weren't bad enough, he was feeling slightly dizzy.

"Lord, don't let me pass out," he muttered. Of course, why the Lord would listen to him was beyond comprehension. More likely his audience was Satan. Gray turned on his heel and made his way slowly, but steadily, back toward the campfire.

Elizabeth lay curled beneath the cloak on her side of the campfire, which was now no more than smouldering pieces of wood. She lay with her head on the wad of petticoat she used for a pillow, and stared at the thin wisps of smoke that curled into the crisp morning air. Unable to resist, she glanced at Gray from beneath lowered gold lashes. Why should she care if he hadn't asked her to marry him? It wasn't as if she'd accept. Perish the thought. She didn't want to marry him. He was wrong for her. He meant nothing to her. Nothing at all. But the thought wasn't quite as convincing as it should have been.

She closed her eyes to block out the sight of him. But it didn't work. She could see him all the same, in her mind. She'd never met anyone exactly like Grayson Cantrelle, and yet she had met other men similar to him. Men who thought they were God's precious gift to this world, and women were put here merely to serve them. She bristled and sneaked a look at Gray again; he was still sleeping, his head propped up against the dead tree trunk, his hat covering his face.

He's a gunslinger, Elizabeth. A drifter. A no-account, shiftless, penniless rake. If he *did* propose marriage, it would probably only be because he figures you have money. Remember that. It certainly wouldn't be because he has any honor. Or feelings. She squirmed restlessly beneath the cloak. There was absolutely no sane reason on earth why she should be so damnably attracted to the man. But she was, and denying it, or pretending it wasn't so, was not going to change anything.

Curse the scoundrel! If she had to be stranded out here on this riverbank, why couldn't she have been marooned with someone else? With one of the older ladies who'd been on the riverboat? Or even one of the men who had obviously been gentlemen? She raised up slightly, pounded a fist into the wad of petticoat, and lay her head back down. Why did it have to be with Grayson Cantrelle? He had made her feel things inside herself she'd never known existed, and now she was having one devil of a time ignoring them.

She punched at the wadded petticoat again. Damn the man! Damn him, damn him, damn him.

"Yo, there, anyone about?"

The loud voice echoed through the forest and into the clearing. Elizabeth shot up and looked around, instantly awake. The first stirrings of morning were still in the air, though dawn had obviously come several hours before. Her hair had come loose from the ribbon she'd used to tie it back, and long golden strands fell across her shoulders in a wild tangle of curls and waves.

She whipped the cloak aside and scrambled to her feet. Thank the saints, someone had come to rescue her! "Here. Here," she yelled back and stared at the surrounding forest.

Gray reached for his gun before he sat up and pushed the Stetson from over his eyes. He cocked the hammer, but kept the gun at his thigh, and waited for their visitor to approach and show himself.

The head of a bay gelding broke through the bushes, and a second later the rider mounted on the animal's back came into sight. Thin waves of light brown hair covered the man's head, as well as his upper lip and the point of his chin. He reined in at the edge of the clearing and slid from the saddle. Gray noticed that the man was short and rather portly, but well dressed, his riding boots polished to a brilliant shine, his greatcoat and breeches made of the finest cloth. The saddle on his mount, as well as the horse itself, also appeared quite expensive.

"Well, I see the reports were right. A runner passed my place day before yesterday. Said there was talk in town of a riverboat wrecked up here, and a survivor on the bank. Thought I'd take a look today, since I was in my east fields anyway."

"Oh, I'm so glad you've come," Elizabeth gushed, and smiled coyly. She moved to stand before him and held out her hand. "I'm Elizabeth Devlin, of Devlin Plantation in Vicksburg." She glanced at Gray. "And this is Mr. Grayson Cantrelle, of Texas." Her last word was pronounced in an acid tone.

The man took Elizabeth's hand and, with a slight bow, lifted it to his lips. He completely ignored any acknowledgement of Gray.

Gray felt a surge of instant dislike for their rescuer. So, he'd heard of their plight day before yesterday, but had just gotten around to investigating it today. Nice guy. People die from that kind of concern and kindness.

"It is both an honor and a pleasure to meet you, Miss Devlin. I am only sorry I could not come to your rescue sooner. Please, accept my apologies. I, ah . . ." he glanced furtively at Gray, "hope there were no other, ah, uncomfortable incidents?"

Gray's granite hard gaze met the man's furtive one, and he felt a surge of satisfaction as he watched their rescuer squirm slightly.

Elizabeth seemed unaware of the brittle but silent exchange between the men. She curtsied. "Oh, the ordeal has been most trying, and I do so appreciate your rescue, Mr.—?"

"Sorens." He bowed deeply. "Damien Sorens of Cypress Grove Plantation, on which you two have, evidently, been stranded since the unfortunate demise of the boat you were traveling on."

"Oh, how lucky for us," Elizabeth gushed. "I was beginning to think we were so far from civilization that no one would ever come to our rescue. I couldn't go in search of help because Mr. Cantrelle," she gestured toward Gray, "was hurt and unable to walk until just recently."

Damien threw Gray a cursory glance. "How unfortunate." A lascivious smile curved his lips as he returned his attention to Elizabeth. "But you look like you've taken the trial very well, my dear." Now he understood Aaron's willingness to marry. Elizabeth was indeed a rare beauty, even in her present state. Damien's smile widened. Perhaps, rather than notify Aaron immediately of Elizabeth's presence, he would offer her his hospitality for a few days, and, if circumstances proceeded according to his plan, would enjoy the pleasures that Aaron had been robbed of. Though the way he'd heard it, Aaron had no one to blame but himself for being jilted.

He patted her hand and his gaze swept over her from head to foot, but Gray didn't miss the direct and prolonged pause as the man's eyes lingered on the swell of Elizabeth's bosom. He also did not fail to miss the fact that rather than seem offended by the man's brazen

122

inspection of her physical assets, Elizabeth appeared to glow at the obtrusive attention.

So, this was the kind of fop she preferred. Gray got to his feet, and with deliberate slowness holstered his gun. "So, Mr. Sorens, how do we get out of here?"

Neither man offered a hand to the other.

"Oh, I've only brought two horses." Damien looked apologetically at Elizabeth, though it was obvious to Gray that the gesture was about as sincere as a three-bit piece. "The reports only mentioned one survivor. If I had known there were two of you, my dear, especially a lady of such obvious quality, I would have brought a buggy, but—"

Elizabeth's hand was still firmly ensconced within Damien Sorens's. "I understand, Mr. Sorens, really. I'm only glad that we're finally being rescued from this . . ." she looked about the clearing, "desolate place."

He smiled widely and slipped her hand into the crook of his arm. "Good, good. Well, if you have no objection, my dear, you can ride with me. And please, call me Damien."

Elizabeth smiled and threw a quick glance at Gray. "Why, thank you, Damien."

"Shall we go, my dear?"

"Elizabeth." Gray's voice cut like a boom of thunder through the still morning air.

Startled, she whirled around to face him. Puzzlement and anger reflected from her eyes. "Yes, Gr . . . Mr. Cantrelle?"

"I think we'd best wait here until Mr. Sorens can bring a buggy."

Elizabeth bristled at his overbearing attitude. *He* thought it best? The last thing in the world she wanted to do was spend another night here on the bank of this river, if she didn't have to—especially with Grayson

Cantrelle. She had to get away from him. She had to. Otherwise . . . well, she didn't want to think about otherwise. Her body had already betrayed her once. No sense tempting fate. "I'd rather go now, Mr. Cantrelle, but I'm sure Mr. Sorens wouldn't mind sending someone back for you later this afternoon, if you feel you're not up to riding."

"Oh, of course. I'd be happy to send a man back for you later, Mr. Cantrelle," Damien said.

"I'll bet," Gray mumbled beneath his breath. When Dana had been younger and had made him this angry, he used to tan her backside. His fingers itched to do just that to Elizabeth now. "Get whatever you want to take, Elizabeth," he growled instead, "I'll make sure the fire is out."

Elizabeth gathered up the cloak and a few pieces of jewelry she'd found after the wreck. Gray kicked dirt over the campfire site, slipped a small sack of coins and greenbacks he'd found into his pocket, tugged on his *calzoneras,* and secured the thong of the Colt's holster to his thigh. He walked to where Sorens stood with the two horses. "She'll ride with me," he said to the plantation owner.

"I beg your pardon, but—"

"I said, she'll ride with me." The quietly spoken words were ground out between clenched teeth and left no doubt that the subject was not open for discussion, as far as Gray was concerned.

"I'm ready," Elizabeth said, and moved to stand before the two men. She held out her hand toward their rescuer. "Damien, shall we go?"

He paled slightly, threw a furtive glance in Gray's direction, and tried to smile, though it looked to Elizabeth more like a sickly grimace.

Gray reached out and took her hand, then pulled her, none to gently, toward him. "You'll ride with me."

124

"I most certainly will not!"

He turned and scowled at her. "You will ride with me, Elizabeth, and that's final."

She yanked her arm from his grasp. "I'm old enough to make up my own mind, Mr. Cantrelle, in case you haven't noticed."

"I've noticed more than your mind, *Miss Devlin,* in case you don't remember."

Elizabeth whipped around to walk away from him. Gray grabbed her arm again and nearly jerked her off of her feet, as he dragged her out of earshot of Damien Sorens.

"Just what do you think you're doing?" she sputtered furiously.

"Watching out for you, though I haven't the faintest idea why I should."

"And who asked you to?"

Gray's hands curled around her arms and drew her roughly to him, her breasts crushed against his chest, her face barely an inch from his own. "You little hellcat! Are you so simple-brained that you'd just ride off into the sun with a perfect stranger?"

"I just spent five days on a riverbank with one," she shot back haughtily, and managed to pull one arm free of his ironlike grasp.

"And took him most graciously, and willingly, to your bed."

The sharp taunt struck exactly as Gray had hoped. Her eyes grew big, and her lips parted in preparation of a retort, but emitted no sound.

"Now, unless you've decided to make that a habit and are planning to work your wiles on Sorens, you'll ride with m—"

WHACK! Her outstretched hand smacked against the side of Gray's face, causing his head to snap back, and his nose to feel as if a horse had just taken its best

125

shot, and connected.

She tried to jerk her other arm free of his grasp, but he had a tight and firm hold on it. Her eyes spit fire as she looked back up at him.

His cheek flamed red, the imprint of her fingers clearly discernible on his flesh. "Was that meant to confirm that you're riding with me, or that I'm right and you prefer to now grace our pompous rescuer with your charms?"

"Ohhh, you're a beast—a cur—a rogue. I hate you, Grayson Cantrelle. I hope I never see you again."

"Unless it's in bed," he said, and had the nerve to chuckle.

Her arm rose in the air, but this time his hand came up and caught hers as it swung toward his face. "Don't ever do that again, Elizabeth, unless you want to suffer the consequences." The threatening words were muttered in a low, guttural drawl.

"Such as?" she challenged.

He released his grip on her hand. "Do it again and find out."

Chapter 9

"Perhaps it is better this way, Damien," Elizabeth said sweetly, practically purring at the man from her seat in front of Gray. She shifted position in Gray's arms, and smiled at Damien as he rode beside them on his own horse. "After all, Mr. Cantrelle has been very weak the past few days, from his injuries, you know, and we wouldn't want him to get dizzy and fall off of his horse or anything."

"Of course not," Damien mumbled.

"That's enough, Elizabeth," Gray whispered into the golden tangles of her mane. A silent string of pithy oaths rattled through his head. There had been several women aboard the riverboat who had openly invited his attentions, and more if he was interested. They had made that obvious, but he, like a fool, had set his sights on Elizabeth Devlin. He must be tired of living.

They rode for over an hour, letting the horses move at a brisk walk, which made each step a moment of agony and a test of self-control for Gray. While Elizabeth chattered almost nonstop with Damien Sorens, her body brushed, rubbed, and pressed against Gray's.

He shifted his own position in the saddle and tried to

scoot back, to put some space, no matter how miniscule, between them. It didn't work. What did happen was that her body settled more firmly into the curve of his.

Gray cursed beneath his breath and clenched the hand that rested on his thigh, while the knuckles of the other hand turned white from the extreme pressure of his fingers wrapped around the reins. Elizabeth was a complete enigma to him. She had the smile of an angel, and the disposition of a little devil. A frown creased his brow, hidden beneath the rim of the Stetson. It didn't matter what she was, he'd taken her and he shouldn't have. It was as simple as that, and now he'd spend the rest of his life feeling guilty about it, because he sure as hell wasn't going to make it worse by asking her to marry him. He almost groaned at the thought. He didn't want to be married. He liked his life just the way it was, and if he ever did decide to get married, it sure as hell wouldn't be to a little spitfire like Elizabeth.

He felt her move against him again, trying to shift her cramped position. Damn, he wasn't any better than the man who'd seduced Dana and then run out on her.

But Elizabeth isn't with child, he argued with himself in an effort to soothe his feelings of guilt. It didn't work, because he wasn't sure she wasn't carrying his child. At least he wasn't sure yet.

As if she had sensed his thoughts were on her, Elizabeth turned her head and glanced over her shoulder at him, then just as abruptly looked away.

Gray found himself suddenly wondering just what it would be like to come home at the end of a long day and find Elizabeth waiting for him in his bed, naked, her body trembling with need. He felt his flesh grow hot with the thought.

"We've only a short distance more to go, my dear," Damien said to Elizabeth.

The words, breaking the silence, brought Gray snapping back to reality like a whip. What the hell was the matter with him? Had he lost his senses? Any man that sentenced himself to a life term with Elizabeth Devlin was crazy. And it wouldn't just be with Elizabeth. What about children? They'd probably all be like her: bullheaded, obstinate, outspoken, and ornery as hell. And if they were girls, they'd be beautiful. Yeah, he answered silently, and probably get their father killed trying to protect their honor.

He sneered. No thanks.

Elizabeth felt Gray stiffen momentarily, and wondered what he was thinking. She took a deep breath and released it slowly, trying to get her own emotions under control. Sitting cradled on his lap was not doing her traitorous body any favors. She had an insane urge to turn and press her lips to his, and that infuriated her. He had turned her into a wanton trollop. She had always been the one to control the situation between herself and her suitors, but with Gray it was different. He would not be controlled by her. He had disregarded her wishes and challenged any and every objection she'd raised against him. And he'd won.

Even now, when her anger at both him and herself was boiling, it was in direct conflict with another part of her that yearned for him to kiss her again, to wrap her in that circle of iron strength that was his embrace. He was everything she had ever wanted in a man; strong, vibrant, and sensual, with a will of steel and a blaze of spirit. He was also everything she had always vowed to stay away from; a drifter, a man who lived by his wits and his mastery with a gun. Grayson Cantrelle was a rakehell, a man with no home, no money, and no more ambition in life than to seize what he wanted and discard what he didn't.

Frustrated by the fact that she couldn't seem to rid her mind of thoughts of him, Elizabeth turned abruptly in her seat to face Damien and strike up a conversation, any kind of conversation. Her elbow rammed into Gray's ribs, and she heard him grunt and flinch away from her, but the arm that held her pinioned against him did not release its hold or loosen its grip. She felt an instant of guilt at having accidently hurt his injured ribs, then ignored it. He had done worse to her.

"Damien, do we have much farther to go?" she asked, her tone practically dripping sugar.

"Actually, the house is right around the next bend."

"And how far is it to town?" Gray asked, his tone surly.

"Oh, not quite half a day's ride. You can catch a boat at Crocker's landing to continue your trip downriver." Damien turned his attention to Elizabeth. "But I'd be most honored if you would stay at Cypress Grove for a few days, and rest before you continue your journey, my dear." He glanced at Grayson and found the man watching him. "Oh, and you, too, of course, Mr. Grayson." He would much rather that Grayson Cantrelle head straight for town, but he didn't see any way to exclude him from his offer without taking the risk that Elizabeth would decline also. And he certainly didn't want that, at least not yet. It would be such a pity to be deprived of enjoying her favors.

"Thank you, Damien," Elizabeth said. "That would be very nice."

"Yeah, nice," Grayson echoed, his tone making it obvious he would rather have declined Damien's offer. He tugged at the inseam of his trousers and shifted his seat on the saddle. "How often do boats dock at this landing in town?"

"Quite often, actually," Damien answered. "There's

130

usually at least one a day."

Gray nodded, and Elizabeth grit her teeth. She was not going to set foot on another boat. If there was any other way to travel, she'd take it. If not, she'd walk. Grayson could sprout wings and fly for all she cared.

Just then the mansion of Cypress Grove came into view. Elizabeth gasped at the sight and stared wide-eyed at the magnificent house. It sat on a small knoll that was completely covered with a blanket of lush, green grass, dotted with magnolias and live oaks. Creamy white flowers bloomed from amid the dark waxy leaves of the magnolias, and curtains of gray Spanish moss hung draped from the sprawling, gnarled limbs of the oaks. The house itself was like a white jewel set amidst the emerald splendor. Corinthian pillars surrounded the house and supported the sloping roof, which was graced with three dormer windows on each side. Green shutters adorned each floor to ceiling window, and a gallery swept around both the second and first floors.

"Oh, Damien, it's magnificent," Elizabeth gushed.

The drive, its surface covered with crushed oyster shells, led in a winding path to the house, giving the caller ample time to appreciate Cypress Grove on his approach.

"Thank you, my dear."

Gray seethed at the endearing term the man insisted on using whenever he addressed Elizabeth.

Once again he wondered at his own actions toward Elizabeth. He had taken her, as he'd had no right to do. He'd ruined her for other men. Yet he didn't feel sorry. He felt a bit guilty, but he didn't feel sorry. He glared at Damien and felt a sensation much like fury swell within him. Suddenly he knew, beyond any doubt, that it wasn't merely anger heating his blood . . . he was jealous. The realization only fueled the anger.

131

He'd felt jealousy when he'd heard her mention someone named Aaron. He still didn't know who that was. And he'd felt jealousy when he'd seen her smile at Damien Sorens and accept his flirtations. A dark shadow swept over his face. He didn't like the feeling. He didn't like it one damn bit. He didn't want to be jealous. That meant he cared, and he sure as hell didn't want to care. Not about Elizabeth Devlin. She was not his type of woman. She was a spitfire, a hellcat, a walking catastrophe. In fact, she was every man's dream and nightmare all rolled up into one package. The dream part he could handle, easily. It was the nightmare part he wanted to run and hide from. She could turn his life upside down with just a smile or crook of her little finger. He almost laughed aloud. Hell, she already had. Hadn't she instilled a burning, simmering hunger within him that just wouldn't be satisfied? And didn't she drive him to rage and a fury like none he'd ever before experienced?

They reined up in front of the brick entry steps that curved toward the drive in the shape of a fan. Azalea bushes lined the front of the house in both directions from the steps, and several wooden rockers graced the first-floor gallery and flanked the front door. A slightly built boy of no more than nine or ten years ran up and took the horses' reins from Damien and Gray.

"G'day, massa." His dark golden lips curved in a wide smile, and Gray noticed one of the child's front teeth had been chipped.

Damien looked at the boy. His eyes immediately darkened, and his smile, which he'd been flashing at Elizabeth, disappeared. "Brush them down, Jason, and feed them well. And make sure you do it right." His tone was brusque, almost threatening.

The boy nodded and mumbled his acquiescence, but kept his head bowed and his eyes averted.

Gray frowned. What the hell was that all about?

Damien turned back to Elizabeth as Gray stared after the boy named Jason. He reminded Gray of a beaten dog he'd seen in a Comanchero camp once.

Damien offered Elizabeth his arm. "Shall we go in, my dear?"

Gray turned at the words. If he heard Damien refer to Elizabeth one more time as *my dear,* he didn't know if he'd be able to control the urge to smash his fist against the man's jaw. He followed them up the steps toward the front door, and tried to ignore the trembling in his injured leg and the fact that his ribs felt as if he'd just been kicked by a mule. He stared at Elizabeth's back. What was the matter with him? Why in the hell didn't he just let nature take its course here? Damien was obviously interested in Elizabeth, and he could give her what she wanted: money and luxuries. It would solve everything. He didn't have to feel guilty anymore. Yet the mere thought of Elizabeth in Damien's arms caused Gray's blood to boil and his fury to simmer.

"Oh, Damien, this is just the most beautiful house I've ever seen. My daddy would have loved it," Elizabeth said. Gray watched her gently squeeze Damien's arm and smile up at him coyly. He felt like grabbing her and throwing her over his knees. "Have you owned it long?"

"I had it built a few years ago, when I decided to move down here from Boston. In fact, I just arrived back home a few days ago myself. I've been in Washington on business for several months."

Gray's attention was piqued at Damien's last comment, and he stared at the back of the man's head as they passed through the entry door and into the foyer of the big house. Damien did fit Dana's description of her lover, kind of, but . . . He shook his

133

head. No, it wasn't possible. It was true he'd been tracking the man for weeks, and had just lost his trail in St. Louis—only a couple day's journey upriver—but, to just happen on him like this? To be rescued by him? Anyway, there was one thing that didn't fit. Gray couldn't picture Dana with this man. Sorens was to . . . to . . . dandified.

Damien turned to a servant who stood nearby. "Zeeanda, please prepare our noon meal, and enough place settings to accomodate our guests, while I show them to their rooms. We'll supper in the dining room in two hours." The small woman nodded and hurried off to do his bidding.

"Nice house, Sorens," Gray said, feeling the need to say something as he watched the servant disappear through a door at the opposite end of the foyer. She had looked vaguely familiar, but it had taken him a few seconds to realize why, and when he did, he noticed something else. She resembled the boy who had taken their horses, and the boy in turn resembled Damien. Gray looked back at Damien with a new feeling of disgust.

"Thank you, Mr. Cantrelle. Now please," he patted Elizabeth's hand, which was still firmly holding onto his arm, "if you will both come with me?" Midway down the spacious second-floor hallway, he paused before a door, opened it, then stepped back. "Mr. Cantrelle, your room."

Gray nodded and entered. It was the most garishly decorated room he'd ever seen. More so than some brothels he'd been in. He forced himself to remain silent. Two of the walls were covered in paper, its burgundy, gold, and white design of ribbons and flowers almost overpowering. The poster bed had a canopy of gold silk with a curtain around each poster, and the bed itself was covered with a burgundy brocade coverlet, its edges trimmed with lace. Against one wall was a fireplace of Italian marble, black with gold veins running through it, and a huge, gilt-framed mirror hung on the wall over the mantel. A huge armoire stood against another wall, its carved and mirrored front reflecting the audacious room, and a huge desk was set between two tall windows. A crystal chandelier hung from the ceiling, its chain surrounded by a plaster medallion that looked like a huge daisy, and an area rug on the floor held a weave of huge yellow flowers that were nearly blinding.

"Your room is down here, my dear," Damien said, leading Elizabeth further down the hall.

Gray leaned across the threshold and watched them pause before a door several down from his own. He saw Elizabeth enter her room, heard her thank their host, and then, satisfied that Elizabeth was in her room alone, stepped back into his own as Damien turned and walked toward the staircase. But Gray did not miss the sly smile that tugged at the corners of Damien's mouth, nor the gleam of lust that sparked within his dark eyes. Damien Sorens was a leech, of that Gray had no doubt, but there was something else about him that bothered Gray, he just didn't know exactly what it was. He'd felt it almost the moment he had set eyes on the man. It was much the same feeling as looking into the eyes of a rattlesnake.

Gray stretched out on the large four-poster bed that dominated the room. Lord, but it felt good to settle onto a real bed again. He might do a lot of sleeping out on the range when at home, running the cattle, bedding down for the night under the stars, but it always felt so good to get back to the house again, and his own room. Sleep swept over him with sudden swiftness.

*　　　*　　　*

Elizabeth rapped her knuckles against Gray's door again. What was the man doing in there? Was he deaf? Or dead? A chill of fear curled up her spine. Had the ride from the river aggravated his injuries? "Gray? Gray, are you in there?" she called, a note of panic in her voice.

The door suddenly swung open. "Yes, Elizabeth, *my dear,*" Gray drawled. He leaned insolently against the doorjamb and crossed his arms over his bare chest. "I'm here. Were you wishing I wasn't?"

Elizabeth couldn't find her voice, but she had no trouble with her eyes. They were darting from his face to the towel wrapped around the lower half of his body, which was all he had on. She felt her face flush, felt her body turn to an instant inferno. Her fingers yearned to touch the muscled wall of his chest, to skip lightly through the dark mat of hair, and slide slowly over the corded muscles of his broad shoulders. She locked her hands together behind her back to hide their trembling, and keep them under control. "I . . . ah, that is, Damien said we should come downstairs to dine when we were ready. I just thought, I mean, since I was on my way, I thought I'd . . ."

A sardonic grin curved his lips. "As you can see, I'm not quite ready to go downstairs. But I won't be long. Why don't you come in and wait for me?"

Before she could respond, Gray reached out, grabbed her arm, and hauled her into his room, nearly yanking her off of her feet. He ignored the pain in his ribs the abrupt movement had brought on, and slammed the door shut behind her.

"This really isn't proper," Elizabeth snapped, and began to turn back toward the door.

Gray did not release her. Instead, he pulled her back until her body was pressed tightly against his. "Nothing has been quite proper between us since we met,

136

Elizabeth. Why change or worry about things now?"
He wanted her, dammit. Damien Sorens might be able
to seduce her with his money, but Gray could seduce
her in other ways. Much more pleasureable ways.

The steel grip of his embrace pinioned her arms to
her sides, locked them there, and rendered her helpless
as his lips trapped hers. She tried to twist away from
him, tried to pull free, but it was useless, and her desire
to do so was not as strong as she wanted to believe.

His mouth was hard and hot on hers, his kiss brutal,
almost savage, demanding her acquiescence. She
sensed the desperate need in him, felt the loneliness that
he denied was there, and in spite of her recent vow to
stay away from him, to put behind and forget what had
happened between them, she opened her mouth to the
assault of his tongue. He kissed her with a firm mastery
perfected from years of experience, a mastery that
drained away her anger, banished all thought of
resisting him, and replaced it with that same churning,
hungry need that always engulfed her whenever he held
her. A trembling weakness spread through her body,
and Elizabeth knew she was lost to him . . . again.

His hands moved over her back, caressing, pressing
her tighter to him, crushing her breasts against the hot,
still wet flesh of his chest. She felt one hand slip
downward, crush the mound of crinolines she wore,
and cup her derriere. He drew her toward him until her
hips pressed against his thighs, and she felt the urgency
of his need, the hard hunger of his passion, against her.

What little sanity she had left was rapidly swept
away by his caresses. His kiss enslaved her senses,
drained her of the urge to resist him, and sparked the
passions that had never flamed within her until his
touch ignited them. His hands roamed her back,
crushing her to him, and his tongue was like a burning
flame within her mouth, dueling with her own tongue,

daring her to respond to him, challenging her to deny him, to deny herself.

A soft knock echoed within the large room. "Supper 'bout to be served," a voice announced from the other side of the door. The retreating sound of footsteps followed, and then another knock on a door further down the hallway, and another announcement.

Elizabeth fought valiantly against the pleasure that had invaded her blood, and threatened to overtake the last shred of rational thought she possessed. She tried to push away from Gray, but he held her firm. "Please, stop," she whispered, her tone one of anguish. She knew, without doubt, that if she didn't get away from him that moment, that very instant, if he kissed her again, she would lose complete control of herself. She would gladly and willingly give in to the swirling ache of desire that had been unleashed within her the moment his lips had claimed hers.

"I want you in my bed, Elizabeth," Gray said raggedly. "I want to love you again. And you want me. You know you do."

"No, I don't." She pushed against him again, purposely positioning her hands over his injured ribs to give her the leverage she needed to free herself of his grasp. It worked. He flinched, and his arms dropped from around her as he stumbled backward.

Elizabeth stood shocked and wide-eyed, unable to look away as the towel that had been draped around Gray's hips fell to the floor.

Chapter 10

Elizabeth couldn't help herself. She stared. Openly. Directly. Her gaze was riveted to that part of his body that she had never seen before, and which had given her so much pleasure. It stood erect, hard, swollen, and pointed directly at her, as if it were a homing beacon and she was its target. Which, of course, she was.

She grew still, frozen to the spot. She was unable to breathe, unable to move, and quite unable to look away.

Gray watched her, and an insolent smile curved his lips. He moved slightly, shifting his weight from one foot to the other, and as he did, a stream of sunlight poured over his shoulder.

Elizabeth blinked as the bright light hit her eyes, and the spell that held her immobile was broken. Her gaze moved over him curiously, slowly, boldly. It was much too late to flee the room in a paroxysm of sudden primness. An aura of energy and purpose surrounded him, exuded from him, and drew her.

She felt her heart give a funny little leap and flutter, but she neither moved, nor met his eyes. His hair, ruffled and wet, fell rakishly onto his forehead. The late afternoon sun, streaming in through the window at his back, cast its golden glow over him, turned his flesh—tanned by long hours under the sun—to burnished copper, and his black hair to strands of ebony satin that glistened as if sprinkled with tiny hidden diamonds. A scar that she had not noticed before, snaked its way in a jagged, curving line, from just below his lowest right rib to just above his right hip. The whiteness of the disfigured flesh was a stark contrast to the cast of his bronzed skin. Only that portion of his body below his hips and above his thighs remained creamy white, unkissed by the sun.

Elizabeth's inquiring gaze rose to meet his, and was caught and held by the bold, arrogant stare of impudent, gold-brown eyes. At the moment they were alive with expression and a message. But it was a missive she was not sure of, and knew she should not seek to define.

She opened her mouth to say something, and nothing came out.

Gray leaned against the bedpost and crossed his arms, making no effort to retrieve the towel or cover himself from her view. "Well, Elizabeth, it looks like you have a choice: supper downstairs, or here."

She looked at him in puzzlement, and then, as if a flash of lightning had sparked her brain, realized what he meant. Suddenly her limbs no longer felt frozen or her voice paralyzed. She whirled around and made for the door. "I . . . Damien is waiting for us downstairs."

Gray chuckled softly, but made no comment as she rushed from his room.

Elizabeth sat in one of a set of green brocade ladies' chairs that flanked the white marble fireplace, and sipped a cup of tea. She was enjoying a light banter of conversation with their host when Gray entered the parlor.

"Sorry I'm late." Gray ignored the rich, almost garish appointments of the room, and directed his gaze toward Elizabeth. She refused to look at him and keep her eyes riveted instead on Damien. She was dressed in a gown of blue velvet, its sleeves fitted to her arms, its décolletage trimmed with a simple ruche of ivory lace and cut low—Gray's eyes took in the revealing swell of bosom—very low.

"Quite all right. No problem at all, Mr. Cantrelle," Damien said. "Elizabeth was just telling me of your harrowing ordeal."

Gray smiled at her. "Which harrowing ordeal?"

Elizabeth blushed and threw him a look meant to kill, but Gray's face remained a smiling effigy of innocence even as his dark eyes sparkled with mischief.

"The riverbank, of course," Damien said. "Did something else happen?"

Gray shrugged and continued to watch Elizabeth. "I wasn't really sure what Elizabeth considered a harrowing ordeal, that's all," he said easily.

Damien rose from his own seat on a nearby settee. "Would you like a drink before we dine, Mr. Cantrelle? I keep a very good stock of bourbon on hand. Whiskey as well."

Gray shook his head. "Actually, I didn't find our ordeal quite so harrowing. I rather enjoyed the time. Peaceful, you know?"

"Yes, well, but I'm sure that you realize a lady of Elizabeth's nature is not used to being in such a primitive environment, as you are." Damien turned nearly purple at hearing his own words, but Gray seemed to ignore the barb.

"Yes," he drawled lazily, still watching Elizabeth. "I do realize that." He finally turned toward Damien, and a quick glance told him all he cared to know about the man. Their host had also changed clothes and was attired in a pair of fawn-colored trousers that hugged his portly form. The leather *sous-pieds* that ran beneath the insole of each shoe and held the hems of his trousers taut did him no favor, but caused the tightness of the breeches to accentuate his nonexistent waist and short legs. His dark brown greatcoat was cut to fit, but the chocolate-brown brocade vest that was buttoned around his girth had obviously been in his wardrobe since a time when Damien had seen slimmer days. Its golden buttons looked like they were under quite a strain, and the lace cuffs of his silk shirt, which was undoubtedly of the finest quality, were out of style. "I'll take you up on that drink later, Sorens," Gray finally answered.

"Well, then, shall we?" Damien held out a hand to Elizabeth.

Gray shot her a look of warning, which she ignored.

"Thank you, Damien," Elizabeth cooed, and sashayed into the dining room beside their host, leaving Gray to follow.

Supper was a virtual gourmet's banquet, of which Gray ate, but tasted nothing. His mind was not on food. He ate only to satisfy his body, which had done a somersault of joy the moment his eyes had registered the food—beef not fish—and sent the message to his stomach. The entire time he ate, his gaze remained riveted on Elizabeth, whose gaze remained stubbornly pinioned on Damien.

Gray could feel his blood boiling, but there was nothing he could do about it. Elizabeth had gotten under his skin, and the only thing that was going to get her out was to bed her again. He was convinced of that. He'd never bedded a woman more than twice, never had the desire to, so he was certain it would be no different with Elizabeth. He'd have his satisfaction, get her out of his system, bid her adieu, and be on his way.

Happily. He'd feel guilty for a while, but he'd get over it. The little lady could then find some other sucker to drive crazy. Probably Damien Sorens, or someone very much like him: rich, pompous, and as phony as a three-dollar gold piece. But the thought didn't make him feel as good as he thought it should have.

"Are the clothes and room satisfactory, Mr. Cantrelle?"

It took Gray a few seconds to realize that Damien had spoken to him. "Uh, yes, fine, thank you. But I'm curious about something, Sorens. Obviously the clothes are not yours." The clothes he'd been furnished weren't a perfect fit, but they were close enough. The black trousers were a bit loose around the waist, as was the white shirt, indicating whoever owned them was a larger person than Damien Sorens. Usually Gray could care less, but he felt the need to know if there was another male in the house Elizabeth could coo over.

Damien smiled smugly. "The clothes belong to my brother. He lives in Washington, but occasionally comes down to visit."

"He's not here now?"

"No. He was, but he left for England just a few days ago. We own several businesses together, including this plantation. Five thousand acres of the richest land east of the Mississippi. Regis prefers to live up north. I prefer it here in Louisiana, but Regis leaves enough clothing here to see him through his periodic visits. I figured you two were about the same size when I saw you."

Gray nodded. "And Elizabeth's?"

The smile left Damien's face, and his eyes turned dark, yet Gray got the impression it was not sadness, but anger he saw in Damien's face. "My late wife, Jane. She's been gone nearly two years now. Died in childbirth."

143

Elizabeth placed her fork on the table and reached to cover one of Damien's hands with her own. "Oh, Damien, I'm so sorry. The child?"

"I had a son. An heir." He sighed deeply. "But he only lived a few hours longer than Jane, and then he joined her." He smiled again, and Gray noticed that Damien's eyes lit on Elizabeth with something more than casual interest. "You remind me very much of my late wife, my dear. She had golden hair, too, but," he leaned forward and covered Elizabeth's hand with his, "she was not a strong person."

"No disrespect," Gray said, drawing their attention, "but you must have had your hands full. If Elizabeth truly reminds you of your late wife, that is."

Elizabeth's mouth dropped open and hung agape. The nerve of the man! He was the most insufferable, most arrogant, most impertinent person she'd ever had the misfortune to meet.

"Why, frankly, Mr. Cantrelle, I find Elizabeth's company quite . . . charming," Damien said.

The compliment didn't help. Elizabeth wanted nothing more than to slap that smug smile off of Gray's face. He infuriated her like no other person she knew.

And he pleasures you like no other person, the little nagging voice of her conscience said.

She felt like screaming. If it wasn't Gray pushing his uninvited and unwanted attentions on her, then it was that nagging little voice inside her head reminding her of her own wanton desires. Damn!

Damien noticed Elizabeth's sudden silence and her intense stare at Gray. "Elizabeth, my dear, are you all right? Do you feel ill?"

She fought a valiant battle and quickly got her runaway temper under control. Grayson Cantrelle was not going to get the better of her. He would not cause her to react like some shrewish harridan in front of

144

Damien Sorens. She turned a sweet smile to Damien. "I'm fine, Damien, thank you. I just feel the need to take some air. If you'll excuse me?"

"I'll accompany you, my dear. I have one of the best gardens in the state. I'll show them to you."

Grayson watched them leave the room through the open French doors, but instead of the elation he should have felt at Damien's obvious interest in Elizabeth, he was seething with the urge to rip the man's heart out. And throttling Elizabeth didn't sound like a bad idea, either.

"Well, if that's who she wants, what do I care?" he grumbled, and pushed away from the table. His ribs burned with pain. It was a slow journey back up to his bedchamber, what with trying not to further aggravate his ribs or put too much weight on his still sore leg. He needed to lie down and sleep for a while. Maybe Damien would propose marriage to Elizabeth, then she'd have exactly what she wanted; a rich husband who could give her every luxury in life her little heart could want.

Gray didn't just sleep the afternoon away, he slept the remainder of the day away, and all through the night. Elizabeth, unfortunately, did not. When she finally disentangled herself from Damien and retired after an early dinner, she did nothing but toss and turn until almost midnight when, finally overcome with exhaustion, she fell into a fitful sleep.

While awake she worried about Grayson. He had gone to his room directly after supper and hadn't come down for dinner. Was he all right? The thought pierced her heart with fear, but she stubbornly refused to go to his room.

The next morning, when she went downstairs,

dressed in one of Damien's late wife's gowns, a pale yellow muslin with puffed sleeves and an embroidered bodice, she saw that Gray had preceded her. Well, at least he's not dead, she thought, then wondered why she cared one way or the other.

Breakfast was an uncomfortable fiasco, with Damien trying to be cheerful and make small talk, while Grayson grumbled and bullied him with one personal question after another, especially about his brother Regis.

"Why'd he go to England?" Grayson asked. "Sudden trip?"

"As a matter of fact, yes. Regis said something about needing to get away for a while." Damien shrugged. "Most likely Melissa is after him to marry her again." He chuckled.

"Melissa?" Grayson echoed.

"A lady friend in Washington, though, I daresay, Melissa would insist she was much more to Regis than a lady friend. She's been trying to get him to marry her for several years now."

"Damien, are we still going riding?" Elizabeth said, interrupting Grayson's interrogation.

"Why, yes, my dear. Any time you wish."

"I wish to go now," she replied and rose from the table. Her gaze fell on Grayson, and there was no question as to the message in her eyes. *You are not invited.*

Of course, he couldn't have gone even if he wanted to, which he didn't. His ribs wouldn't have been able to handle another ride on horseback. Not yet.

He felt a sharp stab of irritation though, at her rejection. She was playing with fire. He could sense it. Damien Sorens was not a gentleman, no matter what kind of trappings he surrounded himself with, but then Elizabeth would most likely have to find that out for

146

herself. She wouldn't believe Gray if he told her, that was certain.

Grayson sat on the gallery nearly the entire time they were gone, and watched for their return. His eyes scanned the horizon, watching for the dust kicked up by horse hooves, or the silhouette of two figures on horseback. By the time they finally returned, he was nearly furious. Damien and Elizabeth enjoyed the noon meal in the parlor, but Grayson went to his room and collapsed on the bed. He hurt like hell, and he was so angry he could punch his fist through a wall. The problem was, he didn't know what he was angry about.

Zeeanda nudged his shoulder gently. Gray opened his eyes and looked up at her. "Dinner's 'bout to be served, Michie."

Elizabeth pirouetted before the tall mirror. She was lucky that she was almost the exact same size as Damien's late wife. Some of the gowns were a bit snug, others a bit too loose, but not enough to make a noticeable difference. She had chosen a soft peach silk tonight. Its neckline plunged a bit deeper than she would have preferred, but she loved the gown. Its skirt was plain except for a flounce of velvet, just a shade darker than the silk, over each hip. The bodice was snug, and her shoulders were left bare by sleeves that hugged her arms tightly down to her wrists. A band of velvet accentuated the neckline and was sprinkled with a field of tiny seed pearls. She was sure Damien would appreciate her in the gown. Gray's tongue could hang out until it reached the floor, for all she cared. She patted the cluster of curls that cascaded from her crown to drape over one shoulder, and sighed. She missed Serena terribly, Damien had offered her the use of a maid, but she'd refused, feeling uncomfortable with a stranger.

Looking in the mirror she suddenly realized how much she had grown to look like her mother. The thought brought on a flood of memories, and with them, the resulting promise she had made to herself so long ago. She had experienced poverty, had felt what it was like not to have anything, and she would never go through that again. Not for anything. Not many people knew, that when she and her sister had been toddlers, their father had gambled away their home in Clarksburg, or that he'd lost all of their money to a gambler a few years later, while traveling home from a business trip. For several years the Devlins had lived by what little good fortune they could find. Then Elizabeth's mother had finally relinquished her pride and gone to her father and begged a loan. With the money he gave her, she purchased a plantation in Vicksburg, and she maintained control of the family's finances thereafter. Eight years later she'd died.

Elizabeth swept a hand over the rich silk of her skirt. "Never again," she whispered to the image that stared back at her from the mirror. Those years of poverty had impressed upon her the need to have things, lots of them. And she was not about to deprive herself of any of the luxuries life had to offer. She could only thank the saints that both she and Eugenia had been left trust funds by their maternal grandfather, otherwise they would have had virtually nothing. Her father had seen to it that there was nothing to leave.

Gray and Damien were already seated at the long dining table when she entered the room. Both men rose. "Oh, I'm sorry. Did I keep you waiting?" Her tone held a note of innocence, though she knew full well she had done just that.

"Your entrance, my dear, and the beauty it brings, was well worth the wait," Damien gushed.

Gray felt like gagging.

Damien walked around the table and escorted Elizabeth to her chair, then reseated himself, as did Gray.

Zeeanda entered and began to serve a meal of rice covered with a gumbo sauce of crawfish and crab, accompanied by green beans and slivered almonds, buttered biscuits, and fresh sliced tomatoes.

"Mr. Cantrelle has been telling me a bit more about the explosion of the riverboat. Sounds as if it was an absolutely dreadful experience, Elizabeth. Absolutely dreadful. You must have been terrified." He reached across the table and patted her hand.

Elizabeth simpered pertly and picked at the food on her plate. "Oh yes, Damien, I was."

"So terrified that she was going to stay on the boat and burn to a crisp rather than jump into the water," Gray said.

Damien turned a puzzled eye to Gray.

Elizabeth stiffened and shot him a scathing glare, then turned back to Damien with a smile. "I can't swim. I was afraid I'd drown."

"But she can burn," Gray said, and smiled the most seductive smile Elizabeth thought she'd ever seen on his face. "Passionately," he added.

Flaming arrows, meant to kill, shot from Elizabeth's gaze as she turned to look at Gray.

For a split second he thought she was going to throw her fork at him, and he prepared to duck.

She rose from her chair and plastered a forced smile on her face. "If you will excuse me, Damien, I'm suddenly not very hungry. I think I'll take a few moments of air, and then retire."

"Of course, my dear, would you like some company into the gardens?"

"No, thank you."

Elizabeth turned to leave the room, but paused at the door and looked back. Her eyes sought Gray's, captured them, and held them prisoner to her own. "Please, Mr. Cantrelle, if you wish to continue your journey downriver, do not think you must remain here any longer and assist me with my arrangements. I'm sure Damien can help me."

For some insane reason that he could not fathom, Gray felt her rejection cut at him sharply. The last thing he wanted was to be responsible for Elizabeth Devlin, to be expected to wait on her, to assist her in anything. Yet now that she had just given him the perfect excuse to leave, to ride off into the sunset and never look back, he found himself hesitant to do so. And he wasn't sure guilt had anything to do with his reluctance to leave her. "I'm sure my business in New Orleans will keep, Elizabeth. Another night or two of rest in a real bed is too inviting to pass up. I'm sure you agree." It wouldn't do his ribs or leg any harm either, he thought, and shifted uncomfortably on the chair. Both were healing nicely, but he wasn't sure if he was up to riding into town just yet.

She smiled, much like a tigress does when she is about to sink her teeth into the throat of her prey. "I'm sure," she purred, and left the room in a swirl of peach silk.

"Quite a woman," Damien said, staring after Elizabeth.

"Yeah, if you like them sharp-tongued and troublesome," Gray grumbled.

"I think your comment rather upset her, Mr. Cantrelle."

"Really?" Gray sipped on a glass of wine. "I suppose I owe her an apology then."

"Yes, I should think so. But, tell me if you will," he leaned forward and made a steeple of his hands beneath his chin, "is there a . . . ah . . . a relationship between yourself and Miss Devlin?"

"Why do you ask, Sorens?" Gray retorted, purposely not preceding the man's name with the proper title.

"Well, ummm, I would like to offer my attendance to Miss Devlin."

"Attendance? Interesting way to put it. Court her, is that what you mean?" Gray prodded.

"Yes, exactly."

"I wouldn't recommend that, Sorens." Now why in the hell had he said that? If he had half a brain, he'd be encouraging the man.

"Oh?"

Gray set his wineglass down with deliberate slowness, sat up in his chair, and leaned forward. He knew he'd be sorry for doing this, but the impulse was too great. Anyway, he just couldn't see Elizabeth hitching herself to this pompous wind bag. He lowered his voice to a conspiratorial tone. "Sorens, despite her sharp tongue and obvious need of a good throttling, Elizabeth and I got pretty close while we were stuck out on that riverbank together. Do you understand what I'm saying?" Why was he doing this? Why in hell was he doing this?

"Of course, of course." Damien glanced toward the foyer door. So, Elizabeth had already given her favors away. Wouldn't Aaron be surprised. And now there was no reason to think she wouldn't be willing to give them away again. "Obviously Miss Devlin's uh, fall from grace, was fortunate for yourself."

Beneath an onslaught of guilt at Damien's words, and at himself for what he'd just done, Gray nailed Damien with a sharp look, but the man was too busy with his own thoughts to notice. "Excuse me, Sorens," he said, and rose abruptly from his seat. He threw his lap cloth down on the table and strode from the room.

Damien watched him exit the house through the front door. He smiled. Perfect. "Zeeanda."

The servant appeared in the doorway almost immediately, her thin hands clasped tightly together, her once pretty face a placid mask that seemed void of emotion, until one looked into her faded brown eyes. They blazed with the contempt she felt for the master of Cypress Grove.

"I'll be upstairs. See that I'm not disturbed."

"Yessah," Zeeanda mumbled, her eyes downcast as Damien made to pass. He paused beside her and nudged her chin with his forefinger. "Don't pout, Zeeanda, I'll tend to you later. Perhaps tomorrow night."

She jerked her head away. Damien chuckled and ascended the stairs.

The moon, a thick golden crescent that hung low in the black velvety sky, was surrounded by thousands of brightly sparkling stars, and turned the formal gardens of Cypress Grove to a virtual landscape of muted colors and hazy shadows. Tall, neatly trimmed boxwood hedges lined both sides of several paths that meandered through and around the gardens, and crisscrossed one another, making a simple maze. True to Damien's claim, more than a dozen varieties of roses dotted the gardens, each a different color. Azaleas, camellias, jasmine, honeysuckle, and several other types of plants and blooms that Elizabeth recognized, but was unable to name, grew along the paths.

She knelt beside a bush and could not resist the impulse to touch one of the huge pink roses that adorned it. "Ouch." She jerked her hand back quickly,

152

and watched a spittle of blood form on the end of her finger from the puncture a small, unseen thorn had invoked. "Oh, piddle." She looked up at the dark sky. "Are you mad at me or something?"

A screech owl broke from his perch on the limb of a nearby tree, and emitted its horrifying scream as it flew over her head. Elizabeth nearly jumped off of the ground. Her heart did fly into her throat, and just as quickly began to calm when she realized what had caused the sound. "Stupid owl," she mumbled, and sucked on her finger to stem the flow of blood.

She moved further down the path and entered the maze. She swiped a hand at the leaves of the hedge. Gray was being a brute. Ever since Damien had rescued them, Gray had snipped at her, taunted her, and acted a total ogre. She meandered between the tall hedges for a few seconds longer, changed direction several times, veering off onto one path or another, and was startled when the light of the moon suddenly disappeared, and she was plunged into total darkness.

"Oh, wonderful," she murmured to herself. She turned around, intent on retracing her steps, and found herself without a sense of direction. It was pitch black no matter which way she looked, even up. She saw no stars or moon. She moved to her left, and walked straight into a wall of leaves and brittle branches. "Ouch!" She jumped back and brushed at the tiny scratches the branches had made on her shoulder. She turned and began to march in the opposite direction, and plowed smack into another wall of foliage. "Ohhh, piddle, piddle, piddle!" The skirt of her gown caught on a branch as she made to step back. It snagged. She jerked it free and heard the fabric tear. Now Damien would be angry with her. She whirled in another direction, but threw out her hands in front of her before taking a step. She met nothing but air. She took

153

another step. Then another, and another. She released the breath she had been unaware she was holding, and continued to walk forward. It didn't get any lighter, she still couldn't see anything, but at least she didn't run into the bush either.

Ten minutes later she was ready to burst into tears. She was lost. She had absolutely no idea how to get herself out of this labyrinth of greenery. Her eyes had adjusted enough to the dark to be able to discern that the twisted, gnarled, thickly leaved limbs of an oak spread over the maze, blocking out the sight of the sky and the light of the moon.

She moved cautiously down the path, felt her way around a corner, and was overjoyed when moonlight broke over everything. Elizabeth almost shouted in joy. She quickened her step, came to another passage that crossed the one she was on, and veered left onto it. A few minutes later she rounded a corner to her right and nearly jumped out of her skin.

Her shriek echoed on the still night air. She threw herself against the hedge to her left, pressed her back into it, and stared at the thing in front of her. Standing within a carved alcove in the hedge, the tall white marble statue of a Greek warrior—completely nude except for the helmet on his head and the sword held in his hand—looked down at her from atop his pedestal.

Elizabeth felt her heart somersault within her breast, and bang against her rib cage. She gulped several times in an effort to regain her breath, and held her hands clenched to keep them from shaking.

"Lord almighty," she mumbled to the statue, "you nearly scared me half to death." She straightened, brushed off her skirt, and stared at the stone figure. He was tall, his body sinewy, shoulders broad, legs long and lean. She looked at him with an assessing eye, and then, when her gaze dropped to the apex of his thighs, was reminded of the scene that had taken place that afternoon in Gray's room. "I think he's built a bit better than you," she said, and giggled softly.

When her legs felt as if they were not going to melt beneath her weight, and were capable of walking without disintegrating, she turned from the statue and continued down the path. Quickly. Moonlight lit her way and stars filled the sky overhead, but no exit to the maze presented itself. She rounded one corner, walked aways, glanced back over her shoulder as she rounded another, and ran right into what felt like a brick wall.

Elizabeth bounced back a step. Her ankle twisted, and she began to fall to one side. Her arms flew up to flail the air in an effort to maintain her balance, and pain filled her leg.

Strong hands grasped her arms and stopped their thrashing, at the same time they held her upright and prevented her sag to the ground.

Chapter 11

"Let me go," Elizabeth screamed, and kicked out with her foot. One of the hooks that kept her laces in place on her shoe caught on the lace trim of her petticoat, and rendered her attack futile.

With the moon at his back, Gray presented nothing more than a huge and—in her present state of panic—menacing silhouette to Elizabeth. She squirmed frantically, twisting and jerking and trying desperately to pull away from him.

"Elizabeth, for cryin'-out-loud, it's only me."

She stopped struggling. "Gray?"

"Yes. Who did you think it was?"

She felt herself flush. She wasn't about to tell him the horrors her mind had envisioned at seeing a huge black shape loom out of the dark and grab her. "I knew it was you all the time. I just wanted you to let me go, that's all."

"Uh-huh, and I suppose you weren't lost in here and ready to panic out of your little mind?"

Elizabeth threw back her shoulders and lifted her chin in a haughty pose. "Of course not. I was just enjoying a walk in the gardens. Alone. Whatever would give you the idea I was lost or ready to panic, as you so graciously put it?"

"I saw you come in here, and I didn't see you come out. But I did hear you shriek, mutter a few very unladylike curses, run into the hedge a couple of times, and talk to yourself about somebody being built better than somebody else." He smiled slyly. "You weren't referring to me perchance, were you? About being better built?"

The seductive question went ignored. "You knew I was in here, lost, and you didn't come in to help me out?"

"I thought you just said you weren't lost."

"Well," she bristled, "I was turned around was all. But you could have been a gentleman and inquired if I was all right anyway."

"If you'll remember, you just about rolled over me like a locomotive out of control a moment ago."

"You stepped in my path," she said defensively.

"I was coming to inquire if *you were all right,*" he said, echoing her own words. "I didn't expect to be attacked for my trouble."

"I think it's time I returned to the house." She tried to brush past him. Gray stepped in her way. "Are you going to force yourself on me again?"

Now it was his turn to be shocked. His mouth dropped open. "Force myself on you? What the hell does that mean?"

Elizabeth lifted her skirts and pushed past him. "You know very well what it means," she flipped over her shoulder.

Gray hurried after her and grabbed her arm, jerking her around roughly and forcing her to pause and look at him. "You and I both know I did not *force* myself on you, Elizabeth."

"You did. I would never have done those . . . those *disgusting* things with you if I'd had my way. And I'll thank you to leave me alone, Grayson Cantrelle. Just leave me alone. You've done nothing but act like a beast ever since I met you, and . . . and you've insulted me numerous times in front of Damien." She pulled her arm away from him and ran toward the house.

Gray started to go after her, and then stopped. If that's what she thought of him, then to hell with it. Let her go to her precious Damien.

"A beast, a nasty, arrogant beast," Elizabeth muttered to herself, as she climbed the steps to the gallery. His conduct ever since they'd arrived at Cypress Grove had effectively told her that he wanted nothing further to do with her, unless it was in bed. "And to think, I actually contemplated the idea of marriage to the man. I must have been touched in the head." Elizabeth shuddered just thinking of what it would be like to be married to Grayson Cantrelle. She'd probably end up following him from one dirty little town to another, sleeping in cheap hotels, doing his laundry, and watching him gun down innocent men.

And letting him do those wonderfully delicious things to your body, that bedeviling little voice in her conscience whispered.

She felt her cheeks burn. "They weren't delicious. They were . . . were . . . nothing." She stormed up the stairs and, after entering her room, slammed the door behind her and began to practically rip off her clothes. "Beast. That's what he is," she grumbled. "A nasty, arrogant, impudent beast." She yanked the coverlet back, blew out her lamp, and climbed into bed. Moonlight filled the room, filtering in through a slight space between the drawn curtains. She stared up at the yellow *ceil de leit* of the bed's canopy. What had happened that last night between her and Gray? Why had he turned so sullen and curt toward her? Had her lovemaking displeased him so? Is that why afterwards he had abruptly gotten up and stalked into the woods? A tear escaped the corner of her eye, and she angrily brushed it away. How could he be so sweet, so loving one minute, and a complete boor the next? She punched the pillow and rolled onto her side. How in heaven's name had she gotten into this situation anyway? Her mind didn't have to search far for an answer to that one. Fury burned in her breast. Aaron Reynaud, that's how. This was all his fault. If it wasn't for him, none of this would have happened to her. None of it. She certainly wouldn't have stormed away from the plantation and boarded that riverboat. And she certainly wouldn't have met Grayson Cantrelle. And if she hadn't met Grayson, she wouldn't have been stranded on that riverbank with him, and he wouldn't have been able to force himself on her.

"He didn't."

"He did," she mumbled into the pillow. "He did."

Damien stood in the shadows at the end of the hallway long after Elizabeth entered her room. He had quietly gone downstairs and turned the lock on the front and rear doors, effectively blocking Grayson Cantrelle's entry to the house. If the man wanted back in, he was going to have to bang on the door, which, if Damien needed it, would serve as his warning. He moved down the hallway quietly and stopped before the door that led into Elizabeth's bedchamber. His fingers wrapped slowly around the doorknob. It did not turn. She'd locked it. Damien cursed softly, and drew a ring of keys from his pocket. He slipped one into the small keyhole below the doorknob, turned, and the door swung quietly open. Repocketing the key, Damien entered, closed the door behind him, and approached the large canopied bed that dominated the center of the room. The mosquito baire had been left drawn open, and because of the warmth of the afternoon, which hung in the still air of the room, the bed's yellow coverlet had been thrown back.

Elizabeth lay asleep in the center of the bed, clad only in a thin, ivory baptiste nightgown. The shape of her body beneath the veil of cloth was quite distinct, and her blond hair spread across the white pillow like a fan of golden threads on a blanket of snow. Only faint streams of moonlight penetrated the room, seeping between the thin crack left by the heavy drapes that had been drawn across the room's two tall windows.

Damien caught sight of his own image in a cheval mirror that stood in the corner, a few feet from the bed. Startled, he jumped, then realized he was looking at himself. He preened, examining himself from first one angle, then another. Satisfied with his appearance, he turned his attention back to Elizabeth.

She shifted her position, and the fabric of the gown was pulled taut over the small perfectly formed breasts whose rosy nipples pushed against the transparent material. Damien's body hardened with desire, and his gaze skimmed over her hungrily. His breath caught in his throat, as his eyes fastened on the golden patch of silken hairs between her legs.

He moved to the edge of the bed and hastily removed his jacket and vest, tossing both on a nearby chair. He yanked on the silk cravat at his neck and pulled the buttons of his shirt free, then let both fall to the floor in a careless heap. He was on fire with need of her, his arousal bulging against the taut confines of his breeches. Damien slid onto the bed beside Elizabeth, and slipped his hand beneath her camisole. His fingers moved to cup the taut mound of her breast. She stirred beneath him. Damien's fingers kneaded the tender flesh, and his thumb flicked the pebbled peak of her nipple. Lord, what that fool Aaron had given up because of his ill-timed philandering! A smile of anticipation spread across his face.

"Umm, Gray," Elizabeth moaned softly. She turned

160

toward Damien and pushed her body up against his. Dreams born of selected memories drifted through her sleep-filled mind. Gray lay beside her, holding her to him, secure and safe against his body. His hands caressed her as he loved her like he had on the riverbank. She snuggled deeper into his embrace, needing him to love her, needing to experience the passion his touch had awakened within her.

Damien's body burned with excitement at her response. He lifted one leg over Elizabeth and lay it atop her hips, pinning her to the bed, then pressed his lips to hers.

Elizabeth's eyes shot open and consciousness hit her like a slap across the face. She looked up into Damien's face and was struck with instant terror, anger, and revulsion all at the same time. She tore her lips from his, pushed at his bare, flabby chest, and tried to twist away from him, but his leg held her pinioned in place.

Gray paced the length of the veranda. His ribs still ached and his leg throbbed, but the pain was at least tolerable now. He ignored both. "Damn," he snapped harshly. What the hell was the matter with him? That knock on the head must have really rattled his brain. Or maybe it had just turned it to mush. He'd as much as told Damien that he'd made love to Elizabeth, had ruined her for other men. At least the type she wanted. Why? Why in hell's name had he done it? Because he was jealous? That was ridiculous. He paused beside one of the massive white pillars that graced the edge of the gallery, and dug a cheroot from his pocket. He scraped the tip of a lucifer against the pillar and cupped his hands around the small flame, as he lifted it to the tip of the thin cigar. The sputtering glare cast his face in a glow of orange light. He'd have to care about her to be jealous, and he didn't. Well, he did, but not that way.

161

He stared out at the dark grounds of the vast plantation and cursed himself for the hundredth time. He should be glad that she'd been flirting with Damien. He should be relieved that she'd turned her attentions elsewhere. He should be thankful that she obviously didn't expect, or desire him to offer a proposal of marriage. Gray inhaled deeply of the cheroot. He should be all of those things, but he wasn't.

Well, he might care for her more than he wanted, but he was not going to propose marriage to her. *That* he was not going to do. And nothing was going to change his mind.

He'd see her to New Orleans, away from the so-obvious lecherous intentions of Damien Sorens. He owed her at least that. Then, if he still hadn't found Carlen Masters, he'd go home.

Carlen Masters. Had he really been hunting the man for over four months? He sighed, remembering the morning Dana had returned to the Cantrelle ranch from her stay in Washington, and told him and his mother what had happened. Gray had been furious. He'd left the next morning and traveled almost nonstop to the nation's capital, to hunt the man down and force him to face his reponsibilities. But he'd failed to find Masters. He'd followed several trails, and finally the one that led him downriver, and then the trail had come to an abrupt end. Carlen Masters had disappeared into thin air.

Yes, it was time, finally, to head for home. Gray closed his eyes and let an image of the Cantrelle ranch, the Bar C, come into his mind. It was one of the biggest spreads in Texas. The country was rough and unforgiving, the land hard, the weather merciless, but he loved it. He had been born and raised on the Bar C, and had taken over its operation when his father died three years before.

He tried to picture Elizabeth on the Bar C, and

couldn't. She wasn't like his mother Celia, or Tori Chisolm, who owned the spread next to his. They were Texas women, strong and independent, as was Dana. She knew what it took, what it meant, to live in Texas. Elizabeth didn't. She was used to grand plantations and a houseful of servants to do her bidding. The Bar C was grand, but it wasn't a plantation, and it had only three house servants, not enough to do everyone's bidding, and not expected to try.

He inhaled deeply of the cheroot. Elizabeth would never survive on the Bar C. She was like a magnolia; beautiful, delicate, and fragile. Magnolias were not abundant in Texas. At least not on the plains of the Bar C. He felt the inseam of his trousers tighten as his mind filled with thoughts of Elizabeth, as he remembered their lovemaking, the feel of her silken, naked body pressed to his.

"Michie, Michie, come quick."

Grayson turned at the child's voice. Jason, the boy who he remembered had taken their horses the day they'd arrived, grabbed on his coat sleeve and tugged at him. "Come, Michie, come, the mistress needs you. Hurry." The front door stood open.

"What mistress?" he said, and glanced into the dark foyer.

"Yours. Michie Sorens, he's in her room. Hurry."

With a quick flick of his hand, he threw the cheroot to the ground and hurried into the house. Damn it all to hell, he'd known Elizabeth was trouble the minute he'd seen her. He took the stairs leading to the bedchambers two at a time.

"Let me go, Damien." Elizabeth's screams bounced off of the walls of the house and filled the hallway. Grayson bolted toward her room. He slammed her door open, and the heavy slab of carved mahogany crashed against the wall. Rage filled his chest and nearly blinded him as his eyes focused on only one thing: Damien Sorens, lying half-naked atop Elizabeth, who was still screaming and struggling to free herself from his weight.

A guttural growl tore itself from Grayson's throat as he strode across the room, grabbed the man by the hair on his crown, and jerked him from the bed. Sorens landed in a sprawling heap on the floor.

"What the hell do you think you're doing, Sorens?" Grayson snarled. He stood with legs spread wide, hands clenched at his sides, and eyes blazing with fury as he stared down at their host.

Damien scrambled up, grabbed his greatcoat from the chair, and held it in front of his bare chest. His eyes widened with fear as Grayson clenched and unclenched his fists. "I . . . I heard Elizabeth whimpering. Crying. Like she was having a nightmare," Damien said quickly, stumbling over his words. "I . . . I came in to console her and she . . . she . . ." he looked at Elizabeth, threw back his shoulders, and puffed out his chest. "She invited me into her bed."

"What?" Elizabeth gasped. She stared at Damien in disbelief.

"She did," he professed again.

"Get dressed, Elizabeth," Gray ordered. "We're leaving."

"But I didn't . . . he . . . I . . ."

"Get dressed."

Damien slunk toward the door.

Elizabeth snatched up a small brass candlestick that sat on the night table next to the bed and flung it toward her retreating host. It hit the wall with a thud.

Damien scurried from the room.

"That blackguard . . . that . . . that . . ."

"Elizabeth."

She quieted at his brusque tone.

"I said *get dressed.* Now." He spun on his heel and walked back into the hallway.

"Wonderful," she mumbled, and slid from the high bed to the floor. "This is just absolutely wonderful." She grabbed her gown and began to struggle her way back into it. "Are all men such . . . such . . . brutes? Are there no gentlemen left in the world?" She had thought Damien a gentleman, a man of breeding, but he was obviously no better than Grayson Cantrelle. Trying to force himself on her like that. Just like Grayson did.

No, he didn't, her little voice of conscience said.

"Yes, he did," she snapped back aloud.

"I will not step foot on another boat!"

"Elizabeth, will you be reasonable for a change? It's the most sensible way," Gray said. He had the urge to pick her up, toss her over his shoulder, and carry her onto the riverboat, but he figured the other people on the small dock wouldn't understand. And he didn't want to have to deal with some overly noble gentleman coming to Elizabeth's rescue.

"No." She whirled around and turned her back to him. The point of her ruffled parasol practically rammed itself up his nose.

Gray jerked his head back, fumed momentarily, and then reminded himself that getting angry with Elizabeth didn't work. What it did do was make her more obstinate. For the life of him, he didn't know why he gave one wit's damn whether she got on the riverboat or not. He should just go ahead and board and leave her here in this one-horse town. But he couldn't. He should. But he couldn't. Especially not with Damien Sorens here. "Elizabeth," he strove to keep his voice both low and calm, "get on that damn boat or I'll carry you on."

"No."

He sighed. Threats weren't going to work. And he'd

165

already tried being nice and cajoling. So what was left? He should leave her, that's what was left. Except that it wasn't. Not really. "All right, Elizabeth, if you won't get on the boat, just how do you propose that we get to New Orleans?" He crossed his arms over his chest and waited for her response.

She turned back to him, a smile of triumph on her lips. "By buggy."

"Buggy? Are you crazy?" He gawked at her. "No, forget I asked. I already know the answer."

Elizabeth's features tightened. "If you do not wish to travel by buggy, Mr. Cantrelle, then by all means, please, board the riverboat and get yourself blown to kingdom come. I am quite capable of handling a buggy on my own."

"Oh, right," Gray scoffed. "You? Travel by buggy, alone, to New Orleans?"

"Yes."

"No."

Elizabeth stiffened and shot him her most scathing glare. "I am traveling by buggy, Mr. Cantrelle. You may join me, if you wish. Good day." She turned on her heel, intent on making her way to the livery they'd passed while heading for the docks.

Gray grabbed her arm and hauled her back before him. His act drew the attention of several people standing nearby. He ignored them. "You are coming with me, Elizabeth, and that's final."

Her feet left the ground, and she felt herself being jerked through the air. She scrambled for balance and landed smack against Gray's chest. She hurriedly pushed away from him and straightened, shrugging her shoulders, tossing her head and brushing the skirt of her gown. "How dare you," she hissed under her breath.

The boat whistle blasted, signaling the packet's imminent departure.

"Dammit, Elizabeth, we don't have any more time for this nonsense. Now come on." He made the mistake of grabbing for her arm again.

She sidestepped to avoid his grasp, swung her parasol around in front of her, and jabbed the point of it into his midsection.

"Aghhh!" His breath flew out in a torrent, his hands went to hold his stomach, and he doubled over slightly.

Elizabeth pivoted and began to walk away. "That will teach you to manhandle a lady."

Gray regained his breath and made a grab for her. "Where do you think you're—"

A fist, which he had not seen coming, connected with his jaw. His teeth clamped down on his tongue, and his head jerked back. With a furious snarl, Gray staggered, caught himself, shook the stars from his head, and looked about for his attacker.

A tall, slightly built, and impeccably dressed young man was bowing before Elizabeth, who was smiling prettily. "Please, mademoiselle, let me introduce myself. Henri LeMeaux, at your service."

Gray launched himself toward the man, who was lifting Elizabeth's hand to his lips. His fist, all grit and muscle, caught the man's jaw and sent him spinning like a top. A gray bowler, that had sat jauntily atop the man's head, rolled across the wharf and propelled itself into the river.

"Grayson!" Elizabeth squealed.

Henri LeMeaux, who had fallen to the ground, jumped back to his feet and hopped into the stance of a boxer, knees bent, arms crooked upward, and fists cocked. "Come, you ruffian, I will teach you not to maltreat a lady."

"Oh, Lord," Gray sighed, looking at Henri's pose. He took a step toward the man. "Listen, mister, I don't want to hurt you, but you've stuck your nose where it doesn't—"

167

A fist caught him off guard, and directly on the chin again. The blow, though not hard enough to do him any damage, stunned Gray and roused his anger further. "All right, dammit, you asked for it." A steely fist whipped up and smashed into Henri's delicately structured aristocratic face, pushing his chin back, his nose in, and his cheeks out. His eyes rolled back in his head, and he immediately slumped to the ground.

"Grayson Cantrelle, you brute!" Elizabeth screamed.

Gray turned away from the unconscious lump that was Henri LeMeaux and confronted Elizabeth. "I am not the cause of this mess, Elizabeth, you are. Now let's go."

Just then the whistle of the riverboat blasted shrilly, and its bell began to clang. Gray turned around and began to curse vehemently. "Dammit all to hell, now look what you've done."

"What *I've* done? Look what *you've* done," she retorted, and stared down at Henri. "He's dead."

Gray looked around, glanced at Henri, who stirred slightly, and then turned the full power of his glare on Elizabeth. "He's not dead, he's just unconscious. But you're going to be if you keep this up. You've made us miss the boat. The only damn boat that is scheduled to leave here today. I ought to just get myself a horse and leave you here."

"Go ahead," Elizabeth challenged. "I don't want to go with you anyway." She tossed her head and lifted her chin in the air. Blond curls bounced around her shoulders. "I'm sure Henri would be more than willing to escort me to New Orleans." She hoped Gray couldn't see through the bravado she was struggling to project. She didn't know the first thing about Henri LeMeaux, other than he'd tried to rescue her from Gray, who—back in his leathers, hat, and low-slung gun—did look threatening and not the least bit gentlemanly. But how did she know Henri wasn't a thief? Or a gambler? Or worse, a murderer?

"Don't tempt me, Elizabeth." He took her by the arm, grabbed her valise from the ground, and steered her toward the street. "We'll get a buggy, but by all that's saintly, don't think up anymore of your shenanigans, or I'll leave you out on the trail to find your own way to New Orleans," Gray said, trying to invoke a threatening tone into his voice in order to scare her.

"Humph. A gentleman would never treat a lady the way you do."

"I never said I was a gentleman," Gray growled, "and I'm not so sure you're a lady."

Elizabeth tried to jerk her arm from his grasp, but his fingers held tight. "Well, I never!"

"No, you probably never have. Maybe that's what's wrong with you."

"Ohhhh." She began to swing her parasol from its resting place on her shoulder.

"Hit me with that thing again, and I'll break it in two," Gray warned in a tone that told Elizabeth he meant exactly what he said.

She marched stiffly beside him until they reached the livery, where he finally released his hold on her.

"I need to buy a buggy, hitchings, and a horse," he told the smithie.

"Buy? You don't want to rent?"

"We just missed the packet to New Orleans, and my . . ." he looked at Elizabeth, "*she* wants to take a buggy. We're not coming back. You want to come down there and get your rig and horse?" Gray inquired acidly.

"Well, no," the man said.

"Then I want to buy. How much?"

"A hundred for the buggy, fifty for the horse."

"What? That's robbery."

"That's the price," the man said.

Gray fumed. He'd already wasted money on two riverboat tickets that were now no good. He dug into a small leather pouch full of gold coins. It was lucky for them both he'd found it in the wreckage on the riverbank, or they'd be walking to New Orleans. He dropped several coins in the man's palm. "Hitch it up," he ordered. "And put a couple of blankets under the seat."

He glanced over his shoulder at Elizabeth who smiled primly.

"Oh, so now you're happy," he snarled.

She continued to smile.

The livery owner led a horse and buggy to the front of the building. Gray threw the small valise he'd been carrying under the seat, and helped Elizabeth mount. "Are you settled?"

"Yes," she answered brightly.

"Good, then I assume we can go?" He took his own seat and snapped the reins over the horse's rump without waiting for an answer from Elizabeth. The animal bolted forward, jerking the carriage into motion.

Elizabeth clung to the seat railing with one hand, and gripped the handle of the parasol that was propped on her shoulder with the other. "Are we in a hurry?" she asked huffily.

"Yes."

The abruptly curt answer aroused her curiosity, but not enough to question him.

They rode in silence for most of the morning.

"I'm thirsty," Elizabeth finally said, breaking the silence. The sun was high overhead; the air hot and humid. "And I'm hot. This parasol doesn't keep the sun off well enough. Why didn't you get a buggy with a hood?"

Gray didn't respond.

"Grayson Cantrelle, don't you dare ignore me,"

Elizabeth said.

"I'm not ignoring you, I'm trying to keep from tossing you out of the buggy."

"You wouldn't dare," she challenged.

"You're tempting me, Elizabeth. I warned you about that."

"Gentlemen don't threaten ladies."

"I told you, I never claimed to be a gentleman, and anyway, I don't see any ladies around here."

WHACK! The velvet reticule that hung from her wrist, which had once belonged to Jane Sorens, cracked against Gray's chest.

"Dammit, Elizabeth, stop hitting me."

WHACK!

"That does it." He reined in, jumped down from the buggy, and stomped around it to Elizabeth's side. He reached up toward her.

"Get away from me, you beast!" she shrieked, and swung the reticule toward him again.

Gray caught it in one hand and yanked it forward. Elizabeth was pulled off of the seat. Gray caught her by the waist and flung her over his shoulder.

"Put me down." She beat on his back with both hands and kicked her legs frantically. Her floundering blows seemed to have no effect on him, and her feet merely became entangled within her petticoats and gown. "Put me down, Gray, or you'll be sorry," she shrieked again.

"I'm already sorry," he barked. "Sorry that I didn't do this a long time ago." He sat on a dead tree trunk at the side of the road, and swung Elizabeth from his shoulder onto his lap, face down, the back of her skirts tossed over her head.

Realization of what he intended to do suddenly struck her. "Gray, don't you dare," she screamed.

WHACK! His hand connected with her derriere.

"Grayson." Elizabeth beat on his leg with her fists.

She made a sound of protest deep in her throat and kicked her legs, trying to connect with his head.

WHACK! "I'm sorry, Elizabeth, but I think you've been in need of this for a long time."

She squirmed desperately, frantic to right herself, furious that he would assault her so. "I'll kill you."

WHACK! "You can try."

She managed to twist her upper torso around, and one hand grabbed the collar of his shirt. It gave her the leverage she needed to prevent the connection of his down-swinging hand to her backside. "Stop it, Grayson. Stop, stop, stop." She twisted further and began to topple from his lap.

Gray caught her around the waist with one arm. The other slipped around her shoulders, and he hauled her weight toward him. He looked into the blue eyes, so dark with fury, at the trembling pink lips, felt her breasts crushed against his chest, and gave in to the temptation that had been hounding him ever since that night they'd made love on the riverbank. His lips descended on hers, smothering her instant protest.

She fought against him, twisting in his arms, pushing at him, trying to break free, but it was no use. Slowly, steadily, she felt the familiar weakness his kiss always wrought begin to invade her body, felt her blood turn hot with need, and knew it was no use. She was fighting her own traitorous body as much as she was him.

He continued to kiss her hungrily, devastatingly, until the blood in her veins turned to burning tributaries, until the spark of need that simmered within her for him, that she so desperately denied, could no longer be ignored, no longer denounced.

The urge to escape him steadily drained away, as his tongue dueled with hers and his hands pressed into her back, crushed her to him, held her close.

A delicious languor invaded her limbs, and rendered

172

both her body and her mind his slave. Her hands, only moments ago beating on him, pushing him away, now betrayed a deplorable tendency to slip over his shoulders, her fingers to tangle within the thick, ragged locks of his black hair.

There was something wickedly exciting about being held in the arms of this dark and strange man. Sensations she had never known before, feelings she had never been aware existed, blossomed to life beneath his touch like a flower beneath the sun. A tight ache of anticipation spread through her body, stoking the fires that already raged out of control within her.

His probing tongue filled her mouth, his lips branded her his, and his embrace melded her body to his lanky frame, until she could feel the desire that drove him. She felt him slide from his seat on the tree trunk to the ground, felt him push her down until her back lay on the cool grass and felt his weight atop her.

She could not help the moan of pleasure that escaped her lips, unbidden, and which, she knew, told him that her need for him was as great as his for her.

His lips left her mouth and moved down the side of her neck. Elizabeth threw her head back, inviting his touch, her body begging for the intimate pleasures only Gray could give her. His mouth pressed against her flesh, and each time his lips pulled away they left behind a small spot on her body that burned with a greater need of him than it had before his touch. A searing heat radiated through her.

One of his hands moved to cup her breast. His thumb flicked over the taut nipple, teasing it. A shiver of reaction rippled over her skin, and unconsciously her body arched under his touch; the desire he had instilled within her—had forced her to accept and enjoy— swiftly destroying what little control she still had left.

The material of her gown proved a barrier Gray could not tolerate. His fingers worked deftly to release the tiny black buttons that ran down the bodice of her blue velvet traveling suit. A few seconds later he gave a gentle tug to the ribbon that secured her camisole and it fell free of its loops. He swept the fabric from her breast, baring the loveliness of her to his warm fingers.

Gray was like a starving man, a man in desperate need of sustenance. His mouth ravished hers, almost devouring her in his hunger, as his hands caressed, soothed, and cajoled the rosebud nipples until they were throbbing and rigid.

Then his lips left hers and moved to cover her breast, his tongue flicking like fire over the pebbled peak.

Her entire body shuddered with shocked pleasure at the touch of his warm probing mouth on her breast. She found herself spiraling into a vortex of pleasure, a color-blinding cavern where nothing mattered but Grayson Cantrelle and the delicious sensations he aroused within her body.

A tearing moan escaped Gray's throat and, unable to help himself, his lips moved to recapture hers, a scorching flame that descended on her like lightning, burning, turning her own fires to a raging inferno that threatened to consume her in its blaze.

As when they'd made love on the riverbank, all reality fled Elizabeth's mind and left her floating in a world of senses-reeling passion and need. His hands, his mouth, his touch, were all that existed, all that mattered.

"Well, howdy there, folks. Guess I caught you at an inopportune time."

Gray jerked upright, stunned, and Elizabeth scrambled to close the bodice of her dress.

"Who are you?" Gray asked, in a not too friendly tone. He leaned so that his torso hid Elizabeth from the man's lewdly staring eyes.

"Thomas A. Coltraine's the name, son. Reverend Thomas A. Coltraine. Sorry to interrupt you and the missus there." The man lifted a hand to the black hat that sat squarely on his thin head and touched its stiff brim. He smiled widely, showing a mouth full of badly yellowed teeth. "Just passing by and figured I'd inquire if you had anything to eat and wouldn't mind sharing. Haven't had a thing to eat all day."

Elizabeth pushed at Gray to move, and, seeing that she'd managed to reassemble the bodice of her dress, he rose and walked toward the buggy.

She stole several furtive glances at the stranger who called himself a man of God. He didn't seem like one, and she had the distinct impression she'd seen him somewhere before.

Gray reached behind the seat and retrieved a picnic basket he'd bought at the general store before they'd left town.

The man remained mounted on his horse, ignored Gray, and stared through small, thickly lensed glasses at Elizabeth. "Heard back in Crocker's that there was two survivors of that packet wreck we had awhile back. A man and a woman. That be you two?"

Elizabeth graced the man with a cool smile and a quickly muttered yes, then hurried toward the buggy, and Gray. "Here," Gray said, and held up a napkin full of fried chicken.

"Ah, thank you, son, thank you. And God bless." The reverend nudged his horse with his knees, and the animal continued its slow saunter down the road.

Gray watched him go, an uneasy feeling niggling at his spine. "If that man's a preacher, than I'm Satan," he mumbled.

"Sounds more than possible to me," Elizabeth snapped.

Gray's head jerked in her direction. Now what the hell was the matter with her? He moved to help her up into the buggy, and she refused his hand.

"I can do it myself, and I'll thank you to keep your

175

hands to yourself." She grabbed the seat railing, propped one foot on the running board, and threw her weight up toward the seat. Her nose hit the side of the seat, and her uplifted knee crashed against the floorboard of the buggy. She toppled back down, and straight into Gray's waiting arms.

"Are you all right?"

She twisted away from him. "Of course, I'm all right. Or I would be, if you'd stop forcing your attentions on me."

"Forcing?" Gray nearly growled. "That's the second damn time you've accused me of forcing myself on you—"

"It's the second time you've done it," she retorted, cutting off the rest of his sentence.

His hands gripped her waist and he lifted her from the ground and deposited her, none too gently, into the buggy. "Stop fooling yourself, Elizabeth. I don't have to force myself on you, and you damned well know it."

Chapter 12

"I have never, ever known anyone as exasperating as you," Gray mumbled, and whipped the reins over the horse's rump. The carriage jerked into motion.

Elizabeth lifted her nose high into the air, and snapped open her parasol. Its ruffled rim smashed against Gray's Stetson, as she swung the contraption over her shoulder.

"Excuse me. Am I in your way?" Gray snarled. "Maybe I should get out and walk beside the buggy."

"Do as you wish," Elizabeth said curtly, and kept her face turned away from him.

Gray threw her a scowl and snapped the reins again, sending the trotting horse into a brisk canter. The sudden acceleration threw Elizabeth back against her seat with a little shriek of surprise.

"Of all the ill-mannered . . ." she muttered.

They rode at that brisk pace for almost two hours, and as a result, made good time on the trail. By late afternoon they were approaching Cheauxville, a small town just up and across river from Baton Rouge. Gray reined up in front of a small building with a sign hanging over its front door that proclaimed it a hotel.

"*This* is where we're going to stay?" Elizabeth said with a sniff.

If her tone hadn't alerted Gray to her disapproval of his choice, the look on her face certainly did.

"We've passed every building in this town, which as you can see for yourself amounts to no more than ten, and this is the only one that claims it's a hotel. Unless you know something about this place that I don't?" Gray retorted, not bothering to hide his own irritation.

Elizabeth graced him with a frosty glance and climbed down from the buggy without waiting for his help. She brushed at her skirt. She felt grimy, dusty, and stiff. She'd take a bath, beat the dust from her gown, and then ask the proprietor where she might dine.

Gray held the door open for her, and Elizabeth entered the hotel. The light inside was dim, but not so that she couldn't see the interior. She stopped on the threshold so abruptly that Gray nearly walked over her. Several chairs were scattered about the room, which obviously was supposed to be a lobby. Their seats were worn, and in a few, the stuffing was protruding or hanging out from rips or worn spots in the fabric. The fireplace, a gigantic rock monstrosity, looked like it hadn't been cleaned of its ashes in years, and the rug that covered the center of the floor had long ago lost whatever design and color the weave had held.

"G'day, folks. Need a room?" an old man asked from behind the desk that was almost obscured within the murky shadows of a far corner of the room. He was short and portly, his shirt, minus a tie, badly stained in several places.

Gray moved around Elizabeth and approached the old man, realizing as he drew nearer that the man was not really as old as he appeared at first glance. It was the bald pate, thick mustache, and waist-length beard that gave the desk clerk the appearance of being elderly. Gray guessed, on closer inspection, that the man was not much older than he was. He leaned on the desk. "Yes, sir, we do, two in fact."

"Ain't got but one. It's got a nice big bed though." He threw a lascivious look at Elizabeth and smiled. "Oughtta be just right for you and the little lady."

"One room? In this bustling town . . ." Gray sneered, "you've only got one room?"

"Yep. Four all total in the hotel, but threes taken permanentlike."

Gray tossed a gold coin onto the counter, and the man handed him a key.

"Two B. Up the stairs and to the right."

Elizabeth gasped when they entered the room. She whirled on Gray. "I am not staying in this . . . this . . . this *hovel!*"

"Fine. Sleep in the buggy," he growled, in no mood to placate her. He threw his saddlebags onto the bed, then unbuckled his gunbelt, tossed it beside the saddlebags, and flopped himself down on the bed, one leg sprawled over the gunbelt and saddlebags.

"Ohhhh!" Elizabeth stamped her foot, and one of the boards of the floor bounced up into the air. She jumped back in alarm.

"Do that again, and you might find yourself downstairs quicker than you want to be," Gray said, and chuckled.

She glowered at him. "You don't—" She cleared her throat and started again. "You don't expect me to sleep in that thing with you, do you?" She stared at the lumpy double bed that occupied the center of the room, its iron head and footboard covered with rust.

Gray didn't answer.

Elizabeth began to pace the room. Gray closed his eyes, drew the Stetson down atop them, and tried to go to sleep. Suddenly he felt movement beside him, and the bed began to bounce and dip. He lifted the Stetson onto his forehead and looked up at Elizabeth, who was kneeling over him. "What are you doing?"

She pushed his saddlebags to the center of the bed and placed his gunbelt next to it, then set her valise down next to the holster. "Making a wall between us."

"Oh, good lord. I'm not going to attack you. Just get some sleep."

"I can't. I'm hungry."

Gray began to silently count to ten. When he reached ten, he extended it to twenty, but at twenty he was still fuming. At thirty he gave up and turned to Elizabeth. "All right, we'll eat. Then you'll lay down and go to sleep, or I'll hog-tie you. Understand?"

What he got for an answer was a look that dripped icicles, and a nasty little *humph*.

The hotel clerk referred them to a boardinghouse down the street that served meals to travelers. They walked to it in silence, sat across the table from each other in silence, and ate their meal in silence. By the time they returned to the room, the sky was pitch black, and so was Gray's mood. Elizabeth, on the other hand, suddenly began to chatter about everything and nothing, busying herself at the mirror and flitting around the room, commenting on this piece of furniture and that piece of bric-a-brac. All of which, Gray knew, were junk.

"Mama would have loved this little chair," Elizabeth said, running her fingers over the rosewood, carved back of a petite ladies' chair that had seen better days. "Oh, and this dressing table. With a little polish, it could look as good as new."

"Which isn't saying a whole lot," Gray said.

Elizabeth ignored him. She pulled the pins from her hair and began to brush it. "I've never seen wallpaper like this," she said, eyeing the paper that was imprinted with wildflower blossoms and a scene of an English countryside manor.

"It's called waterlogged, and I'm called tired and

180

sleepy. Now would you please quit flitting around and come to bed, so I can get some sleep."

Or something else, Elizabeth thought, and felt her cheeks flame. "I'm not tired."

"Elizabeth, I'm warning you."

"Oh, now I have to sleep on command, too, is that it?" she snapped, unable to hold her temper any longer. "First you push your attentions on me, then you get me stranded in the middle of nowhere with you, then you take me to the home of a complete maniac, and now I'm supposed to be nice and . . . and . . ."

Gray jumped up from the bed and marched toward her, a dire look in his eye.

Elizabeth retreated from him until her back was against the dressing table. She held out her hand to ward him off. "Stay away from me, Gray, or I'll scream."

He smiled. "And you expect someone from this rat trap to come to your rescue?"

Her fingers trembled. "You . . . you . . . I mean it, Gray! Stay away from me."

He bore down on her. His hands moved to her waist, then disappeared as he bent forward, slipped his arms around her, and hoisted her over his shoulder.

A small yelp of surprise escaped her lips, followed instantly by a string of very unladylike curses and threats. "You cur. You horrid blackguard. Put me down, you hear? Put me down, you brute."

"Gladly," Gray said, and tossed her onto the bed. The springs creaked loudly, and for a second he thought the whole thing was going to collapse. He leaned over her and pointed a threatening finger in her face. "Now you stay there, and don't utter a peep, Elizabeth, I'm warning you. I've been driving that damn buggy all day and I'm dog tired." And frustrated as hell, he thought silently.

She made to rise, and he pushed her back down. "I'm

not in the mood for any of your shenanigans tonight, Elizabeth. You understand?"

She stared up at him. "A gentleman wouldn't expect—"

"I keep telling you, I'm not a gentleman." He walked around to the other side of the bed and lay down. "Now go to sleep."

She lay still, but she couldn't go to sleep. She had a war going on inside of her body, and she didn't know how to stop it. She wanted to bash him over the head with one of the tiny, chipped and faded statuettes that sat on the dressing table. She wanted to slip his gun from its holster and put a bullet between those hard brown eyes. At the same time she wanted him to hold her, to kiss her and make that delicious feeling that always swept over her at his touch come again.

She listened to his breathing, found it steady, and damned him for being able to sleep while she was laying there in complete turmoil.

But Grayson was about as far away from sleep as he'd ever been, and if his breathing sounded steady to Elizabeth, it sounded ragged and gasping to Gray. His body was on fire from want of her. He wanted to throttle her, to hog-tie her, and take her to a ship leaving port for the Orient and sell her. He wanted to find a box and lock her in it and never let her out, never let her sneak into his life again. And he wanted to make mad, passionate love to her, to caress her body, to let his fingers slide over that satin skin and through the soft, blond curls between her thighs. His fingers ached to cup her breasts, to knead the rosy pink nipples until they throbbed with need for him, and he yearned, hungered, to feel himself slip within her, into that dark, wet cavern of her that held all her sensitivity and pleasure.

He nearly bit his tongue when a moan began to escape his throat and he tried to strangle it.

"Gray?" Elizabeth's voice, soft and hesitant, broke the silence in the dark room.

He let out a purposeful snort and rolled onto his side. Hopefully she would think he was snoring. He might be burning up with need of her, but he would control it. Dammit, if it was the last thing he ever did, he would control that need.

"What the hell do you mean *they left?* You let her go?" Aaron's fist crashed down on Damien's desk. He leaned across the wide surface, his face contorted with rage, only inches from Damien's. "You let her go?" he repeated. "Why? Why didn't you make her stay here until I arrived?"

Damien rose to his feet and moved quickly to a sideboard set against the wall near the door to the foyer. "Because that rogue she was with is a killer, Aaron, that's why."

"A killer," Aaron repeated sneeringly. "Since when has that kind of threat stopped you from getting what you wanted?"

"At the time, Aaron, it was what you wanted, old friend, and as much as our friendship means to me, I didn't relish getting killed trying to hold onto *your* wench." And he wasn't about to provoke Aaron now by hinting that if he had kept her here, it would most likely have been in his bed. He'd seen Aaron's temper flare a few times. The man might be a gentleman, but he was also quite ruthless.

"I'll return the favor," Aaron growled.

Damien poured brandy into two snifters and handed one to Aaron. "But now I have my own reasons for wanting them caught." He smiled, an ugly gesture that instilled no warmth in his eyes.

Aaron's curiosity was piqued. "Oh? Decided you want Elizabeth for your own?"

183

Damien returned to his seat. "No, dear boy, though if you have a mind to share her, after you're done, I would be most pleased with the offer. But my main reason for wanting to go after them is Jason. They stole him."

"Jason? That half-breed you fathered with your housekeeper? What do you care? You were always complaining he wasn't worth much anyway."

"I care because he belongs to me. I also care because Zeeanda won't shut up about it, and hasn't made a decent meal since the boy turned up missing. She thinks I sold him."

"You should have kept them here, Damien."

"Nevertheless, I know where they are."

"Where?"

"They're traveling by buggy to New Orleans. I received a message only hours ago from Tom. You remember Tom, don't you, Aaron?"

"Coltraine?"

Damien beamed proudly. "Yes, the Reverend Thomas A. Coltraine. He came by only hours after Elizabeth and this Grayson Cantrelle left. We talked, and later he sent me a message that he'd seen them on the trail." A shadow darkened his face. "Although he didn't see Jason."

"It would have been easier if you'd just kept her here, Damien. That little hellion needs to be taught a lesson. She practically made me the laughingstock of Vicksburg, running out on our wedding like that."

"A little discretion on your part might have been advisable, Aaron."

He ignored Damien. "When I get through with her, she'll wish she'd never met me, let alone left me standing at the altar like some backriver fool."

"I figure, since we know where they're headed," Damien broached, "there's no real hurry. Why don't we dine, relax, and get a good night's sleep. We'll start

184

out after them first thing in the morning." He moved to stand beside Aaron, and the two men walked toward the dining room. Damien clapped a hand to Aaron's back. "And maybe we can do a little carousing in New Orleans, as long as we're going there anyway. I hear there's a new gambling den in the Quarter."

"I want the cowboy dead," Aaron said.

Damien smiled. "I don't think that will be a problem."

The next morning Gray awoke to find himself almost more tired than when he'd lain down on the bed the night before. One more day, he told himself. One more day, and they'd be in New Orleans. Then he could say goodbye to her and be on his way. He'd visit a brothel. One of the ones in the Quarter. Maybe the damn ache within him to possess Elizabeth would go away then.

Gray was dressed and readying to leave the room when Elizabeth woke. For one brief instant she thought he was leaving without her, and found herself near panic.

"I'm going to go hitch up the buggy," he said at the door. "I'll come up for your valise when you're ready." With that he disappeared into the hall and down the stairs.

She looked in the mirror at herself and almost burst out crying. She looked terrible. No wonder he'd been in such a hurry to leave the room. Her eyelids were slightly swollen, her hair surrounded her face in a tangle of wild curls, and her cheeks were flushed pink. "You look like Medusa," she said into the mirror, and immediately began to brush her hair back from her face.

Within an hour they had eaten, partaking of breakfast at the boardinghouse on their way out of

185

town, and were on the road. All without having said more than a few overly polite and strained words to one another.

The day passed in virtual silence. Gray had purchased a basket of food from the woman who ran the boardinghouse in Cheauxville, and they stopped for lunch beside the road. But this time, they made sure to sit a goodly distance from one another. The stop was short. They were back on the road within half an hour. Gray concentrated on the trail, and kept glancing at the sun high overhead to calculate the time.

Elizabeth, hot, bored and feeling the effects of a full stomach, was having a hard time keeping her eyes open. She tried playing games. How many birds could she count? How many oak trees did they pass? She tried defining the few clouds that drifted overhead into some kind of shape. One looked like a dragon, another like an old man. But with each passing minute, her eyelids grew heavier, her mind duller.

The parasol, resting on her shoulder, slipped from her fingers and toppled off the back of the buggy, as her head slumped onto his shoulder.

Gray looked down at her, surprised, then smiled. So, the little hellcat had lost some of her spunk. Well, it served her right for keeping him up all night. A frown pulled at his brows. But if she was sleeping, where was that sound coming from? He looked around. Someone was crying, softly. He pulled back on the reins, and the horse and buggy came to a stop. Elizabeth's head jerked up as she woke.

"What's wrong?"

"I don't know. Stay there." Gray jumped down from his seat and walked around to the rear of the buggy. He looked at both sides of the road, and behind them. Nothing. Then he heard it again, a soft sob. He reached out and flipped back the blanket that covered Elizabeth's valise. Jason, his cheeks streaked with

186

tears, his eyes full of fear, looked back up at him.

"What the he—?"

The boy scrambled from his cramped position beneath the seat, and stood before Gray. "Please don't send me back, Michie. Please."

Elizabeth turned to look over the seat. "What's *he* doing here?"

Gray ignored her and hunkered down in front of the boy. "Jason, why'd you run away from Cypress Grove? Sorens will be looking for you. You know that."

The boy nodded. "I can't live there no more, Michie. I'm afraid."

"Of what?"

The boy lowered his head and bit on his bottom lip.

Grayson placed a hand on the boy's shoulder. "Jason," he said, keeping his voice soft, "who are you afraid of?"

"Michie."

"Sorens?"

The boy nodded.

"He's your father, isn't he?" Gray had pretty well figured that out almost the moment he'd seen Damien with Zeeanda. The boy had too strong a resemblance to them both.

Jason nodded again.

"Damien is your father?" Elizabeth said.

Gray turned the boy around and peeked beneath his thin rag of a shirt. Jason's back was deeply scarred. He urged the boy to face him again, and sighed. "I won't send you back there, Jason, but we've got to keep you hidden. I'm sure Sorens will send someone after you."

Jason's face lit up with a huge smile, and his eyes sparkled with happiness. "Can I go live with you, Michie?"

"Stop calling me that," Gray snapped. The boy flinched, and Grayson immediately regretted his harsh tone. "I'm sorry. Look, let's take this one day at a time, okay? Call me Gray, and get back up into the buggy."

Jason scrambled to sit on the rear of the buggy, his legs dangling over the side, and Gray returned to his seat next to Elizabeth.

"Do you realize what they can do to you, if they catch him with us? He's a runaway," Elizabeth said. "They'll beat him, and they can send us to jail."

Gray stared at her coldly. "You want to send him back?"

Her eyes met his. "No. I just wanted to make sure you knew what you were doing."

"I usually do." Though since I met you, he thought to himself, I don't seem to know anything.

They spent that night in another hotel. It was a little better than the one the night before, but not much, except that this time they managed to get two rooms. Gray didn't know if he was glad about that or not. Jason slept in the buggy.

The next morning they got an early start.

"How much further?" Elizabeth asked, staring out at the horizon.

"Well, seeing how I don't know this country much better than you do, I'd say, when we see it, we're there."

Elizabeth sighed exaggeratedly. "Well, can you at least tell me if we'll get to New Orleans today?"

"Yes."

"Yes, what? You can tell me, or we will get there?"

"You know, you're enough to drive a man crazy."

"Well, in my opinion, you didn't have far to go. Now," she brushed off the lap of her skirt, "will you please answer my question."

"Yes, I figure we'll get there today."

"Thank you," she said primly.

"You're welcome."

* * *

Two hours later, the city of New Orleans came into view. Elizabeth suddenly stood up in the carriage. "Oh, Gray, it's so beautiful."

The buggy rocked violently from her movement, and Gray had to brace himself in an effort to keep from being tossed out. But her rise to her feet also frightened the horse, who did not have blinders on. The animal lunged forward, jerking the carriage with him, and Elizabeth toppled back into her seat with a great *THUD!*

She jumped around to look at Gray. "You did that on purpose."

"I didn't do a thing. *You* did it when you stopped thinking and stood up in the buggy. It scared the horse."

"Papa always let me stand in our buggy if I couldn't see something."

"Then your father also didn't do much thinking, or he had a steel grip on the reins whenever you were around."

"You're insufferable."

"I know. I'm also arrogant, inconsiderate, ill-mannered, and every other nasty little word you can think of, right?"

Elizabeth looked at him from the corner of her eye. Had she really called him all that?

Gray steered the buggy through the streets of the Vieux Carre. No easy feat considering they were extremely narrow, mostly dirt, and had open sewer trenches lining both sides. To top this off, they were crowded with other carriages, drays, workwagons, street merchants, vendors pushing two-wheeled carts, pedestrians, and romping children.

"Pr'lines. Buy pr'lines," an old lady called from the banquette. She tottered over two planks that had been laid atop the trench to allow crossing to the street, and waved a hand at Elizabeth. "You buy pr'line, lady?"

189

Elizabeth looked questioningly at Gray.

"It's a candy. Mostly brown sugar, molasses, and pecans."

"I know, my nanny used to make them. Could we buy one?"

Gray reined in and dug in his vest pocket for a penny. He handed one to the old lady, and she handed Elizabeth a candy. "Bless you, missy," she said, ignoring Gray, and turned away.

Elizabeth broke the pancake-sized candy in half and reached back over the seat. "Here, Jason, have some."

A few minutes later, Gray reined up in front of the St. Louis Hotel, a grand structure of three stories, surrounded by wrought iron balconies and topped by a huge, stained glass dome.

"Stay here," Gray ordered Jason, as he and Elizabeth stepped from the carriage. She took Gray's arm and allowed him to escort her inside. It had been years since she'd been in New Orleans, over ten in fact, and she was thoroughly enthralled with her surroundings. So much so, that she paid little attention to where he led her.

The lobby of the magnificent hotel was bustling with activity. The center was filled with auctioneers, selling everything from imported furniture to slaves, their loud voices filling the cavernous room and echoing repeatedly. A gallery that ran around the second floor was filled with specialty shops and crowded with people.

Gray pulled a gawking Elizabeth toward the desk. "We need two rooms," he said to the clerk.

The man's face instantly screwed into a mass of wrinkles, and he shook his head. "Oh, I'm sorry, sir, but we have only one room left."

Gray took a deep breath and released it slowly. He was not going to get himself into that situation again. Anyway, this was it. They had to part, to say goodbye to one another. It might as well be now. Yet for some reason, he found himself reluctant.

"Gray! Grayson Cantrelle, is that you, old buddy?"

The deep voice boomed through the huge room. Gray swung around, startled. "Travis? Travis is that really you?"

"I'll be damned," Travis said, and laughed. "I thought you were dead. I mean, I really thought you'd bought the farm back there."

Both men threw their arms around each other, then grasped the other's shoulder and stood back, giving each other a good once-over.

"I thought you were dead, too," Gray said.

"I looked for you for hours, old buddy, but I finally had to give up. Hardest damn thing I ever did. Hey, how about a drink to celebrate another brush with the Grim Reaper, huh? We beat him again."

They began to walk toward the bar when Gray suddenly stopped. "Uh, Travis, I forgot. I'm not alone."

"No? Who're you wi—" Travis's gaze came to rest on Elizabeth, who was staring at Gray. "Elizabeth, lord, I'd forgotten Gray had a wife now." His long arms wrapped around her shoulders, and he hugged her to him. "Thank the Lord you're both safe. Let's all meet for dinner. What do you say?"

"Uh, Trav, listen, I can't explain now, but—" Gray quickly ushered his old friend away from Elizabeth. "Do you have a room here?"

"Sure. Been here about a week."

"Good. Let me bunk with you."

Travis gave Gray a sly wink and a big smile. "Bunk with me?" He peered over Gray's shoulder at Elizabeth. "You got a wife that looks like that, and you want to bunk with me? Are you crazy?"

"Travis."

"Oh-oh, are you two fighting already?"

"Travis, can I bunk with you or not?" Gray snapped, his irritation flaring.

Travis's eyes widened in surprise. "Well, sure, Gray, sure. Tell the clerk to give you the key to 104."

"Thanks. I'll meet you in the bar in about half an hour. We'll talk then, and I'll explain everything."

Gray turned back to the desk clerk. "One room," he said.

"I am not sleeping with you, Grayson Cantrelle," Elizabeth said, only loud enough for him to hear.

"That's right, you're not," he said back.

Elizabeth suddenly looked more dismayed and surprised than pleased. She stared at Gray in puzzlement.

"I'll bunk with Travis," he said, as they followed a porter toward the stairs.

"Oh." She should be elated. Instead she felt deserted. "What about Jason?"

"He'll stay with the buggy."

After the porter set Elizabeth's valise on a chair and left the room, Gray turned and handed her the room key. He stared into her eyes for a long moment, those huge blue pools that threatened to engulf him every time he looked into them. Finally, he forced his gaze from hers. What the hell was the matter with him? It was better that they say goodbye now. Go their separate ways. They were wrong for each other. Deadly wrong. "Well, it's been an experience, Elizabeth. I've got some business in New Orleans I have to tend to over the next few days so . . . well, I'll be busy. I guess we won't see each other again." Why didn't he just get the hell out of there? "I suppose you'll be traveling on to your sister's soon." He couldn't get the word goodbye out.

Elizabeth tried to hide her surprise. She hadn't expected such an abrupt goodbye. "Yes, yes, I will. Huh, thank you for all your help, Gr—Mr. Cantrelle."

192

He nodded and quickly backed out of the room. A deep breath escaped his lungs when he closed the door. It was done. He began to walk back toward the staircase. So why did he feel like such a rake? And why the hell did he have this empty ache inside of him?

Elizabeth stared at the closed door. His words echoed in her mind. *It's been an experience, Elizabeth.* That was it? She moved to stand at the window and look down at the busy street two stories below. But then, what had she expected from him? What more did she want?

"Nothing." She slapped back the lace curtain. "I want nothing from him. Nothing, nothing, nothing." She threw herself onto the bed. "Good riddance, Grayson Cantrelle," she mumbled into the pillow. "I hope I never see you again. Ever." She rolled over and stared up at the sunburst pattern of the ivory silk canopy, and wondered why her words sounded so false and hollow. "I'm just tired, that's why." Her voice sounded irritable even to her own ears. She shrugged. It matched the way she felt. She sat up and pulled the servant's cord at the side of her bed. "I've been through an absolutely horrid ordeal with an absolutely horrid man, and I need to refresh myself. Starting right now."

Minutes later, after sending a message to old friends who lived in New Orleans, the Fordeleaux family, Elizabeth watched as a porter carried a huge, ugly, green tin tub into the room, followed by two maids hauling buckets of hot, steaming water.

Faster than a cow can moo, Elizabeth stripped off her clothes the moment the servants were gone, and slipped into the hot water that had been fragranced with jasmine. Its sweet essence filled the room. She luxuriated in the feel of the soothing water against her muscles, which ached from the long ride in the buggy. She inhaled deeply of the oh-so clean scent, and smiled at the silky feel of the foamy white bubbles on her skin.

She lay her head back against the tub. She was going shopping tomorrow. Theresa Fordeleaux, she felt certain, would show Elizabeth how to get some of her trust money from the bank, and then the two of them would go to the milliner's and dressmaker's. She had a lot of shopping to do before continuing on to Texas, since all of her clothes were at the bottom of the Mississippi River. At the moment she didn't feel in any hurry anyway. She'd had enough of roughing it on the trail.

That thought brought memory of Gray, which she instantly banished from her mind. There was absolutely no good reason on earth to think of him. There was nothing between them. Hadn't he made it clear that's how he wanted it, when he left?

Well, isn't that what you wanted? that horrid little voice at the back of her mind nagged.

"Yes!" she exclaimed loudly, and slipped a little deeper into the water. She wanted some luxury back in her life, and if she had her way, she wasn't ever going to do without it again. But doing without is exactly what would have happened, if she had followed her silly heart and let herself get further involved with Grayson Cantrelle.

A few minutes later, a knock, hard and loud, sounded on the door of her room, and brought a half-dozing Elizabeth shooting up out of the water.

194

Chapter 13

"Are you going to tell me what the hell is going on, or do I have to go upstairs and ask that pretty wife of yours?" Travis snatched the whiskey bottle away from Gray before he could pour himself another drink.

Gray grabbed it back and tipped the long neck over his shot glass. "She's not my wife, thank God."

"Right. And I'm not your best friend."

Gray downed the drink. "You are. She's not."

"Damn it, Gray, talk sense. Now what's going on?"

"I just told you." He poured himself another drink. "Elizabeth is not my wife. Never has been and never will be. And bless the saints for that. I met her on the boat, or rather, on the docks at Vicksburg when she was getting ready to board. I saw her that evening in the dining salon. That little frog of a guy, George something-or-other . . . remember him and his fat brother?" Gray paused and looked at Travis.

He nodded.

"Well, before you got there, they were pushing advances on Elizabeth. I heard her lie and say she had a sick husband in her suite."

"How'd you know it was a lie?" Travis pressed.

"I told you, I saw her board. She was alone." Gray

downed the drink and poured another. He had come to the bar to forget about Elizabeth. On the rare occasions he wanted to temporarily rid his mind of something, whiskey always helped him forget, but Travis's questions were making the whole thing impossible. If anything, they were causing him to remember even more: like what it had felt like to hold her in his arms, to taste her lips against his, to meld his body with hers. He nearly groaned aloud. Instead, he downed another drink.

"And?"

Gray let his gaze wander over the room's occupants. None held his interest.

"And?" Travis persisted.

"And what?" He had completely forgotten what they were talking about, except for the fact that it concerned Elizabeth.

"How did you end up being her 'sick husband'?"

"I walked up behind her and pretended that's who I was, that's how. I just walked up, said 'Hi, honey, I feel better,' and sat down. Then you showed up."

Travis shook his head. "Always the gentleman, huh?"

Gray's glass slammed down on the table. "Hell, no. Why does everyone always think I'm a gentleman?" He leaned across the table and glared at Travis. "I'm not, okay? I'm no gentleman. I'm probably as far from a damn gentleman as anybody could get."

A deep frown pulled Travis's blond brows together. "Come on, Gray, give. What's really bothering you?"

"Nothing, dammit. I just spent seven lousy days in the company of that demanding, spoiled little spitfire, and now I'm trying to relax, which I haven't done since that boat blew up under me. And you're not making it any easier by talking about her, instead of letting me forget she even exists. Okay?" He gulped down his drink.

Travis sat back in his chair, held up both hands as if in surrender, and smiled. "Okay, okay, so relax. Drink yourself into a stupor. I, your best friend since the day we popped out of our mamas' bellies, will carry you to our room when you slide off that chair and fall on your face."

"Thank you," Gray grumbled, and downed another glass of whiskey. "At least now that I'm rid of her, I can get some peace of mind."

"So, tell me," Travis said, deciding to broach another subject. "How'd your search go in Washington for Dana's . . . uh . . . beau? You never finished telling me what you were—"

"I don't want to talk about it."

"Oh, another bad subject, huh? Okay," Travis threw his hands up, "what can we talk about?"

"I sent a message to old man Fordeleaux, when I talked to the desk clerk earlier. He's got a string of stallions he wants to sell, and I'm interested in buying. A messenger brought me an answer, while you were getting us this bottle."

"So, what's the answer?"

"We're invited to a soiree at the old man's plantation tomorrow night. He'll show me the horses then."

"We? What have I got to with this? I'm just a poor gambler drifting around the countryside trying to make a living."

"Yeah, and I'm Davy Crockett." Gray poured them both another drink. "Look, Travis, I know more about horseflesh than you do, right?"

The handsome blond nodded.

"But you know more about how to handle these fancy New Orleans planters." Gray laughed. "Hell, poor gambler, my foot. Anyone whose got half a brain knows what you're worth. You own half the town of Galveston, a gold mine in California, and your own fleet of riverboats. You're about as poor as the king of England."

Travis chuckled and raised his glass in salute to Gray. "All right, we go to the Fordeleaux soiree, and I'll negotiate a price on the old man's horses for you." His smile widened. "Maybe I can do some negotiating with his daughter, too."

An hour later, with three empty whiskey bottles on the table between them, Travis watched as Gray closed his eyes and slumped over in his chair.

"Good thing I was only drinking one shot to your five or six, old buddy," he mumbled, as he hefted Gray from his seat.

"Come on, 'lizabeth," Gray murmured, the words a twisted slur on his lips. "Lemme . . . love you. Ummm, so beautiful."

Travis propped one of Gray's arms over his shoulder, slipped his own arm around Gray's back, and struggled to half-carry his staggering, nearly unconscious friend from the bar. "Come on, old buddy, you need to sleep it off."

"Sleep with 'lizabeth," Gray muttered. He lay his head on Travis's shoulder. "Marry me, 'lizabeth."

Travis paused in his struggle and looked down at Gray's face. "Yeah, you're glad to be rid of her, old buddy. I can see you're real glad."

The stairs were the worst obstacle. It took Travis nearly ten minutes to get Gray up them. He kicked open the door to their room, dragged Gray in, and dumped him on the bed. Gray reached out, grabbed a pillow, and hugged it to him. "'lizabeth," he murmured. His hands caressed the pillow. "Love you, 'lizabeth. Lemme . . . ummmm."

Travis stood looking down at Gray. "Yeah, glad to be rid of her." He pulled Gray's gunbelt off and placed it on the dresser, then turned back and pulled off his boots. The silver spurs jingled in the quiet room. "You just keep telling yourself that, Gray. Maybe you'll start to believe it, in about ten years or so."

Elizabeth jumped out of the tin tub and hurriedly brushed a towel over her wet limbs. "Who is it?" she called, as another knock sounded on the door. The very instant she'd been startled awake by the first knock, an image of Grayson Cantrelle had popped into her mind, unbidden, and a second later, she decided, unwelcome. But she couldn't rid herself of the hope that filled her heart.

"Message, mademoiselle," a deep voice called through the paneled door.

Elizabeth pulled a wrapper around her waist and tiptoed to the door. She opened it just an inch and peered through the crack. A porter stood before her door with a silver tray in his hand, a folded piece of paper lying on its surface. She slipped her hand through the open space and held it open. The porter placed the note on her outstretched palm and she quickly pulled her hand back. "Thank you," she said softly, and closed the door. She unfolded the paper and read the delicately inscribed words. It was a message from Theresa Fordeleaux, apologizing because she could not come to town the next day, but saying that she looked forward to seeing Elizabeth in the evening. Elizabeth flipped open the card that accompanied the message. It was an invitation to a soiree the next evening at the Fordeleaux home.

Elizabeth clasped her hands together and laughed softly. "A soiree. Theresa is having a soiree." Suddenly the smile disappeared, and she pushed away from the door. "Oh, I'll have to go to the dressmaker's first thing in the morning. I have nothing to wear. Mercy, I do hope she has a gown I can purchase. There isn't time to have one made."

The night proved a long one. She'd been nearly exhausted that afternoon when they'd finally arrived in New Orleans and checked into the St. Louis Hotel. Of course, she'd made herself feel worse by the bout of crying she'd allowed herself to wallow in after Gray had abruptly said goodbye. She hadn't expected that. When she'd finally run out of tears and thought about it, she realized she didn't know what she'd expected. But then she'd gotten mad, which was her usual habit when she felt hurt.

But this time her anger had worked against her. It had kept her from falling into a restful sleep. The softness of the bed, the caress of the comforter, the pillow beneath her head, all beckoned her to sleep, but her body wouldn't cooperate, and to her chagrin her mind kept conjuring up visions of Gray. By morning's first light, Elizabeth was already up. She ordered a tray of café au lait and biscuits be brought to her room, which promptly arrived ten minutes later.

For the next hour she buzzed around the room, hastily getting herself together. "Oh, Serena, I do miss you," she muttered, thinking of the servant she'd left behind in Vicksburg when she'd made her hasty departure. She struggled into her camisole and pantalettes, fastened the hoop-cage around her waist, and then fought for numerable minutes to get into her petticoats and get the voluminous folds of her blue velvet gown draped evenly over the bell-shaped hoop. But her worst minutes came when she grappled with the tiny buttons on her bodice, trying to force them into the equally tiny buttonholes.

How in heavens name had Gray so deftly, and quickly, gotten them unfastened? That thought brought a hot blush to her cheeks. "Forget him,

200

Elizabeth," she ordered herself sternly. "He was a bad mistake in your life, just like Aaron. Anyway, he obviously doesn't care about you."

She pinned her hair up on her crown, allowing the blond strands to cascade down in a waterfall of curls that draped over her left shoulder. At the desk downstairs she handed the room key to the clerk. "Can you direct me to a dressmaker's shop? Preferably French?"

"Oh, yes, mademoiselle, of course. Madame Claudette. Her shop is on Dumaine. Three blocks south of the hotel."

"Thank you. Would you arrange a carriage for me, please?" She began to turn away, then paused, and looked back at the clerk. "Sir, I wonder, I have business with the Bank of Louisiana, could you direct me?"

"Yes, mademoiselle. It is just a block from here, on the corner of Conti and Rue Royal."

Elizabeth nodded and moved through the lobby toward the St. Louis street door. The auctioneers had already begun their prattle, and their voices echoed from the big dome overhead. A young black woman stood on the auction block, her head held high, as if she scorned all those standing in the crowd watching her, bidding to possess her.

She reminded Elizabeth of one of the wenches in the slave quarters of the Devlin plantation that her father had made frequent visits to after her mother's death. Elizabeth sniffed and turned her gaze in another direction. Blue eyes suddenly met amber-flecked brown ones and fused. Her heart gave a funny little flutter before she managed to get it, and her suddenly trembling hands, under control.

"Hello, Elizabeth."

"Hello, Gray," Elizabeth answered coolly, pulling a haughty air about her in an effort to keep a distance

201

between them. He looked as if he was about to say something else, but she gave him no opportunity. "Excuse me," she said, and began to brush past him, "but I have a carriage waiting."

"Of course. Visiting friends?" Why in blazes had he asked that? What did he care where she was going?

"No, I'm on my way to the dressmaker's shop."

He nodded. He should have known her first stop in New Orleans would be the shops. She'd probably purchase everything in sight. Grayson tipped his hat to her and disappeared within the crowd.

For one crazy, brief second, Elizabeth thought of asking him to be her escort to the Fordeleaux soiree that evening. She quickly discarded the idea. "How silly of me," she muttered to herself. "What a ridiculous notion. Grayson Cantrelle, at a soiree." She shook her head and chuckled softly.

The carriage, she found, was unnecessary. The bank, as the clerk had stated, was indeed one block from the hotel. One very short block. She had no sooner settled herself into the carriage than she was climbing back out. The bank's attendant was very efficient, and she had no trouble when she requested funds from her trust account. A draft was handed to her almost instantly, along with a promise that all she need do when she arrived in Sweetbriar was to wire them and another would be forwarded.

Ten minutes later the driver reined the carriage up in front of Madame Claudette's shop. "You want I should wait, mademoiselle?" the man asked, and peered down his hawklike nose at Elizabeth from his perch on the carriage.

"No, thank you," she said. "I think I'll walk back to the hotel. It's not as far as I thought."

The carriage departed, and Elizabeth entered the tiny dress shop whose door plaque proclaimed it

Parisian Modes. A small bell tinkled overhead at her entry, and a portly woman Elizabeth guessed to be in her forties appeared.

"*Oui,* mademoiselle?" the woman said.

"I need a gown," Elizabeth answered. "But I need it for tonight, for a soiree."

The woman frowned and began to shake her head.

"I don't care what it costs, Madame Claudette. I have to have one."

The dressmaker began to shake her head again, then stopped, and her face brightened. She whipped around, reached behind a long curtain, and pulled out a gown of Venetian silk, its color the deep royal blue of a midnight sky. Its neckline was plunging, daringly so, and its sleeves were no more than tiny puffs of material that would wrap around the wearer's upper arm, leaving her shoulders bare. The skirt was a mass of flounced blue silk, trimmed with elegant ruches of white Valenciennes lace.

"Oh, my, it's beautiful," Elizabeth gushed.

"*Oui,* Mademoiselle. It was made with great care and style, but," she looked suddenly sad, "the mademoiselle who ordered it, she took the fever."

"Oh," Elizabeth said, sympathically. "I'm sorry."

Madame Claudette's smile returned. "But I can alter it so that it fits you perfectly, Mademoiselle. As if it were made especially for you."

Elizabeth stepped behind the curtain, and the woman immediately began to help her remove her gown. She slipped the blue one on over her hoop-cage, and gasped in delight. It was perfect. Utterly perfect, except that the waist was just a little too loose.

"I shall fix it, and have it to you by five o'clock," the woman promised.

"Send it to the St. Louis Hotel, Room 93," Elizabeth said. "And these, include these." She handed the woman a white ostrich plume, a white satin ribbon, and a string of pearls she picked up from a nearby table, as well as a white fan whose spines were embedded with tiny sapphires. "This will be my first soiree in New Orleans, and I want to look special."

"*Oui*, mademoiselle, you have made a fine choice with the gown, it becomes you. And the plume and pearls, a very wise accent."

Elizabeth left Madame Claudette's and headed back toward the hotel, but she did not go by way of Royal. Instead, she ventured up Rue Chartres until coming to Jackson Square. The bells of St. Peter's Cathedral began to ring, filling the air with a musical chime. Several men stood in front of the Cabildo, arguing politics, while a young couple strolled through the gardens of the Square. Lovers probably, Elizabeth decided, and felt an instant pang of loss as she watched them.

"Oh, poppycock." She changed direction and made for the levee.

The river was a mass of boats: arriving, departing, docked at the wharves, and anchored off shore. One packet, the *Magnolia Queen*, was just debarking. Her name was painted in brilliant red letters across the arched cover of the paddle wheel, and her tall, black, twin smokestacks billowed out clouds of gray white smoke as her side wheel churned furiously. Right behind her was the *Natchez*, and behind that the *Elle Kay*. Arriving from downriver was the *Cairo*, her name emblazoned in huge wrought iron letters that spanned the distance between her smokestacks, and behind her came the *Creole Queen*. Elizabeth neared the French Market, and as she did she looked upriver. At least three dozen packets were docked at the nearby wharves which stretched past Canal and into the "American" section of New Orleans. Beyond that, Elizabeth could just make out the tall sailing ships that crowded New Orleans' upper docks. Too bad she wasn't boarding one of the ships bound for England, instead of going to that godforsaken place her sister had decided to call home.

She remembered Grayson also came from Texas. "Well, if all the men in that place are like him," she mumbled to herself, "I'd rather die a spinster."

"Fresh plantains and potatoes," a voice called out behind her.

"Chickens, get chickens here. Ducks, geese," another hailed just as loudly.

Elizabeth turned and looked at the long rows of tables set beneath a canvas roof. It was some type of market. She approached hesitantly, curious.

"Buy flowers?" An old woman stuck a handful of blossoms in Elizabeth's face.

She shied away, shook her head, and continued on. Pale brown eggs lay on a bed of dried Spanish moss in one booth, while the next table was covered with huge, glistening silver fish, their glassy, lifeless eyes staring at every passerby. An old Indian sat on the ground in the center of an array of baskets, near one of the support poles that held up the canvas top. Nearby a much younger Indian woman was busily working several strips of what looked like thin wood into the shape of another basket. Dead ducks and chickens hung from the rafters, fruits and vegetables of every shape, size, and color filled buckets, barrels, and tables. Elizabeth, her stomach suddenly reminding her with a huge growl that she'd eaten nothing since her meager breakfast of café au lait and biscuits, bought a plantain and two pralines. She ate the plantain and then munched on the pralines as she walked leisurely back toward the hotel.

It was late afternoon by the time she returned to the

St. Louis, feeling the need for a nap before readying herself for the Fordeleaux soiree. "And a bath," she said to herself, remembering how good the hot, scented water had felt on her skin after all those days of washing in the cold, muddy river. But that thought brought with it a memory of the person with whom she'd spent those days, and a sudden ache of loneliness swept over her. She tried to shrug it away, telling herself she was being foolish, but it refused to be dismissed.

Her mood having declined rapidly, Elizabeth discarded her hoop-cage and lay down on the poster bed that dominated her hotel room. It was such a contrast to those she and Gray had stayed in on their journey. The furnishings were all of highly polished cherry or rosewood, the cushions of the chairs and settee covered in a pale green brocade, the drapes of heavy green damask, the panels of the sheerest lace. She willed sleep to come, but when she closed her eyes, instead of the dreamy, mindless darkness she craved, all she saw was the sardonic features of Grayson Cantrelle. In a fit of frustration, she yanked on the bell cord. Two minutes later a porter knocked on her door.

"Order me a bath, please," she requested curtly, and shut the door before the man had a chance to respond.

Her bath arrived momentarily and, as soon as the hotel servants were gone, Elizabeth plunged into it. She lathered her body with the scented soap one of the maids had provided, and then scrubbed herself nearly raw with the washcloth. "He's a drifter," she muttered angrily. "A gun fighter. A man who has nothing. Absolutely nothing." She squeezed the washcloth with both hands, as if trying to strangle it. "He's a rake. A blackguard, a callous rogue with no feelings and no sentiment." She dug her fingernails into the bar of soap. "Didn't he seduce me? Force himself on me when

206

I was stuck on that godforsaken riverbank with him? He's a . . . a Lothario. A devil."

And you'd give anything to be in his arms again.

"I would not!" She threw the soap down and a spume of water splashed up and into her face. Drops of water clung to the wisps of hair that had broken free of the pins that held them to her crown and now curled around her face. She sputtered and shook her head, sending the glistening rivulets in every direction. "In his arms, humph!" She stood and reached toward the washstand for a towel. Sunlight streamed in through the window and gently touched her body, turning the streams of water that snaked down her naked form to rivers of shimmering silver. Elizabeth saw herself in the mirror and paused, turning a hard, scrutinizing eye on herself. Her skin, once the creamy white of pure milk was now more the rich hue of day-old cream. A result of her days in the sun on the riverbank. She ran an assessing gaze over her limbs. She liked the color, though she knew many others would be appalled that she had allowed the sun to tint her flesh. Her breasts were round and firm, as were her hips, and her stomach was taut. Grayson had said he loved her body. That it was beautiful.

"Will you stop thinking about him?" Elizabeth snapped at her own reflection in the mirror. "He's gone, and good riddance."

A knock on the door nearly startled her out of her mind. In a hurry to get out of the tub and into a wrapper so she could answer the door, her foot caught on the rim of the tin tub. Suddenly, the world tilted. Elizabeth felt herself begin to fall forward. A small shriek flew from her lips, and she grabbed for the silk-covered ladies' chair that sat near the tub. It broke her fall as she landed across it, her stomach on the cushion. The tub tipped and crashed to the floor, sending a torrent of warm, soapy water all over the carpet. Elizabeth clung to the chair and gasped for breath.

Another knock sent her scrambling to her feet and diving for the wrapper that lay on the bed. Her foot slid on the wet carpet, and the only thing that saved her derriere, among other things, from crashing to the floor, was her desperate, and successful, grab for the bed's poster.

Another knock aroused her anger. "I'm coming, I'm coming."

She yanked open the door, not giving a fig what she looked like. Whoever was so impatient for her answer could just take her as she was: more a drowned rat than a woman.

Madame Claudette stood in the hallway, the blue gown draped over her outstretched arms, a small valise dangling from one hand.

"I have brought your gown, Mademoiselle Devlin, as you requested."

All of Elizabeth's anger quickly dissipated, and the excitement of attending the impending soiree swept over her again. She took the gown and spread it over the bed. "It's beautiful, Madame Claudette. More beautiful than I remembered. Thank you."

The dressmaker glanced at the lake of water soaking into the carpet. "Would you like for me to stay and help you ready yourself, Mademoiselle Devlin?"

"Oh, could you?" Elizabeth said. "That would be wonderful." She laughed when she saw the direction of the dressmaker's gaze. "I had a little accident with the tub."

"It happens," Claudette said tactfully. "Now, let me help you prepare. You have a young man calling for you this evening, no?"

"No," Elizabeth said, her spritely mood suddenly turning sullen. "I'll be going to the soiree alone."

"Unescorted, mademoiselle? But it is not proper!"

"Monsieur Fordeleaux is an old friend of my family, Madame Claudette, I'm sure he'll understand. Anyway, I do not know anyone else in your city."

"Ah, but I do," the little dressmaker said. "I make shirts for Monsieur Regrette, and I happen to know that he, too, is attending the Fordeleaux soiree unattended." She turned toward her reticule and pulled out a piece of paper, then moved to a desk set against one wall, and picked up a writing quill. "I will send him a message, and he can escort you. I am sure he would be delighted."

"Oh, no, Madame Claudette, please do not bother Monsieur Regrette. I'm sure he would rather not."

The old woman waved a hand at her. "Nonsense. He is handsome, the choice of many of the young ladies in town, but he is foxy, that one. He will choose wisely, and in his own time. And I am sure he would be delighted to meet a beauty such as yourself."

"Are you sure he wouldn't mind?" Elizabeth blushed. "I wasn't really looking forward to going alone."

"Oui, I am sure. Monsieur is an old friend. I have been making his shirts for years, since he was a little boy. He will be delighted." She pulled the bell cord, and minutes later answered a knock on the door and instructed the porter where to take the message she'd written. She turned back to Elizabeth. "I have requested Monsieur to be here at five. It will take you an hour to reach Shadow Glen."

"Where?"

"The Fordeleaux plantation. It is past Bayou Bienvenue, a goodly distance from here."

Claudette insisted on combing Elizabeth's hair, and she proved a master. She drew the long blond tresses up to her crown, and secured them there. Then, with curling tongs she pulled from the satchel she carried, she formed a cascading cluster of ringlets that draped over Elizabeth's shoulder. She broke off the tip of the white plume and inserted it within the curls just behind Elizabeth's left ear, then pinned the string of pearls there, letting the two strands hand down in loops, just grazing her shoulder. The silk ribbon she tied around Elizabeth's neck, creating a small bow at her nape and allowing the ends to dangle down her bare back. She pressed deep red rose petals to Elizabeth's cheeks and lips, lending them a blush of color, and then helped her into her gown.

Claudette stepped back to admire Claudette's work just as a knock sounded on the door. "You look beautiful, Mademoiselle, and," she peered over her shoulder toward the door, "I believe Monsieur Regrette is here."

Elizabeth pulled a black velvet cloak from her own valise, as well as a beaded black reticule. She turned back toward the door just as Claudette allowed Dominic Regrette entry.

Chapter 14

Elizabeth stared into the blackest, deepest eyes she had ever seen. They were like pools of ebony, fathomless and totally unreadable.

"Mademoiselle Devlin, may I present Monsieur Dominic Regrette," Claudette said. She motioned to a tall man, dressed in a black velvet greatcoat that stretched tautly across his broad shoulders, and black trousers that hugged his long, well-muscled, yet lean legs, to enter the room. The dressmaker closed the door behind him and moved to stand beside Elizabeth. "Monsieur Regrette," she waved a hand toward Elizabeth, "Miss Elizabeth Devlin."

Dominic tipped his head toward Elizabeth, and his black hair caught the rays of the setting sun as they streamed through the lace-covered window, allowing brilliant little specks of light to glisten within the raven strands like diamonds. His skin was a golden bronze, the hue intensified by the stark whiteness of the silk shirt he wore. He was a handsome man, strikingly so, but his lean face also held something else, a barbaric quality that sent a little shiver racing down Elizabeth's spine. She had the definite impression that this man would brook no opinion or argument that did not coincide with his own thoughts and feelings. Finely arched brows curved with a wicked slant over his deepset eyes, and she noticed that the tip of his acquiline nose flared just slightly when his lips parted in a smile.

But it was the scar that drew her gaze. She tried not to look at it, to reveal her curiosity, but she couldn't help it. A thin white puckering of flesh curved in a ragged line from the temple over his left eye, slashed across his high cheekbone, and ended at the left corner of his mouth.

Dominic lifted her hand and pressed his lips against the back of her fingers. When he straightened, he maintained his grip on her hand, and smiled. "A duel," he said softly.

"Pardon me?" Elizabeth said, confused by his words.

"The scar. You were wondering about it. How I received it, were you not?"

She blushed, embarrassed at her obvious impertinence.

"I fought a duel several years ago, and nearly lost. I have not made that same mistake since."

"Fighting a duel," Elizabeth said, "or nearly losing one?"

His smile widened. "Losing. When one lives in New Orleans, one cannot avoid the *duello*. But one *can* avoid losing." He turned to Claudette. "Madame Armande, I am forever in your debt for introducing me to such a lovely creature as Miss Devlin."

Claudette smiled.

Dominic turned back to Elizabeth. "Shall we be on our way? It is a somewhat long ride to Shadow Glen."

Elizabeth placed her hand on his offered arm, and they left the room. She did not fail to notice the admiring glances from several women in the lobby as they made their way through the hotel. Even so, she couldn't help but wish, just a little, that it was another ebony-haired man whose arm she held. A man, she knew, she would never see again.

"I haven't worn one of these monkey suits in I don't know how long," Gray complained, as he tried to tie the gray silk cravat at his throat.

"That's your trouble," Travis said, watching him in amusement. "You live in those leathers of yours, and women don't get to see the real Grayson Cantrelle too often."

"That is the real Grayson Cantrelle," he growled back. "This," he glared into the mirror at himself, "is not." Since he and Travis were almost the same build, Gray had borrowed clothes from him, rather than purchase his own for the soiree. He considered that a waste of good money, especially since he had great-coats and trousers at home that he hardly ever wore. Travis's white shirt stretched snugly across Gray's shoulders, as did the steel gray greatcoat. The trousers, held taut by leather *sous-pieds* that ran beneath each insole of the borrowed, black dress boots, hugged Gray's well-muscled legs in an almost indecent display. He finally managed to get the cravat into a proper tie, and turned to Travis. "All right, let's get this over with. I didn't want to go to a soiree, I only wanted to look at the old man's horses."

Travis laughed. "That's how you do things in New Orleans, my friend. You dance, you eat, you compliment the ladies, smoke cigars with the gents, and then you talk business."

Gray shook his head. "Damn slow way to get things done, if you ask me."

"They didn't," Travis chuckled. "And I doubt they'd appreciate your opinion."

"Michie want me to come and take care of your

213

horses?"' Jason asked from his seat in front of the fireplace.

"No, Jason," Gray answered. "You stay here. We can't afford for too many people to see you. Unless you want to be returned to Sorens?"

The boy shook his head violently. "No, Michie, no. Never."

"Then stay in this room, and don't answer the door for anyone, you hear? Travis and I have keys, we don't need you to let us in."

"Yes, Michie."

"I told you to call me Gray."

Jason smiled. "Yes, Gray."

"All right, Travis, let's get this over with." Gray's mood was surly, but not wholly because of being forced to attend a soiree, or even worrying about Jason and whether Sorens had posted a reward on the boy's head. His mood was black because ever since he'd said good-bye to her, he hadn't been able to keep his thoughts off of Elizabeth; wondering what she was doing, if she was all right, and what would happen to her now, tomorrow, and all the days of her life after that.

Travis had two horses waiting at the hitching rack at the Royal Street door of the hotel. A golden palomino with a flowing flaxen mane and tail snorted softly as Travis approached and reached for the reins. The tall black stallion next to the palomino shuffled impatiently.

"Nice," Gray said, giving both animals an admiring once-over.

"They belong to a friend of mine here, but I'm sure I can get her to sell them to you, if you want them, that is."

"Her?" Gray repeated.

"Celestine Tremonte. She operates the Golden Slipper."

Gray nodded. "I'll think on it."

The two men rode in virtual silence to Shadow Glen. They talked occasionally of some memory or other they shared, but generally they remained quiet, each glad to find the other still alive, but not needing to voice those thoughts any further.

"Here it is," Travis said, after about an hour on the road. He steered his mount between the tall brick entry pillars that flanked the drive leading to Shadow Glen. Torches had been placed along the drive every thirty feet or so, lighting the way for the arriving guests. The orange flames flickered against the inky night, casting shadows about the landscape, which was dotted with huge, gnarled oaks, thickly leaved magnolias, and delicate dogwoods. The leaves of the trees were turned gold by the glow of the flames, while high above, where they were touched instead by the light of the moon, they glistened silver.

"How well do you know old man Fordeleaux?" Travis asked as they neared the massive house. It was a brick structure, two stories in height, with a peaked, white portico over the entry, supported by four massive but delicately carved, white Corinthian columns.

"I've never met him," Gray said. "My father used to do business with him, but it was all by mail. I think once or twice my father traveled to New Orleans. Other times he sent our foreman."

"I guess you've never seen his daughter then?"

"No, why?"

Travis chuckled. "Theresa Fordeleaux is just about the most beautiful woman in New Orleans, that's all. The old man's having a hell of a time getting her to settle down though. Evidently the lady doesn't want to just be somebody's wife. He's spoiled her. But then," he shrugged, "he never had a son, and his wife died years ago. There's just the two of them. Way I hear it is that he let Theresa do his books while she was growing up. She made a lot of the decisions about his plantations and other businesses. Now the little lady has a mind of her own, and she doesn't fear speaking it aloud."

"Doesn't sound like your type," Gray said.

"She's not, at least not in the way you're thinking. But then, I'd never turn a beautiful woman away from my bed . . . if she wanted to climb into it, that is."

Both men laughed and reined up in front of the entry steps of the mansion. A butler immediately took the reins of their mounts and handed them to a stable boy, then turned back to Gray and Travis.

"Grayson Cantrelle and Travis Planchette," Gray said.

The man bowed and motioned for them to enter the house.

Theresa and Jonathan Fordeleaux were standing just inside the door, as Gray and Travis entered the spacious foyer. The walls were painted a soft yellow, so that the glow cast by the flames of a hundred candles set in the three-tiered crystal chandelier turned the long room into a brilliant blaze of light. Grayson introduced himself, then Travis.

Theresa Fordeleaux was indeed everything Travis had claimed. Her skin was the hue of a fading magnolia blossom, a creamy, rich gold, while her hair was a luscious sable, pulled from her face and arranged in a thick braid on her crown. Her eyes were pools of darkness, her face a sculptor's masterpiece. She wore a pale yellow gown, adorned with dripping ruffles of ivory lace, a striking complement to her dark beauty.

But all Gray could think of as she warmly greeted him, was how different she was from Elizabeth.

"So, you're Samuel's son," Jonathan Fordeleaux said and shook Gray's hand. "You look like him."

T O   G E T   Y O U R
4 FREE BOOKS
MAIL THE COUPON BELOW.

FREE BOOK CERTIFICATE

GET 4 FREE BOOKS

Yes! I want to subscribe to Zebra's HEARTFIRE HOME SUBSCRIPTION SERVICE. Please send me my 4 FREE books. Then each month I'll receive the four newest Heartfire Romances as soon as they are published to preview Free for ten days. If I decide to keep them I'll pay the special discounted price of just $3.50 each; a total of $14.00. This is a savings of $3.00 off the regular publishers price. There are no shipping, handling or other hidden charges. There is no minimum number of books to buy and I may cancel this subscription at any time. In any case the 4 FREE Books are mine to keep regardless.

NAME

ADDRESS

CITY   STATE   ZIP

TELEPHONE

SIGNATURE

(If under 18 parent or guardian must sign)
Terms and prices subject to change.
Orders subject to acceptance.

HF 102

Heartfire Romance

GET 4 FREE BOOKS

HEARTFIRE HOME SUBSCRIPTION
SERVICE
P.O. BOX 5214
120 BRIGHTON ROAD
CLIFTON, NEW JERSEY 07015

"Thank you, sir. I, ah, I wonder if I could see your horses."

"Later, son, later. Never discuss business at one of Theresa's little parties. Leastways, not at the beginning of one. I learned that the hard way." He laughed heartily. "Anyway, you want to buy those horses, you're going to have to convince Theresa you're the right person to own them. She's kinda funny about selling animals. That way about the slaves, too."

Gray nodded, but refrained from comment. He didn't own slaves. The Bar C and the Cantrelles never had, and never would. He didn't believe in it. An honest day's pay for an honest day's work. That's what his father had always said, and that's how Gray was raised.

"And you," Jonathan said, grabbing Travis's hand and shaking it, "Travis Planchette. I've heard a lot about you, son."

"Not all bad, I hope," Travis laughed.

"Damn good, if you ask me. What say the three of us have a brandy together later in my study? I'll talk to Mr. Cantrelle here about the horses, and I've got some things I'd like to talk to you about, too."

"Papa," Theresa interrupted. "You promised no business tonight."

The old man looked slightly abashed. "Just a little, honey, I promise."

Theresa gave her father a wary look. "All right, but later. Much later."

She glanced toward the open entry door, and then hastily turned back toward Travis and held out her hand. "Would you be so kind as to escort me in and begin the march with me, Monsieur Planchette?"

"I'd be honored, Mademoiselle Fordeleaux," Travis said, with a knowing glance at Gray. He took Theresa's hand and placed it in the crook of his arm.

217

Someone moved up beside Travis and gently bumped him. Travis glanced over his shoulder and met the piercing, ebony eyes of a tall Creole. A jagged scar on the left side of the man's face marred his otherwise classically handsome features. "Excuse me, Monsieur," the man said coolly, but Travis was no longer looking at the man, instead he was staring dumbfounded at the woman on his arm.

The deep voice drew Theresa Fordeleaux's attention. She turned, and her eyes lit with something more than friendship. "Dominic," she said, her tone laced with both surprise and pleasure. "I . . . I didn't expect you to attend."

"My business was concluded with more expedience than I anticipated, *chérie.*" He glanced at Elizabeth beside him, and Theresa's gaze followed the path of his. The smile on her face instantly disappeared. "May I present Elizabeth Devlin," Dominic said. "Elizabeth, this is our hostess, Theresa Fordeleaux."

Gray, who had been conversing with Jonathan, spun around at hearing Elizabeth's name. His eyes sought hers, found them, and held them captive. A clash of emotion assailed him. He wanted to haul her into his arms and capture her lips with his, to bury his face in the silky gold strands of her hair, to feel her body pressed warmly to his. And he wanted to run from her, to get as far away from her as he could, to put as much distance between them as possible and never look back, never think of her again, to wipe all memory of her from his mind and heart. He swore under his breath, inaudibly, and braced himself for what he knew would be a difficult evening.

Theresa quickly caught herself, and the smile that had so abruptly vanished at seeing Elizabeth with Dominic returned. "Elizabeth? Elizabeth Devlin?"

Elizabeth tore her gaze from Gray's and nodded.

218

"Oh, *chérie,*" Theresa said, and laughed softly. "I'm sorry. I didn't recognize you."

"Nor I you, Tess," Elizabeth said, using the name she had called her friend when they'd been children and their parents had visited each other often. "But then, we haven't seen each other since we were . . . what? . . . ten?"

But Theresa was no longer listening, she was staring instead at Dominic.

They're in love, Elizabeth thought suddenly, looking from her escort to her old friend. She felt Gray's gaze on her and tried to ignore it. What was *he* doing here? At a soiree? She tried to concentrate on what Dominic was saying to Theresa, and couldn't. Why were Gray and Travis here? A gambler and a gunfighter. It made no sense. And what was going on between Dominic and Theresa? It was obvious to anyone who cared to notice that they were in love with each other, yet Madame Claudette had made it a point to tell Elizabeth that Dominic was unattached, and somewhat of a ladies' man. She stole a look at Theresa's father. He was staring at Dominic, and his expression was more an angry scowl than one worn to welcome a guest.

The tension in the air was as thick as mud.

Jonathan Fordeleaux was the first to slice through it and end the resulting silence. "Theresa, I think most of our guests have arrived. Perhaps the march should begin?"

She forced her gaze away from Dominic's, where it had been riveted, and looked up at Travis. "Yes, let us begin the soiree, Monsieur." They moved toward the ballroom. Dominic and Elizabeth followed.

"Something has to be done about that rake," Jonathan mumbled to himself, "before it's too late."

Gray caught the softly spoken words and turned a

curious eye to his host, but the old man merely smiled and motioned for Gray to precede him into the crowded ballroom.

It was ablaze with light, a trio of multitiered brass and etched crystal chandeliers that hung from the center of the high-ceilinged room sparkled with the flames of several hundred candles. Twenty-foot-tall gilt-framed mirrors hung on the wall at each end of the long ballroom, to reflect both its length and its light, and a bank of French doors that made up the outer wall stood open, allowing the scent of jasmine, oleander, heliotrope, and roses to waft in on the warm night air.

Travis and Theresa moved to one end of the ballroom. She signaled to the musicians, who had taken their positions on a raised dais in a nearby corner, and they began to play. She and Travis moved onto the dance floor, and everyone, including Dominic and Elizabeth, began to follow, officially opening the soiree.

Gray watched from his position near the door. His scrutinizing gaze raked over Dominic, coldly assessing. Elizabeth was a vision of loveliness in blue and white, and the devil on her arm was a wickedly handsome creature, despite his disfigurement. But Gray was in no mood to coolly size up his competition. The thought struck him like a thunderbolt, smack between the eyes. Competition? Why in the hell had he thought that? There was no competition where Elizabeth was concerned, because there was no contest. He didn't want her. He was lucky to be rid of her. True, he would pay a king's ransom to get the blue-eyed minx in his bed just one more time, but that was it, that was all he wanted. He surely didn't want that little spitfire in his life. He unconsciously shook his head as he watched Dominic glide Elizabeth across the dance floor. No, above all, he didn't want that.

220

The march ended and a waltz began. Dominic whirled Elizabeth into his arms amid the throng of dancing couples. He moved with a fluid grace that was flawless and obviously natural to him. His right hand held Elizabeth's firmly, while his left rested on her waist.

She watched him, but it took no great genius to realize his attention was elsewhere, as was his gaze. "Do you know Theresa well?" Elizabeth asked finally, her curiosity getting the better of her manners.

"We are good friends," he said simply.

"And her father?" Elizabeth asked on a hunch.

Dominic gave her a puzzled look and then smiled. "We are not such good friends."

"Because he doesn't approve of you for Theresa?"

"She has told you?"

Elizabeth smiled, but it was sadness for her friend that curved her lips rather than joy. "No, it was just something I sensed, and a situation I am familiar with."

"Your father did the same?"

"Fortunately for me, I was not in love with anyone when my father decided who I was to marry."

"But Madame Claudette said you were unattached. Have you lost your husband? In a duel perhaps?"

"I am not married, Monsieur. The marriage was called off." Her tone held a note of bitterness, and Elizabeth decided to change the subject before memory of Aaron ruined her evening. "Perhaps Theresa and I can go riding tomorrow, and you might join us? On the trail between Shadow Glen and town?"

"Perhaps," Dominic said, and he smiled.

The waltz ended. Elizabeth slipped her arm within the crook of his and they made their way through the crowd toward the refreshment table, where a huge serving bowl of lemonade sat.

"Elizabeth," Theresa said, rushing toward her. "We

221

have not had one moment to talk and catch up." She slipped her arm through Elizabeth's and guided her toward the foyer. "Come on, let's take a breath of air and talk a bit."

The two women walked out onto the front gallery.

"So, tell me, what are you doing here in New Orleans. How is Eugenia? And what happened with your wedding? Where is your husband, *chérie?* I just arrived home from our trip to France and saw your invitation. I was sick that I had missed it."

"There was no wedding."

Theresa's brows rose in shock. "No wedding? But the invitation?"

Gray moved back into the shadows of the gallery at hearing Elizabeth's voice. He'd been just about to enter the foyer, having stepped out to enjoy a few minutes of solitude and a cheroot.

"I caught him in bed with some trollop only minutes before the ceremony was to start," Elizabeth said, all the loathing she still felt at the memory of the scene lacing her tone.

"Oh, *chérie,* how terrible for you. What a scoundrel! You should have shot him. It would have served him right. Oh—" Theresa clasped her cheek in alarm.

"What is it, Tess?"

"I invited him here, tonight."

"Who?"

"Aaron Reynaud. I saw him in town this afternoon. He said you two had merely squabbled. A mere misunderstanding, he said."

Elizabeth looked suddenly panicked and ready to flee. "He's here?"

Theresa grasped her arm and patted her hand consolingly. "No, *chérie,* no. He did not come. Relax."

222

She steered Elizabeth back toward the ballroom. "Come, let us forget all about this Aaron Reynaud and enjoy the evening. Though," she smiled coyly, "do not make too good of friends with Dominic Regrette, hey?"

Elizabeth laughed. "I fear it is no secret what the two of you feel for each other, Tess. He's safe in my company, believe me."

The two women returned to the buffet table.

Gray stared after Elizabeth. So, that's who Aaron was. Well, now he knew why Elizabeth had been so defensive when he'd first approached her in Vicksburg. Storming away from your own wedding would make a person a bit touchy. Gray wondered what this Aaron Reynaud was like, other than the fact that he'd been caught in bed with another woman by his fiancée. The man didn't know how lucky he was to have escaped that ceremony. But even as that thought tripped through Gray's mind, he felt a twinge of envy for this unknown man named Aaron, a man Elizabeth had loved.

He tossed his cheroot onto the drive. "Oh, for hades' sake, what do I care who she loved?"

Theresa's father summoned her from across the room. "Excuse me, *chérie,*" she said to Elizabeth. "Papa needs me."

Elizabeth stood next to Dominic and watched Theresa move through the crowd of guests toward her father. "Tess and I haven't seen each other in almost ten years, yet I feel as close to her as to my sister."

"She is a wonderful woman."

"Excuse me," Gray said, and touched Dominic's shoulder. "I wonder if I might have this next dance with the young lady?"

Dominic glanced at Elizabeth, who, after a brief

hesitation, nodded her acquiescence. "Of course, Monsieur," Dominic said.

Gray swept Elizabeth onto the dance floor. "What are you doing here?" she asked, the moment they were out of earshot from Dominic.

"I could ask you the same thing," Gray returned.

"Theresa and her father are old friends of my family." She came to an abrupt stop in the middle of the dance floor, and gawked up at Gray. "Did they hire you to shoot somebody?"

He smiled. "No."

"But you are here on business?" she persisted.

"Yes, I am, but I don't want to talk about that." On an impulse he felt helpless to resist, he brushed his lips lightly across hers. "You look lovely tonight, Elizabeth," he said, his soft drawl a tender caress to her nerves.

The kiss was a feather-light touch that both surprised her and sent a thrill of excitement racing through her. She began to lean toward him, wanting to feel the full, hard, ravishing impact of his lips on hers, and then she caught herself and pulled back. She could not allow herself to feel anything for him, or be seduced by him again. The first time she'd had no choice in the matter. She did now.

"I am sure, Mr. Cantrelle," she said, purposely using formality, "that stealing a kiss on the dance floor is quite improper. A gentleman wouldn't—"

His smile stopped her. "I'm sorry, I forgot, you are not a gentleman."

"Who's your escort, Elizabeth?"

Her eyes widened in surprise. "Pardon me?"

"You heard me," he practically snarled. "Who's your escort?"

Her eyes narrowed. "Why?" A flash of panic caught at her heart. Oh, Lord. Was Gray one of those men who couldn't stand for a woman he'd seduced to be with another man, even when he'd discarded her like yesterday's garbage? Was he planning on killing Dominic?

Several couples bumped into them. Gray's hands tightened their clasp on Elizabeth, and he forced her to resume dancing. "Don't look so frightened. I won't kill him. I was merely curious, Elizabeth. You walk out of your own wedding, jilting your bridegroom, make love to me on a lonely riverbank, nearly flirt your way into being seduced by—what did you call Sorens, a maniac? Yes, that was it. And now, only a day after your arrival in New Orleans, you are at a soiree with an escort. I thought you said you didn't know anyone in New Orleans, Elizabeth." Damn, he sounded like a jealous hag, and he couldn't help it. He also didn't care. At least not right now.

"How did you know I wa—" In her surprise she failed to follow his lead and almost tripped. He held her securely in his arms until she regained her feet. "How did you know about Aaron?"

"You mumbled in your sleep," he lied.

"Oh." She looked calm for a moment, then her temper flared again. "And I didn't make love to you. *You* forced yourself on me, just like Damien would have."

"Who is your escort, Elizabeth?" Gray drawled calmly.

Her heart began to return to its normal pace. "I said I hadn't been to New Orleans in years, but my family does have old friends here. Several, in fact."

"Is he one of them?"

"Dominic? Yes, he is a friend."

"But is he an *old* friend?"

Why was he questioning her like this? What did he want? Her heart began to race at the thoughts that were

225

beginning to run rampant through her head. Gray was a gunfighter. Why did he want to know about Dominic? She looked up into his eyes, trying to read them, and nearly groaned at her failure. It was impossible. They were unreadable, at least to her. But she did know one thing: lying was useless. All he would have to do was ask their hosts, or Dominic himself, and the truth would be revealed: that she had not known Dominic before that day. Finally, she shook her head. "I met Mr. Regrette this afternoon, if it is any business of yours."

"And he's already your escort? Fast work."

Elizabeth's temper flared at the insinuation. Or at least, what she thought was an insinuation. "It's not like that, Grayson Cantrelle, and I'll thank you to stop sticking your nose into my business. And my life!" She jerked away from him and marched from the dance floor.

Gray watched her weave her way through the guests. Fine. That was just fine with him. He must have been crazy to ask her to dance anyway. What had he been thinking? The minute he saw her at the Fordeleaux', he should have left. Hell, he should have left her on that damn burning boat.

"Would you care to finish the waltz with me, Monsieur Cantrelle?" Theresa asked from behind Gray.

He turned, surprised. "I thought you and Trav—"

She shrugged. "He's talking to my father. Politics. I'm not supposed to know anything about that."

Gray laughed, took her into his arms, and began to whirl her around the dance floor. "But you do, don't you?"

Theresa joined in his laughter. "But of course, most likely more than a lot of men. But Papa says it's unladylike, and hates it if I join his conversations when

226

others are present. He would find it absolutely scandalous if I broached a political opinion in front of our guests tonight."

"You are an unusual woman, Miss Fordeleaux."

She laughed again, a musical sound that joined melodically with the harmonizing strains of the musicians' instruments. "And you, Mr. Cantrelle, I sense are a very unusual man."

He tipped his head and smiled slyly. "Touché, Miss Fordeleaux."

"Call me Theresa, please."

"Only if you call me Gray, and allow me the pleasure of the next dance."

Elizabeth stood near the buffet table, the glass of lemonade in her hand completely ignored, while her gaze followed Gray and Theresa around the room. She felt a swell of jealousy within her breast, hot and burning, eating at her, its gnawing hunger threatening to devour her.

"Would you like to work off some of that heat by twirling about the dance floor with me?"

She turned to find Travis had moved up beside her. "No, Mr. Planchette, thank you, I'm fine." She whipped open the beaded fan that hung from her wrist, and fluttered it in front of her face.

He shrugged and smiled knowingly. "Just thought you seemed a little *hot under the collar,* as they say."

Elizabeth snapped the fan closed. "As you can see, Mr. Planchette, my gown does not have a collar. And as for being hot, the room is a bit warm, but then tonight is unusually sultry."

He nodded. "Gray said the same thing earlier. About the room being warm, that is. He seems to have found a way to cool off though." He glanced at Gray and Theresa as they danced past. "Or maybe he's getting hotter."

227

She sniffed. "Maybe he'll melt into a little puddle of nothingness and do us all a favor." She turned abruptly on her heel, and marched toward the open French doors that led to a gallery that spanned the rear of the house.

"And a good evening to you, too, Mrs. Cantrelle," Travis muttered under his breath, and chuckled to himself.

Elizabeth stepped outside. Several other couples were milling about, enjoying the air, but she ignored them and moved to the far end of the long gallery and looked out at the dark landscape. Someone stood beneath a tall oak several yards away. She could see the small flame that burned brightly at the tip of the cheroot the man held in his hand, and occasionally lifted to his lips. But he was no more than a shadow himself. Tall and thin, with dark hair, she guessed, that blended with the night. She looked up at the golden moon, a thick crescent of saffron suspended within the darkness of a velvet sky. Why did Grayson Cantrelle infuriate her so? She had never met a man who could so rile her.

And arouse you? that little voice asked.

She snapped open the fan and began to flutter it before her. Yes, *to rage,* she answered her conscience.

Beneath the tall oak tree, Aaron lifted the brandy-soaked cheroot to his thin lips and inhaled deeply. She hadn't recognized him, he knew. If she had, she most likely would have either panicked and ran, left the soiree, or denounced him and flung angry, rage-edged insults at him. She had done neither, which told him she was still unaware of his presence. He and Damien had arrived in New Orleans only that afternoon, and he had not expected to find Elizabeth so quickly. When she'd first left him, he'd been enraged, not because of any deep feelings for her, but because of the humiliation and embarrassment he'd been forced to endure at her abrupt departure from their wedding. He had thought of nothing more than finding her and bringing her home. The boat disaster had left him thinking her dead, until he'd learned that there were survivors. Somehow he'd sensed she was one of them, and he'd been right. Damien had confirmed that.

But then he'd also confirmed that Elizabeth had not survived alone. Aaron burned at the thought of another man savoring Elizabeth's charms. She had belonged to him. He should have been the first, the only one, and she'd be sorry he hadn't been. He'd make certain of that.

An hour later, realizing there was no way he was going to be able to get to Elizabeth with so many people about, Aaron departed. Damien had mentioned he was going to Corey's Rest Stop, a place that offered everything a man could think of but rest. He spotted Damien almost the moment he entered the barroom, seated at a table near the door with another man.

"Aaron, join us," Damien called, seeing Aaron at the door.

He took a chair between Damien and the other man.

"You remember Thomas, don't you, Damien? The Reverend Thomas A. Coltraine?"

Aaron looked at Coltraine. It had been a number of years since he'd seen him. He nodded and shook the man's hand. The years hadn't been especially kind to the reverend. Though his hair was long, his pate was bald, and his nose had obviously been badly broken and not set properly. "Sorry, Reverend, it's been a long time. Didn't recognize you."

"Quite all right, Mr. Reynaud, quite all right,"

Thomas said. "I was just telling Damien about my trip downriver."

Aaron nodded absently and looked around the room. He wasn't interested in either the reverend or his trip.

"Tell him about Elizabeth," Damien prompted.

Aaron's attention shot to the reverend. "Elizabeth?"

Coltraine nodded and smiled widely, exposing several blackened teeth. "Passed her and her man friend on the trail. Pretty friendly they was to each other, too. Leastways from what I saw."

"How friendly?" Aaron prodded.

"Well," a sly twinkle sparked the Reverend's eye, "looked to me like he was intent on getting himself a little husbandly affection, if you know what I mean, and the lady wasn't having no objections."

Chapter 15

"Serena!" Elizabeth squealed as she stood on the threshold of her hotel room, one hand still on the doorknob.

Dominic peered over Elizabeth's shoulder, and saw a generously built black woman sitting on the settee beside the fireplace. She had been dozing, but had wakened when the door opened and Elizabeth shrieked. A fire was burning in the grate, and the room was uncomfortably warm.

"Missy. Oh, Missy." Serena struggled to pull herself from the chair and rise to her feet, and then waddled rapidly across the room toward Elizabeth, who practically ran toward the servant. They flew into each other's arms. "Oh, Missy, I was so scared for you. I thought you was dead. First you run off, then Mr. Aaron left, and just before I got here, I heard about that boat exploding, and thought you was dead. But I come to the hotel anyway, like you told me, and lo and behold, here you is." Tears of joy streamed over Serena's pudgy cheeks.

"A gunfighter helped me get off the boat," Elizabeth said.

"A gunfighter. Oh, praise the Lord, child, that's all I

231

got to say. Praise the Lord. And that man, too, even if he is a gunfighter."

"Oh, Serena, I'm so glad to see you," Elizabeth gushed, and held the woman at arm's length. "Are you all right? You made the trip with no problems?"

"Who gonna give a fat old woman like me problems, child? They too afraid I'd sit on them and squash the life right outta them."

Elizabeth laughed and sat down on the chair opposite the settee, since once Serena retook her seat, there was no room left on the small lounge. "Tell me what happened after I left," Elizabeth said, full of curiosity and excitement. She had completely forgotten Dominic's presence. He moved into the room and stood behind her chair.

"Elizabeth," Dominic said, "I think I shall take my leave now, and allow you two ladies to visit."

She bounced up off of the chair. "Oh, Dominic, I'm sorry. This is Serena, my maid. I had to leave her in Vicksburg when I left, but—"

He silenced her with a raised hand and a smile. "I can see you two have a lot to talk about." He took her hand in his and drew it to his lips. "If it pleasures you, Elizabeth, I would like to call on you again. Perhaps tomorrow, for dinner?"

"I'd like that, Dominic," Elizabeth said, surprising herself. Dominic was not interested in her, she knew that. She also knew that he was *very* interested in her friend Theresa. But dinner would be nice.

"Until tomorrow then." He closed the door softly.

Elizabeth turned back to Serena and clasped her hands together to keep them from shaking the words out of the old woman. "Tell me all about it, Serena! What happened after I left Vicksburg? Was Aaron mad? What did the guests say? What did Aaron tell them?"

Serena laughed again. "He was spitting mad, that

one. Couldn't believe you just up and took off. Said he didn't do nothing that wasn't normal, that everybody didn't do, and you was being silly."

"He would see it that way," Elizabeth said, suddenly sullen. "What else? What did he tell everyone?"

"Said you was sick and couldn't go through with the ceremony. He told them it was just pos—pos—"

"Postponed?" Elizabeth offered.

Serena nodded. "That's it. Postponed. He said you'd all be letting them know when they could come back."

Elizabeth jumped to her feet and began pacing back and forth before the fireplace. "The nerve of that man! After what he did, I wouldn't marry him if . . . if he was the last man on earth." The words seemed oddly familiar, and then she remembered why. She had thought that Grayson would ask for her hand in marriage after they'd . . . after she and he had . . . after he'd forced himself on her, and those had been the exact words she had been prepared to assail him with. She felt a rush of anger. Grayson Cantrelle, in his own way, was no better than Aaron Reynaud. Worse, actually. At least Aaron had money, land, and position. Gray had nothing but his gun. She was better off with neither one of them. So why did she still think of Gray constantly?

Because you want him.

"I do not!"

Serena looked up at Elizabeth, clearly puzzled. "You do not what, honey?"

"Nothing," she grumbled. "Nothing."

"So," Serena slapped her thick thighs, "when we leaving for Texas?"

"I . . . I haven't made the arrangements yet. I'll see to them first thing in the morning."

After the sun had risen well into the sky, and

Elizabeth had enjoyed a leisurely breakfast in her room with Serena, she began to prepare for her day of shopping. There were a million things to do before they left for Eugenia's. But first, she had to send a note to Dominic Regrette. She smiled to herself and sat at the desk beside her bed, taking quill to paper. She wrote first one note to Dominic, and another to Theresa. She would drop them at the front desk on her way out, and ask that they be delivered immediately. Dominic would appear at the Square expecting to meet her for supper, and so would Theresa, but Elizabeth would not be there, and she suspected they would not really miss her too much.

An hour later she had made her way to Madame Claudette's dress shop. One ball gown was not going to see her through the remainder of her journey to Sweetbriar, or the days thereafter. Lord only knows, she thought, if there's a shop in Sweetbriar. She spent the entire morning in the dress shop. Luckily, Madame Claudette had several gowns already made. They required a bit of altering to fit Elizabeth, but it was only a simple matter of taking in a stitch here or there. She picked a half-dozen bolts of cloth to go with the fashion patterns she'd selected, and ordered more gowns be made.

"Now, Madame, I will need accessories, and I want to purchase several bolts of cloth to take with me when I leave New Orleans."

"*Oui,* Mademoiselle. You choose," the dressmaker said, "I will bundle them for you."

Elizabeth chose a yellow taffeta. That was her sister Eugenia's favorite color. Next she set aside a bolt of green brocade silk. A red satin. Pale apricot muslin. A white and lime Caledonian silk. A checked cambric. And a black velvet. By the time she was done, she had a dozen bolts of cloth set aside, four bolts of lace, five pairs of shoes, a half-dozen camisoles and matching pantelettes, petticoats, stockings, gloves, five hats, and two corsets.

"I'll take the new gowns with me now, Madame, if you'll box them, please. And these two hats." She picked up two of the five she'd chosen and handed them to the dressmaker. "Please have the rest delivered to my room at the St. Louis this afternoon."

"Oui, Mademoiselle. I will see to it they are there."

Twenty minutes later Elizabeth left the dressmaker's shop laden down with her bundles. She had donned one of the hats she had picked out, a bonnet really, its wide, yellow-checked brim framing her face, a huge sun-colored taffeta bow holding it secure at her throat. It matched the one-day gown she had taken from Damien Sorens's deceased wife's armoire, and which she now wore.

She stepped out into the light of the bright afternoon sun, squinted, and looked in both directions of the street. She hadn't taken a carriage from the hotel, and she didn't see any of the buggies for hire that usually traveled the streets of the Vieux Carre.

"Wonderful," she muttered in disgust, and began to walk in the direction of the hotel. Before she reached the first corner, she had to stop three times and reposition her grip on the bundles in her arms to prevent them from falling to the ground. Obviously she had taken too much with her. The packages were a cumbersome load, and she could barely see her way over them. Elizabeth didn't worry though. She had a view on either side of her to guide her way to the hotel, and anyone approaching would realize that she couldn't see them, so they'd move out of her way. She quickened her step, hoping to make it to the hotel before she dropped everything.

She was just approaching Pere Antoine, the small alleyway that separated the New Orleans courthouse, the Presbytere, from the cathedral, when she crashed into what felt like a brick wall. The packages flew out of her arms. Some went up, some went out, and others fell straight to the ground.

A soft *whoof* met her ears as the brick wall seemed to topple back away from her, then grabbed her arms as she stumbled in an effort to remain upright and not follow her packages to the ground.

"Please, excuse me, ma'am, I didn't see—"

"Of all the inconsiderate, careless things to—"

"Elizabeth?" Gray gawked down at her. He snatched his hands from around her arms as if fire had suddenly touched his fingertips.

"Gray?" She stared up at him in disbelief, suddenly filled with a mosaic of jumbled emotion, and all centered around him and his sudden reappearance into her life.

"I . . . I'm sorry, Elizabeth." He bent and began to retrieve her packages. "I was just coming out of the alley. I didn't see you." He rose and began to hand the boxes to her.

She reached for them, and her hand touched his. A tingle of warmth ricocheted through her body as her flesh met his, leaving her skin covered with goose bumps and her heart thumping madly in her chest. She fought to regain a modicum of composure. This would not do, she told herself. This would definitely not do.

Gray pulled the boxes from her grasp and held onto them. "Let me carry these back to the hotel for you. It's the least I can do after nearly running you down."

"Thank you," Elizabeth said demurely.

They walked side by side in silence. At the door to the hotel, Elizabeth turned to Gray and opened her arms for the boxes.

"I'll be leaving town in the morning. Travis and I have a wagon train organized," Gray said abruptly. Damn. His mouth had taken off faster than his brain could stop it. Why had he said that? There was nothing between them. They'd spent a few days stranded together on a riverbank. He'd made love to her—a natural thing to do under the circumstances—and he'd made certain she made it to New Orleans without further mishap. He owed her nothing more. He was free to leave, to forget about her, to go his own way and not look back. So why in the hell had he told her he was leaving in the morning? Some sadomachistic urge to hear her tell him what a rake he was again?

"Oh? So soon?" Elizabeth said. Suddenly, as if jarred from the dreamy state of pampered luxury she'd become accustomed to, harsh reality crashed down around her ears. Memory of the passion she had shared with Gray assaulted her senses. She had let him do things to her she had never allowed anyone. Lord, what had she done?! She felt heat rise to her cheeks. At the time, though, it had seemed right, giving herself to him like that. It had been a night of magic that both of them had needed and wanted. A night that obviously meant nothing to him.

"Yes, my business is finished here. I'm going back to Texas," Gray was saying.

"Texas," Elizabeth repeated inanely. He was leaving. Just like that. She didn't matter to him at all. She was just another conquest. "Silly fool," she muttered, totally ignoring the fact that *she* had been doing her utmost to convince herself that he was not the man for her.

"Excuse me?" Gray said, slightly indignant.

Her gaze, which had been a million miles away, suddenly cleared. She pinned him with it. "I said, have a nice trip, Mr. Cantrelle. I hope you fall into a gopher hole and can't find your way out." Elizabeth grabbed her packages from his arm, spun on her tiny heel, and stalked away from him through the lobby of the St. Louis.

"Well, what the hell?" Gray grumbled. He watched

her march away from him, and knew it was the last time he would see her. "I need a drink." He made for the bar. "No," he snarled, "I need the whole damn bottle."

Elizabeth dumped her packages on the bed. "I hope he falls in a river and drowns. No, I hope Indians get him." She ripped off her new bonnet and tossed it on a chair, then began to work on the buttons of her gown. "I hope they tie him to the ground and let the sun burn him to a crisp." She remembered she'd thought of almost the same end for Aaron, but they were two of a kind, so why not?

"Who you talking about getting burnt to a crisp with Indians?" Serena asked as she entered the room. She had several parcels in her arms, which she also dropped onto the bed.

"No one."

"Well, you sure seem mad at someone, Missy." Serena chuckled. "Ain't seen you this worked up since you found Aaron in bed with that trollop." Her eyes narrowed in suspicion. "You got yourself another beau?"

"No." Elizabeth flung her gown on a chair and stepped from her hoop-cage, letting it fall to the floor in a flat heap. She began to sort the packages she'd brought back to the hotel, putting some at the foot of the bed, some at the head.

"What're you doing?" Serena asked.

"Putting my stuff in one place, and Eugenia's in another."

"You figure your sister ain't got a store where she lives?"

"Probably not. Sweetbriar isn't exactly New Orleans or Vicksburg, you know. The way I hear it, we'll be lucky if Texas has a store at all."

Serena sighed. "When we leaving?"

A plan sprang to life in Elizabeth's mind. Grayson Cantrelle may not want her, but he was damn well going to help her get to Sweetbriar, whether he liked it or not. "Tomorrow morning."

"You buy us any satchels?" Serena asked, looking at the purchases Elizabeth had brought back to the room, and knowing instinctively more would be delivered before the day was over.

Elizabeth frowned. "No, I forgot that."

"I'll go fetch them. Store just down the street probably has some."

After Serena left, Elizabeth forgot about the parcels and began to nervously pace the room. She'd show him. She didn't know how she was going to do what she'd planned, but she would. All she had to do was convince Travis. She moved back to the bed and began to tear open several of the packages. Elizabeth lifted a gown of yellow plaid cambric from its wrapping and shook it out. She needed to look her best when she approached Travis. A new gown wouldn't hurt. She moved to the window and peeked out, taking care not to get too close. No sense showing herself, half-dressed, to everyone down on the street.

The sun had already disappeared beyond the roofs of the buildings on the horizon. Evening was quickly approaching. Hopefully she would be able to locate Travis without too much difficulty or delay. If luck was with her, he would also be alone.

Aaron had been sitting in the lobby of the St. Louis Hotel for over two hours, waiting. Damien approached. "She hasn't come back down yet?"

"Would I be sitting here if she had?" Aaron griped.

"Any sign of Jason?"

"No, but then I don't really remember what he looks like."

Suddenly Aaron grabbed Damien's coat sleeve and hauled him toward the far side of the room. Damien slapped at Aaron's hand. "Aaron, whatever are you do—"

"Shut up," Aaron hissed.

Elizabeth descended the wide staircase, approached the hotel desk, and rang for the clerk. Aaron moved closer to hear her words.

"Excuse me," Elizabeth said, when the desk clerk appeared. "I am looking for a Mr. Travis Planchette. I understand he has a room here."

"Yes, Mademoiselle, he does." The clerk looked at the box that held the key to Travis's room. He turned back to Elizabeth. "But Monsieur Planchette is not in."

"Oh." She frowned, then instantly turned it to a coyly hopeful smile. "Mr. Planchette said something about departing tomorrow on a wagon train? Perhaps he's there, getting ready. Do you know where that might be?"

"Yes, Mademoiselle. I believe the wagons for Mr. Planchette's party are at the livery on Levee, by the market."

Elizabeth had absolutely no idea where he meant. "The livery on Levee?" She batted her golden lashes at him. "And where would that be, sir?"

He took a piece of paper from beneath the desk and drew a map. "Here is the hotel," he said, "on St. Louis and Chartres. One block toward the river on St. Louis, and you will find Levee. Go left, like this," he drew an arrow with a flourish of his quill, "and proceed eight blocks. The Mint is directly across the street from the livery. You cannot miss it." He handed Elizabeth the crudely drawn map. "Shall I order you a carriage, Mademoiselle?"

"Yes, please," she said.

The clerk snapped his fingers in the air over his head,

and a porter appeared instantly. "Mademoiselle wishes a carriage. See to it, please."

The man escorted Elizabeth to the door, waved a hand, and a carriage driver, his rig only a few feet away, snapped the reins over his mount's rump. The animal shuffled forward. The porter opened the door of the carriage for Elizabeth and helped her embark.

Elizabeth gave the driver instructions as to where to take her, and the carriage immediately departed from the front of the hotel. She did not look back, had no reason to, and so did not see Damien looking after her from the doorway of the hotel. Nor did she see Aaron board another carriage, or hear him order the driver to follow hers.

It took the carriage less than ten minutes to travel the distance between the hotel and the livery. Elizabeth was surprised to find the huge barn practically surrounded by wagons, all packed heavily. A light shone from within the structure.

"Shall I wait, Mademoiselle?" the young black driver asked.

She glanced at the horizon and nodded. The last thing she wanted to do was walk back to the hotel through a dark and deserted Quarter, which was exactly what it would be in another ten minutes or so. She approached the open door of the livery and stepped in. Several men were busily brushing and feeding the horses and oxen stalled within. She saw Travis immediately, his wheat-colored blond hair turned flaxen by the glow of the lanterns that hung from the beams overhead. She walked up behind him. "Travis?" she said, and touched his shoulder lightly.

He turned, clearly surprised. "Elizabeth! What are you doing here?"

"I came to ask a favor."

Travis put down the brush he had been using on the

241

horse and focused his attention on her. "What can I do for you?"

"I want to go on the wagon train."

His eyes widened. "You want what?"

"I want to go on the wagon train with you. To Texas."

He shook his head. "I don't know, Elizabeth. Gray said—"

"I don't care what Gray said," she snapped. Then another idea struck her, and she instilled a pleading note to her tone. "Look, Travis, Gray and I had an argument while we were traveling here after the boat wreck. I said some things, he said some things, and well, it got a little out of hand. And you know how stubborn Gray is. Please, Travis, he's my husband and I . . ." the words caught in her throat, "I love him."

"Elizabeth . . ."

"Please, Travis, help me save my marriage. Let me go on the wagon train. Please? Don't let Gray leave me."

Travis bit his lower lip. He had to, it was the only way he could keep himself from laughing. This little vixen was just as conniving as Gray had said she was. He stared down at her. He knew she and Gray weren't married, but she didn't know that he knew it. On the other hand, what he did know, or at least felt pretty certain he knew, was that Gray was in love with this independent little sprite.

"He'll have my head if I let you talk me into this," Travis said, finally.

"He'll forgive you. You know he will. You're best friends, Travis. Please?"

He crossed his arms and glared at her sternly. "If I say yes, will you agree to remain hidden in the back of the wagon for the first couple of days? Long enough for us to get well out of New Orleans? Otherwise, if he finds you, he'll send both you and me packing."

242

She nodded, still holding her breath, afraid he might change his mind.

"All right. I don't know why I'm doing this. I'll probably get my head handed to me on a silver platter, but all right. Be here tomorrow morning at 4 A.M."

"4 A.M.?" she squawked.

"4 A.M. I'll find you a driver."

"My maid can drive," Elizabeth offered.

"Your maid?"

"She's very good with a carriage. She can do it."

Travis nodded. "4 A.M., Elizabeth. One minute later, and you can forget it. I don't want Gray seeing me loading you or your things."

"We'll be here. Do you need money to get a wagon?"

"No, I'll take care of it. You just be here on time."

Bubbling over with joy, Elizabeth raised up on her tiptoes and pressed her lips quickly to Travis's cheek. "Thank you," she said, then turned and hurried out of the livery.

"I must be loco," Travis muttered, and turned back to the horse he'd been grooming.

Aaron watched Elizabeth's carriage pull back up in front of the hotel and cursed. He thought he'd have an opportunity to grab her while she was out alone, but there had been none. At least not without being seen. It was unlikely that she would go anywhere else this evening, and he needed a drink. "Take me to the Nom de Plume, on St. Chartres." He felt like playing a little roulette, and also needed to hire himself a guide. The last thought caused him to change his mind regarding his destination. He sat forward in his seat and tapped the driver on the shoulder. "Take me to Magazine Street," he said. The establishments in the Quarter would offer him luxury, but not much in the way of finding a man to guide him into the Texas territory.

Those types crowded the grogshops, taverns, and barrelhouses of Magazine, and the part of town known as The Swamp.

"Stop here," he called out as the carriage rolled past a place whose garishly painted sign proclaimed it The Golden Fleece. Aaron paid off the driver, sent him on his way, and strode into the saloon. It was a crude establishment, at best. The bar was little more than several planks set atop empty whiskey barrels, and a painting of a nude woman reclining on a settee hung on the wall behind the bar. In one corner of the room a crowd was gathered around a well-worn roulette wheel, while others flocked around a wheel of fortune in another corner. The remainder of the room was taken up by gaming tables around which were seated men playing poker, seven-up, and several other games of chance. No one, Aaron knew, would be playing his favorite game of *vingt-et-un* in this place.

He sauntered to the bar and ordered a whiskey, then turned and carefully took stock of the place and its inhabitants. A motley bunch, and that was a compliment. Aaron took the glass from the bar and began to walk toward one of the tables that had an empty chair. He had no intention of drinking the whiskey. He'd heard that some of these places not only watered it down, but then soaked dead rats in the bottles to give the weakened liquor a kick. He paused beside the table. "Mind if I join your game, boys?"

"You got cash?" one of the men asked sourly. He looked like a roustabout from the wharf.

"Enough," Aaron said.

"Then sit, and haul it out."

The man next to where Aaron took a seat reached to the center of the table and pulled the pile of greenbacks that lay there toward him. "Where you from, mister?" he asked.

Aaron looked at the man. He was well dressed, in a

cheap sort of way. His clothes were new, but obviously bought from a general store, not made for him. He was skinny. Not thin, but skinny, his hands looking like flesh covering bone with no meat, muscle, or grit in between. His face had much the same look, and his nose reminded Aaron of a hawk, his eyes of a weasel.

"Vicksburg," Aaron said at last. He threw several greenbacks onto the table in front of him, and picked up the cards that were dealt him. "I'm planning on going into Texas. Need a guide. Anyone here interested?"

Two men shook their heads negatively. Another merely grunted. The skinny man seated next to Aaron was the only one who commented. "How much you paying?"

"How much do you want?"

"A thousand."

"Pretty steep. I could go with a wagon train, a stage, or on one of the packets, for a lot less."

"So go that way then," the man said.

Aaron smiled. "I think I prefer your way. I take it you know Texas well."

"Born and raised there. Do a little business between home and here. Trapping, gambling, trading, things like that." He took the stub of a cigar from his mouth and turned to stare at Aaron. "So tell me, mister, why do you want to go to Texas. And why does someone dressed like you," he flipped a finger under the velvet lapel of Aaron's waistcoat, "want to travel with the likes of me, rather than in a suite on one of them packets?"

Aaron began to spin the tale he'd decided on if asked. "I'm trying to find my sister. She ran away. The man she's with is from Texas. My mother is ill, maybe dying. She wants Elizabeth to come home."

"Elizabeth, huh?" The name piqued George Montrose's attention. The story sounded like a phoney.

About as phoney as the man telling it, he mused. "What's your name, mister?"

"Aaron Reynaud, of Vicksburg, Mississippi." Aaron held out his hand. George ignored it. "And your sister, her name's Elizabeth?"

"Yes."

"How do you know she's around here? Maybe she's in California. Or Boston, or anywhere else."

"She was a passenger on that packet that exploded a couple of weeks ago. She survived and made it here. With her lover. I've just discovered that they're leaving for Texas tomorrow morning. I want to follow them."

George sat back and eyed Aaron wearily. "If she's here, and you know it, why not just grab her now and take her home?"

Aaron sighed and tried to control his simmering temper. The man was asking too many damn questions. "I don't want her lover knowing I grabbed her, or that she's on her way back to Vicksburg. I don't want the heathen to return there looking for her. If I abduct her while they're on the trail, it can be made to look like Indians did it."

George nodded. "Yeah, it can be made to look like that." He downed a shot of whiskey. "Okay, Aary, I'll help you follow your sister."

"Aaron. Aaron Reynaud," Aaron said haughtily.

"Yeah."

Chapter 16

"Argh," Elizabeth groaned. Serena shook her shoulder again. "Missy, wake up. You said we had to be at that livery by four. It's nearly three-thirty now."

Elizabeth tried to burrow deeper into the covers and pull the pillow over her head. Serena grabbed it and tossed it aside. "Missy, you hear me. You get up now, or we'll have to take the boat to Eugenia's."

The word boat did it. Elizabeth sat up and tried to rub the sleep from her eyes. "What time is it?"

"I just told you. Nearly three-thirty."

Elizabeth threw back the coverlet and swung her legs over the side of the bed. "I'm hungry. Go down and get us some coffee and biscuits, would you, Serena?"

The old lady smiled. "They's right there on the table," she said, and pointed to a marble-topped end table near the settee.

"Oh, Serena, you're a dream. What would I ever do without you?"

"Well, seems to me you're pretty good at getting yourself into trouble, that's what."

Elizabeth took the cup of coffee Serena handed her and bristled mockingly. "Well, it wasn't my fault the boat exploded. Or that I got stranded on a riverbank

247

with a gunfighter, who broke his ribs and ended up being good for nothing."

"You a sassy little thing. Anyone ever tell you that?"

"Yes, you," Elizabeth laughed. "For as long as I can remember."

"Ain't done a bit of good though," Serena said, and smiled. "Still as sassy as a tart." She picked up several valises, tucking the smaller ones under her mountainous arms, and moved toward the door. "You want I should come back for the rest?"

"No, I've arranged for one of the porters to transport everything downstairs to a carriage. We've too much here to carry on our own. And I had some things delivered from the general store to the wagon already."

"More stuff?" Serena muttered. "I think you done bought out the stores here."

"I only bought what I needed, and a few things for Eugenia."

"More like a few closets full of things, if you ask me."

"I didn't," Elizabeth said, and softened the words with a sly little smile.

By the time the porter had all of Elizabeth and Serena's satchels, valises, and portmanteaus crammed into the carriage, it was ten minutes to four.

Elizabeth leaned forward in her seat toward the driver. "Please hurry," she said. "We have to be at the livery on Levee across from the Mint in ten minutes."

The man nodded and whipped the reins over the horse's rumps. They arrived at the livery eight minutes later.

Travis was standing beside one of the already loaded wagons, when Elizabeth's carriage reined in beside him. "Cutting it pretty close, aren't you, Elizabeth?"

"Sorry. It took longer to get our things out of the hotel than I expected."

"You mean there's more than what you had de-

248

livered here?" Travis asked in disbelief. He stared at her as if she were crazy.

"Well, yes. Just a bit."

"Elizabeth, these wagons can only hold so much. All that furniture and those trunks you had delivered here this morning are already loaded, and they take up just about the whole wagon. Which, I might add, is mine. I had to put some of my own stuff in Gray's wagon. I only hope he doesn't notice."

"We only have a few more things, Travis," Elizabeth said softly. "Please?"

"Damn it, Elizabeth, I . . ."

"We can still go, can't we?" She turned a worried eye to him. "I have to go, Travis. I have to."

He chuckled. "Calm down, it's okay." He waved to several men standing nearby. "Help me get these things into that last wagon, boys." The men immediately began to transfer Elizabeth's belongings from the hotel carriage to the last of the Conestoga wagons in the train. It took several tries to get it all loaded so that it left enough room in the wagon for Elizabeth to "hide" comfortably.

"I swear, I think you've got half of New Orleans in this wagon, Elizabeth."

She laughed. "Not quite half, Travis, though if there's some room left . . ."

"Forget it. Now, you and your servant—"

"Serena," Elizabeth said.

Travis nodded. "You two better get in that wagon. Gray will be here any minute. He rode out to the Fordeleaux place to get the horses he bought from them. The last thing I want right now is for him to see you here."

"What's he talking about, Missy?" Serena asked.

"Nothing, Serena, don't worry."

"You're driving?" Travis asked Serena as she

approached the front of the wagon.

She nodded.

He gave her a measured look. The fat ladies he'd seen in a traveling circus and a roadside freak show had nothing on Serena. "You ever drive a wagon before?"

"Used to help drive the wagons of cotton to the docks."

"Okay. Let me help you up." He bent over and cupped his hands together to make a stirrup. Serena lifted her skirts and placed her foot in Travis's hands, grabbed hold of the wagon's side, and hoisted her weight upward.

Travis's hands broke apart when Serena put her full weight on them. The pressure nearly pulled him from his feet, and his face rammed into Serena's hip.

Red-faced, he ordered one of the other men to get a wooden box for Serena to use as a step. It creaked under her weight, but it held. She flopped into the raised seat of the wagon, and shifted her weight around until she was comfortable. She looked down at Travis and chuckled. "B'fore he died, my man used to tell me I was woman enough for two men."

"You can say that again," Travis mumbled, still flexing his sore fingers. "All right, Elizabeth, your turn," Travis said. "I left a pretty good space just behind the seat where Serena is. You climb in there, and keep that pretty little face of yours down. Gray won't notice you unless you stick it out in the open. Understand?"

"I understand," she said, and followed in Serena's footsteps. She began to climb over the seat, caught the toe of her shoe on the seat's short back, and nearly fell on her face into the mountain of trunks, furniture, and other stuff crammed into the wagon. She saved herself, and some dignity, by grabbing the back of a washstand she'd bought for Eugenia.

250

"Are you all right?" Travis asked, stepping onto one of the wheel's wooden spokes and peering over the seat at her.

"I'm fine. I just tripped, that's all. How long will it take us to get to Texas?"

"Longer than you want to hear. I'll tell you when you can come out. If ever. Till then you stay put."

The sound of hoofbeats drew Travis's attention. "Gray's back," he said, and jumped to the ground.

"How many horses did he buy?" Elizabeth muttered, peeking around the corner of the wagon seat to get a look at the approaching animals, whose hoofbeats sounded like a roll of thunder against the otherwise quiet early morning. She counted a dozen, and they were all magnificent animals. But one in particular caught her eye: a chestnut mare whose flaxen mane and tail resembled long, snowy white strands of silk.

They began to pass the wagon and Elizabeth ducked down out of sight, only a second before Gray neared. He reined his mount up beside Serena and looked up at her. A frown creased his brow. "Who are you?" he asked, his tone a brittle rumble.

"She's driving my wagon," Travis said, walking up to them quickly. "Serena, this is Gray Cantrelle."

Serena smiled and nodded.

"I met Serena a couple of days ago. She has family in Texas, but had no way to get there. I figured she could drive my rig."

Gray shrugged. "I had some trouble back at the hotel just after you left."

"Trouble?" Travis echoed. "Like what?"

"Jason's daddy had a couple of guys waiting for me, when I made to leave the hotel."

"Did they get him?"

Gray smiled. "You know better than that, Trav. Hell no, they didn't get him, cause he wasn't there

251

to get." Gray twisted in his saddle. "Jason, come up here."

The boy came around the end of the wagon, mounted on a horse that wasn't much bigger than a pony. He beamed proudly.

"I'd sent him down to the back of the hotel. Figured if Sorens was looking for the kid, he'd make his move before we left New Orleans. This morning was his last chance."

Travis nodded. "I should have brought him here with me earlier. Will he try again?"

Gray shook his head. "When he wakes up? I don't think so." he chuckled softly at Travis's puzzlement. "His jaw kind of got in the way of my fist. Anyway, when he does wake up, he'll find five hundred dollars in his pocket. That should be more than enough for this little guy." He smiled down at Jason. "Ready?"

"Yes, massuh."

Gray jerked his horse to a stop even before the animal had made a move to go. "Jason, I'm not your master, you hear? I'm not anyone's master. I paid Sorens off so he'd leave you alone. You can work for me, and I'll pay you, just like anyone else. You got that?"

The boy nodded, looking slightly confused and chagrined, but his dark eyes shone with excitement.

Elizabeth watched from beneath Serena's seat and, in spite of herself, felt a swelling of pride for what Gray had done. Very few men would take the chance of harboring a runaway slave, even a child, and even fewer would take the chances Gray had taken to ensure that the boy wasn't returned to the master he'd fled.

Gray stood in his stirrups and looked around at the others. "Everyone ready to go?"

A dozen heads nodded.

"Then what are we waiting for? Let's move it out. It's

probably going to take us a couple of hours just to cross the river."

Elizabeth's eyes widened. Cross the river? She hadn't thought of that. How were they going to cross the river? By boat? Her fingers clenched tightly, and her nails dug into the palms of her hands. "Oh, god, a boat," she whispered raggedly.

"Calm down, honey," Serena said over her shoulder. "Everything'll be all right." She snapped the reins over the rumps of the team of oxen hitched to the wagon, and the bulky animals began to move forward. The wagon creaked into motion.

An hour later the train was at Chalmette, just south of the city of New Orleans, and at the river's edge. Gray rode down the line, pausing to talk to the driver of each wagon. He reined in next to Serena, whose wagon was last in line. "We're taking a raft across, one at a time. When it redocks for you, just head your team toward it nice and slow. You shouldn't have any trouble at all."

Serena nodded. Elizabeth shuddered. She wanted to scream, to tell him she couldn't go on the raft, that she knew, she just knew, it was going to sink. Instead, she wrapped her arms around her legs and gripped them tightly, buried her head, and nearly bit her tongue off when she clamped her teeth tightly together.

The wagon remained still for what seemed a long time; then just when Elizabeth had begun to relax a little, Serena snapped the reins and yelled for the oxen to move. Elizabeth almost jumped out of her skin. She scrambled to her knees, gripped the back of the wagon seat, and peeked through the small slat of its back. She could see the river, the raft, and Gray. He was sitting astride his horse at the edge of the water, waiting for them. She sank back down in the wagon. "Oh, god," she whispered frantically, "Oh, god, oh, god, oh, god."

The first two oxen stepped onto the raft. It dipped in

the water, then bounced back up. The second pair of oxen stepped on, followed by the wagon. Its huge iron-rimmed wooden wheels rolled onto the raft, and the flat barge dipped again. The wagon lunged forward and swayed from side to side. The wagon creaked, the mountain of furniture shook, and Elizabeth trembled violently. Serena swore loudly, and Elizabeth clamped her hands over her mouth to prevent the scream bursting from her throat to shatter the air. The rear wheels of the wagon rolled onto the raft, and after a few seconds of swaying and rolling, both raft and wagon sat still in the water.

Gray rode onto the raft and moved up beside the oxen. "Okay, Joe, let's go," he said to the man who operated the raft as a ferry service. A rope was untied, and the raft began to drift out into the river. Two men standing beside the wagon began to pull on another rope that stretched from one side of the river to the other. A third man had attached a keel to the rear of the raft, and was attempting to keep it straight in the water.

Fifteen minutes later the raft hit the western shore of the Mississippi. Gray grabbed hold of the two lead oxens yokes and led them and the wagon back onto land.

"Why, that weren't nothing," Serena said.

Elizabeth tried to stop her body from trembling. "Easy for you to say," she muttered. She felt like she'd left her heart and stomach somewhere back there in the middle of the river.

Her fit of panic had worn her out, and for the next few hours, as the wagons passed over endless acres of flat Louisiana plains and skirted around murky bayous, Elizabeth, huddled in a small ball behind Serena's seat, slept soundly.

* * *

"Pull them up," Gray yelled, riding up and down the line of wagons. "We're going to stop for an hour and have supper."

Serena looked up at the sun. "It's about time," she grumbled. "Well after noon, if you ask me. Been driving for seven or eight hours without a break."

"How you doing, Serena?" Travis said, reining his horse up next to the wagon.

"Well, sir, my body feels like every bone done gone stiff. Good thing I got all this padding back here," she slapped the side of her rear end with her hand, "or I'd be one sorry sore." She laughed heartily at her own comment.

Travis leaned forward in the saddle and dropped his voice to a whisper. "How's Elizabeth holding up?"

"Ain't heard a peep out of her since we crossed the river. Think it scared her so bad, she's gonna sleep till we get to Sweetbriar."

He settled back in his saddle. "I'm sorry about that, but there wasn't any other way. Don't let anyone see you giving her food, Serena. We can't risk Gray seeing her yet."

"How come? What's going on?" Serena asked, puzzled.

"She didn't tell you?"

Serena shook her head. "Keeps saying it ain't nothing. I figure if it ain't nothing, why's she hiding down there like a scared rabbit?"

He glanced in both directions before answering, and when he did, his voice was so low, Serena had to lean over and strain to hear him. "She and Gray met on the riverboat before it exploded. They were stranded on the bank together for days. I think they kind of took to each other, you know?"

Serena nodded. "So what's wrong?"

"I don't know. What I do know is that whenever they

255

get together, sparks fly, and they're not always the good kind, if you get my meaning."

Serena chuckled. "I get it. He an independent cuss who got a bad temper, too, huh?"

"The worst," Travis said. "So keep her out of sight until I say it's okay, which might not be until we get to San Antonio, if his mood doesn't improve."

Serena laughed heartily and flicked the reins over the oxen's rumps.

Lunch consisted of biscuits, some dried beef, and a cold can of beans. All provided by Travis, since Elizabeth had not thought about providing food for herself and Serena. Luckily, he had.

Serena slipped a tin plate in to her. "Eat quick, Missy, we ain't got much time. Your man's already grumbling about pulling out, and we ain't been here but ten minutes."

"He's not *my* man," Elizabeth said irritably, and took the plate. She stared at the food. "Is this it? This is supposed to be supper?"

Serena didn't answer.

Elizabeth munched on the biscuit. "I have to . . . to relieve myself."

"You get out of that wagon now, and he's gonna see you for sure."

"I have to relieve myself," Elizabeth said with a touch of anger. "Go tell Travis to distract him."

Serena nodded and waddled off toward Travis, who was talking to one of the drivers a couple of wagons ahead. Elizabeth watched from her vantage point behind the wagon seat, while Travis left Serena's side and moved to talk to Gray. A minute later the two men turned and headed toward the front of the wagon train.

Elizabeth scrambled over the seat and made for a

small clump of nearby bushes. She was just repositioning her skirts about her when she caught a movement out of the corner of her eye. She jerked around quickly and clamped a hand over her mouth to prevent the scream that tried to burst from her throat. A wash of relief invaded her limbs and she chuckled in relief at the sight of a small armadillo rustling about in the brush. She hurried back to the wagon, looking in the direction Gray had gone, to make sure he wasn't returning.

"Hurry up, Missy, and get up in that wagon b'fore that man of yours spots you and sends us back to New Orleans."

"I told you, he's *not* my man," Elizabeth snapped, and scrambled over the wagon seat to her hideaway.

"Head them out," Gray called, just as Elizabeth settled herself in the wagon and Serena began to climb up onto the seat.

The afternoon proved to be just as boring and endless as the morning had been. The scenery remained flat, colorless, and monotonous. The air remained hot and humid, and Elizabeth's little spot in the wagon became more and more uncomfortable. She shifted position endlessly, bending this leg, stretching that one, leaning on one arm, raising the other. She sat up, laid down, tried her side, nestled on her knees. Nothing worked. She was bored, and getting more bored with each passing second. She was stiff and getting stiffer, and she was hungry.

They'd been on the trail for four hours since their stop for supper, when she heard Gray address Serena. Elizabeth scrunched down lower in her spot, desperately trying to become invisible.

"What's the problem back here, Serena? Why is your team dragging so far behind the others?"

Serena shrugged. "Don't know, sir. I'll speed them up, though."

"You do that. We can't afford for the others to slow down, just so you can keep up." He turned his horse and rode back toward the main body of the train.

Nothing had gone right since they'd left New Orleans. Gray reached up and removed the Stetson, wiped his forehead with the sleeve of his shirt and resettled the hat back on his head. It had been one thing after another. Broken wheels, inexperienced drivers, a fallen tree across their intended road, and now this damn woman who couldn't seem to keep her wagon in tow with the others. But that wasn't the worst of it. And it wasn't what was really turning his mood into a black thundercloud that raged over everyone he came into contact with. It was the image of a blond, blue-eyed vixen that would not leave his mind. No matter what he did, no matter what he told himself, how he justified leaving her, it didn't work. He still felt like a snake. And he felt empty. So damned empty.

Elizabeth watched Gray ride away. "Why didn't he just suggest you get down there and hitch yourself to the oxen, so we could go faster?" she snapped sarcastically.

Serena snapped the reins over the oxen's rumps. She didn't respond to the comment, which Elizabeth found strange. Serena always had a laugh or a taunting return whenever Elizabeth gave an opinion on something. "What's wrong, Serena?" she asked, suddenly worried.

"He's right, missy. We been falling behind the others a little more every hour. By nightfall, we'll be so far back, we won't even be able to see them."

Elizabeth looked at the sky. The sun was already quickly sinking from sight. A flash of panic shot through Elizabeth. "We can't lose them, Serena. We'll be lost out here."

*　　　*　　　*

By seven o'clock the sky had turned dusky, the sun only minutes away from slipping below the horizon and leaving the earth enveloped in the black womb of night. Elizabeth peered over Serena's shoulder. Gray had been back to the wagon twice since his first warning. Each subsequent warning had been a bit sterner than the one before it.

Half an hour later a thin sliver of moon offered little light, and she could barely make out the wagon in front of them. "We've fallen awfully far behind," Elizabeth said.

The comment needed no response, and Serena did not give one.

She heard the sound of hooves beating against the hard ground before she saw his shadow emerge from the darkness. His eyes were black with anger, and his features were set hard. Elizabeth could almost feel Gray's fury over the delay their oxen were causing the rest of the train. The others had obviously moved slower that afternoon, so as not to lose them.

"All right, Serena, I didn't want it to come to this, but it has. I need to know what in the hell you've got loaded into that wagon of yours?" His words were a deep, thundering snarl that sent a shiver of apprehension tripping up Elizabeth's spine.

In a moment of stark horror, she scurried to burrow into her tiny space and pull as much furniture and bric-a-brac on top of herself as she could. In the mood Gray was in, seeing her in the wagon would only turn him into a raging bull, and she had absolutely no desire to face that.

Gray dismounted and walked around to the back of the wagon. Serena hurried to follow. Travis rode up, realized what was about to happen, and his eyes rolled heavenward. He approached Gray. "What's the matter?"

"I don't know. That's what I'm about to find out."
He unlatched the rear gate, and it fell open with a loud
thunk. "Serena can't seem to keep your wagon at pace
with the others, and I have a suspicion it has nothing to
do with her ability as a driver."

Travis dismounted quickly. "Why don't you let me
handle this? The others are preparing to make camp for
the night, and could use your help. I'll check this out
while you go up and get them organized."

Gray looked at Travis in a combination of suspicion
and weariness. "This is your wagon, Trav. Something
in here you don't want me to see?"

Travis felt his stomach turn over and plummet
downward. It didn't stop its spiraling descent until it
settled into the tips of his toes. He swallowed hard and
tried to smile. It resembled more of a pain-filled
grimace. "Nah, I just thought, well, since it is my
wagon, I'd see what the trouble is. No need you
bothering yourself."

"It's no bother." Gray turned and—in a move so
swift no one saw it coming—jumped up into the
wagon.

Elizabeth felt the thud of his boots on the plank
flooring, felt the wagon shift under his weight, and
cringed. Oh, god, he was going to find her. He was
going to put her and Serena off the wagon train. What
would they do? Where would they go? She rammed a
knuckle into her mouth to keep from making any
sound.

"So, you keeping a lady love tucked away somewhere that I don't know about, Trav?" Gray said, and
handed him a bolt of red satin fabric.

Travis looked suddenly ill. "It . . . it's for your
mother."

"And this one?" Gray asked. He handed Travis a bolt
of black velvet.

"For Dana."

"And this one? And these two?" He handed three more bolts of cloth to Travis. He picked up a hat box, looked in it, and tossed it out onto the ground. He followed the same procedure with two more hat boxes, then several shoe boxes, a valise of ladies' undergarments, and a box of gloves. He turned and, legs spread wide, hands clenched into fists and rammed onto his hips, glared down at Travis. "Who are you courting, Trav, my mother, my sister, or every woman in the country?" he sneered, his tone dripping with ridicule.

Travis groaned weakly. "Listen, Gray, it's not what you th—"

"Damn right it's not." He turned back into the wagon, picked up a ladies' rocker, its cushion covered with a delicate petit point, and threw it out onto the ground. A marble-topped pedestal table quickly followed, then a portmanteau, and a small étagère.

Elizabeth couldn't take anymore. He was a beast, an absolute beast, and she wasn't going to hide from him any longer. He could send her away from the wagon train if he wanted, but first she'd have her say. She jumped to her feet. "You stop that, Grayson Cantrelle. You just stop that right now."

Shocked at hearing her voice, Gray whirled around and stared into the dark interior of the wagon. "Elizabeth?"

Chapter 17

"Yes, it's me, you brute!" Elizabeth snapped. In a flurry of skirts and temper, she scrambled over the wagon's front seat, jumped to the ground, and stalked around the wagon until she came to where Gray stood on the gate. He towered over her like a giant, his eyes ablaze, face flushed, hands still rammed on his hips. She waggled a finger at him. "You're a beast, Grayson Cantrelle, nothing but a beast. Yelling at poor Serena and Travis like that."

Suddenly the black rage that had darkened Gray's eyes disappeared, the frown faded, and the glower that had pulled his lips downward turned to a smile. When he'd heard her voice, he couldn't believe it was her. But in the brief flash of a second, when she'd actually stepped in front of him, his world, a world that had enveloped him in gloom and despondency all day, had swiftly righted itself. The emptiness that had been gnawing at him abruptly disappeared, and though it was night, it seemed to Gray that the sun was shining brightly.

He jumped down from the gate.

Startled at the abrupt move, Elizabeth squeaked and scurried behind Serena. She cautiously peered around the big woman's girth.

Travis breathed a sigh of relief. Their long years of friendship had allowed him intimate knowledge of Gray's moods and temperment. He sensed that the firestorm of rage that had spewed from Gray only moments before was now gone.

"What are you doing here, Elizabeth?" Gray asked finally, wanting nothing more than to pull her into his arms and cover her face with kisses.

His tone was deep, warm, a velvety drawl that reached out to Elizabeth and caressed her frazzled nerves. Reassured that he was not going to pounce on her, she released her death grip on Serena's arm, straightened, and stepped out from behind the servant. "We needed transport to my sister's in Sweetbriar, and Travis was kind enough to allow us the use of his wagon." She glanced quickly at Travis and realized her ploy of being Gray's wife had just been revealed as a lie. A niggling of guilt gnawed at her conscience, but she ignored it. What did it matter now anyway? They'd traveled too far for Gray to send her back.

Gray's eyes raked over her from head to foot. God, but he wanted her. Every nerve in his body was on fire, every cell alive with need. His muscles felt as if they were straining, throbbing with the desire to reach out to her, and his heart was running rampant in his chest. "Why didn't you tell me you wanted to join the wagon train?"

"I . . . . I thought you'd say no."

"Why?"

She shrugged. She'd be damned if she would admit in front of Travis and Serena, and to Gray himself, that she'd been miserable when he'd said goodbye to her. And that she'd plunged into the depths of despair, when she'd watched him spend almost the entire evening of the soiree wrapped around Theresa Fordeleaux's finger. After that one dance at the soiree, and the heated words that had followed it, he had ignored Elizabeth for the remainder of the evening. He didn't care a fig about her, and she had not been about to ask him to allow her to travel on his precious wagon train.

Travis began picking up the bolts of cloth and furniture and putting them back into the wagon. The movement drew Gray's attention. "What the hell is all this stuff in your wagon?" he asked Travis.

"I . . . uh, I mean . . ."

"It's mine," Elizabeth said softly. "I'm taking a few things to Eu—"

Gray spun back around to face Elizabeth. "Yours? All of this is yours?" His eyes blazed anew. Gone was the soft drawl and look of longing that had given her momentary hope. Instead the fire of outrage turned his handsome face to an angry glower.

"Yes," Elizabeth snapped back, his anger sparking her own. "So what? I asked Travis for a wagon so that I could get to my sister's, and he graciously consented to let me use his. *He's* a gentleman, which is more than I can say for you." She looked around at her things strewn all over the ground. This is not how she had pictured Gray would react when he found out she was on the wagon train. For some nonsensical reason even she did not understand, she'd hoped he'd be happy to see her. She looked at a bolt of white lace lying on the ground several feet away. One end of it was smeared with dirt. The sight banished her silly daydream and brought forth the return of her indignation at his actions. "Just look what you've done, Grayson Cantrelle. No gentleman ever would do—"

"How many times have I told you, Elizabeth?"

She looked at him, clearly puzzled.

"I'm not a gentleman."

"That is painfully obvious."

Gray tore his gaze from hers. "Travis, help me

264

unload some more of this stuff. We'll leave it here for the Indians. If they can't figure out how to use it, they'll torch it to keep themselves warm."

"Leave it?" Elizabeth gasped.

Gray jumped back up into the wagon. "Yes, leave it." He threw out another of her trunks. "It's no wonder these poor animals can't keep pace with the rest of the wagons." A shaving stand flew from within the wagon to crash at Serena's feet. "You've got a damn houseload of stuff packed in here." The drawers of a washstand tumbled off of the wagon's gate.

"Grayson!" Elizabeth screamed.

"I should have known this was your stuff. Damn, where's my brain? The minute I saw your driver, the minute those oxen started getting winded, and this wagon began falling behind, I should have known it was you." He threw out two small valises and another bolt of cloth.

"Grayson, stop it," she yelled, and nimbly dodged a box of stockings that careened toward her from within the wagon.

"Of all the asinine things to do, Travis! I should string you up for this." He had been so damned happy to see her he'd momentarily forgotten all the reasons he knew they were wrong for each other, the reasons why he refused to propose to her even though his guilt was eating him alive, while his desire for her was creating a constant conflagration within his body.

"He didn't do anything wrong," Elizabeth shrieked. She made a grab at another bolt of white lace that flew over her head. She missed and it crashed to the ground, causing a small cloud of dust to rise.

"I ought to tan your hides for this. Both of you," Gray snarled.

Elizabeth turned to Travis. "Make him stop, Travis," she screamed. "Please. He's ruining everything."

265

Travis jumped up into the wagon and grabbed Gray's shoulder. "Come on, Gray, it's—"

Gray shrugged him off and picked up another valise.

"Damn it, Gray, stop this." Travis jerked on Gray's shoulder. Gray whirled. His arm stretched back with lightning speed and shot forward. His fist connected loudly with Travis's jaw. Travis stumbled into the pile of furniture that surrounded him, but quickly bolted back to his feet. His own fist buried itself into Gray's stomach. He lurched, lost his breath, and fell backward out of the wagon. He landed on the ground at Elizabeth's feet.

She glared down at him. "I hate you, Grayson Cantrelle. I swear, I hate you."

Gray struggled to his feet and brushed himself off. Her words stung a part of him he tried desperately to deny. He looked long and hard at her, and in her eyes he saw a reflection of himself, the way she saw him: hard, cruel, taking what he had no right to take, and giving nothing in return. It didn't make him like himself any more, but it convinced him he'd been right all along. They were wrong for each other. Elizabeth needed a gentleman, someone who would take her to exotic places, make her the mistress of a grand plantation with hundreds of servants to see to her every need, and lavish her with the finest of things. And that was not him. That was not his life. "Then I guess there's nothing left for us to say to each other, is there, Elizabeth?" He turned to Travis. "I guess the Indians are out of luck this time. Help me get some of this stuff loaded onto the other wagons. We'll distribute everything as best we can, and hopefully the added weight won't result in an additional damn week in getting to San Antone."

"Are we on a schedule, Mr. Cantrelle?" Elizabeth sneered. "Are we all charged extra, if we make you late?"

"Would it make any difference to you, if we were on a schedule?"

Serena wrapped a comforting arm around Elizabeth's shoulders and drew her toward the front of the wagon. "Come on, Missy, I think you done said enough for one day."

"He's a beast, Serena. A no-good blackguard with no feelings, no manners, and—" She stopped and looked back at Gray. "What's a gunfighter and a gambler doing heading a wagon train, anyway? Where are they going? And what about those horses?" She looked at Serena quickly. "Do you think he stole them, Serena? From Theresa's father? Maybe that's why he's in such a hurry. Maybe there's a posse after him." But for some reason, even as she said it, she couldn't bring herself to believe that Gray was a thief. A man who lived by his gun, yes—his temperament and attire attested to that—but he wasn't a thief.

"I don't think nothing, Missy. All we got to worry about is getting to Sweetbriar and finding Eugenia. That man ain't gonna throw away your things, and you should be awful thankful for that. Now," she urged Elizabeth forward, "let's get this wagon caught up to the others, build us a fire, and get something to eat. Then maybe I can lay this weary old body of mine down and get a little rest."

Aaron saw the glow of the campfires in the distance, small spots of flickering orange against the tenebrous sky and lanscape.

"They've settled in for the night," George said, "which is exactly what I intend to do. Right now."

"I want to get closer," Aaron said.

"You want them to know you're here? That you're following them?"

"No."

"Then do as I say. That's what you're paying me for. Get down and help me make camp."

Aaron grumbled to himself as he dismounted, tossed his saddlebags to the ground, and began to unsaddle his horse. He didn't like being ordered about, but he had no choice. When it came to following someone, and surviving out in the middle of nowhere, he knew nothing.

"Aaron, let's forget this and go back," Damien implored for the hundredth time that day. "My jaw hurts."

"Shut up," George ordered, "and get down."

"We're not going back," Aaron said. "Not until we get Elizabeth. That little . . ." he glanced at George. "We have to get her, that's all."

"I don't care about Elizabeth," Damien whined. He slid from his saddle and thumped to the ground. "Anyway, there's lots of other women. Regis told me about how he's sweet-talked almost every woman in Washington. And you could do the same. He even had one believing he was going to marry her." Damien snickered. "She sure found out different though, when she told him she was carrying his child."

"You do want Jason back though, don't you?"

"Well, yes, but—"

"Then shut up like George said, and make camp."

Aaron threw his saddle on the ground. "What kind of food do we have, George? I'm hungry."

"Beans and jerky."

"Beans and jerky? That's all?"

"You want steak, you shoulda stayed in New Orleans."

Aaron tethered his horse to a small myrtle tree. "I'll get some wood for a fire."

"Can't make a fire."

"What? What do you mean, we can't make a fire? Why not? In an hour or so it's going to be cold as hell out here. And how are we going to heat the food, if we don't build a fire?"

George nodded his head toward the wagon train. "They'll see it, get curious, and come looking to see who we are. If not them, then the Indians."

"Indians? There's Indians out here?" Damien squawked. "You didn't tell me that."

"Figured you knew."

"Are they—" Aaron gulped hard and tried not to show his fear. "Are they, I mean, are the savages dangerous?"

George spread his bedroll and lay down on top of it. "Not if you don't mind dying."

Aaron sat down next to George. "You're not going to go to sleep, are you? What about those savages? Won't they sneak up on us in the dark?"

"They'll scalp us. That's what they do," Damien said, a hint of hysteria in his voice. "They'll sneak up on us while we're sleeping, and scalp us."

"Relax," George said from beneath his hat. "Indians don't like to fight after the sun goes down. They think if one of their braves dies at night, his spirit might not find its way to the happy hunting ground."

"Oh." Aaron lay down, though his body refused to relax.

"Aaron, maybe we should forget this whole thing and just go back to New Orleans," Damien suggested.

Aaron ignored him. He chewed on the jerky, which tasted more like dried leather, and stared up at the sky. This was all Elizabeth's fault, his being out here. Just because she'd seen him in bed with Francine, she'd run off, left him virtually jilted at the altar. Totally humiliating, that's what it had been. He'd been bedding Francine, one of the Reynaud slaves, for years. Why should he stop, just because he was marrying Elizabeth? Anyway, she was no better than he was. Worse, in fact. She had given herself to that cowboy.

A smile curved Aaron's lips, but there was no warmth to the gesture, only icy coldness. He rolled to look at George. "I want to do it tonight."

George sat up and spit the cigar from his mouth. "You want to what?"

"Grab her tonight." He straightened, excited now with his idea. "I don't want to wait any longer."

"Oh, no," Damien moaned.

George slapped open the flap of his saddlebag and pulled out a bottle of whiskey. He jerked out the cork, lifted the bottle to his lips, and took a long swallow. Lowering it, he wiped his mouth with the back of his hand and offered the bottle to Aaron.

Aaron shook his head. "What do you say, George? Tonight?"

George didn't offer the bottle to Damien. "Yeah," he said to Aaron, "tonight. Why not?" He lifted the bottle to his lips again and took another long slug of the dark liquor. He'd help Aaron Reynaud snatch his "sister" from the wagon train, and then he'd enact his own revenge on her. He almost snickered in delight at his good fortune. Aaron didn't know George was also a survivor of the *River Belle*'s explosion. That had been one little detail of his background George had decided to keep to himself. At least for now. He'd been thrown into the river when the boilers had burst and torn the boat to smithereens. It had only been sheer luck that he'd drifted, unconscious, to the shore. His brother, Zachary, hadn't been so lucky. He'd never made it off the *Belle*. He would have, if George had been conscious. If that little hellcat hadn't knocked him senseless just seconds before the explosion. Then he'd have been able to help his brother, to save him. It was all her fault Zachary was dead, and George had every intention of making her pay. But first, he'd get himself a little pleasure from her. After all, she'd given it to the cowboy, why not him? She owed him, after nearly battering his brains in and killing his brother.

Aaron jumped to his feet and began to pace in the darkness. Memory of Elizabeth's desertion filled him with anger, and the thought of her giving her body to another man stoked his thirst for revenge. He felt his flesh begin to burn from want of her, and felt himself turn hard with the hunger of his need. He thought of the man he'd seen at the soiree with Elizabeth, the man he knew she had given herself to. Grayson Cantrelle. Theresa had told him the man's name when he'd pretended to be puzzled over where he'd seen him before. She said he owned a ranch near San Antonio.

Aaron fumed. A rancher. Elizabeth had given herself to a lowly cow drover. He probably owned a handful of cows and lived in a mud hovel. Most likely had a squaw to fill his needs when he was home. Aaron pulled his hand gun from his saddlebag. He released the barrel and spun the cylinder. Fully loaded. Maybe, if the cowboy was foolish enough to try and save Elizabeth, Aaron would have the opportunity to put a bullet between the man's eyes. Serve him right for taking what had rightfully belonged to Aaron.

Then again, a shot would alert the entire wagon train. They might not take too kindly to their guide being killed. Aaron sighed. Better to play it safe. Grab Elizabeth and get out as quietly as possible, hopefully with no one the wiser until it was too late.

He chuckled softly. Wouldn't she be surprised to find herself once again in Aaron's loving arms.

Chapter 18

Serena's snores seemed to fill the air. If Elizabeth hadn't known better, she would have thought a train was approaching and about to roll over her. She stared up at the bottom of the wagon. She couldn't sleep. The camp was quiet. Some people had bedded down for the night, while others remained seated around their fires, talking, and still others were busying themselves checking over their gear.

She rolled onto her side and lay the side of her head on her bent arm. The wagons had been pulled into a circle. Gray and Travis stood in the center of the camp, engaged in conversation with several other men. Elizabeth stared at Gray, willing him to look at her. He proved oblivious to her silent beckoning, and she finally gave up. With a melancholy sigh she lay back down and closed her eyes. The past, with all its hurts and anguish, all its ghosts, loomed forth in her mind to plague her, as they so often had in the last few weeks. With her father's sudden death, everything in her life had changed. She'd had no interest in marrying Aaron before that, not really. Oh, they'd been betrothed, but Elizabeth had been in no hurry to consummate the arrangement. However, her father's death had left her no choice. The plantation had been sold only days before to cover his gambling debts, and although Elizabeth had been left with plenty of money because of her grandfather's trust fund, society frowned on a young woman living alone. It was either marry Aaron or go to live with her sister in Texas. She'd chosen the former.

Elizabeth almost laughed. And now she was on her way to Eugenia's anyway, and still unmarried.

But no longer an innocent.

She opened her eyes and shook her head to rid her conscience of that little devil within her, that always reminded her of things she didn't want to be reminded of.

With a groan of frustration, Elizabeth bunched up the blanket she was using as a pillow, and pummeled it with her fist. No matter what she thought of, no matter in which direction she tried to force her mind, it always ended up on the same topic: Grayson Cantrelle. He had invaded her life, stormed over her emotions like a hurricane; and as its destructive force conquered the land and wreaked havoc on it, he had conquered her resistance and bent her to his will. Then he had deserted her. Tossed her aside with a thank you ma'am and a curt goodbye. Damn him. He had virtually made her his prisoner, taken her to a region of unchartered passion like she'd never known existed, unleashed emotions within her she hadn't realized possible, and then he'd turned his back on her.

But why? That was the question which kept haunting her. It refused to go away and leave her in peace. Why had he walked away from her that night? And thereafter, every time he began to act as if he cared about her, it was as if, the moment he realized it, he threw a barrier up between them, solid and impenetrable. Why?

273

Serena suddenly snorted loudly and her body shuddered. Elizabeth jumped and emitted a faint squeak, startled. She sat up and scooted out from beneath the wagon, where Serena had made a bed for them. It was no use. Her own body was exhausted and sore from being crammed into that tiny space behind the wagon seat all day, but she was not sleepy. There was nothing to drink but water, so making herself a glass of warm milk was out of the question, and she didn't want coffee. She'd take a walk. Grabbing a shawl from the wagon, Elizabeth wrapped it around her shoulders. She glanced toward the center of the camp. Travis was still there, talking with the other men, but Gray was nowhere about.

Elizabeth hugged the shawl to herself and turned toward the end of the wagon. She paused by its gate and looked out at the prairie landscape. A faint sprinkle of moonlight touched the land, creating spots of light and dark on the softly rolling earth, and making it only slightly discernible from the black sky. The horizon was nothing more than a ragged line of inky gray against a Cimmerian sky, sprinkled with stars that reminded her of tiny chips of sparkling, bright diamonds.

She walked into the darkness, into the quiet, tranquil peace of the plains. They had left behind the grand plantations with their acres of cotton, sugar cane, and tobacco plants. They'd left behind the bayous, with their tall cypresses mired in the murky waters, and ancient oaks draped with dripping curtains of Spanish moss. Now the land stretched out in endless plains of tall, wild grasses and scraggly trees.

"You shouldn't be out here," a deep voice said from behind her.

She recognized it instantly, and stiffened, waiting for him to admonish her.

"I'll see you back to your wagon," Gray said instead.

She turned to brush past him, but his hand shot out and steely fingers gripped her arm, holding her still and preventing her escape. She looked up at him and instantly became caught in the whirling vortex of his eyes, in those dark pools that could convey a blistering heat of passion, a cool, raking contempt, or a cold, nipping frost of displeasure. "I thought we had nothing left to say to one another," she managed, after a few long seconds.

"Maybe I was wrong," Gray said. "I was rough on you this afternoon, maybe too much. I shouldn't have been. You had no way of knowing all those little luxuries you brought would be too heavy for one wagon."

"Little luxuries," she echoed. Her temper flared. Who was he to damn her for wanting nice things? She knew what it was to go without, and she didn't like it. She wasn't like him. He obviously liked having only his gun and his clothes, and maybe a horse. But then, he was a gunfighter. A man whose life consisted of owning little, giving nothing, and never staying in one spot. That wasn't the kind of life she envisioned for herself. Suddenly she wanted to hurt him. To make him feel as miserable as he'd made her. He had awakened emotions in her that had never before blossomed, and she didn't know how to control them. She wanted to kiss him, and she wanted to slap him, and the neverending war of emotion only served to fuel her anger. "If that is your idea of an apology, Mr. Cantrelle," she said haughtily, "perhaps you'd better practice a bit before you offer your next one."

He released her arm and gave her a sharp look. "There won't be a next one," he drawled.

She shrugged. "Then I guess, as you said, we haven't anything left to say to one another except . . ." she smiled wickedly, feeling smug, "goodnight."

Gray watched her flounce her way back to the wagon and scoot under it to her bedroll. Damn if that little minx didn't sorely try his patience. And his libido. He'd been trying for days to rid his mind of the memory of her, to force his body to get over its gnawing hunger to possess her again. It hadn't worked in New Orleans, but he figured that was because every time he turned around, she seemed to be there. He'd looked forward to hitting the trail to Texas. That, he'd decided, would make him forget, would allow him to put all thought of her behind him.

"And now she shows up here," he muttered in disgust. He kicked the heel of his boot in the dirt and walked back toward his own wagon, on the opposite side of the camp from Elizabeth's. He settled down on the blanket spread beside the wagon's rear wheel, and leaned back on the wooden spokes. But he couldn't keep his gaze from straying toward her wagon, to the dark, unfathomable spot beneath it where he knew she lay. Of all the women in the world, he had to get stranded on that riverbank with Elizabeth Devlin, a spoiled, pampered, self-centered, little rich girl who couldn't think of anyone but herself and her stupid, inane luxuries. She irritated the hell out of him, her feistiness and independence were enough to drive a man crazy, and her obsession with "things" was annoying, to say the least, but she held an attraction for him like no other woman ever had.

Gray pushed his hat forward with a muted growl and closed his eyes. It was time to forget about Elizabeth and get some sleep. They had a long day ahead of them tomorrow, and a rough trail. He needed his rest and strength.

An hour later he was still begging sleep to allow him entry to its infinite darkness, to soothe his body and

276

allow his mind to rest. And it denied him.

"Why didn't you shoot him?" Aaron said, his voice a snarling whisper of impatience and frustration.

"You want every damn yokel on that wagon train after us?" George snapped. "You'll get your precious Elizabeth, but I ain't getting myself shot to get her." He rolled over, snuggling his shoulder against the saddle he was using as a headrest. "Now get some sleep."

"I'm cold," Damien whined.

The next morning Elizabeth awoke to the sound of a very gruff voice filling the air.

"Wake it up, people, we're moving out in twenty minutes."

She stared through sleep-filled eyes at Gray, who stood in the center of the camp. Twenty minutes? Had the man lost his mind completely? With a groan she lay back down.

"Come on, Missy, you heard him," Serena said, nudging Elizabeth's foot. "Twenty minutes. I don't want no more trouble from that man, so you'd best be getting yourself up."

Elizabeth crawled out from under the wagon. "It's barely light out," she said, looking at the sun that had just, only a few minutes before, peeked over the horizon. A warm haze of yellow bathed the landscape, turned the white canvas tops of the Conestoga wagons a soft amber, and glistened off the pots warming over the campfires. She stood and stretched her arms out wide. "How much farther do you think we have to go, Serena?" She took the cup of coffee Serena handed her.

"According to Mr. Travis, it's a lot farther to San Antone than you want to know."

Elizabeth groaned softly and sipped on the coffee. She wasn't really hungry, but she forced herself to eat the biscuits and grits Serena had prepared. Heaven only knew when Gray would allow them to stop for their noonday meal.

The second day proved as boring and grueling as the first. Grayson stayed well away from her wagon, and Travis visited them only once, during their midday stop.

By nightfall, Elizabeth was more than ready for sleep. In fact, she was so ready, she skipped dinner to crawl under the wagon and snuggle into her bedroll. Having barely gotten a few hours' sleep the night before, she felt the need to make up for what she'd missed. Her body finally cried out for nothing more than rest, and her mind was so dull from exhaustion that Grayson Cantrelle was the last thing it wanted to dwell on. Nevertheless, his image haunted her dreams.

The third day they approached the Sabine River. The sun blazed down mercilessly, its hot, humid rays baking the land and everything and everyone on it. The grasses seemed to wilt under the onslaught, as did Elizabeth. She took off her hoop-cage. Next came her petticoats. She removed the laced-edged pelerine collar of her dress, when her throat felt as if it were being strangled by heat.

"Lord-a-mercy, child, you can't run around like that," Serena scolded, and stared at the plunging décolletage of what was left of Elizabeth's gown.

Elizabeth looked down at her breasts. The gown's neckline scooped low, revealing the swell of her bosom, and just enough cleavage to be scandalous. Well, there was no help for it. She was hot and miserable. "I'm not running around, I'm sitting here on this horrid little seat with you, wilting under the sun, and watching these ugly old oxen walk about as fast as snails." She whipped open a fan and began to flutter it in front of her face. "Oh, when is that horrid man going to let us stop for supper?"

"You mean Mr. Cantrelle?" Serena asked. A sly smile curved her dark lips.

"Yes, Mr. Cantrelle," Elizabeth retorted.

Serena chuckled.

"I don't see what's so funny."

"No, honey, I guess you don't," Serena said, and chuckled again.

As if suddenly conjured up because of their conversation, Gray appeared beside their wagon. "Serena, when we stop for supper, Travis is going to check that lead ox of yours. Looks like he might be developing a limp."

Serena nodded.

Elizabeth strained forward to get a view of the oxen he was referring to. Her breasts pushed against the neckline of her gown, which caused them to swell above its line even more. A thread of alarm squeezed at her heart. "What does that mean, Gray? If he's got a limp?"

"Means we'll probably make stew out of him."

She flopped back down in her seat and stared at Gray in disbelief, and a little disgust.

His gaze moved from her face, which had haunted him all night—to say nothing of the night before and the day in between—to the creamy swell of bosom revealed above the snugly cut bodice of her gown. Visions of her had dwelled within his mind constantly, and given him no peace. This exhibit was his reward for the tortures of sleeplessness she had caused him, he decided. Or was it just more torment in disguise. Whichever, he decided to indulge himself. His eyes feasted there, devouring the sight and taking what little satisfaction, what little sustenance, they could from the display.

Serena noticed the direction and intensity of Gray's stare, and grunted in disapproval. She reached out and slapped Elizabeth's fluttering fan down atop her breasts and held it there, effectively blocking Gray's view.

Elizabeth jumped, and a culpable little smile curved Gray's lips. He tipped his hat with one finger, and nudged the flanks of his horse with his heels. The animal broke into an instant lope.

"Ain't gonna do you no good to be flaunting yourself at him," Serena said, removing her hand from Elizabeth's breast and releasing the fan.

Elizabeth stared at her. "Flaunting myself?" She sniffed indignantly and began to frantically wave the fan in front of her face. "I was *not* flaunting myself. And even if I was, I wouldn't be doing it to attract the attention of *him*, of all people."

"Could of fooled me," Serena mumbled.

"That wouldn't be too hard to do, would it?" Elizabeth snipped nastily. "Really! To think I'd be interested in a . . . a . . . whatever he is."

"Pretty handsome one, if you ask me."

"Well, I didn't, and I'll thank you to keep your opinions to yourself."

Serena chuckled enigmatically. "Sassy little thing lately, ain't you?"

Elizabeth snapped the fan closed and began to rise from her seat. "I'm going in the back to take a nap." She began to climb over the seat.

Gray ordered the wagons to a halt just before sundown. They made camp beside the river, and the women began to make preparations for dinner.

"I'm going to take a bath," Elizabeth announced to Serena.

"Where?"

"In the river." She gathered up a quilt and turned from the wagon.

"You can't do that," Serena protested. "It ain't proper."

"Neither is being dirty and smelly," Elizabeth quipped, and continued to walk toward the river. "I'll be back in plenty of time for dinner."

But at the river she paused. Maybe this wasn't such a wonderful idea. She knelt and slipped her hand into the water. It felt cool, yet for some reason, not that inviting. Elizabeth rose. Maybe she'd just wash off, not actually go into the river.

Gray had spotted her leaving the camp and, angry that she would disregard his warning to stay within the circle of wagons, he followed her, prepared to drag her back by force if necessary. He saw her standing at the water's edge, and began to make his way down the sloping bank toward her. Suddenly it seemed as if they were back on the riverbank after the *River Belle*'s explosion. Just the two of them. His heel kicked a clod of dirt loose, and he slid the remaining way down the bank.

Elizabeth whirled at the sound and, recognizing Gray, tensed.

He closed the distance between them. "You shouldn't be out here," he said brusquely.

"I wanted to bathe."

"It's not safe." He took hold of her upper arm. "Come on."

"No." She jerked her arm free. "Leave me alone. Just leave me alone, Grayson. I don't need you to tell me what to do."

"Damn it, Elizabeth." He grabbed her again. "It's

not safe out here. Now come on, I want you back at that wagon."

She tried to twist away from him again. "I can take care of myself, and I want to bathe." Unable to free herself of his grip, she pushed at him and inadvertently smashed her hand against his still healing ribs.

A groan of agony spilled from his lips. Elizabeth tried to jerk free again, and the movement caused Gray to lurch to the side. His foot slid from the wet bank, and his weight, balanced solely on the other foot, began to sway toward the river.

Elizabeth screamed and tried to pull free. His fingers remained clenched around her wrist. He splashed down into the shallow river. His right hip hit the riverbottom first, sinking into the soft mud, his elbow hit next, then his shoulder. Elizabeth landed on top, and slightly to one side of him. Her free arm, which she'd thrown out in an instinctive effort to break her fall, had disappeared beneath the water, as had one shoulder and her face. She bolted up, sputtering, wiped the mud from her face, and tried to rise. The folds of her gown, now covered with the river's mire, were like weights. She flopped back down, sinking further.

Gray pushed himself upright.

"Look what you've done," she said, and pushed against his chest in an effort to rise again.

"Dammit, Elizabeth, will you stay still and—" He struggled to get to his feet, but her body on top of him prevented his success.

She braced her hands on top of his chest and pushed herself upright. Gray grimaced as her weight bore down on his ribs, but he said nothing. She struggled her way out of the water and back to shore. "I hope an alligator eats you," she said, and sloshed her way up the sloping riverbank.

282

Gray suddenly felt the urge to laugh, and made a concerted effort not to.

After dinner, Serena immediately fell fast asleep, and Elizabeth lay staring up at the wooden slats of the wagon's bottom. She tried counting sheep. She tried ordering her body to relax limb by limb. She tried lying perfectly still and pretending she was stretched out on a elegant, silk-covered feather-filled poster bed. Nothing worked. She was wide-awake and fidgety. She needed to walk, to pace, to somehow rid her mind and body of Grayson Cantrelle. His image haunted her, his sweet words of love echoed in her ears, and the warmth of his touch still burned her skin whenever she thought of it, which was always. Memory of their lovemaking stoked the fire that had simmered deep within her ever since she'd first experienced his touch, a fire that he had ignited, and which only he could extinguish.

"Damn, damn, damn, damn," she muttered, and rolled onto her side.

"Ain't no use swearing about it," Serena said. "Not ladylike."

"Oh, poppycock. Go back to sleep," Elizabeth spat. She threw the blanket off and scooted from beneath the wagon. She had to work off some of this energy, some of the pent-up frustration and anger she felt every time she thought of Grayson. She grabbed her shawl and walked around the wagon.

The landscape had changed drastically from that of the night before. The tall grasses of Louisiana had slowly given way to the harsh, craggy ground of Texas, as the wagon train had crossed into its territory early that evening. Gray had pushed the drivers to keep the wagons moving an extra two hours, just so they could get into Texas before breaking for camp.

"Texas," Elizabeth mumbled. "What's so special about Texas, that we had to get into it tonight?" She meandered out into the darkness, away from the glow of the softly flickering campfires. Within seconds she was no more than another shadow on the landscape. She squinted into the darkness until her eyes became accustomed to it, and she was able to make things out more clearly.

Where Louisiana had been all lush grasses, bayous, and tall trees, Texas was rough, harshly broken ground made up of crevices, planes, and gulleys. Grass grew in sparse patches, and instead of tall cypress and ancient oaks, there were scrub oaks and pines, cactus and gnarled, brittle bushes.

Elizabeth sauntered slowly about, enjoying the solitude and the peacefulness of the night. It was as if she had traveled to a different world, one alien and strange to her. She was used to the softness of Mississippi, the lushness of its green landscape, the sweet fragrance of its many natural wildflowers and cultivated gardens, and the luxuries its societies had to offer. She looked around her. This land was hard. How could it offer anything but a harsh life? She thought of Eugenia, always the belle of the ball, the princess that every man in Vicksburg had yearned to court, and whose hand they'd longed to win. And she'd married a man from Texas instead. How could she possibly have survived in a place like this?

"She's probably turned into an ugly old shrew by now, doing her own laundry on a scrub board, making soap out of lye, and milking cows." Elizabeth shuddered at the mere thought of it. That's what servants were for. *She'd* never allow herself to fall into that predicament.

A shuffling sound nearby drew her from her thoughts. She whirled to face it, anxiety sweeping over

284

her. Suddenly, realization of the folly of her walk in the darkness assailed her. She had moved far enough away from the wagons to be swallowed up by the blackness of the night. What if a wild animal were stalking her? Did she have enough time to run back to the safety of the wagon train? The sound came again, but this time from the opposite direction. She tried to order her legs to move, to sprint into action and take her flying back to the wagon, but they were frozen to the spot, heedless of her command. Her heart hammered against her breast, the sound filled her ears, and her breath accelerated as fear swiftly engulfed her in its grip. She jerked around and peered into the darkness.

Suddenly, from behind, something was thrown over her head. It wrapped around her, scratched her skin and threatened to block off her air and suffocate her, as it was pressed down around her, held tight by strong arms. Her own were pinioned at her sides, rendering her helpless. She tried to jerk free, twisted her body, kicked her legs frantically, and threw herself in every direction she could. Someone swore gruffly and tightened their hold around her waist. She opened her mouth and screamed, but her throat was so paralyzed with fear that the sound emitted was more of a gagging croak.

"Shut her up," a man groused.

"How?" another man whispered frantically.

"Like this." A fist rammed into the side of her jaw. Elizabeth thought her head was going to jerk free of her neck, when the force of the blow caused it to snap violently to one side. Pain filled her head, and stars, brilliant silver stars, swam in a blurry rainbow of color about her eyes. She felt the world begin to slip away, felt the stars begin to fade, and the dazzling rainbow begin to turn to a hazy gray fog. She tried to struggle against her attackers, tried to prevent the blackness that was gurgling up around her from pulling her into its sphere of infinite darkness, but it was a losing battle. Her limbs were quickly going numb, her mind was shutting off, and awareness was slipping away, all too rapidly for Elizabeth to maintain her grip on them.

"Now come on," George said, "we've got to get the hell out of here before someone misses her."

"Elizabeth?"

Both men froze at hearing her name being called out. "It's the cowboy," George hissed, "and he's close. Put her down, Reynaud, we'll get her later."

"What?" Aaron squawked. "Why? We have her, let's just go."

George grabbed the trussed-up Elizabeth from Aaron's arms and let her drop unceremoniously to the ground. "He's too damned close," George whispered. "We ain't got time to get her tied to one of the horses and get moving before he finds us, and frankly, like I told you before, I'm not looking to get myself shot."

Aaron stared after George as the wiry little man ran, crouched, to where they'd left their horses with Damien. He glanced down at Elizabeth, whose face was hidden beneath the wool blanket. With a curse, he spun around and followed George.

Chapter 19

"Elizabeth, are you out here?" Gray called. The anger in his voice was laced with a thread of fear. He'd been making his rounds, checking each wagon, when he'd seen that her bedroll was empty. Fury had instantly assailed him at the thought that she'd wandered off again, after he'd specifically warned her not to leave the camp. He had warned them all of the dangers. But now he was getting scared, and that fed his anger. "Damn it, woman, where are you?" he mumbled to himself. He took a deep breath and yelled again, "Elizabeth?"

In the hazy, swirling fog that her mind had delved into when she'd been hit, Elizabeth heard his voice, a faint, faraway sound that pulled at her senses. She struggled up from the deep recesses of unconsciousness, slowly, painfully, her mind desperately reaching toward that light at the end of the tunnel that would pull her back into awareness. Instinctively, she tried to reach out to Gray, to push herself up from the ground and get to her feet. Her arms were entangled within the blanket that still encased her, and her legs within the voluminous folds of her skirt. She fought to escape, flailing at the blanket, kicking at her skirt, and whimpering in her helplessness.

"Elizabeth. Thank God." He rushed toward her and dropped to his knees at her side. "Hold on, sweetheart, stop thrashing," Gray said. He pulled the blanket off her and tossed it aside. His hands gripped her shoulders, and he pulled her up. She sat on her folded legs as he held her before him, his eyes scanning over her quickly. She was disheveled and scared, and she was trembling, but she was all right. He had begun to fear the Comanches had . . . he shook his head. He didn't even want to think about what they might have done to her. He felt such a rush of relief that she was safe, that he felt suddenly weak.

"Gray?" she mewed. Tears filled her eyes, brimmed over and fell down her cheeks in a steady stream. She clasped her hands in her lap, but it didn't stop their trembling. "Someone . . ." she hiccuped, "someone tried to grab me. They . . . they . . ."

"I know," he said softly. His hand moved to the side of her face, and his finger gently touched the bruise that was beginning to discolor the side of her jaw. She flinched and pulled slightly away from him. Fury exploded within his chest, burning, instilling him with a desire to reach out to whomever had done this to her and kill them. With a groan from deep within him, Gray gathered her sobbing, shaking form into his arms, and cradled her against his chest. His hands caressed her back, trying to ease her fear and calm the violent tremors that still shook her body. "It's all right now, sweetheart," he whispered. "You're with me, and everything's all right."

Elizabeth snuggled against him, feeling a desperate need to get closer to him, to meld with his body, to become one with him. The tears still fell from her eyes, but they'd begun to slow, and the sobs were not as intense. She felt safe again and protected. She had been

288

so frightened, so deeply, bone-chillingly terrified. She'd thought she was going to die. Of their own volition, her arms moved to wrap around his neck. She clung to him tightly, her body pressed against his until it could not press any tighter, her face buried in the curve of his neck.

Gradually Elizabeth's tears lessened until finally they were spent and she lay still in his arms, weak and exhausted, her cheeks damp with tears, as was Gray's neck and chest, where they had fallen. His hands continued to move over her arms and shoulders, lightly, tenderly caressing, soothing, comforting, while he murmured soft words of reassurance, his lips brushing the golden curls at her temple as he spoke.

As the fear began to subside, as his words brought her calmness and pulled her fear-shocked mind back to composure, Elizabeth became aware of his embrace, of the intimate touch of his hands and the softly spoken words of tender concern. But mostly, she became aware of Gray, of his body pressed to hers and of his hands on her back, hands that suddenly felt like spots of fire on her flesh, burning, igniting the need that always simmered within her for him.

His lips pressed to her temple, a soft, light kiss meant to offer her comfort, but instead fed her desire, stoked her passion. She lay still in his arms, afraid to move, to break the spell that held them together, to take the chance that he would pull away from her. Her mind opened the closet where her memories were stored, and gently began to tuck this time within its shelves. She wanted to remember this moment always, to treasure it forever, to be able to pull forth this feeling of comfort and love long after they'd parted.

She felt Gray stir slightly, and raised her head from his chest to look up into his face. She stared into his gray eyes for a long time, an endless time, mesmerized by the lean, dark face that looked back at her, at the rugged handsomeness and chiseled cut of each hard feature. He was everything she wanted, and everything she knew she couldn't have.

Gray felt his heart thudding madly within his chest, beating frantically against his ribs like an Indian war drum. His gaze was shackled by hers, blue eyes that were as clear as the sky and as deep as the ocean, that could pull a man into their depths and let him drown there. With a concerted effort, much like a dying man struggling for his last breath of life, Gray tore his gaze from hers, but his eyes refused to heed the faint warning in his mind, and slipped downward, coming to rest on the low-cut bodice of her nightgown, where the swell of her breasts rose above the plunging neckline, where her proud, thrusting bosom pressed against his chest. He knew in that second of time he could resist her no longer, had no willpower left to deny the desires he had kept pent-up within him, desperately ignored, for the last week.

His conscience screamed at him to try, and he did, but the effort was too great, his resistance to her too feeble. She was what he wanted, had always wanted, and if this were to be their last time together, all that they would ever be able to share, then he would take it, greedily. He eased away from her, only slightly. Not to leave her, or deny himself her pleasures, but to look at her, all of her, and imprint the memory of her on his mind forever, the memory of a woman that was everything he craved in life, and everything he knew would destroy him.

Love was not what she wanted from a man, and it was the only thing he was willing to offer. With a groan, so deep in his throat it was almost unheard by either of them, Gray gathered her back against him, crushing her body to his in an embrace that was all iron and strength. His lips covered hers, his kiss a ravaging claim that left no doubt as to his need for her. The other time he had made love to Elizabeth, he had been gentle, with tender caresses and feather-light touches that had brought her to the edge of ecstasy in slow, tantalizing degrees of sweet torment. But tonight his kiss was a savage brand on her lips, his roaming hands feral tools of possession. They moved over her rapidly, releasing her from the binds of clothing that hid her body from his hungry eyes. He tore his lips from her again as if stunned by the moment, lost in its glow, and stared at her, feasting on the exquisite sight before him, the beauty of her.

All thought to the dangers that had surrounded her, threatened her life only moments before, were quickly forgotten. Elizabeth looked into Gray's eyes, and they were all that existed, all that mattered. Her body ached to press against his, every cell within her begged for his touch, yearned to feel the fiery touch of his hand against her skin, but she remained still, waiting, uncertain of herself.

His eyes grazed over the sight before him, the fragile, delicate body the mere thought of which turned his own to an inferno of need and hunger. His gaze followed the curve of one shoulder, then dropped to the small breasts, swollen and pink with passion, each rosy pink nipple hard and pebbled, as if reaching out for his touch. Subtly curved hips flared from a slim waist and framed a flat, taut stomach that eventually gave way to a silken triangle of golden hairs at the juncture of her thighs.

Gray felt himself hardening further, his body turning to a fervent shell of armor that only her touch could melt and turn back to human flesh. Hunger for her consumed him, filled every fiber of him with a craving so intense it threatened to destroy him if not satisfied.

He gave into this need readily, easily, with no thought to the consequences, or tomorrow. He lowered his head, brushing his lips against the soft curve of her shoulder, over the delicate swell of one breast. He heard her breath catch as his mouth descended over a pink nipple and his tongue curled around the begging, hard peak, felt her body arch toward him, her arms slip around his neck, her fingers slide through the dark tendrils of his hair. His teeth nipped the tiny mountain of flesh, tasting its woman flavor, while his hands slid over her body, exploring, exciting. One hand moved to cup her other breast, and his thumb began a rhythmic caress over and around the stiff pinnacle of flesh. He heard her small, faint cry of pleasure and Gray lifted his head, his mouth once again claiming hers, his tongue plunging between her lips, flicking flame wherever it touched.

Urgently, not taking his lips from hers, and for the first time in his life not giving any thought to where they were, or the possible dangers that lurked around them, Gray struggled out of his own clothes, shrugging away the shirt, unbuckling his gunbelt, slipping his feet from his boots, and grappling his way out of the leather *calzoneras* and trousers that encased his legs. His naked body melded to hers, hot flesh fused with hot flesh, communicating their need for one another, their uncontrolled desires, through their bodies.

Losing the inhibitions of her innocence, emboldened by the courage his desire gave her, Elizabeth's hands returned his caresses, her fingers skipping lightly over his arms, his hips, his stomach. His groan of pleasure heightened her daring and spurred her newborn brashness. She needed to know him completely, to explore, experience, and remember everything about him. She needed a memory that would last her a lifetime, a memory of the man who fired her passions and filled her with an all-consuming need, whose touch turned her body to fire and pushed all rational thought from her mind.

Instinctively, mimicking his movements, Elizabeth's hands traveled his body, sliding over the muscled chest, her fingers gliding through the silken carpet of black hairs that curled there, over the corded shoulders whose breadth seemed to go on forever, and the sinewy arms that held her crushed to him. In a brazen move that surprised even herself, Elizabeth's hands moved over his hips, through the thick forest of ebony hairs just below his flat stomach and, trembling with a mixture of excitement and fear, her fingers wrapped around the solid evidence of his need.

Gray nearly doubled over as a shock of pleasure seared through him, jolts of lightning that raced through his body on a blinding, mindless course. It was too much to endure, this sense-routing spasm of euphoria that her hands were invoking upon him.

"Do you know what you're doing to me, Elizabeth?" Gray gasped weakly. "Do you have any idea at all?" He did not wait for an answer. Instead, his mouth captured hers in a kiss that was at once punishing in its demand as well as a surrender to the invisible chains she had wound around him. His tongue dueled with hers, feeding on the sweetness of her, the exotic lure that she, like no other woman he had ever known, held over him.

His hand moved to the juncture of her thighs and with a gentle nudge, he encouraged her to open her legs for him. His fingers sought the warm, satin sheath that surrounded the center of her womanly charms, that hid her sensitivity from the world. His finger found the small nub, flicked over its summit, and then began to encircle it, caressing the over-sensitized flesh, teasing.

Elizabeth twisted beneath him, and a moan slipped from her mouth into his as her desire mounted, building to a crescendo she neither could nor wanted to stop.

His finger moved to slip inside of her, and Elizabeth was suddenly filled with an exquisite torture of need so intense it seemed to explode within her, leaving her no other awareness, no other thought or feeling. His mouth left hers and moved to recapture first one breast, and then the other, his tongue laving each nipple, his teeth nibbling, grazing, teasing them.

"Why can't I get enough of you, Elizabeth?" Gray whispered, raggedly. "Why?" His mouth roamed over her body, showering her with kisses, and finally, when Elizabeth thought she would be forced to cry out for him, to beg his lips to take hers, his mouth returned to claim hers.

"Love me, Gray," Elizabeth pleaded, the words murmured from her lips to his. "Love me."

She felt his weight settle atop her, felt his legs push hers farther apart and, as her body rose to meet his, she felt the hard, hot-flesh spear of his need penetrate the aperture of her own hunger. A brilliant, star-filled explosion of ecstasy washed over her, wave after wave of bliss. But rather than satiate the yearning that gnawed within her, it teased, taunted, and fed it, threatened to engulf her, to absorb her until that was all that was left of her.

He moved over her, his thrusts within her hard, each deeper than the one before it. Her hands slid over his body, drawing him closer, loving the feel of the hot, sweat-covered flesh that drew taut over the rippling muscles of his body. She matched his rhythm, her hips rising to meet his, her tongue returning each blaze of flame that his ignited.

A frantic need to once again scale the mountain of pleasure they had traversed together as they'd lain on the riverbank enveloped her. She thrashed beneath him, her mouth returning the ravishment of his kiss, her body pushing hard against his, aching for the release she knew would eventually come.

"Yes, Gray," she murmured against his lips, "Yes, love me."

Her plea was his undoing. Even with the intensity of need that was searing within him, he had wanted to prolong this last time with her, savor it, and make it last for as long as he could. But he could hold himself back no longer, felt unable to deny himself, for one more second, the spiraling flight over the summit to the ecstasy he knew awaited him.

He moved deep within her, a savage thrust that brought a cry of joy from her lips. She clung to him, her legs entwined with his, her fingernails digging into the flesh of his back, as she rode the throes of pleasure he'd caused to burst within her. At the same instant that she plunged from the mountaintop, Gray felt his own body quiver, felt an explosion of heat fill his insides. A rain of pleasure cascaded over him, through him, and into the deepest reaches of his body, until it touched the very depths of his soul.

For long, endless moments Elizabeth lay in his arms, content, spent from the passion that had erupted between them. Her fingers played with the black curls of hair at the nape of his neck, sliding through the silken tendrils and reveling in the satiny feel against her skin. Gray shifted his weight so that he lay half on her, and half on the ground. His head was cradled in the curve of her neck, and his hot breath blew over the bare skin of her breast. She felt her nipple harden at the unintentional teasing, felt the knot of desire coil within her again, and nearly moaned with her need.

Gray lifted his head, as if he'd heard the little sound that had begun to fill her throat, or perhaps he'd felt it. His lips moved over her face, a sprinkle of feather-light kisses so tender, so gentle, that Elizabeth felt a swell of emotion fill her throat and tears sting the back of her eyes. She stared at Gray, a dark, handsome stranger who lay beside her, whose body had just taken her to a world she yearned to return to, longed never to leave. Was she wrong about him? Was she destined to love him, no matter what type of life he led her into? No man had ever made her feel the way he did, and she suddenly knew, beyond any doubt, that no man ever would.

The realization filled her with a warm, comforting glow. How could she ever have thought she didn't care about him? That she could walk away from him and continue on with her life without him?

Something rustled in the brush nearby, and she felt Gray stiffen in her arms, felt the solid muscles beneath her fingers tense. He shot upright, his dark eyes narrowed and scanned the moonlit landscape that surrounded them. He grabbed for his trousers. "We'd best get back to camp, Elizabeth. This was a foolish thing to do."

Foolish? The man had just made love to her, and he called it *foolish?* Her heart felt as if he'd just sliced it in two. Fury swept over her in a blinding wave of heat, as intense and swift as a prairie fire on a Kansas plain. She pulled her gown over her head and jammed her arms into its sleeves. She should have known. She should have known better than to let her silly heart care about him. He was nothing but a crude, arrogant cow drover. A gunfighter, with no heart and no feelings. Hadn't he proven that to her time and again?

"Go back to the wagons, Elizabeth," Gray said. He stood, tied the thong of his gunbelt to his thigh, and looked out into the darkness as he buttoned his shirt. "I'm going to have a look around."

She scrambled to her feet, holding her shoes in one hand, and stormed toward the wagons without a backward glance. Foolish! She'd show him what was foolish. How could she have thought she cared about him? She must be touched in the head.

Gray watched her stalk away. What in the hell had he been thinking to make love to her again? Was he insane? Hadn't he already decided that the best thing was to stay as far away from that little hellion as possible? She'd made it clear all she wanted out of life were the things that money could buy, to drape herself in silks, satins, and diamonds, and live on a grand plantation and be waited on by a dozen servants. That was *not* the type of woman he wanted for a wife. "Hell, I don't even want a wife," he muttered, disgusted with himself. But he couldn't rid himself of the guilt. He had left Texas to hunt down a man for seducing his sister and then rejecting her, and he had done exactly the same thing to Elizabeth. Maybe he should just put a bullet in his head. That would end the turmoil of his feelings, and probably make her as happy as a little lark.

After a quick look around, and finding nothing, though he hadn't really expected to, Gray returned to the campsite. He walked past Elizabeth's wagon and, unable to help himself, glanced under it to assure himself she was there. She was. He walked across the open space the circle of wagons created and sat beside his own wagon, leaning his back against the wooden spokes of one front wheel.

"Can't sleep?" Travis said, from the darkness beneath the wagon.

"Yeah," Gray mumbled. "Can't sleep."

"Want to talk?"

"No."

Travis shrugged and lay back down on his bedroll.

Gray stared off into the darkness, then his gaze dropped to the outline of Elizabeth's wagon, a gray

297

shadow against the black night. He had been struck cold with terror when he'd heard her muffled scream, when he'd thought something had happened to her. Relief had swept over him like a tidal wave when he'd finally found her, safe and unhurt, but frightened half out of her wits. Gray snapped in half the small twig he held in his hands. He had made love to her, allowed the desire that had been eating at him to take over his senses—if he had any, which he was seriously beginning to doubt. He'd been a fool . . . again.

He threw the pieces of twig to the ground and, with a soft curse, got to his feet. It could never work between them. She'd end up hating him. They would do nothing but fight. Hell, they'd probably end up killing each other. Or she'd spend all of his money, and they'd end up in the poor house. "Lord help me, I'm going to do it anyway." He stalked across the camp toward her wagon and hunkered down beside it. "Elizabeth?"

"What?" she snapped instantly.

"I need to talk to you," he whispered.

"No."

"Elizabeth."

"I have nothing to say to you."

"But I have something to say to you, and if you don't come out here, I'm going to come in and get you." Heaven help him. She drove him into near blind rages, but she was the only woman he had ever failed to banish from his thoughts.

Elizabeth slid out from under the wagon. Gray rose and, taking her hands in his, helped her to her feet. He guided her to the center of the encampment, where a fire still crackled softly. "Look, Elizabeth, I know I shouldn't have . . . I mean, I know you were never with a man before me and . . . well, what I mean is, I want to do the honorable thing and—" Why was he having so much trouble saying it?

Elizabeth stared at him. *Honorable thing?* He wanted to do the honorable thing? He sounded about as enthusiastic as a lamb being led to its own slaughter. Her temper began a slow, but steadily rising burn. In a sugary tone she said, "Are you perchance trying to ask me to marry you, Grayson?"

"Yes." There, he'd said it. Surprise swept over him at the realization that he didn't feel as if he'd just fallen into a bottomless black hole. In fact, he felt kind of good.

"Thank you, Grayson," she said, "but no." Her fist rammed into his stomach. A loud *whoof* of air escaped his lips, and Gray doubled over gasping for breath, his eyes wide. "Honorable thing? *You* want to do the honorable thing? What do you know about honor? You are a rake, Grayson. A rake. You forced your attentions on me when I had no choice and no help against you, and now you have the audacity to think I would marry you?"

"Elizabeth, you are the most infuriating female I have ever met. I did not force myself on you, and you damn well know it."

"You did, and I wouldn't marry you if you were the last man on earth."

Grayson's temper snapped. "Well, fine, that's just fine with me. You'd probably drive me crazy anyway."

Tears stung at the back of Elizabeth's eyes. She turned and fled back to the sanctuary of her wagon. She hated him. He hadn't felt anything when he'd seduced her but lust, and now because he felt guilty, he wanted to do the honorable thing. Tears streamed down her cheeks. She didn't want him to want her because he felt guilty. She wanted him to love her.

The next morning the wagon train moved deeper into Texas, and the landscape continued to change.

The last vestiges of the tall grasses of Louisiana, the magnificent oak trees with their draping curtains of moss, the tall bayou cypress, and the blossoming magnolias, were left behind. Instead, scrub oaks and pine, scraggly dogwoods, tumbleweeds, and cactus now began to dot the landscape. The wild grasses seemed to grow in patches instead of meadows, and an occasional log cabin or mud hovel dotted the horizon rather than the elegant, multipillared, plantation homes Elizabeth was accustomed to seeing.

She tried to keep her thoughts off of Grayson and on the scenery, and what she was going to do with her life. She watched all this pass with a sense of despair. *This* is what Eugenia had moved to? Spent her days looking at? Contending with? Elizabeth shuddered and tried to picture herself living in this land. How would she ever stand it?

The answer came in a flash. She wouldn't. There was no reason she had to. She could visit with Eugenia for a few weeks, maybe a month or so, and then she'd leave and go back to New Orleans. She'd get a town house and live in the Quarter. Eugenia would object, Elizabeth knew, but she'd contend with that when the time came. It wasn't proper for an unattached young woman to live alone, but that couldn't be helped. Her parents were dead. Her fiancé might as well be. "Ex-fiancé," Elizabeth grumbled softly to herself. And her only sister lived in this godforsaken country. A shadow darkened her blue eyes as a frown creased her forehead. She wasn't a *proper* young lady anymore, anyway.

"What you thinking on so hard?" Serena asked, shifting her weight on the wooden seat and rearranging the reins she held wrapped around her pudgy hands. "How I'm going to explain to Eugenia that we're not staying here," Elizabeth said without thinking, and instantly regretted the way her tongue, too often,

300

trekked along without benefit of her brain.

"Ain't staying? What do you mean, we ain't staying?"

Elizabeth grimaced. Now she'd done it. Serena would nag her for the remainder of the trip. "I don't like it here, Serena. I think we'd be better off taking a house in New Orleans."

"Humph. Ain't proper, you being on your own like that."

"You'll be there. Unless . . ." she paused, suddenly unsure "you'd rather not?" Elizabeth looked at Serena anxiously, the sudden thought filled her with alarm. What would she do if Serena didn't want to go to New Orleans? She could refuse. She had every right to do so, since she was not a slave, but a free woman of color. That was one of the few right things her father had done before his death.

Serena shot her a sharp look. "You think I'd let you go traipsing off all alone? Humph. You just get yourself into one mess after another when you're on your own, Missy. Just look what happened when you done left Vicksburg like that, all huffy and such."

Elizabeth smiled. Serena would accompany her back to New Orleans. A feeling of security warmed her.

"Oh, lawdy," Serena gasped, her eyes fixed on the softly rolling horizon to the north of the train.

Elizabeth instantly forgot her daydreams and looked in the direction of Serena's gaze. Icy manacles of fear clutched at her heart, and her fingers instantly gripped the edge of the seat. "Do . . . do you think they're going to attack us?"

At the head of the wagon train, Gray had noticed the same sight that had sent chills down the spines of everyone in the caravan. With a jerk on the reins he brought his mount to a sudden stop, and lifted a hand over his head in a signal for the drivers to halt. The wagons came to a slow stop, each driver remaining nervously in his seat and awaiting Gray's next move. Travis rode up to the head of the procession and paused beside Gray.

"Looks like we got company," he said. "Want me to order the wagons to camp?"

Gray shook his head. "Not yet. If we do that, they'll think we're itching for a fight, which we're not. Anyway, there's not that many of them." He pulled the brim of his hat low across his forehead. "Let's ride out and see what they want."

Travis nodded and nudged the ribs of his horse.

Both mounts broke into an easy canter in the direction of the waiting Indians.

"Oh, Serena," Elizabeth said, and clasped the black woman's huge arm. She stared at Gray approaching the Indians and felt a shudder of terror. What if they killed him? She felt like running after him and forcing him back to the safety of the wagons.

"It's all right, honey. There's only a handful of them, ten or so," Serena said patiently. "If they was going to attack, there'd be a lot more than that coming toward us."

"Then what do they want?" Elizabeth felt her heart beating against her breast, a mad thumping that she felt certain even the Indians could hear. She stared at the men whose skin color was little different than that of the red brown earth. They wore their black hair long, braided, and decorated with bits of cloth, beads, and feathers. Deerskin mocassins, adorned with designs painted in blue, as well as beads and bits of silver, reached from toe to hip.

Gray kept his horse in a steady and easy pace alongside Travis's, as the two men rode slowly toward the back of the train, their eyes fixed on the Indians, who were also approaching them. "They're *Kwerharrehnun* Comanches," Gray said, eyeing their attire, and wondering if they were the ones who had attacked Elizabeth the night before.

"Yeah, but what are they doing this far south? This is Waco territory. Little out of the *Kwerhar-rehnun* homeland, isn't it?"

Gray nodded. "Could be hunting up north isn't too good this year, though I haven't heard of any problems. Or maybe they've been out raiding. If it's that, whether they're raiding Wacos or whites, we could be in trouble."

"Oh, boy," Travis mumbled.

"They're not wearing war paint though. No war shields or headdresses. That's a good sign—I hope."

"I won't hold my breath."

"Good idea," Gray whispered, as they neared the Indians. "If this doesn't go well, it could be the last one you take."

"You really know how to make a guy feel better, don't you?" Travis said.

Gray held up his hand in a gesture of friendship. The Comanches had stopped about one hundred feet from the last wagon—Elizabeth's wagon. He felt a silent groan fill his throat. They couldn't have picked a worst spot. "Travis, wait for me near Elizabeth's wagon. The last thing we need right now is for that little spitfire to panic and think the Comanches are going to scalp her."

Travis nodded, veered his horse away from Gray's, and urged it in a slow walk toward Elizabeth's wagon. He had to move slowly, so as not to spook the Indians into thinking he was doing something that he wasn't—like preparing an attack.

"What's happening?" Elizabeth asked, the second Travis was within earshot. She stood in front of her seat. "Is Gray all right? Are they going to attack us?"

Travis reined in beside the wagon and turned his horse to that he could keep an eye on Gray should his friend need him. "Gray's fine, and I think we're all right, too. If they were going to attack, I doubt they'd have approached for a pow-wow."

"What's a pow-wow?" Elizabeth asked, and looked at him blankly.

"A discussion. A few minutes' chat so that each side can tell the other what they want."

She watched Gray nervously, noting the shake of his head, a hand motioning back toward the wagons. They were close enough so that she could hear them, but the language they were speaking was totally incomprehensible to her. One of the braves kept looking in her direction, which made Elizabeth even uneasier. Her hands began to tremble, and she quickly looked away. But she couldn't keep her gaze averted. The Indian's brow arched upward when Elizabeth looked back. He leaned slightly and nudged the brave next to him, then pointed toward Elizabeth.

Her heart nearly jumped out of her chest. They were talking about *her!*

Serena noticed Elizabeth's nervousness and reached over to pat her arm. "Calm down, Missy. Everything's going to be all right."

"What are they saying, Travis? Are they talking about me? I can't understand them? They might as well be speaking Greek."

Travis smiled. "They want to trade. They claim they've got furs they're willing to trade."

"For what?"

"Liquor probably. Or guns."

"Do we have them?"

"Not to trade."

"Then what will we do?" She refused to look back at the two Indians that were still talking together and motioning toward her. "They'll kill us, won't they? If we don't give them what they want?"

304

Travis took a deep breath and turned a patient smile on Elizabeth. "What we do is pray that Gray can talk some reason into them. That we can trade something else for their furs."

"Why not just give them what they want, so they'll go away?"

"Liquor makes Indians crazy, and guns enable them to kill people, including us."

Elizabeth fell silent at that and listened to Gray communicate with the Indians. He began shaking his head vehemently and gesturing in jerking, sharp movements with his arms and hands.

"Oh, boy," Travis said, barely above a whisper.

"What?" Elizabeth asked, nearly jumping on his soft comment. "What's he saying? What's wrong?"

Travis chuckled. "They want to trade all right, but they don't want liquor or guns."

"Then what do they want?"

He looked squarely at her for a long moment before answering. "You."

Chapter 20

"What?" Elizabeth gasped. She stared at Travis as if he'd just taken out his brain and thrown it on the ground. "What do you mean, *me?*"

"Ain't making no trade like that," Serena said. She reached behind the seat for the shotgun that lay there. "Leastways not as long as I'm around." She propped the weapon across her lap and stared at the Indians, her huge brown eyes hard and full of indignation.

Travis chuckled. "They like your hair, Elizabeth. The way it turns flaxen under the sun, like pure gold. In fact, they're calling you the golden one. They probably think you're the daughter of the sun, or the moon, or some such nonsense."

"I'll show them whose daughter I am," Elizabeth snapped, then climbed down from the wagon before Travis could get a grip on what was happening.

"Missy, you come back here," Serena ordered. She stood up so quickly, shifting the heavy weight of the gun upward, that her feet slid out from beneath her. She toppled backward, over the seat into the bed of the wagon, and landed with a hard thud on her back. The shotgun, still gripped tightly in her hands, fired with a thunderous roar as Serena's impact jarred her hands and her finger pulled down on the gun's trigger.

The wagon shook violently, the air exploded, and buckshot smashed into the velvet cushion of a ladies' sitting chair that had been crammed into the wagon.

All four oxen, momentarily scared, lunged forward a few steps, jerking the wagon. Serena, who had half-risen, fell back to the floor. Travis's horse reared and whinnied, its front legs flailing the air.

He ignored Serena's plight. "Elizabeth," he yelled instead, to absolutely no avail. She didn't even pause. He watched her stalk away from him as he fought to get his mount under control.

Gray heard the commotion behind him, heard Travis yell Elizabeth's name, and nearly groaned aloud. This was it, he knew it. They were all goners. By morning their scalps would probably be dangling from some brave's war lance. He should have known she'd do something. He chanced a look around and instantly wished he hadn't. No, what he really wished was that the minute he'd seen the Comanches he had ordered Travis to hog-tie Elizabeth inside the wagon and stuff a sock in her mouth. If he had, they wouldn't be in this predicament now, and she wouldn't be barreling down on them like a crazy person who was about to get them all killed. Gray jerked the reins of his horse. He had to get to her and make her go back to the wagon. His mount began to turn and was suddenly halted by one of the Indians, who reached out and gripped the animal's bridle. Gray looked back at the brave who held his horse. Unless he wanted an arrow in the back, he couldn't do a damn thing. "Except watch Elizabeth bring the world down around our ears," he grumbled to himself.

One of the Comanches stared at him in curiosity, but since Gray had spoken in English, the Indian hadn't understood his words, just his tone, which was obviously angry.

Elizabeth stalked straight past Gray, throwing him a quick I-hope-you-drop-dead look, and paused beside the mounted Indian Gray had been conversing with. She glared up at him. "How dare you think you can buy me, you stupid, savage beast," she said, and jabbed his thigh with her fist.

"Elizabeth," Gray snarled, wishing he could reach out and entwine his fingers around her pretty little neck.

"How dare you," she hit the Indian again, "even think that I would consent to go off with a vulgar, half-clothed, unkempt animal like you." She swung her arm out, preparing to smash her fist against his thigh for the third time, but the Indian reached down—his movement as swift as lightning—and grabbed her wrist. His black eyes bore into hers, and his fingers squeezed her flesh in a near bone-crushing grip.

Elizabeth winced in pain, but only for a second, then she began thrashing about, smacking at him with her other fist and twisting herself about frantically. "Let me go, you savage! You heathen. I'll kill you, all of you. Do you hear me? I will. I'll kill you in your sleep and leave you for the buzzards."

The Indian looked down at her in puzzlement, then back at Gray. He asked Gray why the golden one was so upset with him.

Speaking in the tongue of the Comanche, Gray answered: "She is angry with you. She says that she's spoken for, that the gods have promised her to another man. A great white chief. She says if you try and stop her, death will come to your tipi and prevent your spirit from ever leaving this earth."

The Indian instantly jerked his fingers from around Elizabeth's wrist, and pulled his hand away as if it had been suddenly scorched by fire. "Take her away," the Indian said. "Make her go back to your wagons, away from us. We want nothing to do with the golden one. Her power is too great, her tongue too sharp."

Elizabeth looked from the Indian to Gray, unable to understand their words.

Gray nodded but forced himself not to smile. That wouldn't do, not yet. "Elizabeth, go back to the wagon," he ordered in a stern voice.

"I will not," she snipped. "You are not going to sell me to these heathens, Grayson Cantrelle. I will not be traded for a few measly pelts of fur, so that you can have your own miserable hide. I won't go, you hear me? I won't, and you can't make me."

"Elizabeth," Gray growled, "go back to the wagon—now." His voice boomed, resounding on the air like a roll of thunder.

She stood her ground and, to her credit, did not even flinch. "I won't go with these . . . these beasts, Grayson. Serena has a shotgun, and if you try to make me go, she'll shoot you."

"Elizabeth," his eyes bore into hers, "if you don't shut up and go back to your wagon right now, I swear, I *will* trade you to them."

Like a guardian angel swooping down to save her, Travis rode up beside Elizabeth, approaching more swiftly than he normally would have under other circumstances. But he had seen her attack on the Indian, and he had heard the rage in Gray's voice when he'd ordered her back to the wagon.

"Take her out of here," Gray said, his voice filled with fury.

Before she could protest further, Travis reached down and lifted Elizabeth from the ground. She made to scream and bit her tongue instead. Tears filled her eyes as pain filled her mouth.

Holding her dangling off the side of the horse, her hands gripped tightly to his arms, her feet swinging wildly in the air, Travis headed back for the wagon. "I can't believe you did that," he said to her. He reined his mount up beside the wagon. Elizabeth grabbed onto the seat and hoisted herself up and onto it. "Hell and tarnation, Elizabeth, you could have gotten us all killed." He glanced back at the Indians and Gray. "Course, it's not over yet. We could still end up as decorations for their war shields."

Serena had picked herself up off the floor of the wagon and resumed her seat. When Elizabeth climbed back onto it, the old woman wrapped a hefty arm around her and hugged her close. "I won't let them take you, Missy."

"No one's taking anyone," Travis said, not taking his eyes off of the Indians. "The *Kwerhar-rehnun* will wait 'til nightfall, if they're going to attack us. I doubt they wanted to before, but after your little tirade, Elizabeth, I'm not so sure."

"I thought Indians didn't attack at night. Didn't you say that?" Elizabeth said.

Travis nodded. "Normally they don't, but the *Kwerhar-rehnun* are different, they're the fiercest of the Comanche bands, and if they want to attack, they're not going to let a little thing like nightfall stop them."

Gray turned his mount away from the Indians and rode back toward Travis.

"So, what do we do?" Travis asked when Gray neared.

"We give them what they want, unless you want to hand them that fancy scalp of yours."

Elizabeth bolted up from her seat, her fury having returned twofold. "You brute. You've sold me to them, haven't you? To save your own lousy skin, you went and sold me to those savages!"

He couldn't help it. The temptation to teach her a lesson was too great. He struggled to keep a straight face as he talked. "I'm sorry, Elizabeth, but the offer was too good. They said they'd give me four horses for you." He glanced back over his shoulder at the waiting Indians. "They're good horses, too."

"You—you—" Elizabeth sputtered, too outraged to even form a protest.

Travis looked at him in total shock. Serena glared, while Elizabeth was beginning to turn purple.

The stern look dissolved into a smile, which in turn gave way to a soft laugh. "Calm down, Elizabeth, I know your opinion of me is low, but I just couldn't bring myself to stoop quite that far down. I didn't sell you."

"But—you just said—"

"What I said was that we're going to give them what they want, and we are."

She stared at him in confusion.

"What do they want, Gray?" Travis asked.

"Things for their women and themselves. Jewelry, trinkets, cloth."

Travis nodded. "Good. Let's get to it and get out of here, before they change their minds and decide they'd rather have a few scalps for their lances."

Gray rode around to the back of Elizabeth's wagon, dismounted, and opened the gate. It settled into place with a resounding thud that shook the entire wagon, including the seat Elizabeth was settled on. She whirled, suddenly understanding where they were going to get the things the Indians wanted. "You can't take these things, Grayson." Scrambling from her seat, she ran around the wagon. She grabbed a bolt of velvet he had in his arms and jerked it away from him, then threw it back into the wagon. "That's my stuff. Mine. You can't give it to those—those people." She slapped both hands to his chest and pushed him. "You can't."

Unprepared for her attack, Gray stumbled backward against his horse. He righted himself instantly and bore down on her, fire spitting from his eyes and a grimace a mile wide stretching his lips. He stopped barely an inch from her, rammed clenched fists onto his hips, and glared down at her. "Elizabeth Devlin, I swear, sometimes I think you are the devil's own curse. If we don't give those Indians what they want, they're going to go back to their camp and get their friends. Then, when they return, there won't be any talking or bargaining, but there sure as hell will be a lot of killing, and I doubt we'll be the ones standing when it's all over." He moved to turn away from her, thought better of it, and whirled back. "And as for you, my sweet, I'd bet my last dollar, after that little trick you pulled out there, if we do end up firing at each other, those Indians won't be in any mood to take you back to their camp as a squaw, when it's all over. More than likely, your bones will end up rotting on the prairie, while that nice long blond mass of curls hangs from one of their war shields."

"Ahh!" Elizabeth squeaked. Her eyes turned huge, her mouth dropped to hang agape, and she stared at him in horror, an image of what he'd described vivid in her mind.

"Now go back and sit beside Serena, and for god's sake, be quiet," Gray thundered.

She began to turn away.

"Don't even breathe if you can help it." He grabbed a bolt of cloth from the wagon and handed it to Travis. "I swear, that woman could make the angels spew fury and God slam the pearly gates shut on us forever." And to think, he thought to himself, I offered to marry her. In spite of his black mood, an almost silent chuckle rose from his throat. Passion and trouble, that's what

312

marriage to Elizabeth would bring him. Passion and trouble, and most likely not one day of peace and quiet. But then, was peace and quiet what he really wanted?

"Hell, yes," he muttered beneath his breath.

"What?"

He looked at Travis and handed him several pairs of Elizabeth's gloves. "Nothing."

When their saddlebags were so loaded with bolts of cloth and lace and half of Elizabeth's jewelry, gloves, stockings, and underthings that they couldn't hold anymore, Travis and Gray rode back toward the Indians.

"Imagine," Elizabeth muttered to Serena, glaring at Travis and Gray as they passed, "giving all my beautiful things to those . . . those primitive heathens. It's a downright disgrace, that's what it is. A disgrace. Now I won't have anything for Eugenia."

"It's our lives, Missy, and don't you forget it. We can buy new things for your sister, but an arrow through the heart ain't gonna buy you nothing but a pine box and a hole in the ground."

For the remainder of that day and the next, Elizabeth saw little of Gray. The wagons moved steadily behind the slowly plodding oxen, the sun beat down mercilessly, and the landscape all looked the same: brown. At night when they made camp, she stayed up late, walking about the inner circle of the wagons, sitting beside the center campfire, and even, once or twice, passing by Gray's wagon. But he was always gone, or somewhere else other than where she was. If she approached a group of people conversing, of which he was one, Gray quickly walked away, as did most of the others. If he was sitting near the campfire

313

enjoying a cup of coffee, he'd mumble an excuse to leave as she approached.

The scare with the Indians, and the long days of doing nothing but riding beside Serena and staring out at what seemed an unchanging view, had given Elizabeth a lot of time to think. She'd been wrong, she could see that now. Ever since she'd met him, Gray had protected her, and cared for her. He would have never traded her to the Indians, but her anger, that impulsive fury that always got the better of her tongue, to say nothing of her brain, had given her little time to think, only to act. And she'd acted all wrong, as usual.

She'd watched for him all day, and each time she'd gotten a glimpse of him, riding in front of the wagon train, or moving from wagon to wagon to make sure each was all right, her heart had done a funny little leap within her breast, and a smile had pulled at her lips. But he'd never noticed. Once, while he'd been talking to Serena about their wagon, she had tried to interrupt and apologize to him, but he'd turned his horse and ridden away before she could utter more than two words. She sat down beside the campfire that was still simmering in the center of the camp, and poked a stick at the softly glowing flames.

With a flick of her wrist, she tossed the stick into the fire and stood. What difference did it make if she saw him again anyway? He didn't care about her. Hadn't he made that painfully obvious? The hurt that filled her heart turned to angry indignation. And what did she care? Did she really want to spend her life following him from town to town? Watching him get into one gunfight after another? The answer was no. Definitely not. Wasn't it? She stared into the flames as if she could find an answer there, and finally she did. She'd visit with Eugenia for a while, a few weeks maybe, and then return to New Orleans. Someday she'd marry a gentleman, a man who had property and money. She'd be mistress of a grand plantation, like her mother had been, and she'd give fabulous soirees and dinners. Her husband would see to it that she had dozens of beautiful gowns and jewels, and everyone who was anyone would want to be on her guest list. Grayson Cantrelle could go flitting about the countryside like he always had, hiring out his gun to kill people and being a nobody. A nothing. And that was just fine with her.

Gray watched Elizabeth from his position in the shadows of one of the wagons. The moon was barely a sliver in the sky tonight, a thin arc of pale gold that did little to illuminate the earth. Only the tiny glow of Gray's cheroot distinguished him from the blackness, the thin spot of burning tobacco turning a brilliant orange whenever he lifted it to his lips and inhaled.

She could very well have gotten herself and everyone else on the wagon train killed with her little tirade, yet all he could think of was how much he wanted her, how desperately he needed to feel her body pressed to his, the sweet taste of her lips, the warm caress of her fingers as they slid through his hair. His body was rigid with the hunger that gnawed at him, but his mind was cool, his thoughts crystalline clear and hard. He might covet her, might crave her more than any woman he had ever met, ever desired, but it was something he would have to learn to live with, and eventually forget. She could never stand the rigors of life on the Texas plains. Even with the luxuries the Cantrelles' Bar C ranch offered, he knew Elizabeth would not be satisfied, would long for more. He had known all this when he'd made love to her on the riverbank, he had known she was inexperienced, had not been with a man before, and yet he'd done it anyway. He was no better than the man he had been trying to track for the last few months.

Gray bristled against the thought. No, that wasn't true. He had not denounced Elizabeth, he had proposed marriage to her. Granted he had taken his time doing it, and he hadn't been very enthusiastic about it, but he *had* proposed. It was she who had rejected it, she who had refused his proposal.

Nevertheless, he would damn himself for a thousand days for what he'd done, for a hundred years. But if he had to do it all over again, he knew he would not change one thing. And it was better that she'd turned down his proposal. They were wrong for each other. It would never work. He frowned into the darkness. So why did he feel so damn empty inside?

A shadow, quick and fleeting, moved beside a tree that stood just a few feet beyond the perimeter of the wagons. Gray caught sight of it from the corner of his eye. He tensed, and his hand moved to settle lightly on the butt of the Colt that rested low on his thigh. He turned and disappeared into the darkness.

Chapter 21

"What the hell are you doing out here?" Gray asked, in a none too friendly tone. "I was just about to put a bullet in your head."

"I was making sure there wasn't anyone else out here," Travis said. "I thought I heard someone moving around."

Gray nodded and reholstered his gun. "Yeah, me, too. Tell the guards to keep alert. Our Indian friends might not have been satisfied with the little goodies we gave them this afternoon, and I'm still not sure they weren't the ones who tried to abduct Elizabeth the other night."

Travis chuckled. "Well, I wouldn't want to be the one to tell Elizabeth the Comanches want more of her cloth, if they've come back."

"Maybe we should have just given her to them, when that's all they were asking for," Gray grumbled.

Travis smiled. "Really gets to you, doesn't she?"

"Go to bed, Travis," Gray snapped, as he moved off into the darkness.

"Serena, if I never see another wagon, another ox,

or the damn plains of Texas again, I won't care."
Elizabeth swatted at a bug that flew before her face,
and then pressed her forehead against the sleeve of her
dress. The moist blanket of perspiration she wiped
onto her sleeve instantly reappeared on her flesh. At
the same time her lips felt dry, parched, and cracked.
Wisps of hair keep slipping from the ribbon at her
nape, the cloth of her gown felt as if it were stuck to her
back, and she so longed for a bath she could scream. If
she had the energy. Which she didn't. "They gave this
place the wrong name," she grumbled. "They should
have just called it Hell."

The sun, a brilliant orb of orange-gold light, hugged
the horizon, ready to slip behind it at any moment, but
its descent had done nothing to cool the fierce heat of
the day.

"Ain't no worse than where we come from," Serena
said.

"Humph. Maybe you've gone blind in your old age,"
Elizabeth muttered, waving a fan in front of her face in
an effort to cool off. Suddenly she sat bolt upright in
her seat. A second later, after squinting into the
distance, she gave a small shriek and jumped up.
"Serena, look, we're there! We're finally there."

"Now maybe you can get that bath you been
dreaming about all day," Serena said.

"Oh, lord, we can sleep in a bed tonight. A real,
honest to goodness bed, with a mattress and pillows!"
Elizabeth clapped her hands together and laughed.
"We can stay in a room with walls, doors, and
windows, and I can wash this grime off my body." She
sat down and hugged Serena's arms. "And tomorrow
we'll see Eugenia."

Ten minutes later Travis approached their wagon.
"We're camping here for the night, Serena. We'll go on
into San Antonio in the morning."

Serena began to turn the team. Elizabeth, instantly angered by Travis's words, jumped up from her seat and nearly toppled from the wagon as it veered to the left. She grabbed hold of the canvas and glared after Travis. "Why can't we go into town tonight, Travis?" she called.

He reined in and looked back at her. "Only thing that'd be open by the time we got there is the saloons and cantinas, Elizabeth, and believe me, you don't want to be there then. It will be better in the morning."

Elizabeth flopped back down in her seat. "He did this on purpose, Serena. The rake. He got us this close just so we could see the town and want to go in, and then he says no. He's getting even with me, that's all."

"Getting even for what?" Serena questioned, turning a suspicious eye on Elizabeth. "What'd you do to that man, Missy?"

"Nothing," she mumbled. "I didn't do anything to him."

"Uh-huh."

Elizabeth snapped around. "Well, I didn't."

Except fall in love with him, her conscience nagged. Suddenly she felt like crying.

The smell of food filled the air: beans, ham, biscuits, and coffee. The mood in the camp was high, everyone excited about finally reaching their destination. It had been a long trip, and, except for their encounter with the Comanches, an uneventful one. Everyone breathed a sigh of relief.

One of the party brought out his fiddle. Another a harmonica. Another a banjo. Suddenly music filled the air, and people were dancing, laughing, and having a good time.

Elizabeth watched as Gray danced with one of the

other women, the daughter of a family moving to San Antonio from South Carolina. A frown creased Elizabeth's brow, and she held her arms crossed tight under her breasts. The girl kept looking up at Gray as if he were her knight in shining armor. "Well, she can have him," Elizabeth said peevishly, so filled with jealousy she was about to turn green. "Poor thing, doesn't know what she's getting herself into."

"You say something, Missy?" Serena asked, moving to stand beside Elizabeth.

"No."

A man on horseback suddenly appeared between two of the wagons. He rode right up to the edge of the dancing couples, reined in, and dismounted.

Gray excused himself from his partner and went to greet the rider, whose long gray duster hung over his lanky body like a blanket and obscured it from view. Only the silver star pinned to his breast gave indication of who or what he was. The two men moved away from the others.

"You'd best have your people pack up and move into town," the man said, with no preamble at conversation or polite greetings.

"What's happening, Ned?" Gray asked.

The other man wiped a hand across his mouth, brushing at the whiskers that covered both his upper lip and chin. "It's not safe for you to stay out here, Gray. The Comanches have been raiding."

Travis moved to stand beside Gray. "Hi, Sheriff."

Ned Thompson nodded.

"We ran into a small party of Comanches just yesterday, Ned. All they wanted to do was trade," Gray said.

The sheriff shrugged and Elizabeth, who was watching, had the impression that every bone in his body moved with the gesture. Several people approached to stand behind Gray, both curious and alarmed.

"Maybe they were only a small party, not enough of them to overtake you," the sheriff said. "Or maybe they were a different band. I don't know."

"Or maybe whoever's doing the raiding ain't Comanches," Gray offered. "It's happened before."

The sheriff shrugged. "All I know is that we got word a few hours ago that Sweetbriar was under attack. People in San Antonio figure if Sweetbriar's got Indian trouble, it might soon be on us, too."

Gray nodded. "You're probably right. Anyone know what started this?"

Elizabeth heard the word Sweetbriar and was instantly filled with apprehension. She pushed through the crowd now surrounding the trio, and slammed into Gray. She grasped his arm. "What's happened in Sweetbriar?"

Gray felt her panic and remembered that Elizabeth's sister—the only family she had left in the world—lived in Sweetbriar. With a determined effort he forced her grasp from his arm and gripped her shoulders with his hands firmly. "There's been some trouble there, Elizabeth. We don't know how much yet." He slipped an arm around her shoulders and tried to turn her back toward the campfire. "Come on, I'll see you back to your wagon. We have to move into San Antonio tonight."

She jerked away from him, her gaze darting from him to the sheriff, and back again. "What kind of trouble, Gray? What's going on? Please . . ." her voice rose as she spoke, "tell me. What's happened there?"

He shook his head and pulled her to him, forcing her to walk toward her wagon. "We don't know yet, Elizabeth. The Indians have—"

"Indians? Oh, my lord! Eugenia's dead, isn't she?"

321

He felt the shudder that rippled through her body, felt her flesh go cold, and heard the thread of hysteria in her tone. His arms closed around her, and he pulled her to him. "No. Don't think that."

He felt her tears fall onto his chest, where the open vee of his shirt left his skin revealed. His heart ached for her. "I'm sure they'll hold their own, angel. There's a lot of good men in Sweetbriar, don't worry. As soon as everything calms down and it's safe, I'll take you down there myself, I promise."

She pulled away from him and shook her head. "No. I have to go now, Gray. Immediately. Eugenia might need me!"

"Elizabeth, do you understand what I've been saying? The Comanches are raiding both Sweetbriar and the homesteads between there and San Antonio. You'd never make it. They'd pick you off before you got halfway. Or worse, take you captive."

His last words brought back a memory of the Indians they'd encountered the day before, of the gleaming, savage looks the braves had given her before she'd thrown her tantrum. There may have been a lot of emotion in those dark eyes, but warmth had not been one of them.

"I could hire a scout. Someone who knew how to get around the Indians. There must be someone!"

"No. Don't you understand? No one can get through. When it's safe, I'll take you. Until then, you'll stay in San Antonio."

Gray took her silence for acquiescence. "Now, Serena's already in the wagon. Everybody's loading up. We'll be leaving in just a few minutes." He helped her up into the wagon. "I'll see you when we get to town."

Elizabeth climbed onto the seat beside Serena without another word, though her mind was racing. She had to get to Sweetbriar. She just had to. How did he expect her to just sit and wait for word, not to know if her sister was safe or . . . she shuddered at the thought of what might have happened to Eugenia, sweet, always smiling, loving Eugenia.

The caravan began to move. Serena—knowing that whenever Elizabeth fell completely silent, it meant trouble—kept throwing her wary glances, and with each one, the frown tugging at her brow grew deeper.

Finally, more than an hour and a half later, as the first wagons of the train rolled onto the main street of San Antonio, Elizabeth straightened, her shoulders lost their sag, and her blue eyes brightened.

Serena knew instantly that something was up, and she suspected whatever it was, she wasn't going to like it.

The caravan passed several saloons, and though it was late, nearing midnight, they were lively with noise. The tinkling of piano music competed with loud shouts, laughter, and the calls of faro dealers and boisterous drunks. Men lazed on the benches that sat before the saloons and cantinas, or slouched against hitching racks and support poles. They stopped their arguing, talking, or laughing as Elizabeth's wagon rolled past, all turning an appreciative eye toward her.

"Hey, honey, hope you're staying in San Antonio," one called out, the words slurred on his lips. The others all laughed and began to jeer at the man.

"Ignore them," Serena ordered, and flicked the reins over the oxen's rumps.

Gray brought the wagons to a halt at the open square in the center of town. He conversed with the sheriff for a few minutes and then rode down the line, telling everyone this was it, they'd disassemble the caravan in the morning.

Elizabeth knew that if she were going to act, it had to be now. She climbed down from the wagon and moved

323

toward the center of their circle. "Everybody!" she called loudly. "Everybody, listen to me, I have an offer to make."

The other members of the procession, most of whom had begun to climb from their wagons and prepare for the night, turned toward her, curious. A few ambled to stand before her, and a few cowboys from a nearby saloon sauntered over.

Gray, still mounted, turned to look at her. He'd had a hunch she would ignore his warning and pull something. And he knew just what he was going to do to stop her. While everyone was busy watching her, he jerked on the reins of his horse and rode to the rear of Elizabeth's wagon. Thankfully Serena had gone with her mistress. He climbed into the wagon and knelt before her trunk.

"I need to get to Sweetbriar," he heard her call out loudly, "and it's imperative that I get there *now.*"

Gray shoved a small velvet bag into the inside of his shirt and left the wagon.

"I'll pay five hundred dollars to anyone who'll guide me there," Elizabeth said.

Gray saw a few men shake their heads, and heard a couple snicker at her offer.

"Let's see the money," one of the cowboys who'd been sitting in front of the saloon called out.

Elizabeth hurried to the back of the wagon and made her way to the small trunk. She fumbled with its latch and finally got it open. She stared down in shock. The small velvet bag that she'd so carefully put in the trunk with her jewelry, the bag that held every cent she'd drawn from the bank, was gone.

"Serena!" Elizabeth shouted. "Serena!"

The old woman lumbered to the back of the wagon and peered over the gate. "What?"

"The money—it's gone!"

324

"Then we ain't going to Sweetbriar?" Serena tried to keep the relief she felt from her voice.

"Serena, someone stole our money. All of it. We have nothing." Elizabeth slammed the trunk lid down. Getting to her feet, she climbed back out of the wagon. "*He* did this, I know it."

"So where's the money, lady? I'll take you to Sweetbriar for five hundred dollars," one of the cowboys called out, his words slurred.

"Oh, shut up," Elizabeth snapped.

Gray rode up beside her. He struggled valiantly to keep from laughing, by reminding himself the situation wasn't really funny. Anyway, what he had done was for her own good, though he knew she wouldn't see it that way. "Is there a problem?"

She glared up at him. "My money's gone and—"she bit her bottom lip and looked away. Suddenly she felt like crying and clamped her teeth together, hard. She'd be damned if she'd cry in front of him. Everything was going wrong. Her whole life was nothing but one big mess, and every time she tried to fix it, things only got worse. She'd lost her respectability, she'd lost her money, and she'd lost her heart. And there was nothing she could do to get any of them back.

"Elizabeth?" Gray said softly.

She lifted her chin. Obviously she'd just have to wire the bank in New Orleans for more money, but how would she pay for the wire? And where were they going to stay? She looked at Gray. "Do you think the hotel will let us stay there without paying, until I can have the bank in New Orleans wire me more money?"

"No."

"No?" she repeated in surprise and stared at him. A slow burn of anger crept over her. "This is all your fault, you know. If you hadn't made me jump off that stupid boat and leave everything behind, I

325

wouldn't be in this fix."

Gray felt his own ire instantly provoked. Damn. Even when he was trying to be nice to her—which he should know better than to do—she acted like a little hellion. What he ought to do is give her back her damn money, but he knew, instead of a hotel room, she'd hire a guide to Sweetbriar and end up shot full of arrows. He couldn't let that happen, even if it made her hate him more than she already did. "If I hadn't made you jump off that stupid boat, as you put it, Elizabeth, you'd have burnt to a shriveled pile of bones and then sunk to the bottom of the river."

"Well at least I wouldn't have to put up with you!"

"You don't have to." He started to turn his horse away, then looked back. "If you'll remember, Miss Devlin, *I'm* not the one who invited you to join this wagon train in the first place."

"You're not gentleman enough to know how to invite a lady to do anything," Elizabeth spat back.

Gray jammed his heels against the sides of his horse and left Elizabeth standing in the dust of his abrupt departure. She flailed her hands at the dirt-filled air. How did that man always bring out the worst in her? And to think she'd even thought for one second that she loved him. Huh! She turned back toward her wagon.

"Now what are we going to do, Miss Smarty Pants?" Serena said, looking down at her from the seat of the wagon.

"Don't sass me, Serena. Not unless you want to stay in Sweetbriar with Eugenia, instead of returning to New Orleans with me."

"Might not be a bad idea. Probably be more peaceful, even with the Indians around."

Elizabeth shot Serena a scathing look. "I'm going to the hotel. Are you coming?"

The old woman climbed down from the wagon. "Can't let you go alone. No telling what might happen."

"Serena," Elizabeth said in a warning tone. She began to march down the street in the same direction Gray had taken. Within minutes she was in front of the door to the hotel. She stalked in.

"I need a room," she said smartly to the wiry little clerk who stood behind the desk.

He tossed a key onto the registry. "That'll be five dollars in advance."

Suddenly Elizabeth lost all of her bravado. Uncertainty washed over her. "Well, I, uh, that is my money was stolen."

The clerk grabbed the key back.

"But I'm having more funds wired here from New Orleans. Tomorrow. I can pay you then."

"Sorry. We don't take credit. Cash only."

"I'll vouch for the lady," Travis said, entering the hotel.

"No credit, Mr. Planchette. We don't give credit."

Travis dug several five-dollar gold pieces from the pocket of his trousers, and tossed them onto the counter. "I need a room, too." He took the keys from the man and handed one to Elizabeth. "Pay me back when you can," he said. "Order the ladies up a bath, too, would you, John," he said to the clerk. "It's been a long trip." He bent and kissed Elizabeth's cheek. "I'll see you in the morning, beautiful."

She watched him bound up the stairs and disappear.

Serena leaned over her shoulder. "Looks like that other one ain't the only man who's taken a fancy to you, Missy."

Elizabeth brushed her away. "Don't be silly, Serena. He's just being a gentleman."

"Uh-huh, and I'm George Washington."

327

An hour later, Elizabeth lay half-asleep in the big green tin tub the desk clerk had dragged into the room and filled with hot, soapy water. Her head rested against the tub's raised back. She'd washed her hair and then pinned it atop her crown, but a few tendrils had fallen loose of their pins and lay draped over her shoulder.

"I'm going downstairs to get us some coffee," Serena said, throwing a wrap around her wide shoulders. "No sense getting into bed now. Sun gonna be coming up in another hour or so."

Elizabeth opened her eyes and watched the older woman leave the room, then sighed. The water had cooled, and her fingertips were crinkled from their lengthy drowning. It had been so long since she'd had a real bath, that she'd been unable to bring herself to leave it. But now it was time. Unless she wanted to look like a shriveled-up prune. Grasping one side of the tub, Elizabeth rose and, with the other hand, reached out for the towel that lay folded on a nearby dresser top.

In the room on the other side of the wall that was to her right, a loud crash sounded, followed by a grumbled string of oaths. Elizabeth looked at the wall and frowned. What in heaven's name was going on in there? Something thudded against the wall, and it seemed to shake. She stepped hurriedly from the tub, rubbed the towel over herself, and moved to the side of the bed. What was going on in that room? A fight? She began to pull a batiste nightgown over her head when a knock behind her caused her to jump.

"Elizabeth, are you—"

She jerked around and stared at the door that led to an adjoining room. A door which she'd assumed was locked. Gray's tall figure filled the doorway, one hand still on the doorknob. The look of surprise etched on his face was no greater than the surprise that jolted her body.

In momentary shock at his sudden appearance, she stood still, staring at him, her eyes shackled by his, pinioned in place and unable to tear themselves away. She felt the breath catch in her throat, her body warm under his assessing gaze, and a hot, burning, aching sensation burst to life deep within her.

Gray stared at Elizabeth in awe, mesmerized. She was a vision of loveliness. Moonlight streamed into the dimly lit room from the window at her back to touch her body. It filtered through the sheer fabric of her gown, turning it to a translucent veil, her creamy white flesh to subtle planes of shimmering gold, and her curves to mysterious valleys of shadow.

Gray felt his body ignite into a flame of desire, and then harden with the gnawing hunger that always consumed him whenever he looked at her. His fingers clenched as they ached with the need to reach out and touch her. Memory of every kiss they had shared, every caress, came rushing back to assail him, to tease and haunt him, and stoke the hunger that threatened to engulf him.

Another crash against the wall behind her jerked Elizabeth from the hypnotic spell that held her. She jumped, startled, and let out a soft shriek.

Her movement also broke the stupor that held Gray in its grip. He felt a shiver ripple through him, like a wave of need unsatisfied. He shook it off. "Elizabeth, I'm . . . I'm sorry. I knocked, but you didn't answer. I thought . . . I mean, I heard the noise and wanted to see if you were all right, and . . ."

Elizabeth, while he'd been stammering, had managed to regain a modicum of composure, along with her indignation. She'd also rediscovered the anger she felt toward him, unreasonable as it might be. She knew she'd be dead if it wasn't for Gray, just as surely as she knew that he hadn't forced himself on her. Nor had he invited her on his wagon train, and she couldn't believe that he'd stolen her money. Yet he had made her feel things she'd never felt before, and he'd caused her to feel vulnerable. That's what fueled her anger. She had sworn when she'd left Aaron, that no man would ever make her feel that way again, and then she'd met Grayson, and all her barriers had crumbled like dust. She hurriedly grabbed her wrapper from the bed and pulled it around herself. "As you can so obviously see, Mr. Cantrelle, I am just fine, though I don't normally receive gentlemen callers in the dead of night, when I am preparing to retire." She remained across the room from him, not daring to go near him. "But then, I seem to have forgotten, you aren't a gentleman, are you?"

Gray held a tight rein on the anger that had bristled to life at her words, and tried only to think of why he'd come into her room in the first place. "Only enough to offer you a place to stay, until you can continue on to Sweetbriar," he growled softly.

Surprised, Elizabeth's answer was little more than a few stilted words. "A place? To stay?"

"Yes. My place. Travis and I will be going there in the morning. It will be days before you can travel to Sweetbriar. Maybe more. There's no way of telling. And I doubt your wire for money will result in any getting here sooner than two weeks. Travis has reminded me that you have no money and need a place to stay."

His cold tone infuriated her, and his mentioning that Travis had reminded him of her situation bristled on her nerves. The man was insufferable. Inconsiderate. Uncaring. He'd most likely leave her sleeping in the streets, if it were up to him. She squared her shoulders.

330

"Thank you, but we wouldn't want to put you out, Mr. Cantrelle."

"You won't. The Bar C has plenty of room." He made to close the door, paused, and looked back in. "We'll be leaving at dawn. Be ready."

Elizabeth stared at the closed door. Her heart was hammering so hard she thought it was ready to burst from her throat and take flight, and her fingers trembled so badly that she had to clutch the wrapper around her just to steady them.

He's like Satan, she decided, still staring at the door. Dark, handsome, alluring, mysterious, and hateful. "And not for me." She threw herself down on the bed and began to cry. "Definitely not for me."

Chapter 22

"Now what's wrong?" Serena asked, leaning back in her seat on the wagon to look at Elizabeth.

"Nothing," Elizabeth grumbled, refusing to meet the older woman's gaze.

"Nothing," Serena echoed. "You been snipping and snapping all morning, but nothing's wrong. Child, you're a wonder."

"Don't call me child. I'm not a child anymore."

"You act like one, I'll call you one," Serena said.

"I can fire you, you know."

Serena chuckled. "Then who'd you sass at? Him?" She nodded toward Gray, who was riding beside the buckboard in front of them. Travis was driving it, and he and Gray, for the past few minutes, had seemed deep in conversation. Jason rode in the back, sitting atop a pile of flour sacks and nodding off every once in a while.

Elizabeth stared at Gray's back. As if he felt her eyes on him, he twisted around in his saddle and looked at her. She met his gaze squarely, her own eyes blazing with, she hoped, defiance. "I don't have anything to say to *him*." She knew she should be grateful for his invitation to accommodate her and Serena until their wired funds arrived from New Orleans, but she couldn't help be suspicious of him, despite her conviction that he wasn't a thief. He and Travis were the only ones who'd been inside her wagon. The first time when they took some of her things out and distributed them to the other wagons to ease the load on her oxen, and the second time only a few days ago when they'd had to trade some of her goods to the Indians. Either man could have taken the small satchel of money, but she guessed it had been Gray. It was probably an attempt to get her into a compromising position again, so that he could take advantage of her. Seduce her. Elizabeth's jaw set hard. Well, that wasn't going to happen.

Serena smiled a knowing smile. "Nothing to say, huh?" she mumbled softly. "Time will tell."

Elizabeth's head jerked up, and she glared at Serena. Anger had always been her best defense against hurt, and it would remain such. "Poppycock," she snapped. "The sooner we can leave and get to Eugenia's, the better I'll like it. Then we can go back to New Orleans, and Mr. Cantrelle," she threw a glance at Gray again, "can go back to shooting people, or whatever else it is he does for a living."

Aaron reined his horse up beside George's and looked at the two wagons far ahead of them. "How are we going to get her now?" he whined. "They're going to his ranch. It'll be impossible."

"There's Jason," Damien said, pointing toward the buckboard.

"Nothing's impossible," George said to Aaron. He smiled and ignored Damien. The gesture caused his thin face to take on the appearance of a ferret. "Not out here."

"But there'll be others now. We can't just ride in and—"

"Stop your whining, Reynaud. We'll get her, when the time's right." He chuckled derisively. "Don't you worry. That little blondie and I got some unfinished business."

"Aaron," Damien said, "look, there's Jason."

Aaron's head snapped around, and he stared at George. "What do you mean by that? What business? How do you know my sister?"

George smiled. "Cut the jawin', Reynaud. That little hellcat ain't your sister, and we both know it."

Aaron stiffened. "All right, so she's not my sister. But how do *you* know her? And what do you mean you have unfinished business?"

"All I was trying to do was be nice to her, and she damned near killed me. Almost split my skull open. Then she killed my brother."

Aaron's mouth fell open. "Killed your brother? How? What are you talking about?"

George waved off his question. "Ain't important how. She just done it, that's all you need to know. And she's going to pay. You can have your fun with her, then it'll be my turn."

Aaron began to protest and then stopped. He shrugged. What did he care if the man had Elizabeth . . . so long as he got her first. "How much farther do you think they have to go?"

"Aaron," Damien cut in. "We have to get Jason back."

"Shut up," Aaron snapped.

"Man at the general store said the ranch was five miles out of town," George said. He paid no attention to Damien, but then he hadn't since the moment they had ridden out of New Orleans. "I'd reckon we're on his property right now. House should be coming into view

334

any time. Most likely, right around that little hill there." He pointed to a raised knoll of land off in the distance.

Gray turned his horse and rode back toward Elizabeth, circled again, and came to ride beside her wagon. "We're almost there," he said. He leaned forward in his seat and looked past Elizabeth to Serena. "When we get there, just pull your wagon up in front of the house. I'll have it moved and the oxen taken care of later."

Serena nodded her understanding. Gray nudged his horse and moved back up beside the wagon which Travis drove.

"Just pull your wagon up in front of the house," Elizabeth mimicked angrily. "I'll have it moved."

Serena chuckled. "Lordy sakes, Missy, I ain't never seen such hot sparks and cold icicles fly between two people as I been seeing between you two."

Elizabeth glared at her.

"I swear, you two either got a great big hankering for each other, or you're hungering to kill one another."

"Hand me a gun and I'll give it a try," Elizabeth said.

Serena laughed, her big body shaking with tremors at her mirth.

The road they were traveling curved around a tall knoll, and as they passed a long, narrow copse of scrub pine, the Bar C ranch house and its outbuildings came into view. Elizabeth immediately forgot her conversation with Serena, as well as her anger at Gray. Her eyes grew wide with surprise, her mouth dropped open, and she stared, unbelieving.

"This . . . this is the Bar C?" she mumbled. She had expected a mud hovel and maybe a few corrals. She had expected windows of cloth and a roof of sod. She

335

had not expected this. The soft pink walls of a Spanish hacienda glowed before them beneath the shimmering hot rays of the morning sun. With a roof of red brick tiles, the house was two stories, and huge wings branched off just behind and on either side of the main body of the structure. Tall windows were framed by shutters painted a soft deep rosy color, a wide veranda swept before the length of each storey, and four fat, squat pillars graced the front of the main part of the house. There were several outbuildings on either side of the house: barns, bunkhouse, and stables, as well as corrals. Several hundred yards before they reached the house, the wagons rolled under an arched wooden entryway which had the words Bar C carved into it.

"I can't believe this is *his* home." Elizabeth said, her voice barely more than a ragged whisper.

"Guess it ain't what you expected, huh, Missy?" Serena said.

She had thought he had nothing. That he was a drifter. A gunfighter. Confusion gleamed from her eyes. Where had she gotten the notion that he made his living by hiring out his skill with a gun?

Serena pulled the wagon up before the house as Gray had instructed.

"Welcome to the Bar C, ladies."

Elizabeth and Serena turned at the unexpected female voice.

At their looks of surprise, a light tinkling of laughter escaped the woman's lips. The sound drifted away on the gentle morning breeze that wafted through the brilliantly white bougainvillea, which clung to one of the pillars.

Elizabeth returned the woman's smile, feeling an instant warmth toward her. She was tiny, barely five feet tall. Her skin was tanned to a golden hue, her dark hair was as black as the night, and her eyes were a soft brown with slight tinges of gold within their depths. She wasn't young, attested to by the tiny lines around her eyes and mouth, but she wasn't old either, Elizabeth mused, looking at the woman's hair and spotting not one strand of gray. She was dressed in a gown of muslin almost the same shade as her eyes, its piping trim the color of a pristine cloud.

Travis jumped down from his wagon and hurried toward the women. He bent his tall frame and kissed the short woman's cheek, whispered something in her ear, then quickly turned to help Serena from the wagon. When Elizabeth stood and moved to climb out, expecting Travis to turn back to assist her, too, she was taken aback to find Gray standing beside the wagon, his hand outstretched toward her.

Reluctantly she placed her fingers on his hand. She tried to steel herself against his touch, but it was no good. Searing flames of heat shot through her fingers, raced up the length of her arm, and swept through her chest to collide in a crashing blow with her suddenly racing heart. Get a hold of yourself, Elizabeth, she ordered silently. He doesn't care about you. He only invited you here because Travis made him feel he had to. She knew it was true, and yet she found herself wishing desperately that it wasn't.

Gray's hand disengaged itself from hers, as she balanced precariously on the edge of the wagon wheel. For one panic-filled second, she thought he was going to let her fall, then his hands clasped her waist, his fingers spanning its breadth easily. He lifted her from the wheel, and Elizabeth found herself forced to place her hands on his shoulders for balance. When her feet touched the ground she barely noticed. Gray's hands remained on her waist, warm and firm, their touch burning through the fabric of her gown, and her hands

337

remained on his shoulders, as she unconsciously reveled in the sensation of his strength, the iron hardness of his muscles beneath her fingertips.

"Travis, Gray, are you boys going to introduce me to your friends?" the woman said, drawing everyone's attention.

Gray, suddenly embarrassed, dropped his hands from Elizabeth's waist. At the same time she pulled her hands away from him and stepped back, then turned to face the woman who'd greeted them.

"Sorry," Gray mumbled, but whether to Elizabeth or the woman who'd spoken, neither were certain.

The woman reached out and took one of Elizabeth's hands in her own. "It seems my son has forgotten his manners." She smiled and threw Gray a sly little look. "I'm Celia Cantrelle," she said to Elizabeth.

Son? This beautiful woman was Gray's mother? Suddenly, staring at the woman in open wonder, Elizabeth began to see the resemblance between mother and son. The same ebony hair, almost the same amber-flecked brown eyes, and definitely the same smile, though Gray didn't use it often enough, she thought.

"Mother, this is Elizabeth Devlin, and her servant," Gray nodded toward the older woman, "Serena." Celia Cantrelle smiled and took one of Elizabeth's hands in hers, as Gray continued to talk. "They were on their way to Sweetbriar—Elizabeth has a sister there—when we heard the news of the town's attack. I invited them to stay here until it was safe to travel again."

"That was good, Gray," she said. "Now, you and Travis go on and take care of the wagons and animals, and the ladies and I will go inside and get acquainted. We'll see you both later, for supper."

Travis and Gray started to turn away, as did the women. Celia Cantrelle looped one arm through

Elizabeth's, and led her and Serena toward the entry door. Before entering she paused and looked back at the men. "Don't disappear on us again, Travis."

"No, ma'am, I wouldn't think of it," Travis said, and though his words sounded demure, Elizabeth didn't miss the little wink he sent Gray's mother.

Celia led Elizabeth and Serena into a large foyer. "Now, let's see, Gray will have someone bring your things to the house from the wagon, and when he does, I'll show you to your rooms." She paused. "Oh, that is, unless you want to go to them now. Are you tired?" Celia looked from Elizabeth to Serena.

Elizabeth was too filled with curiosity to want to go to a room and rest. She could have been ready to faint dead away from exhaustion, and she'd still have said no. This was Gray's mother. This was his home, his land. Why hadn't he ever told her? Why had he allowed her to believe he was nothing but a drifter—a man who lived by his gun—a nobody?

Because he doesn't really care about you, and didn't want you getting any silly notions about him, said the little voice that popped up in the back of her mind whenever she *didn't* want to hear it.

But this time she couldn't argue with it, because she knew it was right. Elizabeth shook her head.

"Good," Celia said. "I want you to meet Dana."

"Dana?" Elizabeth echoed.

"Yes. Didn't Gray tell you about Dana? Or the baby?"

"No, he didn't. I mean, well, the subject never came up and . . ." Elizabeth felt her insides contract—hard. Gray had a wife. And a baby. The miserable, lying, low-down blackguard. All the while he'd been with her, flirting with her on the boat, making love to her on the riverbank, and again on the prairie, all that time, he'd had a wife and child waiting for him! And the blackguard had proposed to her. She felt a volcanic swell of rage begin to seethe deep within her. The rogue. Her fingers itched to scratch his eyes out.

"Missy, this old body is screaming for a cup of coffee," Serena said. She turned to Celia. "Ma'am, if I could impose on you?"

"Of course, Serena. Just go through that door there," she pointed to a door at the end of the foyer, "and you'll find the kitchen. Maria always has a pot of coffee steeping on the stove. Just help yourself."

Serena waddled off and disappeared through the door Celia had indicated.

Gray's mother turned back to Elizabeth and suddenly frowned. "Elizabeth, I couldn't help but notice the tension between you and Gray. Is something wrong between you two? I mean," she laughed lightly, "I don't wish to sound like a prying mother, but, I know my son, especially when he gets around a beautiful woman. Did he . . . well, there's no delicate way to put this, so I'll just say it. Did Gray mind his manners around you?"

Elizabeth felt like laughing. Mind his manners? What would his mother think if she told her the truth? Well, Mrs. Cantrelle, let's see, your son seduced me once while we were forced to camp out on a bank on the side of a river, and nearly managed to do so again on the road to New Orleans. He kissed me beneath the moonlight of a Texas sky and did such magical things to my body that I didn't have the strength or the will to deny him. But, yes, Mrs. Cantrelle, your son remembered his manners. The only thing he didn't remember was to inform me that he had a wife and child.

"Elizabeth, dear?"

Elizabeth blushed and tried to push the memory of Gray's kiss from her mind. "Yes, Mrs. Cantrelle, Gray was a perfect gentleman," Elizabeth said. No sense destroying the woman's illusion of her son, and having her realize she'd given birth to an incarnate of Satan himself.

"Good. He hasn't always, and I was afraid . . ." She waved a dismissing hand in the air. "Never mind. Come, let's go see Dana and the baby. Randy's almost four months old now, and Gray hasn't even seen him yet. He left when Dana was just a little over five and a half months pregnant."

Elizabeth followed Celia Cantrelle, though her step was anything but lively now. She wasn't looking forward to this. She had never been much of an actress and, as Serena always said, most people could see her true emotions written across her face, no matter what she was acting like.

They entered a room that Elizabeth realized through the haze of her muddled mind was a library, obvious by the tall shelves of books that reached from floor to ceiling on three walls, the other being comprised of two windows framed by drapes of burgundy damask. A woman, small and slender, with brilliant dark brown eyes and full, sensuous lips, her dark hair spread across her shoulders like a silky black veil, looked up as they entered the room. She handed the baby a toy he'd dropped, and then pushed the sleeves of her white blouse higher on her arms.

Elizabeth realized instantly that they were about the same age.

"Look, Randy," the young woman said to the baby, who lay on a brilliantly colored Indian blanket on the floor at her feet. "Grandma's here, and she's brought company."

The baby gurgled happily, threw the toy down, and began to play with his toes.

"Dana, this is Elizabeth Devlin," Celia said. "She was on the wagon train with Gray and Travis, and has a sister in Sweetbriar. She's going to be staying with us for a while, until it's safe to travel again."

"Hi," Dana said. "Welcome to the Bar C."

"Hello," Elizabeth said softly, staring at the baby. Gray's baby.

"Dana, your brother also brought Travis home with him," Celia said.

"Travis?" Dana jumped up from the settee. "He's here now?"

"Relax," Celia chuckled. "He'll be joining us for dinner. You can see him then."

Dana tried to hide her disappointment, but it was still obvious, at least to Celia. Elizabeth wasn't paying any attention. She was too deep in shock at Celia's earlier comment.

Brother? Elizabeth thought, looking at Celia and Dana Cantrelle in confusion. Brother? Gray is her brother?

Celia turned to Elizabeth. "Tell me, Elizabeth, do you know where Gray found Travis? We haven't seen him for, my goodness," she looked at Dana, "what is it, three or four years now, Dana?"

Dana nodded.

"You're Gray's sister?" Elizabeth said in a weak voice, completely ignoring Celia's question about Travis. She couldn't think about Travis right now, or anything else for that matter. Her heart felt as if it were suddenly flying. Dana was Gray's sister, not his wife, as she'd assumed. Why she felt so exuberant, she didn't know. It really made no difference. Gray didn't care for her. But she couldn't help it. She was so glad Dana wasn't Gray's wife, she felt like throwing her arms around the girl and hugging her.

"My brother is almost ten years older than me. Mama always says I was her late-in-life baby." Dana laughed softly. "Our father died quite a few years ago,

342

and Gray had to take over the running of the ranch. He kind of took over as a father to me, too."

"He . . . he's not a gunfighter?"

Both women looked at her in astonishment, and then, after a long moment, began to laugh.

"A gunfighter?" Dana said, finally, gasping. "My brother?" She shook her head.

"I'm sorry," Elizabeth said, wishing Gray were standing before her, so that she could swing her reticule against the side of his head. "I just assumed that, from some of the things he said." *And didn't say,* she added silently.

The baby began to cry then, and Dana turned her attentions to him.

"I'll see about getting us some coffee and biscuits," Celia said, moving from the room.

Elizabeth felt assailed by a seige of emotions, all of which were in conflict with one another. She sank down on a chair opposite Dana. Everything she had assumed of Grayson Cantrelle—that he was a drifter, a man who lived by his gun, a man who had nothing— was wrong.

And it doesn't matter, because he doesn't care one twit about you.

Elizabeth didn't want to hear that voice right now, didn't want to acknowledge what it had to say. But it wasn't going to give her a choice. She gave a mental shrug. The voice was right, but what did she care? So what if he had money . . . and land . . . and position. He wasn't a gentleman. He'd made her catch and cook those slimy, icky fish, he'd made her take care of him, had lulled her into a state of comfort and then seduced her, and had promptly tried to leave her in New Orleans like so much unwanted baggage. No, she had lied to his mother. Grayson Cantrelle was no gentleman. She sniffed. If she took a husband at all—which

343

after her recent experiences with men she was beginning to highly doubt—he definitely would have to be a gentleman.

"I'm sorry about your sister, Elizabeth," Dana said, laying the baby on the floor again. "But I'm glad you'll be able to visit with us a while." She smiled knowingly. "I'll bet Gray is, too."

"I rather doubt it. Gray and I don't exactly . . . well, we don't get along very well with each other. Does your husband work on the ranch, too?" she asked.

A shadow fell over Dana's face, and her brilliant smile faded. "I'm not married."

"Oh," Elizabeth looked at her in surprise. "I'm sorry, I just thought . . ."

"Didn't Gray tell you?"

Elizabeth shook her head. "Tell me what?" Had the girl's fiancé died?

"That's why he was away from home, he was looking for the man who . . . he was looking for Randy's father."

"Oh, he's missing?"

Dana shook her head. "He decided he didn't want a wife and child."

"I'm sorry," Elizabeth said, and she was. She knew exactly how Dana felt. She thought of Gray, and knew she felt almost the same way. He didn't want a wife either. At least he didn't want Elizabeth as his wife.

Dana's smile returned. "But it's okay, really. I tried to make Gray see that, when he said he was leaving to find Carlen and bring him back here to face his responsibilities, but he wouldn't listen."

Elizabeth rose. "I think I'll find your mother and have her show me to my room. I'm really very tired. Please excuse me, Dana, I'll see you later." She felt a heaviness in her heart. That was why Gray had asked her to marry him. That was the only reason: because he

344

felt guilty. It was as she'd suspected all along. He didn't care for her, he'd only wanted to face his responsibilities. She threw back her shoulders. But what did it matter, she didn't care for him either. She began to turn away.

"Elizabeth," Dana called softly.

She turned back. "Yes?"

"Does Gray know you're in love with him?"

Elizabeth's mouth almost dropped open. She caught it just in time, and stared at Dana in absolute disbelief. A thousand denials raced through her mind. In love with him? With Grayson Cantrelle? The thought was totally insane. Crazy.

"I can see it in your eyes, Elizabeth. A woman can always tell when another woman is in love. My mother taught me that."

Elizabeth stiffened, squared her shoulders, and pointed her perfect little nose high in the air. "I'm afraid you're mistaken, Dana," she said evenly, refusing to allow Dana to see how much the statement had unnerved her. In love with him, indeed. How ridiculous. True, she'd wanted to believe he cared for her, but only because of what they'd done together. "Gray and I have nothing in common, nor do we even like one another. Circumstances threw us together, and . . . and that is all."

"Does he know you love him?"

Elizabeth felt a swell of anger. "I don't love him, Dana. I don't. And he doesn't love me."

Dana remained silent. She didn't comment. She couldn't. Not until she talked to her brother.

Chapter 23

The nerve of the woman. In love with Gray. Was she crazy? Elizabeth stormed around the room she'd been shown to, pulled a gown from one valise, a petticoat from another, shoes from yet another. The man was an insufferable rogue. What was there to be in love with? His arrogance? His conceit? His bullying?

Elizabeth sniffed. In love with him indeed. How ridiculous. She'd more likely fall in love with a toad than Grayson Cantrelle.

A knock on the door stopped her short. She whirled around, startled.

"Missy? Missy, you in there?"

She released a sigh of relief. Serena. For some insane reason, she'd been afraid it was Gray. She hurried to the door and flung it open.

Serena waddled into the room. "A man just rode in from town. Said they dispatched a troop of Rangers down to Sweetbriar, but we probably wouldn't hear anything for several days."

Elizabeth felt a sweep of guilt. For the past few hours she'd been doing nothing but thinking of herself, and, if truth be told, Grayson. Not once had she thought of Eugenia.

Tears welled up in Elizabeth's eyes. "Oh, Serena, whatever are we going to do? What if something happens to Eugenia?" She flopped down on the huge pine bed that dominated the room, her fingers absently poking at the crocheted coverlet. "I just couldn't stand it if something happened to her, Serena. I just couldn't."

Serena began to hang Elizabeth's gowns in the tall armoire that stood against one wall. "Ain't nothing going to happen to Eugenia, so don't go fretting about it." She turned back to Elizabeth. "She's been living down here in this country for some years now, she'll be fine, but I don't know about you."

Elizabeth bolted from the bed to glare at Serena. "And just what is that supposed to mean?"

"Nothing. Take a nap. Mrs. Cantrelle said dinner would be ready in a few hours." Serena moved toward the door. She opened it, began to step into the hallway, then paused, and looked back at Elizabeth. "Wear that new blue satin gown tonight that you showed me, Missy. It's your best color. Shows off your eyes."

"Why? There's no one here to show off for."

Serena chuckled and shut the door behind her as she left.

"I couldn't find him, Dana," Gray said. He held his finger out to the baby, all the while avoiding his sister's gaze. Randy promptly wrapped his tiny fingers around his uncle's larger one and gurgled happily. With the other hand Gray slid a finger beneath the stiff white collar of his shirt, and tugged at it in an effort to loosen the black string tie at his neck. His mother had always insisted on dressing for dinner.

"It's not really important, Gray. Not anymore."

He looked up then, surprised. "What do you mean?

347

The man seduced you. He left you while you were with child—just walked out on you! And now you say it's not important that we find him?"

"What for?" Dana asked. She smiled at the way Gray continued to play, absentmindedly, with Randy.

"Dana, the man fathered your child."

"A child he doesn't want, and as far as I'm concerned, a child he has no right to know. Randy is mine, Gray. He's a Cantrelle. He has you, me, and Mama. He doesn't need Carlen Masters."

"Or whatever his name is," Gray said derisively.

"Or whatever his name is," Dana echoed. "Look, I don't want him here, Gray. I don't want him to share any part of my life, or Randy's, whether he wants to or not. We were wrong for each other, I know that now. We were too different."

"But he—"

"Would you want a wife who didn't love you, Gray? Who didn't share your interests? Who didn't want to live here, on the Bar C?"

He thought instantly of Elizabeth, and sighed. "No," he said softly. "You're right."

She watched her brother for a long moment, and finally got up the courage to ask the one question that had been on her mind for the past few hours. "Gray, how do you feel about Elizabeth?"

He took a long breath, released it, and continued to play with Randy. She thought he wasn't going to answer, but finally, he spoke. "She's the most infuriating woman I have ever met, Dana, and the sooner she can leave for Sweetbriar and I can get my life back into some kind of order, the better I'll like it."

Dana smiled. "She said almost the same thing about you. . . ."

"Well, at least we agree on something."

A bit of devilment sparked in Dana's eyes. "Well, if

348

you don't care for her, maybe we could match her up with Travis. If he got married, he'd probably stick around a little more." She watched Gray carefully. "What do you think?"

"I think you're crazy," Gray said, and got to his feet as his mother entered the parlor.

"Why do you think your sister is crazy?" she asked.

"Do I have to have a specific reason?" Gray said, chuckling. He bent over and kissed his mother's cheek.

Travis entered the room almost on Celia's heels. "Dana, you look beautiful tonight." He moved to stand before her. "But then, you always do. And yellow certainly does become you." He gave her an exaggerated bow, lifted her hand in his, and pressed it to his lips.

Dana laughed softly. "And you, my errant friend, obviously still have that silver tongue that always used to get you into trouble."

Elizabeth stood in the large foyer, just out of sight of the parlor entry door. Her stomach was in flutters. Serena had insisted on eating with the Cantrelles' servants, leaving Elizabeth alone to face her hosts. Why in heaven's name was she so nervous? "You're being silly, Elizabeth," she admonished herself softly. Taking a deep breath, and unconsciously sliding one hand across the blue satin flounces of her skirt to smooth them, she smiled widely and stepped around the corner of the entryway.

As if he could feel her presence, Gray, who'd had his back to the door, turned. His gaze met hers and, for one long, seemingly interminable minute, held it his captive. The sight of her nearly took his breath away, and the repercussion within him was anger. He didn't want to notice her beauty, he didn't want to desire her, but he couldn't deny the flames of hungry passion that swept through him every time she came near, or the need to possess her, to make her his and never allow another man near her for as long as they lived. "Damn," Gray breathed softly, the curse no more than a whisper.

His gaze slid from hers and dropped to the deeply plunging neckline of her gown. The soft swell of her breasts rose enticingly above a ruche of snow-white lace, the delicate fabric dripping in crisp folds over the snugly fitting bodice of royal-blue silk. His hands yearned to caress the bare shoulders revealed above the puff of sleeve that encircled each upper arm, or span the breadth of the tiny waist that was encased within a wide sash of blue velvet.

"Elizabeth," Celia said, hearing Gray's expletive and noticing his sudden change in attitude. She hadn't seen a woman unnerve her son for a very, very long time, and never with such intensity. "Please, come join us. We were just visiting, while we wait for dinner to be served."

Elizabeth tore her gaze away from Gray's, but not without some difficulty. The man was a boor, yet everytime she got near him, she felt drawn to him like a magnet. It was infuriating. Her skin turned to a prickly blanket of hot shivers, her heart nearly beat itself right out of her chest, and her pulses felt as if they were racing out of control.

Behind her a loud knock suddenly sounded on the main entry door. Everyone turned toward the foyer expectantly. Gray jerked himself from the spell Elizabeth's appearance had cast over him, and brushed past her toward the door. He swung it open wide, allowing the sweet scent of the night, of jasmine, bouganvillea, roses, and prairie sage, to invade the house.

"*Señor,* I have a message," a young boy said hurriedly. His thin brown fingers kneaded at a straw hat he held in his hands.

Gray nodded. "Go ahead, Pedro. What is it?"

"The sheriff in San Antonio, he said to tell you that the town of Sweet—Sweet—" the boy looked suddenly panicked.

"Sweetbriar?" Gray prompted him with a little smile.

The boy's brown eyes lit with happy relief. *"Sí, señor,* Sweetbriar. It is all right now. The town. But the road, she is still closed. Too many renegade Indians."

Gray took the boy's hand and placed a coin in it. "Thank you, Pedro. Tell your father to come by tomorrow, we can use his help with the new horses I brought back with me."

"Sí, señor, I will tell him. *Gracias."* The boy bowed and quickly disappeared into the night.

Elizabeth hurried to stand beside Gray. "Does that mean Sweetbriar is safe? The town is safe?" Elizabeth asked, anxiously. "Can we get through now?"

"The town is safe, Elizabeth, but the road's not. It's still too dangerous to travel, unless you're not as fond of that blond hair of yours as I thought."

Dana watched Gray furtively, measuring every word he spoke to Elizabeth, every nuance of movement he made.

For an answer, Elizabeth turned on her heel and walked back toward the others. The small group was just returning to the parlor, when another knock sounded on the entry door.

"Now what?" Gray growled, turning back and stomping to the door. He swung it open with a snap. "Yes?"

"Well, if I had known I'd get such a heartwarming reception, or that I'd be dining with a bear, I think I would have declined the invitation and stayed home."

Gray smiled sheepishly as their neighbor, Tori

Chisolm, swept into the room in a swirl of lavender silk and ivory lace. "Sorry," he murmured.

"Humph, you've been gone more than six months, and *that's* the kind of greeting I get?" With a little frown creasing her brow, and a mocking glare in her green eyes, Tori drew a silk shawl from her shoulders and handed it to a servant who had quietly appeared at her side, then turned to Gray. She shook her head slightly, causing her red hair to cascade in long, loose waves over her shoulders, then stood on tiptoe, placed both hands on his shoulders, and pressed her lips lightly to his. "Now that's a proper greeting," she said, and smiled widely. Her eyes sparkled with mischief.

Gray's hands lingered on her waist as he smiled down at her. "You're right, and one I like much better myself."

"Tori?" Travis said. He pulled himself from Dana's clasp and hurried to the woman's side. "You little minx, it is you!"

Laughing lightly, Tori kissed Travis's cheek. "I missed you too, Trav," she said, and looped an arm through his.

Elizabeth felt a swell of instant dislike for the new arrival. Who was this woman anyway? She obviously had both men under her spell, though Elizabeth couldn't for the life of her see why. Oh, she was beautiful enough, there was no denying that. But she was so . . . so . . . Elizabeth searched for a word to describe her impression of the woman, and couldn't think of one. All she knew was that the way the woman was simpering over Gray and Travis was nauseating. And they were lapping it up like two attention-starved puppies.

"Dana," Travis said, "look who's here. Oh, and Elizabeth, you don't know Tori." Travis pulled Tori toward Elizabeth. "Elizabeth Devlin, this is Tori

Chisolm. Her ranch borders the western edge of the Bar C."

Elizabeth forced a smile to her lips.

Behind them a servant approached Celia Cantrelle and announced that dinner was being served in the dining room.

Travis immediately spun around and offered one arm to Dana. Tori released his other arm to turn to Gray, and Travis offered his now free arm to Celia. Elizabeth glanced from Travis to Gray, feeling suddenly awkward.

Gray, looking as if he'd rather be offering his arm to a hungry tiger, paused before Elizabeth. "Miss Devlin?"

"Thank you, but I can see myself to the dining room," she said haughtily, and spun around. Miss Devlin. The nerve of the man. What was he trying to do, convince this little tart that he and Elizabeth were virtual strangers? That there was nothing between them?

Well, there isn't.

"Shut up," she snapped at the voice inside of her head.

"Pardon me?" Celia said, turning to look at Elizabeth.

Her cheeks burned, and she just knew she had turned as red as the threads weaved within the Indian blanket that hung from one of the dining room walls. Why did Grayson Cantrelle always cause her to act like such a . . . such a *ninny?* "Oh, nothing," she mumbled, embarrassed to the core. "I was just, ah, just thinking out loud."

Dana bit down on her bottom lip to keep from smiling.

Celia sat at the head of the table with Dana on her right, and Travis beside Dana. Gray pulled out a chair for Elizabeth to Celia's left, then, after seating Tori in the third chair, settled himself between the two women.

Elizabeth nibbled her way through a salad, forced herself to down a cup of soup, made a halfhearted attempt to eat a biscuit, and picked at her steak, jabbing it with a knife she secretly wished she could jab into Gray's ribs. Maybe then he'd remember she was sitting next to him, too. Of course, he was so preoccupied with Tori Chisolm, that he seemed oblivious of anyone else at the table. Maybe she could stand abruptly, as if she'd been startled, or felt sick, and accidentally fall against his chair and knock him over backward. Or perhaps she could, in reaching for her napkin, knock over her glass of wine. A wet lap would certainly cool his ardor for the impudent Miss Chisolm.

"Gray," Celia said, drawing her son's attention, "why don't you and Travis go ahead and make your rounds for the night, make sure everything is locked up, and then join us in the parlor for coffee?"

Elizabeth rose from her seat as Gray and Travis left the room. "I think I'll retire for the night, Mrs. Cantrelle, if you'll excuse me?" The last thing she wanted was to sit and watch Gray drool over Tori Chisolm again. At least Travis seemed to have gotten control of himself.

Gray watched Elizabeth leave the room, and Celia watched Gray. She saw the light leave his eyes, and knew that Elizabeth Devlin had definitely found a place in her son's heart, even if he didn't realize it.

Elizabeth woke the next morning to sun streaming in through the two tall windows of her bedroom. The heavy drapes of yellow damask had been pulled back, and her clothes were already laid out on a gold brocade settee that sat near the armoire. At that precise moment, the door to the hall opened and Serena entered carrying a tray laden with a pot of steaming coffee and a plate of hot biscuits.

"Well, it's about time you woke up. I was beginning to think you was going to sleep all day."

Elizabeth yawned and pulled herself up to a sitting position, then leaned back against the mound of pillows propped against the bed's headboard. "What time is it?"

"Almost noon." Serena handed Elizabeth a cup of coffee.

"Any word on Sweetbriar? Can we get through yet?"

Serena shook her head. "You'd best get yourself up and outside."

"Outside?" Elizabeth looked clearly puzzled. "Why?"

"'Cause that pretty little thing that was here last night is back."

She knew instantly that Serena meant Tori Chisolm. An image of Gray hovering over Tori's every word the previous evening flashed in her mind. "So?" she responded coolly.

Serena didn't answer. Instead she busied herself digging Elizabeth's new riding habit out of one of the valises.

"And just why are you presuming I'm going to wear that?"

"'Cause you're going riding, that's why."

"I am not."

"Miss Tori and Miss Dana are, and so are Mr. Gray and Mr. Travis."

"I prefer to stay here," Elizabeth said sullenly. "I'll visit with Mrs. Cantrelle."

"You can't. She's going, too."

"Oh, pooh." Elizabeth flung the covers from her legs and slid from the bed. "We never should have come to this horrible land. I should have stayed in Mississippi and married Aaron. At least he was a gentleman."

"With every skirt in sight," Serena added.

"I'm beginning to believe all men are like that." Elizabeth wrestled herself into her pantalettes and camisole, then struggled her way within the confines of a lightweight riding habit. The skirt was a pale brown muslin, while the jacket was a darker shade. Black velvet trim edged the cuffs and lapels.

She pulled her hair to her crown and pinned it, allowing it to fall free in a mass of tiny wild curls.

"Her outfit's more for turning a man's head, but I guess this will do," Serena said, fluffing Elizabeth's skirt.

"Well, thank you so much for the compliment. I feel much better now."

"Save your sass, Missy, you're going to need it."

Elizabeth tugged at the black kid gloves she wore and flexed her fingers inside of the leather, as she made her way down the stairs. She stepped onto the shaded veranda and began to make her way around to the side of the house toward the corrals. Why she'd let Serena talk her into accepting the invitation to go riding, she didn't know. Even though it was barely mid-morning, the sun was blazing mercilessly and the air was already suffocating. At the corner of the house, Elizabeth stopped abruptly. Gray was standing beside a horse within one of the nearby corrals, his hand resting on the animal's mane. His right hand held that of Tori Chisolm, who sat astride the horse. The rich, sonorous sound of Gray's laugh seemed to suddenly fill the air, as she watched a smile light his face at something Tori said to him.

Dana, Travis, and Celia stood nearby, conversing,

but Elizabeth paid little attention to them. She stared at Gray, searing bolts of irritation, like lightning, snapping through her body. Well, they certainly had no hesitation at flaunting their relationship in everyone's face. Elizabeth's fingers suddenly ached to wrap themselves around Tori's neck.

She moved toward Dana and the others, a bundle of raw nerves, confused emotions, and white-hot indignation. She tried to ignore Gray, to keep her gaze averted from him, and failed miserably. Her eyes just would not obey her brain's command, and kept sneaking back in his direction. What in tarnation was the matter with her? The man was a beast. An arrogant, bullying, insensitive brute. Just because he wasn't a lowly drifter or gunfighter like she'd thought, didn't change any of that.

Her gaze rose to take in Tori, bent over in the saddle, her face to come in close proximity with Gray's, and saying something to him Elizabeth could not hear. Elizabeth sniffed and quickly yanked her gaze away. This was all too ridiculous. Why should she care *what* Gray did, or what kind of woman he was attracted to? If Tori Chisolm wanted Grayson Cantrelle, well, she could just have him. And good riddance.

Elizabeth stomped up to the trio. Dana and Travis exchanged what Elizabeth considered a somewhat knowing glance, which only added fuel to the already blazing conflagration raging within her, and Celia smiled complacently.

"I'm so glad you could join us this morning for a ride," Celia said.

Elizabeth forced herself to smile, though she felt as if her lips were ready to crack from the effort. What she really wanted to do was think of an excuse not to go, but she couldn't. She wanted to pick up one of the boards she'd seen lying near the corral fence and crown

357

Gray with it, giving him a permanent wooden hat. She wanted to do anything but stand there and listen to the lilting sounds of Tori's laughter drift over to her, accompanied by the soft chuckling of Gray's deep baritone.

"Elizabeth."

She spun around, startled at hearing his voice so near her ear. Her heart hammered, her breath caught in her throat, threatening to strangle her, and she had the instant and insane feeling of sudden joy.

"I didn't know you were going riding with us," Gray said. A frown tugged at his brow, shadowed by the brim of the black Stetson he wore. "We don't have any sidesaddles. Every one here rides astride."

She stared up at him, drawn by the almost overpowering aura of virility and strength that surrounded him. The anger she'd felt only seconds before was instantly forgotten, as was her conviction that the sooner she was permanently away from Grayson Cantrelle, the better. Suddenly memories of their times together, of his lips on hers, his hands caressing her body, his length pressed tightly to hers, filled her mind. She felt a hot coil of heat spark to life deep within her, felt a flush of warmth sweep over her, searing her insides and prickling her skin.

She had given him what she had given no other man—herself, and he had awakened within her passions she had never known existed. Grayson Cantrelle had taken her to an unchartered world of passion and desire, and she wanted to go there again, with him.

"Elizabeth, are you all right?" Gray asked. He stared at her as if a pair of golden horns had just popped from her blond curls.

His voice broke the spell that had held her in its illusionary grip. Her heels dropped back to the ground and, abruptly aware of what she'd been about to do, Elizabeth felt her face burn with embarrassment. God, she'd been about to kiss him! Right in front of everyone! Like some wanton harlot.

Celia moved up beside her and laid a hand on Elizabeth's arm. "Are you all right, dear?"

"Oh, uh, yes." She pulled her gaze from Gray's and pinned it on Celia, grateful that she had someone else to divert her attention. "I'm sorry, I guess I'm still upset about my sister. I can't seem to stop worrying over her."

"Would you rather go back to the house, dear? And rest a while?" Celia's eyes held a deep note of concern.

Elizabeth shook her head. "No, thank you. I really do want to ride. It will help keep my mind off of things."

Yes, like Gray.

She ignored the voice inside of her head. She had to, because it was right, whether she wanted to admit it or not. And she did not.

Gray, who'd moved away while Elizabeth had been talking to Celia, grabbed the reins of a horse and drew the animal up before Elizabeth. "Are you sure you can ride astride?"

Elizabeth looked at the horse. His long legs seemed to go on forever. The little mare she'd ridden at home was a pony compared to this animal. Her gaze moved to the saddle, and she felt as if she were going to faint. It was a man's saddle! And not the gentleman's type she was used to seeing her father and Aaron use. This was a cowboy's saddle. The kind Gray and Travis used.

"Elizabeth?" Gray said.

Her eyes were riveted to the saddle: its huge, curved horn, the sloping cantle, and the stirrups, large carved wooden stirrups booted with a skirt of scalloped leather. She'd never ridden astride—ever. It wasn't proper. It was unladylike. It was scand . . . She stopped her runaway mind and looked up into Gray's eyes again, then glanced past him to where Tori sat waiting, wearing trousers and sitting astride another tall gelding. Determination filled her. She moved toward the horse and reached up for the saddle horn.

"Are you sure you want to do this?" Gray asked softly, his voice only loud enough for Elizabeth to hear.

She threw him a scathing glance for an answer, and reached up to grasp the saddle's cantle with her other hand.

Gray bent over beside her and cupped his hands together. "Let me give you a foot up."

Elizabeth raised her foot to place it in his hands, and instead got it tangled within the folds of her skirt. She pitched forward and her nose crashed against the stirrup's strap. She jerked away from the saddle and turned a scowling gaze on Gray. "You moved," she accused hotly.

His jaw set and his eyes hardened. "Maybe you'd be better off staying here," he growled softly.

His words made her more determined to go than ever. "No." She lifted her skirt so that her left leg was free, and rammed it down into the cup of his hands. She heard a sudden grunt and felt him give slightly. Grasping the saddle again, Elizabeth pushed off of the ground with her right foot, while pressing down on Gray's hands with her left, and propelled herself upward. Her head shot past the saddle. She tried to swing her left leg outward and over the horse's rump. The skirt of her riding habit hampered the move. Her stomach bounced against the saddle, hard, so that her breath was temporarily knocked from her lungs, and suddenly, horrified, she felt herself falling downward.

She caught a quick glance of Tori Chisolm sitting on the horse several feet on the other side of the one she was trying to mount, and heard a soft gasp from someone behind her. Her weight pulled her back. Her left hand clung to the saddle horn, her fingers wrapped tightly around its fat girth, and her right began to flail the air.

Gray, having just begun to rise from his bent position and at the same time move to stand behind her as she mounted, looked up at Elizabeth's sudden thrashing. Her elbow shot directly toward him and smashed against his cheekbone. A curse shot into his mind as his head snapped backward from the blow and his hat flew off, but before he could regain his balance or react, Elizabeth's plummeting body crashed against his chest.

Gray's backside hit the ground, his tailbone doing a nosedive into the earth, driven harder by the extra weight of Elizabeth's body and the force of her fall. Dirt flew up around them in a cloud.

"Elizabeth, are you all right?" Celia said, running up to stand over them.

Mortified, Elizabeth scrambled to her feet and began to brush off her skirts.

"Are you hurt, dear?" Celia asked. Concern etched her face. "We really shouldn't have expected you to ride this type of saddle. You're clearly not used to it. I don't know what Gray was thinking."

"Thank you, I'm fine, mother," Gray grumbled from his sitting position on the ground. His eye was already swelling, and the skin just below it turning an ugly purple.

Dana lifted a hand to cover her mouth to keep from laughing.

"What happens to them when they get around one another?" Travis muttered to her. "It's like this every time."

Celia looked down at her son. "Oh, blazes, Gray,

361

you're fine. You've suffered much worse than that. Now, get yourself up here and see Elizabeth back to the house."

"No, please, I want to ride," Elizabeth said quickly.

Gray got to his feet and shot her a look that was meant to wilt, but said nothing. He turned away and yelled at one of the ranch hands repairing a nearby corral fence. "Ben, bring that box you've got over here."

The man carried a wooden box across the corral and handed it to Gray, who turned and placed it on the ground next to the horse. He looked back at Elizabeth. "There. Step onto that."

"It isn't high enough for me to mount from," Elizabeth said, looking at the box dubiously.

Gray felt his anger begin to strangle him. It gurgled up from his chest, choked off his throat, and began to turn his blood to boiling molecules of fire. "I only have two eyes, Elizabeth," he said evenly. "I'm not going to give you a shot at the other one." He lowered his voice to a menacing whisper. "Now get on the damn box."

Chapter 24

The inside of her thighs felt as if they had been rubbed raw. Her ankles, she was certain, had no skin left to cover the bone, her derriere felt as if someone had beaten it with a wooden paddle, and the sun had just about baked her to well done. She would probably be as dark as Serena by the time they got back to the ranch. She looked down at her exposed forearm. It was pink—bright pink—not the pale alabaster it should be.

She stared at Gray's back and, as she'd been doing for the past hour, silently called him every evil name she could think of and damned him to the heavens. The man was a sadist. A devil. A mean, bullying, insensitive cur.

She watched as Tori reached out and playfully punched Gray's arm, and the two of them broke into another gale of laughter.

"I wish they'd both choke," Elizabeth mumbled.

"Pardon me, dear?" Celia said. She rode beside Elizabeth on a small dapple gray mare.

"Nothing."

"Are you doing all right, Elizabeth?" Dana asked, twisting around in her saddle to look back at Elizabeth and Celia.

Travis, riding beside Dana, looked back, too, but said nothing. Neither Gray nor Tori glanced back, or acted as if they'd heard anything.

Elizabeth nodded, tried to straighten her skirts, which were bunched up in a most unladylike manner around her calves, and clenched her jaw tight. She would not let any of them know that her body felt as if it were being tortured beyond reason. If the other women could ride on these horrible saddles, beneath the pounding rays of a merciless sun, in air that felt like it contained no oxygen whatsoever, then so could she. To make matters worse, she was used to riding the smooth-gaited Walkers her father had bred and used as saddle horses, not these *mongrel*-type horses Gray seemed so pleased to own. She might fall over dead when they finally made it back to the ranch, but at least she'd have made the ride with no complaints.

She tried to concentrate on the scenery, which she'd been attempting to do for the last couple of hours, but to no avail. Everything looked the same. Flat planes of endless earth broken by jutting plateaus, craggy gulleys, and here and there a poor excuse of a stream. Occasionally the monotonous landscape was broken by a dogwood, pine, or oak tree. Sometimes the trees grew alone, with only a spot of wildgrass or cacti nearby for company. In other places they grew bunched together like a group of old friends, providing a blanket of shade for a patch of grass or a bend in a stream.

Gray turned his horse away from Tori's and rode back to Elizabeth. "Tori thinks you might have had enough for today, since you're not used to riding astride. I just wanted to let you know we'll be heading back now." Without waiting for a response, Gray nudged his horse and rode back to Tori's side.

"Tori thinks you might have had enough for today," Elizabeth mimicked, staring after Gray as he rode away.

Beside her, Celia smiled. Ahead of her, Dana chuckled softly, and Travis merely shook his head in wonder.

After another agonizing hour in the saddle, the ranch house came into view. Gray led them directly to the corral they'd departed from. Elizabeth felt such sudden relief, she wanted to cry. Gray and Tori rode side by side to the corral fence and began to dismount. Elizabeth stopped her horse near the gate, stood in the saddle, swung her leg over the horse, and slowly slid toward the ground. Her feet touched earth, and she let go of the saddle and made to turn away from the horse.

Pain, hot and fervent, engulfed her. It shot through every muscle and fiber of her legs, robbed her of what little strength she had left, and turned her body limp. With a soft shriek of both surprise and alarm, Elizabeth sank to the ground.

Gray caught Elizabeth's collapse out of the corner of his eye, and abruptly dropped the blanket he was taking from his horse's back. He took the distance between them in only a few long, hurried strides. "What's the matter?" he growled, sounding, to Elizabeth, more irritated than concerned.

His deep voice, which rang out in the quiet corral like the peal of a church bell announcing mass, drew everyone's attention. Elizabeth looked up, a fresh feeling of mortification washing over her as she saw the others turn toward her, watching.

She began to struggle to her feet. Her rubbery legs gave way beneath her again, and her derriere crashed soundly back to the ground.

"Let me help you," Gray said. He bent down beside her and grasped her under one arm.

Elizabeth jerked away. "I am very capable of taking care of myself," she spat indignantly.

"Yes, I can see that."

She struggled to her feet, her legs wobbling,

trembling, and threatening to collapse under her again. She willed them to stand erect. "I merely slipped."

"Slipped," Gray echoed.

Elizabeth graced him with a scathing glare. "Yes, slipped, if it's any concern of yours, which it isn't."

A deep scowl drew Gray's dark brows closer together. Her tongue was as sharp as a knife, and as stinging as the bite of a whip. Her attitude usually left him wanting to throttle her, while her obsession for the luxuries in life annoyed the hell out of him. That annoyance had grown to even bigger proportions when, on the morning they'd left San Antonio, he and Travis had taken her possessions back from the other wagons and reloaded them onto hers. Gray's temper had soared ever higher with each item he'd repacked. Yet he couldn't help the feelings that stirred within him whenever he thought about her, and which burst into a firestorm whenever she was around. At night she haunted his dreams, giving him no rest, and even in the light of day, no matter how hard he worked in an attempt to rid his thoughts of her, or tried simply to avoid contact with her, the image of her was always with him, teasing his senses and stirring his emotions.

What the hell was there about Elizabeth Devlin that drove him crazy? That made him want to possess her? That awoke feelings deep within him that he had felt for no other woman? And which he damn well didn't want to feel for *her!*

He watched her whirl away from him and march toward the house, her head high, her back held ramrod stiff. The scowl disappeared, and a smile that he couldn't prevent pulled at one corner of his mouth. Her legs were shaky, and a couple of times she wobbled and nearly lost her balance, but he had to give her credit, she made it to the house without another fall. Maybe there was a bit more to Elizabeth Devlin than he'd thought.

"So how's Elizabeth?" Travis said, moving up beside Gray.

"Stubborn. Bullheaded. And," he chuckled softly, "most likely sore as hell."

"Why'd she do it?"

Gray looked at his friend. "Ride?"

Travis nodded.

"Probably because I suggested she not ride. For some reason that woman always seems to do exactly the opposite of whatever I say." Gray shook his head. "Hell, if I was smart, I'd probably tell her not to jump off the roof of the house."

"Sounds like she's gotten under your skin, old buddy."

"What?" Gray spun on Travis. "Are you crazy? The last thing I want is a woman like that. Hell, she can't even ride! What would she do out here—sit on the porch and sew all day? Or maybe run back to New Orleans every chance she got, and buy up half the town with my money? No thanks."

Travis chuckled. "Well, if you ask me, it sounds like you've been thinking about it."

"I didn't ask you, and I haven't been thinking about it." Gray stomped back to his horse, grabbed the animal's reins from the fence, and led him into the barn. "Right, I could just see her living here," he mumbled to himself. "The house would probably turn into some frilly museum with fancy furniture meant for looking, not sitting. And most likely we'd have to import one of those French cooks, and, of course, she'd insist on another half-dozen maids. Probably a seamstress, too. Can't have the lady of the house wearing the same gown more than once or twice."

"What are you grumbling about?" Celia asked, pausing before the open end of the stall Gray was in.

He swiped a brush over his horse's back. "Nothing."

"Grayson," she moved to put a hand on his arm,

forcing him to stop his frantic grooming of the stallion's back and look down at her. "I've seen you in a lot of moods, but this is a new one."

"I'm just tired . . . from the trip." He began brushing the horse again. "I didn't sleep well last night."

"Are you in love with Elizabeth?"

"In love? With Elizabeth?" The hand holding the horse brush paused in midair, and he stared down at his mother in disbelief. With what Celia could see was a great effort, he regained control of his emotions and began to brush the horse again, but kept his gaze averted from hers. "Of course not."

"Why of course not, Gray?"

"She doesn't belong here. She belongs in a big fancy house with a lot of servants."

"People said that about me, when I married your father and came here."

Gray's brush strokes became long, hard, and intense. "That was different."

"Why?"

"It just was."

"Why?" she persisted, unwilling to let him shrug the subject aside so easily.

His arm stopped and he whirled around to face her, his dark eyes ablaze with anger and frustration. "Damn it, Mother, you're different, that's why!"

"I wasn't always, Grayson. Before I met and married your father, I was very much like Elizabeth." With that, Celia Cantrelle turned and walked from the barn.

Gray watched his mother leave, and stared at the empty doorway for a long time. His mother didn't understand, and he couldn't explain it to her. Elizabeth needed luxury and softness. She needed parties, servants, and lots of places to go shopping. She had been raised in that environment, was a creature of it, and needed it in her life, just as much as he needed the Texas plains, the beauty and ruggedness of the land,

368

the harshness of life running the ranch, and its rich rewards. Even if he wanted to, he couldn't change her, couldn't make her into someone she wasn't. And he couldn't change himself either, not even for her. He stroked the animal's back. Maybe his mother had come from a background similar to Elizabeth's, but he would bet she'd never been a spoiled, pampered, self-indulgent little hellion like the blond minx whose image seemed always in his mind.

On impulse he resaddled the horse, mounted, and rode from the barn. There were a few good hours of afternoon light left, and needed to check on the stock in the south canyon. The chore could have waited until the next day, or even later, considering his foreman had a good handle on everything that happened on the Bar C, but it was an excuse to get away by himself. He wanted, needed, to be alone for a while, to feel the sun on his back, the wind in his face, and do the things he normally did, instead of fretting about some troublesome female who was hell-bent on turning his world upside down and inside out.

Elizabeth sank back into the depths of the deep tub and allowed the bubble-topped water to encase her body, the steaming, penetrating hotness to soothe her sore, aching muscles. She lay her head back on the tub's edge and closed her eyes, inhaling deeply of the violet fragrance which emanated into the air from the bubbles, and blocked out the waning rays of the late afternoon sun that streamed in through the dressing room window. Images of Grayson Cantrelle astride his huge black stallion, as he'd looked that afternoon on their ride, filtered into her mind's eye. The sun, blazing in the sky high overhead, reflected brilliantly off of the silver conchos that adorned both his leggings and the leather band of his hat, and the leather vest he wore stretched taut across the width of his broad shoulders. He moved atop the horse as if rider and animal were one, both strong yet graceful, full of power, yet sensitive, brave, yet wary of the unknown, the unchartered.

Memory of his unclothed body pressed to hers, his legs entwined about hers, his arms holding her close as his hands caressed her sensitive flesh, brought a soft moan, unbidden and unexpected, from her lips. She stirred slightly in the water, her body remembering even more than her mind. His hands had worked a magic on her that was dark and sensuous, had drawn her into a realm of desire that had allowed her soul to fly among the stars and touch the heavens.

Need of him, of his touch, his passion, stirred deep within her, a gnawing hunger that turned to an insistent ache.

Then, suddenly, out of the darkness that surrounded the image of Gray astride his horse, another rider appeared and sidled up beside him. Tori Chisolm. A woman who was the epitome of everything Elizabeth was not. She had grown up on the western range, experienced its beauty and harshness firsthand. She knew how to ride as well as any man, as well as Gray. She knew how to handle a gun, a rope, and everything else it took to run a ranch in this severe but beautiful territory. In her mind's eye, she saw Gray look at Tori, saw the warmth and love that glistened in his eyes as he gazed down at the woman, and Elizabeth wished with all her heart he would look at her that way.

The image brought her eyes open with a snap, and she sat up. Soft mounds of bubbles slid from her shoulders to slip over the smooth swell of her breasts, which were now only barely concealed by the foamy whiteness that covered the water's surface. Jealousy filled her, burning, searing, white-hot waves of resentment that raced through her body and took over every molecule, every fiber of her being.

"This is impossible," she mumbled, her voice etched with shock. She shook her head. "He's . . . he's the most inconsiderate brute of a man I have ever met."

A knock sounded on the bedroom door, but Elizabeth, too deep in thought to hear, paid no heed.

She shook her head again. "I can't really care about *him.*" Her eyes snapped shut, hard, and her hands, resting on the edge of the tub, closed into fists. "No, I can't. I won't." But even as she said the words aloud, even as she denied the feelings that had taken root within her, that had come to possess her heart, she knew it was too late. She was in love with Grayson Cantrelle, and she wanted him, wanted him more than she had ever wanted anything, anyone, in her life. With a flush of determination, Elizabeth stood up and reached for a towel.

Gray paused in the doorway of her sitting room. He had come to her room against his better judgement. But she had a right to know right away what he'd learned about Sweetbriar from the rider he'd encountered on his way back to the ranch from the canyon. He had planned to tell her in the parlor before dinner, but she hadn't come down, and his mother had requested that he see if she was all right, or whether she wanted a tray brought up to her room. He had knocked, loudly and repeatedly, but evidently she had not heard. He entered, assuming she'd lain down and fallen asleep. He stepped into her room and realized immediately his assumption was wrong. The huge bed was empty. He turned to leave, but paused as he heard someone talking in the dressing room. His mind ordered him to leave her room, to flee as fast as his legs could carry him, but something else, some force that he could not control, moved him instead toward the open door of her dressing room.

His gaze moved over her slowly as she stood in the

center of the tub and stared back at him, frozen in place, her eyes wide, her arm outstretched toward the towel that lay folded on a nearby washstand, her face flushed. The brilliant saffron rays of the setting sun streamed in through the twin windows across the room, touched her skin, and gilded it a creamy white gold. It danced within the curls of her long blond hair, which now spread across her shoulders like a shawl of flaxen silk, and reflected from her eyes, turning them to deep lagoons of fathomless blue.

Silver rivulets of water glistened atop her skin as they snaked their way downward. A small dab of foamy white bubbles slipped from her bare shoulder. His eyes followed its jagged course as it slid toward one breast, met the subtle swell of flesh and changed its path, curving inward. It moved out of sight within the valley of her cleavage, only to reappear a second later to snake past her waist, over the flat, taut plane of her stomach, and finally disappeared in the triangular and shimmering patch of golden curls that lay at the apex of her thighs.

His breath caught in his throat, and he felt the tormenting ache of desire that he'd tried so desperately to control and conceal for the past few days, sweep over him. He had made love to her, his hands had explored every curve, every plane, every valley of her body. He had tasted the sweetness of her lips and the exquisiteness of her passion, and yet at this moment, in this eternity of time stood still, he wanted her more than he had ever wanted anything in his life. Nothing mattered to him but that she allow him to possess her, to love her. He moved toward Elizabeth slowly, not wanting to break the spell that bound them, held them.

She waited for him, not moving, not daring to breathe lest he disappear like all her other dreams. His gaze held hers, golden-lashed blue shackled to ebony-lashed brown, unwavering, melding. It pierced through her, within her, to touch her fiercely independent spirit, to tame it, at least momentarily, and brand it his.

Gray moved toward her, paused, and without a word, reached out for her. His hands encircled her waist, their heat, their touch, more searing than the hot water she had just abandoned.

"Gray . . . please . . . I want . . ." Her lips moved on other words, but no sound murmured from her throat; the passion that was fastly consuming her, engulfing her, rendering her incapable of further speech or protest.

His left hand slid upward to cup her breast, his thumb moved over her nipple, softly, an air-light touch that sent a jolt of raw desire through her. "Let me love you, Elizabeth," he whispered hoarsely. "I need you, Elizabeth. I need you to be mine."

His lips descended on hers, and the hot, lambent strokes of his tongue stoked and fueled the sweet inferno that was consuming her. She melted against him, her hands sliding up his muscle-hardened arms, and moaned his name, the sound lost within the dark recesses of his mouth.

Her surrender fired his own need and made his desire for her all-consuming, an obsession that controlled him and left him without the will to turn away from her. But then, he didn't want to. His lips left hers, an abandonment that left him aching for want of her. He lifted her from the tub, and in one swift movement, his right arm wrapped around her back while his left slipped under her legs. He hefted her into his arms and held her against his chest.

For an endless second Gray's gaze searched her face, and then, in a movement so fluid she was barely aware of it, he carried her to the bed and, bending slowly, lay her on it, and slid to join her. The thick, heavy fabric of his *calzoneras* was rough against her bare skin, and the silver conchos that decorated it as well as his vest were icy cold, but Elizabeth barely noticed. He was with her, holding her in his arms, and she knew, was finally able to admit to herself with no reservations, no thought of denial, that Grayson was all she cared about, all she wanted and would ever want.

His mouth covered hers in a slow, tantalizing kiss, a caress that teased her senses and stoked the fires that burned within her. It was a strangely gentle kiss, a tender touch that left her shaken to the core, yet it was also a kiss that demanded everything of her, total acquiescence, wanton response, and passion, hot, white, and intense. His tongue in her mouth was like a flick of fire, exploring the dark, moist caverns of her sweetness, while his roaming hands wreaked such sense-shattering havoc over her that she moaned in pleasure, the sound echoing deep within her throat. His lips left her softly bruised mouth and traveled with feather-light touches across her cheek, her jaw, and down the slender column of her neck. He moved with tormenting slowness, leaving small realms of burning flesh behind where his lips had touched, and prairies of tingling skin where the heat of his breath had wafted.

Her breasts ached to feel the caress of his hands, her lips longed for the return of his, and the hot moist center of her pleasure yearned to feel his invasion, to know the melding of their bodies again. Her hands slid over his shoulders, feeling the rock hard, corded muscles beneath her fingers until they slipped within the ragged curls of his black hair, moving caressingly among the silken strands and holding him to her as his mouth gently nuzzled between her breasts.

A wash of pleasure sped through her, and she drew in a sharp intake of breath as his mouth moved across one breast and covered its pebbled nipple. She arched instinctively toward him at the touch of his hot wet tongue, like a darting flame on the aching rosebud, and her body unashamedly, wantonly, begged him to continue his assault.

"Love me, Gray," she whispered, her tone one of desperate need and released passions. "Please, love me."

Her words were almost his undoing, and the control he held in such tight rein nearly escaped him. His mouth moved to capture hers again, to silence her pleading words, but only for a brief, fleeting moment. Rolling from the bed, Gray tore off his clothes, snapping the buttons from his shirt in his haste, their broken threads dangling free as the buttons fell to the floor. He lowered himself back on the bed, his long, lean length moving to press against hers, hot flesh melded to hot flesh. His lips claimed hers, his tongue plunged into her mouth to spar with her own, a duel of pleasure giving and receiving. He slipped one arm beneath her neck, held her to him, as the other explored her body, cupped her breast, his thumb moving rhythmically over her nipple, teasing the sensitized flesh until she moaned with pleasure. His hands tripped lightly over her stomach, her hips, her thighs, each touch an exquisitely sweet torture that left her body yearning, aching for more.

His fingers nestled within the silky gold curls at the juncture of her thighs, causing her hips to rise up to meet him, to plead with him to further his exploration, his ravishment of her body and senses. Passion held her prisoner, desire rendered her helpless, and his touch, his kisses, instilled a need within her that craved only his caress.

Gray's body trembled with the force of passion that engulfed him as her body invited and responded to his lovemaking. She angered him, irritated the hell out of him, and made him curse all women in general, but she also aroused him deeper than any woman ever had, turned his body into an inferno of need that only she could satiate. His mouth moved over hers with more urgency now, his demand more intense, his lips nearly devouring her in his hunger. His fingers slipped from their nest within the short curls below her stomach and slid between the satiny folds of flesh that enveloped the hot, throbbing center of her passion.

A shock of lightning sharp desire coursed through her, wracked her body, sent a shudder of need through her, and left her shivering with pleasure in its wake. She was being swept away on a tidal wave of ecstasy, and the intense force of the sensual emotions he had awakened within her, combined with the newly acknowledged conviction that she was in love with him, was almost more than she could stand. His name left her lips as a softly muted plea, "Gray. Oh, Gray."

This time he could no longer maintain the control he had struggled to hold over himself. With a growl of need deep within his throat, Gray lifted himself to cover her body with his. He had made love to dozens of women, ladies and whores alike, but none of them had ever inflamed him as Elizabeth did. She had become a drug that his body needed and craved. She was forever on his mind, in his thoughts. Her legs parted willingly, eagerly, and the hard, swollen length of his own need plunged into her inviting warmth.

Her arms, wrapped around his neck, held him fiercely, and her lips sought his, craving the fiery assault of his tongue as her body craved the fervent invasion of his shaft.

Chapter 25

In that instant, that mind-shattering, star-bursting moment of time, Elizabeth could not understand how she had ever denied her feelings for Gray. "Love me, Gray," she whispered, the softly spoken plea tumbling from her lips in a breath of emotion. Her hands slipped beneath the fabric of his shirt and pushed it away. His mouth caressed the long column of her neck, nipped at the shell-like curve of her ear, as he lifted his body slightly away from hers and shrugged first one arm, then the other, out of the shirt. Elizabeth's fingers played across the mountains of flesh that made up the wide, rock-hard breadth of his shoulders, and tripped caressingly over the sinewy length of his back.

Intoxicated with desire and need, Elizabeth joyously accepted the warm intrusion of Grayson's body, her own trembling with the passion only he seemed able to awaken within her.

"You are so beautiful, Elizabeth." His hands roamed her body, kneaded her breasts, caressed her hips. Roughly he murmured against her flesh. "You have bewitched me, princess. How could I help but want to love you?" He lifted his head and looked down into her eyes, blue fathomless pools that reflected his own passion. "When you are in my arms, nothing else matters, Elizabeth, nothing, except ... except that you are mine." His lips claimed hers, a half-savage, half-gentle assault that gave as much as it took, that shattered whatever doubts Elizabeth was still experiencing over her feelings for him. She was in love with him, in love with everything about him. His arrogance, which had so angered her, she now saw as steely pride. What she had viewed as inconsiderate, she realized had been nothing more than his way of making her responsible for her own actions, for herself. And his ungentlemanly behavior, what she'd taken for crudeness, was merely the iron strength and resolve of a man who faced life on its own terms, who chose to live life on a harsh land, without luxuries, and surrounded by constant danger and hardship. This newfound realization seemed to deepen her newly acknowledged love and strengthen it.

His lips moved over her face, showering her with kisses that were as fiery as a raining cascade of wild sparks. Elizabeth writhed beneath him in reckless abandon, the blazing need his assault had created within her craving more from him with each movement, each joining. She belonged to him now, she knew that with a certainty beyond reason. She would follow Grayson Cantrelle anywhere, live any way he chose, any place he wished. It didn't matter anymore, none of the things she had thought so important to her life, nothing mattered but this darkly handsome man whose hands, mouth, and body were like a shroud of hot velvet, enveloping her, engulfing her, possessing her. His touch was sweet torment, his kisses exquisite agony. His hands pulled her closer to him, and they moved in unison to the ancient cadence of man and woman's unification, letting the molten passions of their lovemaking flow freely from one to the other to meld them body, mind, and soul. Elizabeth arched to follow the rise of his hips and meet their fall, every fiber of her being aching for the soul-stirring release that she knew only he could give her.

Gray shuddered, every muscle and cell of his body filled with the essence of her, every emotion a tangled web of desire. With the rising tempo of their passions, the feel of flesh moving with flesh, Gray steeled himself against the almost overwhelming urge to release himself into her, wanting nothing more than to prolong the sweet, body-trembling pleasure that being within her gave him.

Instinctively, Elizabeth wrapped her legs around Gray's, pulling him deeper into her as she felt a torrent of sensation rush through her, lava-hot and scalding. It carried her upward, toward the skies, the heavens, a sweet ride of rapture that brought a moan of his name from her lips, caused her body to arch upward against him, and her arms to tighten around his shoulders.

He heard the whisper of his name, felt the involuntary shudder of her body, and with a deep thrust into her, filled her with himself, with the seed of his life. He gave up the taut rein of control he had held so desperately, and a wave of ecstasy broke over him and wracked his body violently, as it, too, rode the crests of desire.

They lay together for long minutes, silently, bodies entwined, their labored breathing slowly returning to a more normal state. Gray lay with his face turned toward her on the pillow, his once rigid organ still embedded deeply within her. "Each time with you, Elizabeth, seems better than the last," he whispered, his warm breath stirring the wispy tendrils of golden hair at her temples. "Or is it just that I need you more with the dawn of each new day?"

She smiled and ran her hand lightly up his arm,

letting her fingers caress the hot moist skin that stretched taut over the sinewy mounds of muscle. She felt him instantly begin to harden within her and, surprising herself, felt a white-hot shock of need fill her. Elizabeth inhaled deeply, breathing in the scent of horses, leather, and Texas dust that emanated from him, and blended with the erotic fragrance of their lovemaking that clung to both of them.

A knock at the door brought Gray jerking away from her and bolting from the bed.

"Elizabeth? Elizabeth, dear, are you all right?" Celia called. The knock sounded again.

Gray cursed beneath his breath, glanced up at the clock on the mantel of the oak-faced fireplace, and cursed again. It was an hour since his mother had suggested he look in on Elizabeth. He had agreed to the task begrudgingly, having just that afternoon made the determination that the only way to deal with Elizabeth, to dampen the stirrings that simmered within him every time he neared her, was to stay away from her . . . far away. But the moment he'd stepped into her room, had encountered her rising from her bath, rivulets of glistening water clinging to her body, he had forgotten everything except his need to possess her again, to hold her in his arms and taste her passion.

He scrambled to pull his trousers on while Elizabeth clutched the sheet to her breast and stared, her eyes wide, at the door.

"Elizabeth?" Celia repeated, a note of anxiety in her voice now.

"Answer her for god's sake," Gray snarled acidly, ramming his arms into the sleeves of his shirt. He grabbed his boots and *calzoneras* from the floor, glanced around to make sure he'd forgotten nothing, and turned toward the windows that faced the second floor gallery.

"Just a minute, Celia," Elizabeth called out, her gaze on Gray.

He shoved one of the windows upward and, bending, stepped over the sill to the gallery. In the split second it took for Elizabeth to blink her eyes, he was gone.

Slipping into a baptiste wrapper that lay on the bed, she moved to the door, opened it a crack, and looked out at Celia Cantrelle. "I'm sorry, I laid down for a nap, and I guess I overslept."

Celia put a hand on the door and with gentle pressure, forced Elizabeth to open it. She breezed into the room. "That's all right, dear. I was just worried about you, after that long ride this afternoon." She paused in the center of the room and looked around. "Would you like me to send up a tray for you?"

"Oh, did I miss supper?"

Celia's gaze dropped to the floor beside the bed. A silver concho lay atop the carpet. Its curved and highly polished shape caught the soft glow emanating from the oil lamp that sat on the dressing table, and reflected it like a fallen star. Celia's lips curved in a knowing little smile, and she turned back to Elizabeth. "Supper hasn't been served yet, dear. It will be shortly, but I can have Maria hold it a bit, so that you can join us, if you wish?"

"Yes, I'd like that," Elizabeth answered. "I'll dress quickly, I promise."

She moved with the haste of a hurricane, pulling one of the new gowns she'd had made in New Orleans, a pale blue-green silk, from the armoire, and struggling her way into pantalettes, corset, camisole and hoopcage. "Oh, where is Serena when I want her?" she muttered, forgetting that she'd told the servant earlier that she wouldn't be needed. Upon returning to the

381

house after her ride that afternoon, she'd informed Serena that she would be bathing and going straight to bed. She hadn't realized she'd be disturbed, though thinking back on it, she couldn't imagine a more pleasureable way of being disturbed.

She pulled the dress over her head and down around her bodice, fluffing out the flounced and ruffled skirt. With trembling fingers she fumbled with the tiny pearl buttons that ran up the front of the bodice, and were nearly obscured by tiny rows of pleating done in a darker shade of blue silk. The neckline was cut daringly low, exposing more cleavage than Elizabeth had ever dared before. It hugged her shoulders and left them bare, while puffed sleeves encircled the upper portion of her arms and flared into thick ruffles of lace just above her elbows. With hasty strokes of a brush, Elizabeth pinned her hair into a wild, cascading waterfall of curls, cursing every second her lack of expertise. Serena always did her hair.

She gave herself one final look in the cheval mirror that stood in a corner of the room. A smile curved her lips. The dress was prettier than she'd remembered. She slipped a fan, its spines delicate carvings of rosewood, onto her wrist and left the room.

A few feet from the dining room entry she slowed her pace, touched a hand to her hair to reassure herself it was still in place, and smoothed the skirt of her gown. She wanted to look perfect for Gray. Voices echoed from the dining room and Elizabeth paused, suddenly unsure of herself.

"Gray, that was a terrible thing to do," she heard Dana say. "Taking Elizabeth's money."

"I only took it to prevent her from doing something foolish, which is exactly what she tried to do."

"Yeah," Travis said. "If he hadn't taken that money out of her wagon, she would have traipsed off to

Sweetbriar and most likely would be decorating some Comanche's tipi by now."

Elizabeth began to tremble with fury. He *had* taken her money. He had actually taken her money. The cur. Every warm feeling she had toward him, every memory of what they'd shared only moments ago, was suddenly dissipated by the urge to slap his face, to scream at him that he'd had no right.

And if he hadn't, you'd be dead.

She squeezed her eyes shut and ordered the nagging little voice to go away and leave her alone. Plastering a smile on her face, she stepped into the room, but only Celia, seated at the head of the long table, looked up.

Gray sat to the right of his mother, flanked by his sister and Tori Chisolm. The three were laughing, but his attention, his gaze, his smile, were definitely riveted on Tori. Despite her rage, Elizabeth felt a flash of jealousy, its impact so intense it nearly rocked her from her feet. Pride kept her head held high, and determination moved her into the room and to the empty chair beside Travis.

He stood and pulled back her chair. "Good evening, Elizabeth," he said. "How are you?"

"Fine," she snapped a little too curtly.

"Hello, Elizabeth," Dana said.

Gray glanced at her, but his attention was drawn instantly back to Tori.

"Gray, do you remember that night we followed your father out to the south canyon?" Tori asked with a chuckle and a knowing gleam in her eye. "And our horses got loose after we dismounted, and decided to return to the ranch on their own?"

Gray laughed. "My father nearly whipped my backside raw for that one." His hand rested lazily on the back of Tori's chair.

Elizabeth desperately fought the urge to stand, move

around the table, and lift his hand away from the woman and return it to Gray's lap where it belonged.

" 'Course, I guess that was better than being scalped by the Comanches, which could just as well have happened."

"I don't remember that," Travis said with a frown. "Where was I?"

"Sleeping, which is what you always wanted to do at night," Tori said.

"No adventure in his spirit," Gray added, and received a playful slap from Tori as they both broke into laughter.

Elizabeth seethed quietly, but whether over the discovery that Gray had taken her money or because of the attentions he was paying Tori, she wasn't sure—and she didn't care. She was just plain furious with him.

"You two were always running off and leaving me behind," Travis accused, sounding a bit pouty.

"Gray," Tori rested her fork on her place and turned suddenly serious, "have you tried breaking any of those horses you brought back yet?"

"No, haven't had time. Why?"

"I'd like to buy that chestnut mare with the flaxen mane and tail, but I want to break her myself, before we make a deal. That way, if I decide she's a little devil, you can keep her."

"Oh, some deal," Gray said, but the smile that curved his lips belied the sarcasm of his words.

Elizabeth shot Tori a scathing glare. That mare was the one she liked. She didn't want Tori to have her.

"How about first thing in the morning, Gray?" Tori urged.

"I thought perhaps we could go for another ride in the morning, Gray," Elizabeth interrupted, drawing everyone's shocked attention and surprising even herself at her boldness.

Gray stared at her for a long moment before answering. The dark gaze held her pinioned to her chair, and refused to allow her to look away.

This was exactly what she'd wanted, and now that she had it, she wished she'd never opened her mouth. Her eyes searched his for the warmth and passion she had seen there only a short while ago, when he'd held her in his arms, and a little part of her seemed to die inside when she failed to find it. Coldness, she thought. All she saw was haughty, arrogant coldness.

"Another ride?" he murmured. He glanced at Tori, then back at Elizabeth. "If you really want to ride, perhaps my mother could accompany you. I have too many things I have to see to tomorrow."

Yes, like Tori Chisolm, Elizabeth's little inner voice said.

She felt her face grow warm and struggled to maintain her composure. For the remainder of the meal, Elizabeth played with her food, pushing it around on her plate with her fork and trying desperately to suppress the anger and resentment that had begun to burn within her. But it was fear that was eating her up. Deep, gnawing, all-consuming fear. Had she fallen in love with a man who didn't care about her at all? Had she truly been nothing but a body with which to satisfy his lust?

She felt tears fill the corners of her eyes at the thought, and hastily blinked them back. She couldn't cry, not now, not in front of everyone, not in front of Gray. She dropped her fork to her plate with a clatter and stood so quickly that she nearly knocked her chair over. "I'm sorry, I really am not feeling too well," she mumbled, and hurriedly left the room.

"Grayson, that was terribly rude of you," Celia said, not caring one wit if she sounded the scolding mother in front of the others.

His rancorous growl brought a strained silence to the table. "She'll get over it."

Elizabeth paced her room, her emotions in such a tangled weave she didn't know which she felt more: anger at Gray for making her love him and then turning his attentions to Tori Chisolm, or fury and disgust with herself for opening her heart to him in the first place. For long minutes tears filled her eyes and streamed down her cheeks. When they were finally spent, she stood at the window and stared out at the black Texas night.

The transformation was a slow and steady one, but the longer Elizabeth's gaze roamed the dark landscape, the longer her mind replayed the scene at the table, the harder her resolve became. As her breast was filled with rage and her mind with indignation, so her heart was filled with determination.

"All right, Gray, if that's what you want, then that is exactly what you'll get," she muttered softly.

If Tori Chisolm was the type of woman Gray wanted, and that seemed obvious, then that was the type of woman Elizabeth would become, because if there was one thing she knew, it was that she wanted Grayson Cantrelle. No matter what he was, no matter how much or how little he had, she wanted him . . . and she was damn well going to have him. Dabbing a fluff of rice powder over her nose and cheeks in an effort to conceal the redness caused from crying, Elizabeth left the bedchamber and went back downstairs in search of Serena. She found the woman sitting at the kitchen table across from an bonily thin, old black man whose cord-decorated sombrero looked as if it were ready to slip over his ears, fall down around his shoulders, and devour him.

"Serena, I need you to find me a pair of trousers. I don't care what they look like, but I need them first thing in the morning." She eyed the old man. "A pair his size would probably do just fine."

Serena's mouth dropped open, and she looked up at Elizabeth as if she'd lost her mind. "Trousers?" she echoed.

"Yes. And a belt. I'll most likely need a belt." She turned to leave the room, paused, and looked back. "And a hat. I'll need a hat, something with a wide brim."

Before Serena had a chance to question her, Elizabeth left the room, anxious to get back to her bedchamber before encountering anyone. Well, not anyone, she admitted to herself. Gray. She didn't think her heart could take another encounter like the last one.

Long hours after Tori had been seen home by Travis and the rest of the family had retired for the night, Gray prowled around the outside of the ranch house, moving about the corrals, the barns, even his mother's small garden with its many varieties of cactus, roses, and flowering fruit trees. He couldn't sleep, for he found it impossible to quiet his mind and quell his thoughts, or rid himself of the image of Elizabeth.

Why hadn't he left her in New Orleans? He picked up a pebble and absentmindedly began turning it over and over between his fingers. Of course, the answer to that was easy, he hadn't known until it was too late that she was on the wagon train. But he could have left her at Damien Sorens's plantation. He shook his head. No. The thought of Elizabeth with that pompous, overweight fop was more than he could stomach.

Yet, what did he want? That was the question that had been plaguing him for days, only now it wouldn't leave his mind for a second. It nagged at him, haunted him, and gave him no peace. The idea of marriage to Elizabeth was unthinkable, and the mere fact that he *was* thinking of it was enough to send his mind and body into battle against one another. There was no question they were perfect for one another—in the bedroom. Elsewhere all they seemed to do was spar and spit at one another. Yet she made him feel alive, more alive than he'd ever felt before.

Gray threw the pebble into the night. What the hell was he supposed to do? The conflict within him was not something that was going to go away, nor was it going to be easily reckoned with. He wanted Elizabeth, wanted her with a passion like no other. From the moment he'd seen her, he'd known she was different from the women who'd sashayed their way through his life before. And, if he hadn't been sure, she'd proven it during their stay on the riverbank, and again on the journey from New Orleans to Houston. She was soft, gentle, and refined. At the same time, Elizabeth Devlin possessed a will of iron and more grit and stubbornness than the good Lord should have allowed in one woman. And it was all those things about her that he cherished, and which drew him. He wanted to possess her, to protect her, to keep her by his side forever. A soft snort escaped his throat. At least he admitted that much to himself. At the same time, he fought desperately against the feelings she stirred within him.

He moved further into the dark shadows of the garden. But even if he overlooked the fact that out of the bedroom they seemed to do nothing but get on one another's nerves, there was one thing about Elizabeth he could not overlook: the fact that she wanted— needed—luxuries in her life. If he were ever to marry, it had to be to a woman who loved him for who and what he was, not because he owned the Bar C, and not because he had more money and wealth than Damien Sorens, or almost any other plantation owner in Louisiana or Mississippi could even dream of.

The mere thought that Elizabeth might feel that way enraged him. But it did nothing to quell the hungry yearning to take her in his arms again, to taste the honey-sweet passion of her kiss, and to lose himself within the fathomless blue of her eyes. He wanted her to stay, but if she did, would he ever know whether she loved him for himself, or because of what he could give her?

He turned and looked back at the house, his eyes searching for her window and finding it dark. Its panes glistened softly beneath the moon's pale glow, but he could detect no movement behind the silver glass. He willed her to appear at the window, and he ordered her to stay away, and then, in the midst of his inner turmoil, the thought that had been at the back of his mind since the first time they'd made love loomed forth and refused to be ignored. What if Elizabeth was with child? His child.

Chapter 26

"How do I look, Serena?" Elizabeth asked, twirling about in front of the older woman.

"Like a trollop," Serena grumbled in answer. She eyed Elizabeth's attire in distaste. "Ain't proper, you wearing trousers. What would your mama say?"

"Mama's not here," Elizabeth said, and sniffed. "Anyway, it's more practical for what I have to do this morning."

"And just what is that?"

"Never you mind." She walked to the door, but before slipping out, paused. "I'll be out most of the day."

At the bottom of the wide staircase, she was met by Dana, who kept looking around furtively. "Hurry, Elizabeth," she whispered, "or someone's bound to come out of the dining room and see us."

Dana's outfit was much more practical, and complimentary Elizabeth thought, than her own. Gray's young sister was dressed in a white silk blouse, as Elizabeth was, but not hastily altered and ill-fitting trousers. Instead, she wore a skirt, unencumbered by petticoats and sewn in the center to create leggings. Beneath the calf-length skirt, she wore tall riding boots, which looked much more comfortable and sensible than Elizabeth's lace-up ankle boots.

The two women tiptoed from the foyer, and, once out of the house, hurried to the stable. One of the ranch hands stared openly at Elizabeth's choice of attire, but said nothing as Dana shushed him away after his offer to help the two women saddle their mounts.

"Are you sure you want to do this?" Dana asked.

"Yes." Elizabeth struggled to prop the saddle on the horse's back. Lord, it had to weigh fifty pounds! "If I'm going to live here, uh, in Sweetbriar, I need to learn to ride. And not sidesaddle."

"Gray could teach you," Dana said coyly, watching Elizabeth.

"I'd rather be with you."

"I bet," Dana muttered.

Elizabeth caught the softly murmured words, but refrained from commenting. Everyone knew how she felt about Gray, it seemed, except Gray. Or maybe he knew and just didn't care. She felt her heart nearly plummet to the bottom of her stomach, and prayed that her last thought wasn't true.

Using a small box to stand on, Elizabeth mounted her horse. "Where are we going?"

"Not far. It's not safe to go too far from the ranch house without Gray or one of the ranch hands along."

Elizabeth frowned. "Why not?"

"Comanches."

Her eyes widened. "Indians? They'd attack us?"

Dana shrugged. "You never know. There's also bandits from Mexico."

"Wonderful," Elizabeth mumbled.

After an hour, her derriere felt as if it had been pummeled with rocks, to say nothing of her ankles. But she was starting to feel a bit more comfortable with her seat. It had been over twenty minutes since she'd last lost her balance. Of course, they were only trotting.

Her mind shied away from the prospect of what would happen when Dana decided it was time to lope. She straightened her shoulders and gritted her teeth. She was not going to give in. She was going to learn to ride the way Tori Chisolm did—astride. And she was going to learn to do it well. She had to.

Aaron peered over the small rise of land he, George, and Damien knelt behind, his gaze riveted on Elizabeth. "We could snatch her now."

"No. The other one would go screaming back to the ranch and alert everyone. We wouldn't get five miles," George said. Lord, didn't the man ever use his head? "Though I guess we could snatch her, too. Have us a little more fun with two of them." George snickered.

"But Jason's not with them," Damien said, protesting. "We have to get Jason, too. And teach that cowboy a lesson."

Aaron eyed George in disgust. He should never have admitted that Elizabeth was not his sister. Of course, he wanted the same thing from her that George seemed to want, but still, when George talked about it, the whole thing seemed sort of . . . repugnant. Aaron shrugged the thought away. What did it matter? He wanted revenge against Elizabeth, and damn it, he'd have it. If that enabled George to invoke revenge against her, too, well, so be it. What did he care? But Damien was starting to get on his nerves.

"So when are we going to get her?" George hissed, not looking away from the two women on horseback only a few dozen yards away. "We been here for two days now."

"As soon as the opportunity arises. I don't want that cowboy coming after me. Or the law either," Aaron snarled grumpily.

*   *   *

"Come on, Elizabeth, it's time to go back. We're much farther from the ranch house than we should be, as it is," Dana said, turning her mount around.

"All right, but I want you to teach me how to shoot a gun when we get back."

"A gun?" Dana echoed, looking at her in astonishment.

"Yes. I mean, I know how to use a gun, but not the kind you carry here. The kind Gray has. I may have to defend myself some time."

"You mean against my brother?" Dana said with a sly smile.

"No, against Indians," Elizabeth answered a bit too coolly.

"Elizabeth," Dana said, as they rode side by side back toward the ranch house. "Have you told Gray yet that you're in love with him?"

Elizabeth's head jerked around and she stared at Dana, then a sigh of resignation escaped her lips and her shoulders sagged. Why lie? she thought. She had been doing that to herself for too long already. "No, but I doubt he wants to hear it anyway."

"Why do you say that? I've seen the way he looks at you, Elizabeth, and it's not the same way he looks at me, or Mama."

"Or Tori Chisolm?" Elizabeth offered.

"They're only friends," Dana said.

"Humph."

Dana smiled. "Elizabeth, listen to me. Gray, Tori, and Travis grew up together. Her mother was my mother's best friend. Anyway, if Tori was in love with Gray, believe me, she'd have snared him long ago. She's not the type to be proper and wait for a man she's interested in to ask to court her."

393

Elizabeth looked at her through narrowed eyes.

"He loves you, Elizabeth," Dana said. "Remember, he's my brother. I know him."

An hour later, having dismounted and handed their tired horses over to one of the wranglers to brush down and cool, Dana and Elizabeth stood in the center of one of the corrals and faced the side of the barn.

"All right, start shooting," Dana said.

Elizabeth lifted the heavy Colt, one of Dana's father's and almost identical to the one Gray carried. Holding the gun in both hands, something she was forced to do because of its weight, she pointed it toward the bottles Dana had set up on the fence a few feet from where it connected to one corner of the barn. Her finger tightened on the trigger, and a second later the air exploded in a blast of sound. The gun jerked upward in her hands, and Elizabeth stumbled back, losing her footing and balance and falling to the ground—right on her already sore derriere.

Dana couldn't help the laugh that bubbled from her throat. She moved to help Elizabeth back to her feet.

Elizabeth looked up at her, ready to snap angrily at Dana. Instead, at Dana's smile, she began to laugh. "I guess," she chuckled, "if my attacker was about twenty feet tall, I'd have just pierced his heart. Thank heavens I didn't need this skill while we were on the wagon train."

"You'll learn, but that reminds me. Did Travis get that bolt of cloth from your wagon like you wanted?"

"Yes, but I didn't use it after all. I really brought those things for my sister. I figured living out here—" Elizabeth paused, not wanting to insult Dana.

She giggled. "I know. You figured that anyone who lived out here, with the Indians, probably ran around in rags, right?"

Elizabeth nodded self-consciously. "I just wanted her to have some pretty things."

"Well, from what little I've seen, I'd say your sister will be very pleased. But enough of that, let's get back to your practicing. When you take aim, look at the raised notch on the end of the gun barrel. Point it a little below your target. That way, when the gun kicks, you'll hit what you want to hit."

Elizabeth nodded, lifted the gun, and aimed it toward the bottles again. She fired, this time managing to stay on her feet, though she stumbled back and fought to keep her balance.

"Son of a—" Gray yelped, and jumped back behind the corner of the barn. A second later, as both women stared in horror, he reappeared, holding his hat in one gloved fist. He stalked toward them, anger emanating from every muscle, his dark eyes ablaze with rage. "Of all the insane, stupid things! Just what in the hell do you two think you're doing? Trying to get me killed?"

"Gray, we didn't know—" Dana started.

"I see Miss Catastrophe is at it again," he snarled, and glowered at Elizabeth. He had been so engrossed in eavesdropping on their conversation, and shocked by Elizabeth's comment that the things in her wagon were gifts for her sister, he'd unconsciously stepped out to greet them and forgotten what they were doing. "Look at this," he demanded, and held the Stetson up before them. He poked a finger through the bullet hole that had pierced its brim. "I could have carved my initials on the damn bullet, it came so close. Or is that what you intended?"

As usual when Gray turned his temper toward her, Elizabeth's rose to meet it head on. "I wasn't aiming at you, but now that I see what a wonderful target you'd make, maybe I should." She began to lift the gun toward him.

Gray, unable to believe what she was doing, reacted instinctively. His hand shot toward her, his fingers wrapped around the gun's barrel, and he yanked it from her grasp, jerking a surprised Elizabeth right off her feet and into his arms. Exactly where he didn't want her.

Gripping her shoulders, he fought the urge to wrap her in his embrace, and pushed her away from him. Once assured she had regained her balance, he readily released her. "The road to Sweetbriar should be clear in another day or two," he said, his gaze boring into Elizabeth, his tone icy cold. "I can have a couple of my wranglers escort you to your sister's place then." With that, he rammed the bullet-pierced Stetson down on his head, abruptly turned on his heel, and strode away.

Elizabeth stared openmouthed after him. "Well, if that isn't an invitation to leave, I've never heard one," she muttered after a few seconds.

"Oh, nonsense," Dana said. "He's just mad because he wasn't watching where he was going, and walked into our target area."

But Elizabeth wasn't convinced. Gray wanted her gone, of that she felt sure. Tears stung the back of her eyes, and a sob caught in her throat. He had made love to her last night, had murmured sweet words in her ear, had been gentle and loving—and moments later, in the dining room, had totally ignored her to lavish his attentions on Tori. She had never felt so miserable. "I . . . I think I'll take a nap," she said.

"Elizabeth," Dana called after her as she ran toward the house. "He didn't mean it."

She wished she could believe Dana's words, but it was no use anymore. She had to face the truth. He had used her. She had been nothing more than a convenience for his bed, and now he didn't need or want her anymore.

* * *

Gray sulked around the stables for the rest of the day. He was acting like the back end of a mule and he knew it, but he couldn't seem to help it. He'd ignored Elizabeth over dinner last night and turned all of his attentions on Tori, because he'd been so mad at himself for falling into Elizabeth's bed again. It wasn't bad enough that he'd seduced her once and ruined her for other men, but he kept on doing it! Around her he seemed to have no control over himself. And now, to make matters worse, or better—he couldn't seem to resolve which—he'd found out that everything he'd thought about her, assumed to be true, wasn't. Why hadn't he just asked her if all those things were hers?

That evening Elizabeth had Serena bring her dinner to her bedchamber, feigning a headache. A rear ache, thigh ache, or ankle ache though, would have been closer to the truth. She was so sore, even after a bath, that she could hardly walk.

"Why you hiding up here in this room?" Serena asked, staring pointedly at Elizabeth.

"I'm not hiding out."

"Yes, you are. You two have words again?"

"Who?" She looked at Serena and tried to look confused.

"You know exactly who I mean. Michie Cantrelle. You two have words again? Been spattin' like two cats in a cage, haven't you?"

"No. He invited us to leave, that's all."

"Hah. After you near took his head off with a bullet, way I hear it." Serena began to chuckle, her whole body bouncing with the gesture.

"It wasn't my fault! He wasn't watching where he was going and almost walked into it."

"So, you're going to leave and let that little filly

from next door have him?"

"Yes! And good riddance. I don't want him."

"You'd best think on that one, Missy," Serena said. "You think on it good, less'n you want to end up with someone like Aaron Reynaud again."

"Aaron," Elizabeth spat. "This whole mess is his fault. I wish I could see him again, I'd put a bullet through *his* head." She pounded a fist into her pillow and threw herself down atop it.

By the time the morning sun streamed through the windows of her room, Elizabeth had gotten little more than a couple of hours sleep, her mind refusing, for the most part, to turn off and relinquish its image of Grayson Cantrelle.

She skipped breakfast, having absolutely no desire to sit across the table from Gray or Tori, who always seemed to be there. Instead, she went straight to the barn and asked one of the wranglers to saddle her a horse. Last night she'd been about to give up. This morning she was fighting mad, and filled with more determination to make Grayson Cantrelle notice her, want her again, admit that he loved her, than she had been the day before. But she wasn't ready to face him yet—or his beautiful next-door neighbor, who was obviously the epitome of the type of woman he wanted, if not *the* woman.

Elizabeth rode south, away from the rising sun and toward the plateaus she and Dana had skirted the day before. It was a beautiful area of the ranch, and one she wanted to see again. The soft, golden rays of the rising sun touched the earth all around her, turning the harsh, rugged landscape to a panorama of soft, dazzling pastel colors and brilliantly rich earth tones. The tall cacti seemed greener, their small blossoms blooming a brighter white, a more radiant red, a richer pink, or purple or yellow. A stream she crossed glistened gold, and the sky was a diorama of endless clear blue, unbroken by clouds, while the earth itself was a lush blanket of weaving sienna, chestnut, and mahogany hues.

It was a beautiful land, so different from the one she had known all of her life, yet as magnificent and exotic in its own way. She could understand, finally, why Eugenia loved it so. Why Gray loved it.

When she reached a small plateau, Elizabeth dismounted and tied the reins of her horse to a small bush. She'd had enough riding for a while, now she wanted to practice with the gun. She opened her saddlebag and pulled out the Colt Dana had loaned her. Moving a few feet away from her horse, she raised the gun, aimed at a cactus several yards away, and fired. Her first three bullets missed by a mile. The fourth hit the arm of the cactus. The plant shuddered violently. Her fifth bullet struck the dirt in front of the tall plant.

She heard a scuffling sound behind her and turned.

Two men, Indians, were running toward her, one holding a blanket stretched out in front of him.

"No," she screamed, raised the gun, and fired.

One of the men jerked to the side, stopped, and then stumbled forward.

The man with the blanket crashed into her, nearly knocking her to the ground. He threw the blanket over her head, and she screamed.

"Shut her up," one of the men hissed.

Something clamped down on her mouth, forcing the rough fabric of the blanket against her lips and nose. She tried to jerk away. She couldn't breathe! They were suffocating her. She twisted frantically and kicked out, thrashing within the confines of the blanket.

"Damn it, control the little bitch, or I will," the same voice threatened.

Something struck her on the side of the head as she twisted again, and the world exploded in a shower of stars: brilliant, blinding stars whose light hurt her eyes. She shied away from them, from their glare, and plunged headlong into a dark, cavernous void, an abyss of endless, impenetrable blackness.

"So, throw some water on her. Wake her up," George barked. "What are you waiting for? We ain't got all night."

Aaron turned back from where he'd been standing, looking out into the darkness, trying to discern if they had been followed. As far as he could tell, they hadn't. Evidently no one had witnessed the abduction, and by the time they would discover her missing, perhaps just before nightfall, it most likely would have been too late to start a search party. He smiled. Things were working out quite nicely after all.

The blanket had been removed, but Elizabeth kept her eyes closed, afraid to open them, fearful of what would happen if her abductors knew she was awake. She had thought they were Indians when they attacked her, but now, after hearing one of them speak, she knew they weren't. Indians didn't speak English. Her arms and legs ached terribly, but when she tried to move them, just a bit, Elizabeth found that she couldn't. They had been tied, her legs at the ankle, the rope wound tightly about her boots, her arms drawn behind her and secured at the wrists. Her hands were nearly numb, though she could still feel the roughness of the rope that bound her, cutting into the flesh of her wrists. It felt raw and her shoulder blades screamed in pain.

"Come on, dammit, do something," George snarled. The voice of her abductor sounded familiar, yet she couldn't place it. She felt certain now that the men weren't Indians. Thank heavens. At least they wouldn't skin her alive, like Dana had said Comanches had been known to do to white captives. But who were they? Why had they taken her?

"You promised we'd get the boy," Damien said.

Aaron poured a bit of water from his canteen onto a rag of cloth, and moved to stand before Elizabeth. He crouched before her and patted the wet rag to her cheeks and forehead. "Come on, Elizabeth, time to wake up," he cooed.

Elizabeth's whole body went rigid. Aaron! Her eyes flew open, and she tried to twist her face away from his hand.

He smiled. "Hello, sweetheart."

"What—" She coughed. Her throat felt dry and raw. "What do you want?" she croaked, her gaze pinned to Aaron's. She had never seen him look so ugly, so vile. It was as if, suddenly, every ounce of humanity he once had, or she'd thought he had, was gone.

His eyebrows raised in mock surprise, and he stood. "Why, we want you, my love. Nothing more. Just you."

Panic swirled within her breast, and Elizabeth struggled to tamp it down. She couldn't give in to it, not now. She had to keep her wits about her. "What do you want, Aaron?" She damned the quaver in her voice.

"As I said, my love, you. I figure you owe me that much. And George here," he crooked a thumb over his shoulder at the other man, "he figures you owe him, too. Says if you hadn't knocked him unconscious on that riverboat, he could have saved his brother."

George moved to stand behind and slightly to one side of Aaron. "Hey, *Missus* Cantrelle, pleased to see you again," he said, his voice dripping with sarcasm.

She looked up in horror at the weasal-like face of the man who stood behind Aaron. His eyes were like pinpoints of hatred, his lips drawn back from yellowed teeth in a grimacing smile. He held one hand to his right shoulder, and Elizabeth noticed that his shirt was stained dark with blood. She cringed away from their leering stares. "What do you want of me, Aaron?"

"Why, I thought that was obvious, my dear. Since you've been sharing your favors with that . . ." his nose wrinkled in disgust, "that cowboy, George and I figured that you wouldn't mind sharing them with us, especially since you owe us so much anyway. Damien would like to enjoy you, too, of course, when George and I are through."

"You're . . . you're crazy, Aaron!" Her gaze jumped to George and then Damien, who sat a few yards away. "You're all crazy."

George snickered.

Aaron shrugged. "Perhaps. Now," he turned to George. "Listen, old man, would you mind giving us a bit of privacy? Then, when I'm done, you can do with her what you want."

Elizabeth felt nausea rise within her, and her limbs began to tremble violently. She struggled against the rope that was twisted around her wrists, and felt it cut deeper into her flesh.

"Yeah, just don't take all night."

George walked to the other side of the campfire and settled down on the ground near Damien, but his gaze never left Elizabeth, and a shudder of revulsion coursed through her.

Aaron knelt beside her and took a silver flask from his breast pocket. He opened it, took a long swig, and then offered it to her. "Have some, my pet, it will help to relax you. Anyway," he continued when she turned her head away, "it's not like you hadn't once planned to share my bed."

Tears filled her eyes, and she damned them. She

didn't want to cry, didn't want him to see her fear. "Aaron, please," she whispered, "don't do this."

"It's a little late for that, Elizabeth," he said, his tone suddenly becoming ugly and vindictive. "You made a fool of me in front of the whole town." He took another swig from the flask. "Everyone was talking, wondering what was wrong with me that you'd run off only hours before our wedding. They're whispering about me, Elizabeth, saying ugly, nasty things."

"Aaron, please, I was upset. I wasn't thinking," she whispered again, realizing even as she uttered the words, that it was useless to plead with him.

"That's too bad, Elizabeth, but it's too late for 'thinking' now."

His hand snaked out and grabbed the neckline of her blouse, his fingers moved against the swell of her breast and gathered the fabric in a wad. She flinched away from his touch, a violent shudder of disgust shaking her entire body, nausea welling up within her throat. Aaron laughed softly, jerked his arm back, and the front of her blouse tore open, its pearl buttons ripping from their threads and falling to the ground.

"Aaron, please," Elizabeth screamed, shocked at his cruelty and more scared than she'd ever been in her life. He was crazed. He was truly crazed with his rage and jealousy.

"Beg me, Elizabeth." He grabbed the other lapel of her blouse and tore it from her shoulder. "I think I like it when you beg, though you don't do it near as well as Francine." He laughed wickedly, the sound echoing on the still night air. His fingers began to play with the thin blue ribbon that held her camisole closed over her breasts. "I always wondered what it would feel like to undress you, Elizabeth."

"Then get on with it," George growled.

Aaron's hand moved to the belt that held Elizabeth's

403

makeshift trousers up, and he flipped the buckle open, jerking the belt away from her before she even realized what he was doing. She jumped back.

"Maybe I should spank you, Elizabeth, for running off from me. Would you like that?" Aaron chuckled. "Would you enjoy it?" He grabbed the loose end of the belt in his other hand, and snapped it before her face.

Fear caught in her throat, and she looked about wildly. God help her, there was no way to escape them. Even if she screamed, who would hear? She had no idea how far they'd traveled while she'd been unconscious, no idea how far they were from the Bar C, or even if anyone knew she was missing.

Aaron slowly unbuttoned the front of her trousers, his tongue sliding over his lips with the release of each button, his eyes meeting hers as his hands drew the pants open. He chuckled and eyed the bindings around her ankles. "I guess I'm going to have to untie your legs, aren't I, Elizabeth?"

Instead, he reached toward her bosom. She cowered and tried to lean away from him, but found a large rock at her back that prevented her further movement.

Aaron smiled, a lewd curve of his lips that sent another shudder of revulsion through Elizabeth. His fingers tugged at the thin blue ribbon of silk that held her camisole secured. The bow fell loose, and with another tug the ribbon was pulled from its loops and the sheer fabric dropped open, exposing her breasts to his leering gaze.

"Now that's more like it," George said, his cackling laugh echoing on the air.

Elizabeth screamed and kicked out at Aaron, while at the same time she tried desperately to scoot away from him. He merely laughed. Elizabeth tried to squirm away from him, as his fingers brushed lightly over her bared flesh. Gut-wrenching nausea filled her, churned her stomach, and tears of fear and loathing blurred her eyes. She jerked her shoulder to the side, trying to avoid his touch, lost her balance and fell over, the side of her face landing on the hard ground. A small cloud of dust rose up to sting her eyes and choke her breath.

"It's no good trying to fight me, sweetheart," Aaron cooed, and reached to pull her upright by her shoulders.

An arrow struck the ground directly in front of Elizabeth's face, and only inches from Aaron's outstretched arm. A grunt of surprise broke from his throat. He yanked his hand back and jumped up.

George scrambled to his feet and grabbed his rifle, firing several shots into the darkness. Another arrow pierced the air, its wheezing sound alerting them to its approach, but not soon enough for them to react. It sliced into George's arm just below the elbow, the flint-carved point protruding from one side of his forearm, the wooden shaft and feathers that decorated its end from the other.

"Aghh! Comanches," he screamed, clutched his arm, and fell to the ground, his eyes wide with both fear and pain.

Aaron, never one to be a hero, began to tremble. He looked around wildly, scrambled to his feet, and threw his hands up in the air. "I surrender," he yelled loudly. "Don't shoot me. I'm not armed. I'm not armed."

Damien rolled up into a ball and covered his head with his arms.

Hoping against hope, Elizabeth tried to scoot away from Aaron. Maybe the Indians hadn't seen her, hadn't noticed her lying on the ground. If she could just get to the rocks, to the shadows that they and the scrub pine beside them offered, maybe the Indians wouldn't see her. She inched her way across the ground.

She was almost to the trunk of the pine when she lost her balance again and fell over. A moccasined foot hit the ground before her face. With fear caught in her throat, threatening to strangle her, her gaze traveled up the lone limb. The deerskin covering reached from the Indian's foot to his hip, and ornamental pictures and designs were painted on it in a pale blue hue. It was also covered here and there with beads, bits of bones, and pieces of silver. The silver reminded her instantly of the conchos on Gray's *calzoneras.*

"Oh, God," she mewed softly. She was going to die. These savages were going to kill her, and she'd never even told Gray that she loved him.

She forced herself to look up at the Indian who stood over her. His other foot rested atop a large rock. The only other garment of clothing he wore besides the moccasins was a breechclout of deerskin, and dangling down beside it was a small sack of leather. Her gaze continued upward, the terror that filled her breast tempered only by the curiosity that mesmerized her and held her spellbound. His bronzed chest was bare, but slipped over one arm was a war shield, its round face painted with colorful designs, its edges trimmed with what looked to Elizabeth like teeth and locks of human hair.

Hysteria shook her limbs, clogged her throat, and burned her eyes. His hair was long, reaching almost to his hips, and braided into two tails, one draped over each shoulder. The braids, like his war shield, were decorated with bits of silver, beads, cloth, and feathers.

He looked down at her then, his hard, black gaze meeting hers and sending another shudder of dread coursing through her. His nose was broad, his face almost flat, his skin dark. His cheeks were painted with black stripes, as was his chest.

A movement behind her caught his attention. He

406

stiffened instantly, and raised the lance he held in his hand over his shoulder.

"No," Elizabeth screamed, realizing that he was pointing the deadly shaft at Aaron.

The Indian hesitated, and looked from Aaron back to Elizabeth.

"I was only going to lower my arms," Aaron cried. "They hurt."

Suddenly the camp filled with Comanches. Two grabbed George by his arms, hauled him roughly to his feet, dragged him toward the fire, then threw him to the ground. He screamed in agony as one end of the arrow, still lodged in his arm, hit the ground before he did. Another Indian roughly pushed against Aaron's back, jabbing him with a lance when he stumbled, then beating on his shoulders until he, too, fell to the ground next to George. Damien remained huddled in a ball, trembling and mumbling incoherently.

"*Taitbay-boh,*" one of the Indians spat, and then spit on the ground beside the two men, as if to rid his tongue of the very word he'd spoken.

The Indian standing over Elizabeth hunkered down in front of her, balancing the weight of his sinewy body on the balls of his moccasined feet. He reached out toward her and she cowered back, in spite of her sudden resolve to maintain some small degree of pride and dignity and face him bravely. His fingers lifted a thick curl of her blond hair, and held it up as his eyes studied it. A smile suddenly curved his lips, and he let the silky tendrils slide through his fingers until they once again rested against Elizabeth's shoulder. He stood abruptly and walked to the fire where George and Aaron sat, surrounded by several other braves.

The Indians conversed for long minutes, their voices raised, in anger, their words punctuated with flailing hands and other gestures.

An hour later Elizabeth sat against the rock she had tried to scoot toward at the Comanches' first appearance. She was still bound hand and foot, and her camisole remained draped open, her trousers undone, but the Indians, other than setting her upright, had paid her no attention. That had been directed solely and unerringly at the three men.

They were now spread-eagled on the ground to one side of the campfire. Moments before doing this, the Indians had—amidst taunts and laughter—stripped them of their clothes, using their knives to snip and swipe at the fabric until it hung in shreds on the men's bodies. Then, as George, Aaron, and Damien had stood huddled beside each other, each clearly terrified, the last bits of their clothing were torn from them and they were thrown to the ground. Wooden stakes had been pounded into the hard earth and the men's wrists and ankles were tied by thongs of leather to the stakes.

Elizabeth shuddered, trying not to think of what they might still do to her. Dana had told her stories of how some women had been kidnapped by Comanches and never seen again, while still others who either escaped or were later rescued, had shown evidence of being badly beaten, raped, and tortured. Some had returned with virtually no faces, their noses and lips burned off, while still others lacked fingers or toes. She glanced furtively at the Indians, who were now hunched together around the fire.

As if feeling her gaze on his back, the Indian who had stood over her earlier rose to his feet, turned, and directed his black eyes toward her.

Chapter 27

"Gray!" Dana yelled. "Gray!" She snapped the reins over the flank of the carriage horse to urge it to more speed. Her dark hair whipped free of its chignon as the carriage careened in a wide arc through the entry gates of the Bar C, balancing precariously on two speeding wheels. Its other wheels crashed back down, jostling Dana and nearly throwing her from her seat. "Gray!" she yelled again, yanking back on the reins and bringing both horse and carriage to a stop before the barn. She jumped up and scrambled to the ground.

Gray ran out from the barn, at hearing his sister's cries, a look of alarm on his face. Travis, having also heard the commotion, appeared from within one of the nearby corrals where he had been working with one of the new horses. Seeing Dana and the speeding carriage, he jumped over the corral fence and hurried to where Gray stood.

"What the hell's the matter?" Gray asked, the moment the carriage pulled up before him.

Dana jumped down. "They've got Elizabeth, Gray," she said, hurriedly, the words coming in between gasps to catch her breath. "I . . . I was on my way back from the Walker place, and I saw them. Out by the canyon.

They grabbed her off of her horse."

Gray felt a swell of panic wash over him, invade every cell, every fiber of his body, and leave him nearly weak with fear. He fought it, clenched both his fists and jaw, and his eyes turned to hard, flinty orbs of blackened amber. He reached out and gripped his sister's shoulders, his fingers biting into her flesh. "Who took her, Dana?" he demanded. "Comanches?"

Without a word, Travis turned and ran into the barn. He grabbed several bridles and moved toward the stalls.

"No—I mean, yes—I mean, I don't know! They were dressed like Indians, but, well, one did look like an Indian, kind of, but I don't think they were. I mean, the other, he . . ." Tears filled Dana's eyes, the fear she'd felt for the past twenty minutes while racing toward the house, now overcoming her.

Gray shook her by the shoulders. "Don't break down on me now, Dana. The other *what?*" His voice was steel hard. "Tell me, Dana. The other what?"

"The other man didn't really look like an Indian. I mean, his skin, it was too white, and . . . and his hair was short and brown."

"What else?" Gray demanded. "Did they hurt her?"

Dana shook her head. "She got off a shot at them when they rushed her. That's what drew my attention. I think she hit one of them. I heard him scream."

Travis moved up beside Gray. "I've got three horses saddled, as well as two packed with blankets and extra saddlebags for food," he said, offering the reins of one to Gray. "You want some of the other boys to go with us?"

Gray shook his head. "No. Dana said there's only two of them. Anyway, they'd see our dust if too many of us go, and we can make better time if it's just the two of us." He turned back to Dana. "Tell Ma—"

"I'm going with you."

"No, you're not." He took the reins from Travis and turned to mount his horse. He yelled at one of the other wranglers who was standing nearby, to get them some food from the house; the man took off at a run.

"Gray, I saw where it happened, and I saw them," Dana said. "I can help, and I'm going. Elizabeth is my friend." She grabbed the reins to one of the other horses from Travis.

Gray looked down at her. "Damn it, Dana, I don't have time to argue."

"Then don't," she said, and hefted herself up onto the animal's back.

A few seconds later, both the wrangler Gray had sent to the house and Gray's mother ran toward the barn, their arms wrapped around heavy burlap sacks.

"Shall I send for the sheriff?" Celia asked, as she crammed one of the food sacks into the packhorse's saddlebag. She looked up at her son, and for one brief flash, wanted nothing more than to weep for him. His dark eyes, usually so vibrant and full of warmth and life, had turned to glittering black pools of anguish. Pain exuded from him, naked and torturous, and if Celia Cantrelle had harbored any doubt that her son was in love with Elizabeth Devlin, she had it no longer. She reached up and covered one of his work-roughened hands with her own satin-soft one. "Be careful, my son."

"Here," Dana yelled, twenty minutes later. She reined in. "This is where they jumped her."

Gray swung a leg over the pommel of his saddle and slid to the ground, then hunkered down and studied the earth. Long seconds later, he stood. His features had turned hard. During the ride, he'd closed off his

411

emotions, the stabbing, gnawing pain and fear that had gripped his heart the moment Dana had told him what had happened, and forced himself to concentrate on nothing but getting Elizabeth back. "Three horses," he said. "Elizabeth's, and two others. There's no blood, so they haven't hurt her . . . yet." He remounted. "But you're right, Dana. It wasn't Comanches. These horses were shod."

A rider suddenly appeared from around a jutting plateau of earth. Gray's hand moved with lightning speed to the holster at his hip and drew the Colt free of its confines, at the same time his thumb cocked back the hammer. "Hey, its only me," Tori said, laughing softly. "I was just coming over to your place to look at that horse of mine. What are you three doing out here?" Tori pushed back the beige Stetson she wore, identical in style to Gray's, and looked from one worried face to the next. "What's wrong?" she asked finally.

"Someone grabbed Elizabeth," Travis said.

"Comanches?"

He shook his head as Gray nudged his horse into movement.

It had been early afternoon when Dana had returned to the ranch with the alarm that Elizabeth had been abducted. Now, after several hours of tracking, they were running out of daylight.

"Gray, we're going to have to stop for the night," Travis said. "We can't track them in the dark."

"No," Gray said. "They've been traveling in a direct line south. You make camp with the girls. I'll go on. You can catch up with me tomorrow."

"I'm going with Gray," Dana said.

"Then I guess we all keep going," Travis said.

Two hours later, aided by nothing more than the pale glow of the moon and Gray's uncanny ability to track anything anywhere, they reined in abruptly at the sight of a small fire flickering on the horizon. They dismounted quietly and hunched down close to the ground, their horses at their backs.

"Think that's them?" Travis whispered.

"More than likely," Gray answered. "Either that, or we've got some Comanches out here just waiting for some poor stupid white man to venture onto their camp so they can pull him apart."

Dana shuddered. "That's horrible."

"Yeah," Gray said, but his gaze never left the distant flames. "Stay here," he said to the other three, and handed his reins to Travis, then bent down and pulled the spurs from the back of his boots and looped them over his saddle horn. "I'm going to get a closer look."

Gray moved across the flat Texas plain, his knees bent, his body stooped low, so as not to be a noticeable object on the still landscape for any watching eyes. Thankfully, the shirt he wore was dark, not his usual white, so that it did not pick up the glow of the moon; and the Stetson with the silver conchos was back at the ranch house in his room, the one on his head had no adornments that could reflect the light.

He heard laughter long before he neared the brush surrounding the campfire, and then a Comanche war cry. The sound sent a chill of alarm up his spine. Had he been wrong? Had it been the Comanches who had abducted Elizabeth after all? His mind argued with him, with the sound he had just heard. No, he had lived on the Texas plains all of his life. He knew the Comanche ways. They had not been the ones who had taken Elizabeth, and yet there was no denying the cry he had just heard. He inched his way closer to the camp, careful to stay in the shadows, out of the light of the moon. Moving up behind several large rocks, he peered over them at the scene below.

Gray felt his body nearly collapse with the rush of

relief that swept over him at the sight of Elizabeth, sitting directly on the other side of the rocks. All he could actually see was the back of her head and her shoulders, but it was enough to know that it was her, and that she was unhurt. His gaze moved over the camp. He counted eight Comanches, all huddled around the fire. To their right, three white men were staked, naked and spread-eagled, to the ground. Thin red lines slashed their bodies where the Indians had used their knives to slice the men's skin. Gray could see small pools of blood, having dripped from the as yet superficial wounds, glistening a blackish red on the ground beside the staked men.

Cautiously, Gray pushed himself away from the rock and hurried back toward where Travis, Dana, and Tori waited.

"Is it them?" Travis asked.

"Is Elizabeth all right?" Dana whispered.

"Yes, but she's not going to stay all right, if we don't get her the hell out of there . . . and fast."

"Comanches?" Travis said.

Gray nodded. "The men who took her are staked to the ground. They're white, probably drifters or army deserters. Evidently the Comanches surprised them after they'd made camp. I don't know about the men, but I think I can talk the Comanches into releasing Elizabeth." Gray stood, unbuckled his holster, and then, rebuckling it, hung it over his saddle horn atop the spurs.

"Talk them into it?" Travis echoed.

"Gray, what are you doing?" Tori asked, a thread of alarm in her voice as she watched him remove his gun belt. "You can't go in there alone. Unarmed."

He ignored Tori and turned to Travis. "Remember those Indians who approached the wagon train and wanted to trade?"

"The ones who wanted to trade for Elizabeth?"

Gray nodded. "It's the same ones."

"What makes you think they'll give her up?"

"They believed me then when I said she was spoken for." He began to unsaddle the packhorses. "And nothing's changed," he added with a low growl.

"How will we know if you need help?" Dana asked.

He looked at his sister for a long second before answering. "If I'm not back in thirty minutes, I'd say the odds are I won't be coming back."

He grabbed the reins of the two packhorses and turned to go, but Dana stopped him with a hand on his arm. "Gray—"

"It's the only way, Sis. I have to get her out of there." He leaned forward and pressed his lips to her cheek, and then he was gone, swallowed up by the blackness of the night.

Elizabeth felt her heart lurch within her breast, as the Indian who had met her curious gaze moved toward her. His features were a blend of roughly chiseled curves and sharp, flat lines, while his eyes were as black as the night and his flesh the color of burnished bronze. He bent down before her and muttered something she did not understand, then motioned toward the other Indians, still sitting around the fire.

When she didn't answer, his hand grasped the handle of the knife that was sheathed at his waist and pulled it free.

She tried to cower away from him, suddenly terrified that her life was a breath away from being ended.

The Indian reached behind her, grabbed her arms, and slit the rope that held her wrists bound together. Her hands fell to her sides, each instantly filled with a painful, hot, tingling sensation that raced up her arms

415

as circulation returned. The knife slipped between her ankles, and, with a swift upward movement of his wrist, the Comanche freed her of her leg bonds.

He smiled again, mumbled some more incoherent words, and motioned with his hand, lifting it from his palm to his mouth and back again.

She watched him carefully, and suddenly understood what he was trying to convey to her. *Eat,* she thought, in wonder. She frowned in confusion. He wants to know if I want something to eat. She looked from the Indian to where George and Aaron and Damien lay, and then back at the Comanche. The Indians had done nothing for the past hour but taunt and torture George and Aaron, and ignore her—she felt a wave of surprise wash over her—and now one of them was offering her food? As if she were their guest, rather than their prisoner. She looked into the black eyes, trying to understand what was happening, and the Comanche's smile broadened further.

"Can . . . can you speak English?" Elizabeth asked.

The blank look on his face was her answer. He rose and walked back to the campfire, then returned to her a few seconds later. He squatted down and handed her a bowl.

She returned his smile, trying to ignore the whimpering sounds coming from Aaron and George and Damien. She hated them all with a passion, had wished Aaron dead a thousand times, but she never would have wished this fate on him. On any of them. "Thank you," she said to the Comanche. She held the bowl cupped in her hands and looked down into it. "I think," she mumbled, staring at a mound of what looked like congealed fat of some type lying on the bottom of the bowl, steaming. Her nose wrinkled in distaste. Did he really expect her to eat this?

A sudden rustling of brush behind them brought

the Indian upright to his full height. He whipped out the knife again and stared into the darkness.

A deep, drawling voice broke the night stillness with muttered words she did not understand. Elizabeth almost fainted with relief at recognizing his voice. Gray walked from the darkness into the light of the campfire, his hands held away from his hips, his head bare of a hat, and continued talking to the Comanches in their tongue. The one standing before Elizabeth turned and approached Gray, and the two talked while the others around the campfire mumbled, grunted, and motioned among themselves.

After several long minutes, Gray walked toward Elizabeth, but paused when Aaron cried out. He turned and looked back at the staked men.

"You can't leave us here. They'll kill us. Please . . . please, help us."

Gray began to turn away, but Aaron, on the verge of hysteria, screamed out again. "Please, I'm Aaron Reynaud. And that's my fiancée, Elizabeth Devlin. I'll pay you anything you want, just get me out of here."

Elizabeth sputtered madly at Aaron's bold lie.

Shocked, Gray stared at the naked man. Aaron. This was the man Elizabeth had been about to marry, the man she'd discovered in bed with another woman on their wedding day. A seething rage filled his chest at the thought. Gray turned to the Indian and, though at the moment he didn't really care—for he wanted nothing more than to slit the man's throat himself—asked in the Comanche tongue what Aaron had done.

"Elizabeth, please," Damien begged, "help me. You know I didn't do anything to you. It was only Jason I wanted. Please, Elizabeth, tell him to help me." Tears rolled down his cheeks, and his entire body trembled with fear.

The brave mumbled a few angry words, and with

417

each his rage seemed to grow.

"Listen," Aaron said, "I haven't done anything to them. It was George."

"The chief says you shot two of his braves," Gray said, his own brown eyes almost as dark and hard as the Indian who stood beside him.

"George shot at them. George did it."

"Why did you follow us, Aaron?" Gray growled. "Why did you come after Elizabeth?"

"I . . . I love her," he mumbled quickly. "I do. I wanted her to come home with me."

"That's a lie," Damien said. "He only wanted to get revenge."

"Shut up," Aaron screamed.

"He was angry because she gave herself to you. He was going to share her with George."

Gray looked at George and suddenly recognized him. "You were on the *River Belle*."

George sneered. "If it wasn't for her, my brother would be alive."

"Forget about him," Aaron pleaded. "He's been selling guns to the Mexicans and the other Indians around here and . . . and he's got a gang of men that rob people and make it look like the Indians did it."

"Shut up, you little weasel," George hissed.

Aaron ignored him. "He told me. He sold guns to . . . oh, what were their names?"

George tugged viciously on his bindings. "I'll kill you for this, Reynaud," he growled. "I'll kill you."

"Humph," Aaron snorted, and threw George a dismissing glance. A frown pulled at Aaron's brow, and then suddenly his eyes lit with excitement. "The Wacos, that's what he called them. He's been selling guns to some Indians named Wacos, and raiding with them, too. I just hired him as a guide. That's all, just a guide, to help me find Elizabeth."

The Indian standing beside Gray mumbled something, his temper flaring almost out of control at Aaron's mention of the word Waco. His eyes blazed with hatred.

Gray realized that what he was about to do would seal George and Aaron's fate, yet he had no choice, not if he wanted to walk away from this alive, and get Elizabeth back to safety. He hurriedly interpreted Aaron's words. He couldn't take the chance of lying, of telling the Indian that Aaron had said something other than what he'd actually said, for fear that, just possibly, the Comanche understood enough English to know that Gray was lying. Then, he felt certain, none of them would see another sunrise.

When he finished, the Indian's response was little more than a savage snarl. He whirled away from Gray and stalked toward the other Indians. Angry words from the group filled the night air within seconds.

Gray hurriedly turned back to Elizabeth. "Are you all right?" he asked.

She nodded, not trusting her voice for the tears of relief that filled her eyes and threatened to choke her.

He bent down, balanced on his haunches, pulled the laces of her camisole together, took her hands in his, and pulled her weight gently toward him.

"Can you stand?"

She nodded again, but when she made to move, Elizabeth found that both her wrists were weak with pain, and her ankles were still nearly numb. Gray helped her to her feet, slipped an arm around her waist, and held her tightly to him.

Two of the Indians disappeared from the camp, and when they returned a moment later, they were leading the two horses Gray had brought in payment for Elizabeth. A curt remark was flung at Gray by one of the braves. He nodded, then bent, and swooped Elizabeth up into his arms.

Too exhausted to think, act, or feel, Elizabeth lay her head against Gray's chest, content merely to know that he had come for her, that she was safe and in his arms.

"I thought I had lost you," he said softly, his lips moving against the silken tangles of her hair.

"Wait," Damien screamed. Gray looked up. One of the Indians was bending over Damien with a knife. He slashed the leather bindings that held him to the ground and yanked Damien to his feet, then pushed him roughly toward Gray. He motioned for Gray to take him, saying that Damien had done nothing, and then turned back to the other braves.

Turning, Gray walked into the darkness with Damien stumbling behind him. They had not gone far before the sounds of George's and Aaron's screams filled the air, anguished cries and pleas for help, guttural moans and inhuman shrieks that told Gray, and anyone else who could hear, that someone was dying . . . slowly . . . painfully.

Gray clenched his jaw and steeled himself against the sounds, thankful that Elizabeth—so spent and drained of energy from her ordeal—had fainted almost the moment he swooped her up in his arms, and could not hear the men's cries.

He had tried to help them, but it was no good. The *Kwerhar-rehnun* chief had been adamant. The braves had approached the camp merely to trade goods, just as they had with the wagon train, but Aaron and George had opened fire on them. Two braves had been killed. If there had been any chance of getting either of the men out, Aaron had destroyed it when he exposed George's selling guns to the Wacos. The Indians looked on the two men as partners, and no amount of refuting the point was going to change their minds. Why they

420

had released Damien Sorens, Gray didn't know and didn't care.

At the sound of footsteps on the rough ground, Travis drew his gun and crouched low. He held one arm out to keep the two women behind him, while the other held the gun pointed into the night, as his gaze scanned the darkness for whatever threat was approaching them.

"It's me," Gray called out to alert the others. The last thing he needed now was a bullet from his best friend, parting his hair or ventilating his forehead.

Dana rushed up to meet him, as Travis reholstered his Remington.

"What the hell are those screams, Gray?" Dana asked. "What's happening back there."

"Someone's dying," Tori said softly, looking out into the darkness.

Gray accepted a blanket from Travis and gently wrapped it around Elizabeth's shoulders. "She's exhausted, and most likely terrified out of her mind, but I think she's okay. I want to get her back to the ranch as soon as we can."

Damien staggered into the camp, holding what was left of his trousers in front of his naked body.

"Carlen!" Dana shrieked, and stared at him.

Gray stared at her as if she'd lost her mind. "That's Damien Sorens, Dana," he said.

She stared at Damien. "He looks so much like . . ." She shook her head. "No, you're right, I'm sorry."

Gray handed Elizabeth to Travis and mounted his horse, then reached out and pulled her into his lap as Travis handed her up.

"Dana, ride with Travis and let Sorens ride your horse. Let's get going."

"Yeah," Travis said, looking back in the direction from which Gray had come. "I don't think it's going to be very pleasant around here tonight anyway."

Gray cradled Elizabeth in his lap and mumbled soft, soothing words of comfort in her ear. She remained unconscious for the ride back to the house, a combination of physical exhaustion and the after-effects of experiencing a deeper fear than she'd ever known before. But he whispered to her anyway, on the chance that, somehow, in the shroud of darkness where her mind dwelled for the time being, she could hear him, and know that she was safe.

He looked down at her face settled against his chest, her golden lashes turned to a ruche of flaxen silk by the touch of soft moonlight. This was all his fault. If he hadn't interfered with Damien Sorens, if he'd just shut up and let the man court her, she would most likely, this very night, be enjoying a soirée, perhaps as Damien's fiancée. He felt a wave of disgust at the thought and forced it down. He should have sent her back to New Orleans, when he'd discovered her on the wagon train, forced Travis to escort her. None of this would have happened to her if he'd done that. But he hadn't. He'd been selfish. He'd wanted her with him, even though he had known it was wrong, that she didn't belong in the kind of life he led. He had wanted her nearby for just a little longer.

It was a long, slow, tormenting ride back to the house. The screams of the two dying men traveled with them for several miles, echoing on the still night air. But they could not move with any speed, for Gray refused to jostle Elizabeth. So they rode at a steady walk, and grimly endured the sounds of death.

Chapter 28

Celia met them at the front door, alerted by the wranglers who had seen their approach. Serena hovered at her shoulder, her eyes pink from what had obviously been hours of crying.

Gray entered with a still unconscious Elizabeth cradled in his arms.

"Is she—?" Celia stared up at her son, her heart nearly breaking at the look of anguish she saw in his eyes.

He shook his head. "Just exhausted," he mumbled.

"Thank God," she muttered, then quickly assumed an air of efficiency. "Take her directly up to her room, Gray. I've sent for the doctor. He should be here shortly."

He brushed past his mother and began to take the wide stairs effortlessly, two at a time.

"Serena and I will get her into a nightgown and cleanse whatever cuts or scrapes she has," Celia said, following him.

They entered the large bedchamber, and as Gray lay Elizabeth on the huge poster bed, Serena finally spoke.

"Who did this?" she asked, her voice as hard as steel. "Who took my baby?"

"Aaron," Gray said simply, knowing the servant would recognize the name.

Serena's entire body shuddered at hearing the name. "I should have killed him before I left Mississippi," she said. "He swore he'd come after her, but I didn't believe him. He was always such a talker, saying how he was going to do this and that, and never doing any of it." She shook her head and her dark eyes filled with tears again, as she looked down at the woman she had helped to raise. "I should have killed him." She looked back at Gray. "Did he hurt her?"

Gray shook his head. "No."

Celia gave him a hard look, but Gray offered no further explanation.

Gray paced the parlor while the doctor, called out from town, examined Elizabeth. Travis stood at the sideboard, Damien Sorens sat on a settee, having clothed himself in a pair of trousers and a shirt that had once belonged to Gray's father, and Dana stood by the window. She stared at Damien, as she had been doing ever since they'd entered the room an hour before.

"You look too much like Carlen for it to be coincidence," she said at last.

Gray stopped his pacing and looked at Damien. "You have a brother. Does he look like you?"

Damien nodded. "He's taller," he mumbled. "And slighter."

"Does he sport a mustache?" Dana asked.

Damien nodded again.

Gray looked at Dana. "His brother is Randy's father?"

"No," Dana said, with more fire in her tone than Gray had ever heard before. "Randy's father is dead."

Gray opened his mouth, and then closed it again.

424

She was right. The man had no right to his son. It was better that he never know he had one. Gray felt a rush of regret and guilt. If Elizabeth had been heavy with his child, and he'd let her leave, would she feel the same as Dana did? Would she have told their child that his father was dead?

Jason, dressed in a fine pair of trousers and a white shirt, walked into the parlor carrying a tray laden with coffee cups and a steaming pot. When he saw Damien, he abruptly stopped, and the tray began to shake as his hands trembled. His eyes shot to Gray.

"It's okay, Jason," Gray said. "He's not going to take you back. Are you, Sorens?" His dark eyes pinned the man to his chair.

"Uh, no," Damien shook his head. "Of course not."

An hour later the doctor had finished examining Elizabeth, pronounced her fit but exhausted from her ordeal, and left, leaving behind a bottle of laudanum in case she needed it to sleep. Some people who'd had run-ins with the Comanches, he told Gray needlessly, experienced fitful nights full of nightmares and jitters.

But Elizabeth, although unable to sleep, was not suffering from nightmares or a delayed reaction to her ordeal, as the doctor had also suggested might happen. Instead, her thoughts were filled with memories of Grayson Cantrelle, her mind haunted by his image, her body tortured by the memory of his arms wrapped around her, his lips on hers.

She had lost him. The thought hung over her like a black cloud on a pristine clear day, nagging, threatening. If ever she had truly had him, her behavior, her actions, her selfishness had killed whatever he'd felt for her. She knew that now, knew it with a certainty that tore at her heart and left her insides a bleeding, aching mass of yearning for what would never be. She had acted foolishly this morning, riding so far from the ranch, unconsciously placing herself in danger. Something Tori Chisolm would never have done. Gray had been forced, by mere decency, to come after her. A longing ache for what would never be filled her chest. She could never be like Tori, she saw that now, even though that was the kind of woman Gray wanted, the kind he deserved. She couldn't do it. She'd proven that today by getting herself abducted—twice! She loved him, and she had lost him. It would be better for them both if she left first thing in the morning.

She flung the coverlet from her legs and rose. The room suddenly seemed stifling. She needed some fresh air. Slipping into the sheer folds of a batiste wrapper, not bothering to tie the ivory ribbons that dangled loose from its delicately embroidered yoke, Elizabeth slid her feet into a pair of satin slippers she'd purchased in New Orleans, and left the bedchamber. She walked swiftly down the dark hallway toward the stairs. Pale yellow rays of the night's light filtered through the narrow windows on either side of the front door, and shone softly on the highly polished cypress floor. Opening the wide entry door, Elizabeth stepped out into the shade of the gallery and the blackness of the night. As she moved, walking around the house toward Celia's garden, tears filled her eyes, but this time she did not bother trying to stem their tide. Moonlight caught the threads of her sheer gown and reflected off of the thin ivory strands that made up the voluminous folds, as she walked slowly across the grounds. The material became a mist of diaphanous fabric that floated about her body, failing to totally conceal the subtly rounded breasts that ached for Gray's touch, the long, slender legs that yearned to entwine themselves around his, and the tiny waist that ached to be encircled by his arms.

He had lulled her fear and calmed her ragged and frayed nerves with soothing words on the ride back to the ranch after leaving the Indian encampment, but she knew they had been hollow words, spoken because he knew she'd needed to hear them, not because he'd meant them. He had held her in his arms, cradled against his strength, but he'd also held something back, something she longed for from him, and which he was not willing to give, not to her. All the things she had always thought so important to life, to her happiness— the luxuries, the gowns, fancy soirees, and living on a grand plantation—seemed now so very insignificant.

If she hadn't known that before tonight, it was painfully clear now. But it was too late. She had lost the one thing that could make her happy. She had lost Gray's love.

She paused in the center of Celia's garden and looked up at the moon, a pale sliver of gold nestled low in a sky of midnight velvet. Its light reflected on the tears that filled her eyes and streamed down over her cheeks, and turned them to glistening paths of silver. She tried to brush them away, but they were only replaced with still another stream of moisture.

From the shadows of the gallery, Gray watched her, a pale white spectre moving amidst the gardens and the night's blackness. He lifted a cheroot to his lips and inhaled deeply of the whiskey-soaked tobacco. Its burning tip glowed red against the darkness, the only evidence of his presence in the dusky shadows. His eyes studied her, and he felt his body instantly react to her, felt the burning heat of need that always simmered within him for her, its coiling tentacles move through his body, turning it to a flame of desire that only her touch could satiate and cool. But there was another feeling within him now, a need to protect her, a need to keep her close to him, forever. When he had thought

427

he'd lost her, that he would never see her again, never hear her laugh, or snap at him again, he had found his world suddenly empty and colorless.

All during the afternoon, when he had been tracking her abductors, thoughts of Elizabeth had haunted him. But it had been an image of a broken woman, a woman whose mind had delved into almost insane hysteria because of her ordeal. He had expected to find her that way, like a fragile doe frightened beyond endurance. Instead, he had found the woman that had been there all the time, a woman of strength and grit, a woman with an iron will and stubbornness that matched his own. He had been so wrong about her.

He heard a soft sob break from her throat and escape her lips, and when she turned in his direction, he saw the glistening trails her tears had left on the high cheekbones. A wave of fierce protectiveness washed over him, almost violent in its intensity. The need to shield her, to keep her safe, to ward off, at any costs, anything or anyone who would harm her, was almost overpowering. His hands ached to touch her, to pull her into his arms and feel the soft, magnolia ivory of her flesh against his. He nearly groaned with the need to kiss her, to capture her lips and feel her tongue duel with his own. Never had he wanted a woman so much, or so completely.

And then, at that moment, Gray realized the depth of his love for Elizabeth, and knew he could not let her walk out of his life. He had never before been willing to give his life for another person, never been willing to die to save them, but he had been willing, almost anxious, to risk his life to rescue Elizabeth . . . because she *was* his life!

Pushing himself away from the stuccoed wall of the house, Gray threw the cheroot to the ground and crushed its burning tip with the heel of his boot. Moving over the earth as silent as a cat, as unobtrusive to the surroundings as the Comanches who claimed the land as their brother, Gray approached her.

Sensing she was not alone, Elizabeth turned and stared into the night's blackness, but there was no fear in her eyes when Gray appeared from out of the Cimmerian shadows. She had known, sensed, it was him, and her heart had stalled within her breast, fearful, even while a thread of hope clogged her throat.

"Elizabeth . . ." His voice broke on the softly spoken word. He wanted to tell her he loved her, that she was his life, the very breath that moved within his lungs, the beat that kept his heart pounding in his chest. She was his sun, his moon, his night and day. Nothing mattered anymore but that she remain at the Bar C, that she remain a part of his life. But he had never been one for fancy words. He was a man of action. It was the way he had been raised, the way he lived.

She looked up at him as he stepped before her, their bodies so close that little moonlight filtered between them. Glistening, tear-filled eyes of blue melded with hard, determined brown, but this time there was no cold arrogance in the tawny depths, no haughty disregard or cool insolence.

Her heart pounded rapidly within her breast. She saw what she had feared she would never see again: flames of desire, like tiny sparks of gold, danced within the eyes that stared down at her, but there was also something else, something she was almost afraid to acknowledge, to believe was truly there.

She reached toward his face, letting her fingers trace the chiseled line of his cheekbone, the strong, square curve of his jaw. "For a while today, I was afraid I would never see you again," she whispered.

"Never," he growled softly. "I would never let that happen."

A sad little smile curved her lips. "I wasn't sure you'd come. That you cared what happened to me."

A moan, deep in his throat, like a cry of agony, rumbled through him, and tears glistened in his eyes. He pulled her into his arms and crushed her to him. God, he'd been so afraid, so damned afraid he'd lost her. He had moved through the day like a man whose heart had been ripped from his chest, whose blood had turned as cold as the rivers that flowed from the mountains. Nothing had mattered to him. Nothing. Not even if he died trying to save her. As long as she was all right.

He felt her arms wrap around his shoulders, her hands slide over the nape of his neck, warm and satin soft, and felt her fingers slip within the tendrils of hair at the back of his neck. She held him to her, pressed her body to his, and a shudder of sheer joy raced through his body at experiencing her touch again. His lips claimed hers in a deep, ravishing kiss, a kiss that told her more than words ever could of what was in his heart. It both demanded her acquiescence, and begged for her love. It was a demand to possess her soul, and a gift of his to her—and she both gave and accepted gladly.

Long minutes later, when he finally tore his mouth from hers, Gray held her away from him, just slightly, and looked deep into her eyes. "I've done a lot of things wrong in my life, Elizabeth, a lot of things wrong between us . . ." He put a finger tenderly to her lips when she tried to interrupt. "I said I would never ask you this again, but I find I have to. I have no choice anymore." He brushed his fingers across her cheek, a feather-light touch that sent a shiver of longing through her. "Marry me, Elizabeth," he said huskily, "Be my wife."

Joy filled her heart, lifted it toward the heavens, and

then abruptly released it, letting it plummet earthward. Fighting back her tears, she tried to calm her racing heart and steady a voice she knew would break on her words. He hadn't said he loved her. He was only proposing because he felt sorry for her and responsible for her, because of what had happened between them. Despite her efforts, a tear slipped from the corner of her eye, and she looked away from him. "You don't have to marry me, Gray," she said softly. "I'm not with child. I know you want a woman like Tori. I can't be that for you. I tried, but I just can't."

Her words tore at him, but he understood why she'd said them. He cupped her chin with his fingers and turned her face back toward him, forcing her to look at him. "Elizabeth, when we met, when I proposed to you before, it was out of a sense of guilt, I admit that. You had never been with a man before. I knew it, and I took you anyway. Afterwards, I remembered why I'd been on that boat: to find the man who had seduced my sister, and then deserted her. I'd sworn I would never do that, and then I took you, and I felt we were so wrong for each other. But we're not."

"Gray, you don't have to tell—"

"I don't feel guilty anymore, Elizabeth, and I don't give a damn if you can ride a horse astride, or shoot a gun, or rope a calf." He pulled her into his arms. "This time I'm asking you because I know I can't live my life without you. I need you, Elizabeth. I love you."

Tears shone in her eyes again, but this time they were tears of happiness.

But Gray wasn't completely certain. Fear stabbed his heart. "I'll sell the ranch. We can live in New Orleans, if you want. In the fanciest house you can find."

Elizabeth smiled. He truly did love her. So much so that he was willing to leave the land and ranch that had been his whole life, the home that he loved, that was a part of him. She slipped her arms around his neck and shook her head. "No," she said softly.

"No?" His echo of her word was almost a thunderous roar in the still night. He jerked away from her and began to pace, circling her. "I don't believe this. I fall in love with the most stubborn, hell-raising, troublesome female on the face of the earth, I risk my neck to save her at least three times in as many weeks, practically offer to turn my world upside down just to please her, and when I ask her to marry me, for the second time, mind you, she says *no!*"

When he was through, Elizabeth caught his arm as he made to pass before her again. He turned, his eyes blazing with frustration, and she slipped her arms around his waist and pulled him back against her. "What I meant was, no, we are not moving to New Orleans. We're not moving anywhere. I love it here, and I love you. This is your home, Gray, and I want it to be my home, and our children's home."

One of the French doors of the parlor opened. Celia Cantrelle stood on its threshold. "Do you two think you can finish your argument in the morning?" But her tart words were softened by the smile that lit her face.

Gray looked at his mother while his arms held Elizabeth against him. "How soon do you think you can get a wedding arranged, Ma?"

"Tomorrow," she announced, and chuckled softly.

"Only if I can help," Tori said, from behind Celia. The door closed with a soft click.

Gray turned back to Elizabeth, bent down, and scooped her into his arms. "Not soon enough," he growled, and with a brush of his lips across hers, turned back toward the house.